N
S
Land of Lost Promises
Village of Despair
Gates of Heaven
Isles of the Dragon's Lair
Rock of
Salvation
Lighthouse
Bay of the Martyrs
Straits of the Dragon
Mountain
of Fire
Cavern of
Ancient
Mysteries
Precarious Pass
Formidable Mountain Range
Deeper Life Commune
Field
of Blood
Comfort Cove
The Potter's
House
Abundant Life
Falls
Potter's Field
The Father's Vineyard
Tent
of the Lord
Valley
of
Indecision
River of Life
Settler's Mill
Still Water Bridge
Watered Down Village
Bay of the Lost
Kadim
The Land
of
Earthen
Vessels

Master Potter®

From Brokenness to Divine Destiny— An Allegorical Journey

JILL AUSTIN

 Unless otherwise identified, Scripture quotations are from the King James Version of the Bible. Please note that Destiny Image's publishing style capitalizes certain pronouns in Scripture that refer to the Father, Son, and Holy Spirit, and may differ from some Bible publishers' styles.

Destiny Image Fiction

An Imprint of

Destiny Image® Publishers, Inc.

P.O. Box 310

Shippensburg, PA 17257-0310

ISBN 0-7684-2172-1

For Worldwide Distribution
Printed in the U.S.A.

7 8 9 10 11 12 13 14 / 10 09 08

Dedication

I dedicate this book to the loving memory of my mother, Elizabeth Isabelle Austin, a pioneer and forerunner. You were the only graduating female medical doctor in your class at the University of California, Berkley. You practiced medicine for 46 years and attained excellence as a woman in a male-dominated profession. You are my hero!

I know at first you didn't understand why I stopped being a professional potter and "wasted" my teaching degree by going into full-time ministry and traveling with a rag-tag, struggling Christian performing arts group. But you stood in my corner and encouraged me to run for my dreams, and even made up the financial differences when love offerings were low or nonexistent.

I'm glad you came to know Master Potter like I do and that you laughed your way into glory as you departed this world. You stand today with the great cloud of witnesses—still my cheerleader.

Your sacrifices in the beginning enabled me to move into the global ministry I have today. I know that you will one day share in these rewards.

You are my inspiration. Mom, I love you forever.

Acknowledgments

I want to thank the many faithful people associated with Master Potter Ministries over the last 25 years.

There have been so many generous supporters, friends, office staff, actors, musicians, counselors and intercessors. You were willing to be radical and on the cutting edge when it wasn't popular. You were truly glorious comrades, always challenging the status quo. I love your abandonment for Jesus and your love for the Holy Spirit's ministry. You have faithfully stood with me through both blessings and adversity. I love you all for your courage and loyal friendship.

Linda Valen has been my ministry assistant for the last ten years. She is the left lobe of my brain; without her I could accomplish very little. She is truly a woman of excellence and integrity. Linda serves sacrificially and unrelentingly, and has a tenacity and hunger to press into Jesus that few people possess.

My mentors through the years include Lonnie Frisbee, who was the catalyst behind the Jesus People and the Vineyard movement. I am grateful that he gave me the revelation that the Holy Spirit is a person and taught me how to move in the anointing. Thanks to John Wimber who taught me how to "do the stuff" and also how to train and equip others to "do the stuff." Mike Bickle still inspires me with his radical, passionate love for Jesus. His humility in the midst of outstanding revelation is astonishing. His intercession, love for the Word and for the Holy Spirit continually inspire me.

A big thanks to the following contributing editors who hammered out the plot with me and gave voices to Beloved and the vessels that I love so much. Your invaluable writing skills and profound insights have significantly molded this book. What a delight to work with such gifted people: Madeline Watson, Jackie Macgirvin and Peggy de Alminana.

Thanks to Don Milam, Don Nori and the rest of the staff at Destiny Image for believing in Master Potter. Thanks for taking a risk on this prophetic, untraditional allegory.

Blessings to you all.

Jill

ENDORSEMENTS

To me, there are two powerful things in this tremendously profound book. One is the Master Potter's remolding us in ways we can't do for ourselves. The other is writer Jill Austin's masterful storytelling ability. I predict God Himself will get hold of the reader in ways he or she has never dreamed of.

—Oral Roberts
Founder/Chancellor, Oral Roberts University
Author, *Still Doing the Impossible*

As I read this book, not only was it a great prophetic journey and in the same caliber as *Harry Potter* or *Lord of the Rings*, but this is a Christian novel that took me in the Spirit. I was able to experience God and see in the Spirit as I read. This book opened my eyes to the reality of Heaven. I actually felt I was reading a prophecy. I highly recommend it as good Christian reading, prophetic story and revelation.

—Todd Bentley
Evangelist, Fresh Fire Ministries
Abbotsford, BC, Canada

Jill Austin is a living parable of her writing on the *Master Potter*—a woman who has literally been formed, crushed, reformed, glazed, fired, set aside, and fired again. *Master Potter* is a must read for every person who seeks a deeper walk with a living God.

As a testimony to her life, Jill, once a handful of broken and discarded earthen shards, is herself a compliment to any situation. She adorns the company and lives of all who know her in much the same way that a masterpiece of art graces a room. The fire of the Holy Spirit that emanates from Jill's pen will warm even the coldest heart and make the soul farthest out sense the draw of the Almighty.

Every chapter holds the voices we all know so well, and some we have either been spared or taken prisoner by. *Master Potter* catches up the reader. It's as though we have been placed, again or for the first time, on the Potter's wheel. The transformation, wet with the kindness and power of the Word, begins lovingly.

There is not a scenario or relationship, a set of circumstances—high or low—that afflicts the human situation, that Jill has not brilliantly allegorized in her book. To read *Master Potter* is a living experience with the effect of a thousand inspiring and soul-searching tales.

We have all been Forsaken, felt her shame, used her excuses, and been chased down by Antagonist. But not everyone has completed the journey of encounter and transformation to Beloved. And that is just the beginning! On to the Potter's House, and the great adventure begins.

Master Potter is a refreshing allegory of the rarest personal kind. For anyone who is interested in the spiritual dimension, *Master Potter* is a personal footpath on which to recognize oneself. It is as if the characters are there, just a few steps ahead, beckoning.

As a practical tool, this book, much like the parables Jesus used, is an asset to every minister, lay and ordained. From "Rock-a-bye baby, never grow up" to the lovesick Bridegroom pacing up and down the aisles waiting for His Beloved, *Master Potter* is a triumph. We await Mountain of Fire!

For any man, every woman, life has a way of putting us on the Potter's wheel for formation and re-formation. A literary journey through *Master Potter* can arrange even the most confused fragments of the heart into a kaleidoscope of grace and beauty and guide the reader to becoming a vessel fit for a King! I hope you will read it, give it to your friends, send it to your enemies, and share it with your children.

—Mahesh and Bonnie Chavda
Pastors, All Nations Church
Founders, Mahesh Chavda Ministries International
Charlotte, NC
Authors, *The Original Sin* and *The Hidden Power of Prayer and Fasting*

People of all ages will love this book. Open its pages and slip into the realm of the supernatural—the real realm. Explore deep recesses of the unseen that will draw you close to a loving Father. This book proves that biblical reality is more exciting than occult fantasy!

—Cindy Jacobs
Co-founder, Generals of Intercession
Author, *Possessing the Gates of the Enemy*

Jill is a prophetess. Her life, ministry and this book will cause you to fall more in love with Jesus. This is the greatest endorsement I could give about any book.

—Ché Ahn
Senior Pastor, Harvest Rock Church
Pasadena, CA
Author, *Into the Fire*

With the skill of a true artisan, our dear friend Jill Austin descriptively paints a vivid picture with words that will captivate your attention and create an increased hunger and insatiable desire to know your Creator. In the hands of the Master Potter, you will find your heart gripped with love. You will weep with gratitude and rejoicing that you are chosen! This book is a modern day classic right at your fingertips!

—Jim (James) W. and Michal Ann Goll
Co-founders, Ministry to the Nations
Nashville, TN
Authors, *The Lost Art of Intercession* and *A Call to the Secret Place*

The ability to blend the realm of the supernatural with the natural in a way that doesn't confuse, compromise, or offend is truly unique. Jill has painted spiritual truth with such artistically clear strokes that it reminds one of the Master Himself. What an insightful, gripping book!

—Dr. Dutch Sheets
Founder, Dutch Sheets Ministries
Senior Pastor, Springs Harvest Fellowship
Colorado Springs, CO
Author, *Intercessory Prayer* and *Praying for America*

Jill Austin masterfully writes this deeply impacting allegory with artistic penmanship. The journey will truly capture the attention and heart of the reader. Many life-changing truths are wonderfully portrayed in the pages of this book.

—Chris Mitchell
Middle East Bureau Chief, CBN News
Jerusalem, Israel

We love Jill Austin. She truly is an intimate friend of the Holy Spirit. This story really isn't just a rich allegory, but rather an invitation to embark on a journey into the very heart of our lovesick God. *Master Potter* is an insider's guide to the supernatural glory realm. May you be empowered in your daily Christian walk as you realize God's great love for each of His vessels and the glorious future you have in Him. May this profound book lead the *Harry Potter* generation into the loving arms of *Master Potter.*

—Wesley and Stacey Campbell
Founders, Revival Now! Ministries
Pastors, New Life Church
Directors, HOPE for the Nations
Kelowna, BC, Canada
Author, *Praying the Bible! The Book of Prayers*

Jill Austin, through the use of artistic penmanship, intricately and passionately describes a prophetic journey unto wholeness and calling throughout the pages of this amazing allegory. The reader is sure to find hope and healing in the truths portrayed in *Master Potter.*

—Pat Cocking
The War Room
Kelowna, BC, Canada
Author, *Third Heaven, Angels and Other Stuff*

Jill Austin is a unique treasure to this world. She puts language to the innermost desires—and often misgivings—we all experience on this journey called life. Jill's book puts it all in perspective. It is profound yet simple, pure yet passionate. It will shine a light on the path each of us must walk to see warmth and peace touch the hurting areas of our hearts. Jill takes wisdom, truth, and compassion and weaves them into a profoundly powerful story that will grip your heart. You will find yourself in these pages. Better yet, you will find the restoration and freedom you need to seize your future and fulfill your destiny.

—Melody Green
President and Co-founder, Last Days Ministries
Kansas City, MO
Author, *No Compromise*

This book goes straight to the heart! *Master Potter* excellently conveys the mighty, yet merciful, nature of God and His undying desire to "put us back together again." Jill Austin's story line is so vivid and touching, moving the reader to visualize and relate to the personalities portrayed. This work certainly prompts soul-searching! I highly recommend it to those who desire to be yielded vessels for the Master's use.

—Dr. Kingsley A. Fletcher
International speaker, author
Kingsley Fletcher Ministries
Research Triangle Park, NC
Author, *Prayer and Fasting*

Jill truly understands the power of narrative! *Master Potter* allows the reader to touch the world of the supernatural in a way that promotes understanding and insight, and through allegory helps the reader view life's twists and turns with a "God's eye" view. I highly recommend both the author and her book!

—Lisa Ryan
700 Club, CBN
Nashville, TN
Author, *For Such a Time as This*

An intriguing look behind the eternal curtains of the spirit world, where the true daily battles are won or lost within the thoughts of the mind and the motives of the heart.

—Dr. Terry Lyles
"The Stress Doctor"

May the Holy Spirit's fiery angels swirl around you as you read, and when you're into it, may you find it difficult to put the book down, as we did. In the end, we pray you may find yourself breathing fresh air, looking forward again with hope (rather than dread), anticipating life again, whether in the fires, on the shelf, or into the heights of spiritual warfare. Wherever He is, it's worth it, which is one of the grand themes of the book. God bless you as you read.

—John and Paula Sandford
Co-founders, Elijah House International
Hayden, ID
Authors, *The Elijah Task* and *Prophets, Healers, and the Emerging Church*

Jill Austin is someone whom I have come to love and respect over the last several years. She is someone who not only allows the Potter to have His own way in her personal life, but also allows the Spirit of the Lord to bring the fresh fire and oil of His Spirit to His ministry and services. The Lord uses her to bring people out of their old religious traditions and to prepare them to break out of their old wineskins so they are able to allow the new wine of His Spirit to flow more freely in their own personal lives.

She also leaves a major deposit and impartation in the ministries and lives of everyone with whom she comes in contact. Jill has been and continues to be a real blessing in my own personal life. Her sincerity and walk of holiness, as well as her character and integrity, are the reasons I am proud to endorse her and have her as my friend.

Jill also attends and is a part of a major church where prayer, intercession, holiness, and passion for the Lord are of primary importance. She has an amazing ability to dig into the Word and to pull out nuggets of revelation in a very simple yet practical way that makes even a child able to comprehend the truths that are being revealed.

It is with much delight that I endorse and recommend Jill, as I have seen new depth come in my own life since becoming acquainted with her.

—Suzanne Hinn
Benny Hinn Ministries

Jill Austin's books draw you in as you read them—she creates imagery with hope. No one can write like this unless they have been in the presence of the Lord. Of all the portraits of God in the Bible, that of the Potter and His clay is one of the most familiar and vivid. In Jill Austin's ministry there is a dynamic of the Holy Spirit that leads to a fresh understanding of a very intimate God who chooses His clay, molds and shapes it, even breaks it, and resurrects it for vision, and powerful anointing. My teenage daughter, Abby, saw me reading Jill's book and declared: "Mom, it is because of Jill Austin that I'm saved!"

—Rev. Linda Oakland, D.D.
Senior Pastor, The Well
Northridge, California

CONTENTS

PROLOGUE

The word which came to Jeremiah from the Lord, saying, "Arise and go down to the potter's house, and there I will cause thee to hear My words" (Jeremiah 18:1-2).

One of the most powerful biblical images describing the relationship of the Almighty God to humanity is that of a potter to the clay. The roots of the image are found in man's creation in early Genesis. God carefully and tenderly shaped the clay of the earth into the form of man. Mankind was fashioned not of precious materials, but of mere dust. Contrast God's handiwork with the mimicry of human rulers. Nebuchadnezzar fashioned an image of himself out of gold, and Caesar casts his image in silver coins, but God housed His image in the clay of the earth, and takes His delight in an earthen vessel. He caused the lowly earth to wear greater glory than the Nebuchadnezzars or Caesars of this world can house in precious metals!

In the story of redemption, once again the image of potter and clay emerges. The redeeming love of Heaven again takes the lowly clay of the earth and patiently, lovingly labors over it to fashion a vessel unique in elegance, beauty and purpose. Time becomes a potter's wheel and a kiln carefully arranged for the fashioning of vessels. But the great designs of Heaven transcend time. These vessels are fashioned for eternity. They will stir unending praise to the wisdom and care of the Heavenly Artisan whose love drives Him to create manifold likenesses of His own glory.

The house of the Master Potter becomes a place where life is imparted, callings are shaped, stories are fashioned, and destinies are celebrated. It is a place of deep revelation, where the Lord causes His heart and His word to be discerned. It is a place where the broken and rejected are reclaimed and made new, fitted for the Master's use.

You are about to embark on a memorable journey into the house of Master Potter. We are conducted on this journey by one who has served many years, first as a faithful apprentice, now on her way to becoming a clarion voice whose very words are being used to shape and call forth destinies in the heart of God. The prophetic voice of Jill Austin is now captured in story form! Through the vehicle of a story, the author draws you into fresh encounters with the wisdom and love of the Triune God.

The genius of this story is that it is an allegory framed within the disciplines of the potter's trade. The power of allegory is its ability to create vivid pictures in the imagination that release unexpected insights into the story of our own redemption being written by the finger of God. *Master Potter* is a storied reflection of Jill Austin's ministry.

The book graphically portrays the story shape of our salvation! Each of us is a story God is writing! He marvelously interlaces our particular history, our temperament, our gifts, our gender, our family, our culture and our time as the raw materials for retelling the story of redemption patterned in His Son, Jesus Christ. As you read the powerful allegory of Forsaken, rescued from destruction and despair in the Potter's Field, marvelously transformed into Beloved, and prepared to walk out a new destiny, you will experience the full spectrum of human emotion while seeing resemblances to your own life story.

On the dark side, the adversity she endures, the snares she faces, the lies she believes, and the demons she battles are all painfully close to realities in our own lives. On the redemptive side, both the joyful surprises of divine love and the equally surprising mysteries of pain and suffering appointed in the wise counsels of Heaven closely touch the story of our own salvation. The contours of her story belong to everyone whose lives are being fashioned by the loving hand of the redeeming God.

The story unfolds on many levels—the divine and the human, the angelic and the demonic, the good and the evil. These layers are expertly woven together as the composite setting for the full telling of the story. Not since the release of Frank Peretti's *This Present Darkness* has a book appeared that so deeply stirs the heart to consider the multiple levels on which the story of our salvation is being written.

In this story a broken pitcher by the name of Forsaken finds herself at a final place of despair in the Potter's Field. She reflects on the slippery road that has led her to this desperate place. We feel her anguish and desperation, even as the realms of darkness close around her to bring her life to an end. But meanwhile, Heaven has other plans. The intercessions of Master Potter enlist the angelic realms to carry out an eleventh-hour rescue, and Forsaken is snatched from the clutches of darkness, given the new name of Beloved, and carried away to the house of Master Potter. She finds a love she has been searching for all her life but has never known. She celebrates the miracle of Master Potter's life entering her broken clay vessel!

Her rescue from sure destruction fills her heart with unspeakable joy! But her initial exhilaration is only the beginning of Master Potter's appointed journey into the full joy of her salvation. That journey comes in divinely orchestrated seasons that the Potter's wisdom only reveals in stages. She is graciously crushed, reshaped, pruned, and sent back into the wilderness where her heart and faith are tested. She makes choices that seem to thwart God's purposes, only to be redeemed again to her destiny years later.

As we walk this journey with Beloved, we observe Master Potter's loving oversight of her life even in seasons of disobedience. He is intent on fashioning her into a beautiful vessel of honor and preparing her for a new destiny birthed of His sure prophetic word. He patiently shapes her with His loving hand. She is taken into deep places of healing from painful memories that have left her broken, fearful, and wounded, full of anger, bitterness, and shame. Her heart is gradually secured from all the places where she is still vulnerable to the subtle seductions of the world, the weakness of the flesh, and the fiery darts of the enemy. She learns the healing power of forgiveness, and the supernatural reversal of dark designs against her by deepened repentance and purified love.

You will find in the characters that make up Beloved's journey through life curious resemblances to people in your own history. The abuse of Antagonist, the lies of Madam False Destiny and Pastor Compromise, the treachery of Mayor Lecherous and Pastor Beguiler, and the infidelity of Enchanter. The oppressing demons of Fear, Shame, Self-Pity, Despair and Death, and her heavenly companions, Valiant and Amazing Grace who war against them—these all give shape to the common spiritual struggles of the redeemed.

Unlike most fiction, this book invites a slow reading. In fact, there are profound encounters with the healing Lord awaiting a thoughtful and reflective reading of *Master Potter*. So vivid, so real, so human is her journey that if you dare to leave your heart open to the workings of the Holy Spirit, you will experience measures of healing and deliverance yourself. Beloved's journey into wholeness can be replicated in the careful reader! The book invites you to read it prayerfully and expectantly—to anticipate healing and cleansing encounters with the love of Master Potter who is fashioning us for a bridal destiny at His right hand.

—Steve Carpenter
Th.M. Dallas Theological Seminary
President of Word and Spirit Ministries
Director of the Forerunner School of Prayer
with Mike Bickle's International House of Prayer, Kansas City, Missouri

Foreword

Too many today are starving.

In a modern society longing to experience the reality of the Holy Spirit, they have relentlessly pursued nearly anything supernatural. People are so disillusioned and jaded by the lack of the Holy Spirit's power and demonstration in Christendom that they have resorted to hunting for it wherever they can. So thirsty for living water, they go to the desert and, instead of finding living streams, they have learned to drink the sand. The wild success of *Harry Potter* testifies how easily people get ensnared into the occult, New Age, and witchcraft simply from their hungering for something more.

Jill's book offers something authentic, something more, by countering the current counterfeit imitation. She leads the reader into the arms of the true source of all the mysteries of the supernatural—the Master Potter Himself—the glorious man Christ Jesus. She demystifies some of the *mystical* by pulling back the curtain of the spiritual realm, as the reader is caught up in the battle between angels and demons and whisked into the transcendent splendor of the throne room of the beautiful God.

Warning, dear reader: You are not merely beginning a book but rather entering into your own journey into the ravished heart of Jesus, the Master Potter. With the unfolding of this prophetic journey, we watch the adventure of a broken little pitcher named Forsaken, who is renamed Beloved as a vessel of honor fit for the King's use.

Mirroring the Shulammite woman in The Song of Songs, Forsaken's tale begins with a spiritual crisis. Distraught with desolation, Forsaken is wounded and discarded in the Potter's Field—the garbage dump on the outskirts of town. In the debris and rubble of her deferred hopes and dreams, Master Potter pursues Forsaken. Like us, Forsaken simply desires to be loved and to love in return. She is obviously a picture of what happens in our own hearts. In her weakness, she realizes that she is "dark" yet altogether lovely to the Master Potter—Jesus Christ. Her heart is tenderized; the first commandment is restored to first place in her heart; her name and identity are forever changed from Forsaken to Beloved.

Yes, Beloved emerges from her wilderness as one victoriously leaning on her Master Potter. She is no longer an echo; now, she is a voice. Beloved is not one who has memorized a message, for her authority comes from the secret place of being "shelved" for the Master Potter's use. Living for an audience of one, in this very place of intimacy, she gains great authority in the Spirit. The Master Potter can then challenge her to go to the deeper places in Him—the "Mountain of Fire."

This prophetic allegory reveals the greatest mystery in the universe: Christ and the Church are betrothed to be married forever! Because you are His favorite and He is crazy about you, He doesn't want to just bless you; He wants to give you Himself! In the turning of these pages, you will hear the love songs of God's heart for you. Learn to listen; learn to return them back to His heart.

God is going to change the understanding and expression of Christianity in this generation. My conviction is that this book will help catalyze this transformation process that God desires for all His people. Jill's message is not merely for the Church but also a call for the lost to enter into God's grace, which is abundantly available through Jesus. This story transcends the walls of the church to meet a generation exactly where they are. In a world where most do not know Jesus, we must respond with a "yes" to God's desire to revolutionize how the world sees the man Christ Jesus. From Barnes and Noble to prison cells, this book sounds an alarm that our hunger must not be met in *Harry Potter* but rather in the *Master Potter* Himself.

So come, eat and drink deeply! Beloved, you will not walk away the same; this book will ruin you for Jesus! Therefore, it is with great excitement that I wholeheartedly introduce to you Jill's book. I pray that with the turning of each page, this book will root you and ground you in the reality that *you* are the one He desires.

With passion for Jesus,

—Mike Bickle
International House of Prayer
Kansas City, MO

Greetings From the Author

From Potter to Preacher

...O Lord, thou art our Father; we are the clay, and thou our potter; we all are the work of thy hand (Isaiah 64:8).

For years I was an award-winning, professional potter before the Lord ambushed me and called me to full-time ministry. One day, as I was demonstrating on my wheel how to make a clay vessel at a Christian art festival, I heard His audible voice. Tenderly He began to speak to me of His love for the clay vessel. I repeated what He said, and the people listening were powerfully touched. Through pottery the Lord gave me insight into His great love and tender mercies for us, His vessels.

This was the beginning of my wonderful prophetic journey, which is known as Master Potter Ministries, a performing arts group combining music, drama and art. It's hard to believe that this began over 25 years ago. For those first ten years I used the potter's wheel and portrayed Jesus as the Master Potter, while actors spoke for the clay vessel. The last 15 years the Lord transitioned me away from these dramas into preaching and moving in signs, wonders and miracles around the world.

Pottery is still a passion of my heart. I love the yieldedness of the clay as I sit at the wheel. I'm always aware that any abrupt movement of my hands could tear the vessel.

The pottery process parallels our prophetic journeys. Jesus is the divine Potter and we are the yielded clay. Each vessel is His handiwork, unique and loved by Him.

Through our lives our sinful choices are manifested as cracks, chips and brokenness. When a vessel becomes too broken it is pronounced "worthless" and is discarded. That's when Master Potter comes on the scene, rescues the pot, and begins to remake it. He does not disqualify us because of our weakness and vulnerability. He whispers in our ear His great love and incredible destiny for us—transforming us from weak broken vessels into His victorious Bride.

Unfortunately, much of this process is quite painful. We find ourselves back on the wheel of life and then impatiently sit on the shelf to dry. Can't you relate to the testing of your faith when you are in the kiln and fired for the purposes of God? What an incredible, tailor-made journey God has for each of us!

This allegory is the story of weak broken pots powerfully loved, redeemed and re-created by Master Potter. May the book give you encouragement for whatever stage of the prophetic journey you're in. As a potter I promise you this—if you submit to Master Potter's gentle touch, you'll end up as a vessel of honor fit for the King's service.

—Jill Austin
Master Potter Ministries

Frail dust, remember, you are splendor!

MACRINA WIEDERKEHR

Settings and Characters

Settings

Comfort Cove, a quaint nineteenth-century seaside fishing village
The Potter's Field, the garbage dump outside Comfort Cove
The Potter's House, Master Potter's home overlooking Comfort Cove
Deeper Life, a religious commune in the wilderness
Formidable Mountains, a rugged mountain range behind the Potter's House
Precarious Pass, a dangerous pass through the Formidable Mountains
Mountain of Fire, a mountain kiln deep within the Formidable Mountains
Madam False Destiny's Inn, an entertainment establishment

Major Characters

Father in Heaven
Master Potter/Son of God
Holy Spirit
Beloved/Forsaken, a pitcher
Satan/Prince of Darkness

Demons and Angels

Michael the archangel
Gabriel, the messenger angel
Valiant, Beloved's guardian angel
Death
Suicide
Fear of Man
Religious Ritual
Law 'n Order

Comfort Cove

Antagonist, Forsaken's former boyfriend
Madam False Destiny, spiritualist and owner of the inn

The Fire Chief
Mayor Lecherous
Pastor Compromise, pastor of the Country Club Church
Grandma Pearl, Beloved's deceased grandmother
Beloved's father, the town drunk

Pottery Tools

Unrelenting Love, a large stone used to crush clay pots
Servant, a reddish-brown bowl
Soaking Love, a sponge
Piercing Love, a needle-like tool used to puncture air bubbles
Rite of Passage, a cutting wire used to remove the vessel from the potter's wheel
Pruning, a metal trimming tool used to take excess clay from the bottom of pots

The Wilderness

Amazing Grace, a mysterious guide
Pastor Beguiler, pastor of Deeper Life Community Church
Mrs. Beguiler, Pastor Beguiler's wife
Enchanter, Pastor Beguiler's son
Purity/Promiscuous, Beloved's daughter
Crusader/Rebellious, Beloved's son

Beloved's Friends

Turncoat/Faithful, (a sugar bowl), a card dealer at Madam False Destiny's Inn
Comrade/Friendless, a squatty mug
Harvester, a large canister
Sweet Adoration, a perfume vial
Long Suffering, a tall, willowy vase
Golden Incense, a teapot
Fearless, a wine carafe
Joyful, a wine goblet
Patience, a beautiful vase
Steadfast, a large serving platter
Diligence, a sturdy casserole dish
Abundance, a large fruit bowl
His Desire, a glazed pitcher

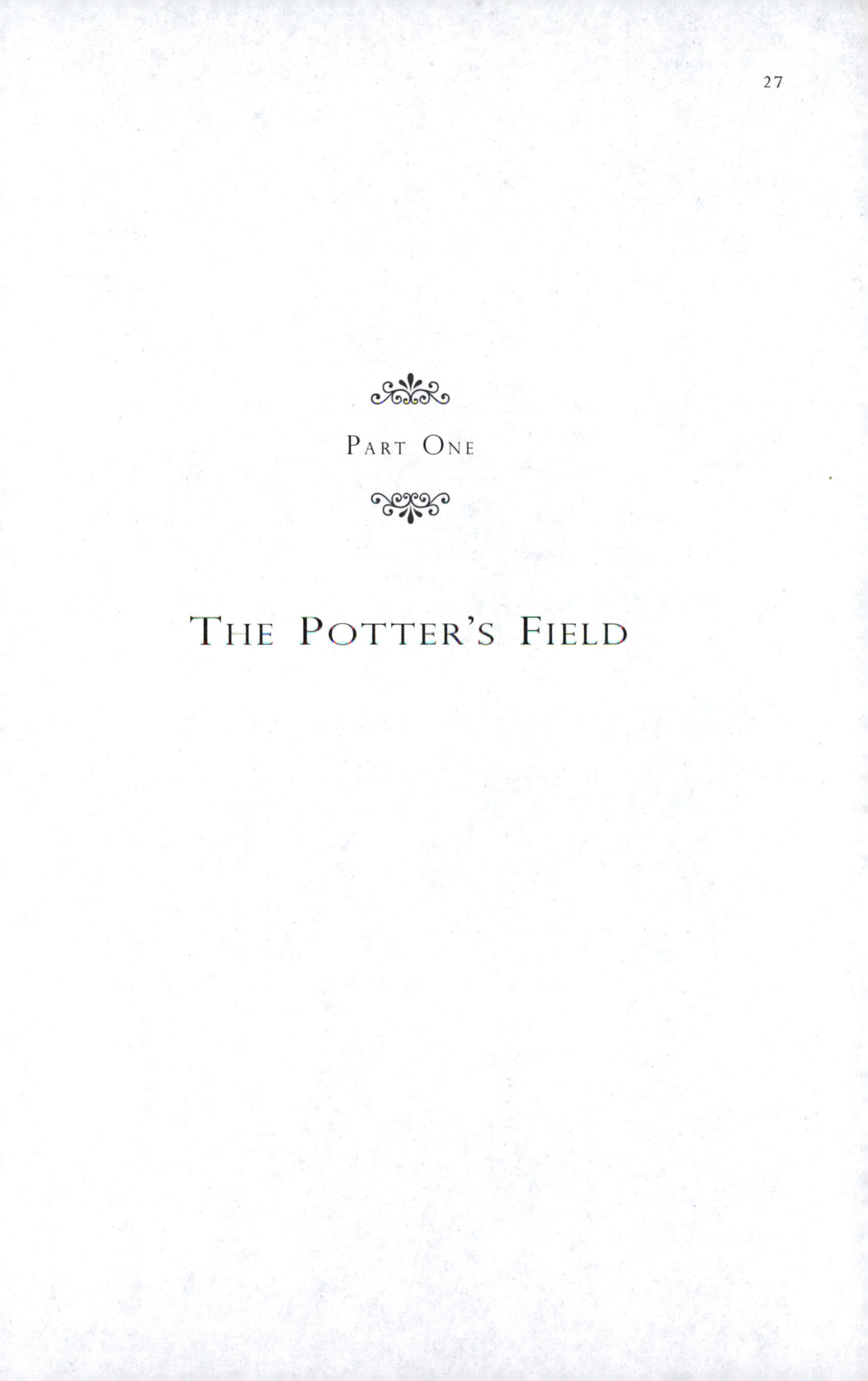

Part One

The Potter's Field

Chapter One

Jill's Studio

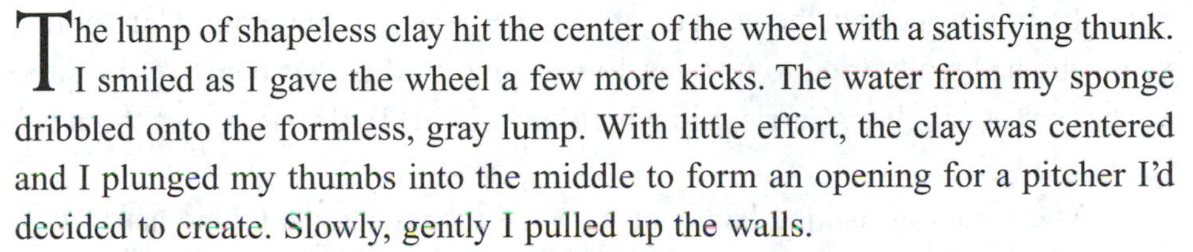

The lump of shapeless clay hit the center of the wheel with a satisfying thunk. I smiled as I gave the wheel a few more kicks. The water from my sponge dribbled onto the formless, gray lump. With little effort, the clay was centered and I plunged my thumbs into the middle to form an opening for a pitcher I'd decided to create. Slowly, gently I pulled up the walls.

I let out a big sigh. I love this creative process. Transforming a worthless lump of clay into a beautiful, highly prized vessel has been a passion of mine for more than 25 years.

I'd had this pitcher on my mind for a week or more but hadn't found time to slip off to my studio. Although I didn't understand it, I had a sense of urgency about creating this piece. I felt as if I was birthing something. I smiled as I imagined the finished form, glazed white with royal blue filigree and trimmed in gold. Before I'd started forming it, I knew where it would go—on my mantel with fresh flowers spilling over the sides. In joyous anticipation, I'd already cleared the space.

I felt comfortable, even secure, sitting at the potter's wheel, cocooned away from the world, lost in my affection for this pot. Outside my studio it was raining, and lightning flashes highlighted the rain hitting the skylight. Even the thunder claps sounded warm and friendly.

But life can be so capricious. Reveling in my work, I had no way of knowing that someone was dialing my phone number, and her message would send me spinning into turmoil. My fervency for this piece was so great that I almost didn't answer the phone, but I yielded to an inner voice urging me to pick it up. Thick gray clay coated the receiver and tangled into my sun-streaked, blond hair. Brushing the matted hair from my face with my forearm, I heard the distraught voice of Jennifer's mother on the other end. It was tragic news—there had been a terrible car wreck....

I hung up the phone, leaned my head back against the window and looked into the sky as rain washed down the window in streaks, forming little rivers on the glass. I slumped over and began to weep. After a few minutes I lifted my wet face upward and asked God, "Why?"

Jennifer had been like the sister I'd never had. We grew up together through grade school and high school. Her dad was an alcoholic, and it seemed as if she spent more nights at my house than she did at her own. She dropped out of high school with just two months left to marry a 27-year-old *alcoholic*! I begged, pleaded, and cried, but I couldn't talk her out of it. Then she got pregnant, the beatings began, he went to jail, and she was a single mom. The last few years she had really tried to turn her life around. I think that being responsible for her sweet daughter, Carrie, had a lot to do with it. To Carrie, I was "Aunt Jill the pot lady."

After years of making bad choices, even though she had done her best to leave that life behind, the destructive patterns kept controlling her. It seemed that she couldn't escape, no matter how hard she tried. I spent years crying and praying for her, but she kept rejecting God's love.

Unbelievably, a drunk driver had hit her car on the passenger side as he ran a red light. She was sober, but it seems that the demon of alcohol never let her get far from its wretched grasp.

Now little Carrie was teetering between life and death, and Jen, whose life was not in danger, had broken bones from her skull to her ankles. They'd both need surgeries, but of course Jen couldn't afford health insurance.

Still sobbing gently, I looked down at the pitcher slowly turning on the wheel. "Here is Jennifer," I said, motioning to the half-completed form, "and here is the world." Angry at the world and at God, I brought both fists crashing down onto the pot. I scooped the mangled vessel off the wheel and hurled it into the refuse pile with the other discarded pots. I'd had a unique design for each of these pots, but they'd never realized their potential and had become nothing but rubbish.

Hurt and disgusted, I turned off the lights at the studio and plodded through the rain back to the house.

After washing up, I threw a few logs into the old stone fireplace while the kettle on the stove came to a boil. Settling into an overstuffed leather chair in front of the fireplace, I put my feet up and waited for the cup of tea to cool enough for a first sip. I tried in vain to push the image of the car accident out of my head—surely this hadn't happened. Then I noticed the vacant spot I'd prepared on the mantel, and hot tears cleared the rims of my eyes and spilled down my cheeks.

"Lord, why does life have to be so hard? Jen suffered so much and now this. Why did You make Your people so weak? We're just dirt and water mixed together and formed into fragile clay vessels. So breakable, so vulnerable—so expendable...."

I stared at the dancing flames and took a sip of tea. Ouch, still too hot! A bolt of lightning struck close outside, and the immediate thunderclap was right overhead. I took several deep breaths to help slow my racing heart and went back to prayer. "Oh Lord, what if Carrie dies? How will Jennifer ever recover? It's not fair—life's too hard. Sometimes it seems as if we're all pots on a potter's wheel spinning out of control."

In an instant, the room became pregnant with the presence of God. Deep in my spirit I heard a voice, "Fragile, yes, but there is a mystery in why I created earthenware vessels. When they realize their great weakness they will call out to Me. Each one's journey takes them through much joy and pain—but no person or situation is beyond hope. There is no tragedy that can't be redeemed. I am the God of second chances, and I passionately love every one of My vessels. Each one is a unique piece of beautiful art, designed before the foundation of the world and fashioned by My loving hands.

"Let Me take you to Kadim, the land of earthen vessels, and to a village called Comfort Cove and show you another little wounded clay vessel. No one believed she had a future or hope either, but My Son, Master Potter, fought to redeem her as His Bride. This young woman's name is Forsaken, but to Him she has always been Beloved."

Chapter Two

Master Potter

The burning logs in my fireplace give way to an open vision. A quaint nineteenth-century fishing village appears before my eyes. Ships docked at the harbor for the night roll with the waves, and their crisp, white sails whip in the wind. The last sliver of sun is disappearing over the horizon. The cobblestone streets are deserted. Looking in the distance I see beautiful, snow-covered mountain peaks.

Suddenly I am transported toward the mountain range and to the edge of a jagged cliff which overlooks Comfort Cove. The low-lying clouds reflect the vibrant reds and oranges of the sunset off the white-capped sea below.

I turn away from the cliff and I can see an alluring and mysterious light flickering through a fragrant cedar forest. I know that my purpose for being here is to approach this brilliant, fiery glow. As I pick up my pace, the atmosphere becomes alive.

When I step out from the ancient grove I get my first unobscured glimpse of this old-world, stone and log house. A pillar of fire, terrifying in its beauty, broods over it. The pillar engulfs but does not destroy this mystical dwelling. A heavy mist of radiant glory surrounds it like a blazing whirlwind. A dazzling display of light and golden mist permeates the environment.

I have no fear; in fact I feel drawn to this fiery, yet inviting dwelling. As I walk closer I feel life emanating from this amazing house. With each breath of the heavenly atmosphere I feel I'm leaving my stress and cares behind. I feel like I'm home, even though I've never been here before. In the soft mist of this glory the whole world seems to be bathed in magnificence. I can't wait to look in the window.

I stand on my tiptoes and my eyes are immediately drawn to a huge stone fireplace where a blazing fire crackles and dances. Each weather-beaten stone is hand-hewn and has been placed artistically on top of the next. Several large, graceful vases, elegant pitchers, and sturdy platters are prominently displayed on the great cedar mantel above.

I can feel heat radiating from the fireplace and I can smell the earthy aroma of clay mingled with the fragrance of brewing tea. Everything about this house is bright, alive and inviting.

I force myself to look away from the fireplace to see the rest of the room. The back walls are lined with old wooden shelves displaying hundreds of vessels in different stages of completion. The ceilings are supported by rustic beams of aged cedar. Flickering kerosene lanterns add to the cozy, intimate quality of the room.

As I continue to watch, unsure whether I'm till in my house seeing a vision or whether I'm actually outside this fiery supernatural home, Master Potter enters the room and settles into His big leather chair.

The cozy fire from the stone hearth casts flickering light onto the dark waves of His thick, shoulder-length brown hair and His plain brown robe. He leans His head back and sighs, relaxing after a long, satisfying day creating vessels of destiny. The spicy aroma of freshly brewed tea tempts Him to another sip, and He slowly places His sandaled feet on a low wooden footstool. As He gazes over His cup, deep in thought, dancing flames reflect in His sad, brown eyes.

Fervent Prayers of the Son

"Father, there are so many broken and devastated lives! Oh, how I long to rescue and heal them." Master Potter kneels at the footstool, folding His callused hands. Soon the room fills with loud groans as His prayer turns to deep travail. "The enemy is fierce and delights in their torment. My heart aches when I hear their agonizing cries for deliverance. Oh, Father, bring those who are Mine into the Kingdom! Stir the prayer warriors as the battle increases."

Terrible loneliness sweeps over Him. "The waiting is unbearable! My heart burns with passion for those broken vessels that will one day become My Bride. She will be so beautiful on our wedding day."

Centuries of waiting and longing erupt into fervent intercession.

Before the Father's Throne

Master Potter's fervent prayers thunder into the throne room. Heaven pauses, waiting for the Father's response to His Son's prayer. He turns toward the myriad of worshiping angels, all lovesick in extravagant devotion to Him. As far as the eye can see, shimmering light reflects from their wingtips, creating a heavenly rainbow.

This beauty realm of the throne room—with vistas of celestial colors, rare fragrances and surges of radiant light—fills the heavens. Twenty-four elders surround the great throne, arrayed in white robes and adorned with crowns. Each elder holds a harp and golden bowl representing heavenly worship and intercession. These bowls contain the prayers of the saints and are sweet incense rising up to the Father.

Four living creatures, full of eyes and blazing with fire, guard the throne. These burning ones glisten with dazzling light as they fly around the face of God. They are glorious blazing fires of worship consumed and alive with the fire of His presence. Lightning and fire shoot back and forth among them in magnificent splendor.

Night and day, they never cease their adoration and ministry as they receive greater revelation of His beauty. Overcome by each revelation, they cry, "Holy, holy, holy! Lord God Almighty" and release the new vision of His beauty to the 24 elders, who fall down and cast their crowns at His feet.

They join all of creation in worshiping the One who sits on the throne.

Holy Spirit manifests as seven torches of blazing fire moving throughout the atmosphere in a beautiful symmetry of movement.

Millions of words and harmonies become one magnificent song! A symphony of sounds never heard by human ears resounds throughout the throne room. And yet at the same time there is silence. Silence, yet sound.

GABRIEL, COME FORTH!

"Gabriel, come forth!" the Father cries. From the myriad of worshipers, this glorious messenger angel steps forward. He has fine, chiseled features, long golden hair and piercing eyes of fire. Rays of brilliant light emanate from his heavenly being, and the intensity of glory increases with each step he takes closer to the throne. Magnificently powerful in spirit and body, the angel bows low.

"Gabriel, I'm overcome by His cries. I long for His presence." He hands Gabriel a burning scroll of divine secrets and tells him to summon Master Potter to the throne room. The magnificent archangel bows again after receiving his orders. The Father smiles at his trusted messenger and motions for him to rise.

He signals His warring archangel to join them. The glint of Michael's flaming sword fills the heavenly atmosphere with golden, reflected light. This mighty warrior comes before the throne fully armed with godly wisdom and experience culled from many ancient victories. Michael's eyes are like pools of fire and his hair is light, almost flaxen. His skin is deeply tanned, a kind of burnished bronze. It radiates from having been in God's presence from eternity past. He wears a white tunic with golden embroidery and a belt encircles his waist. Dangling medallions embellish his shoulders, signifying his governmental rank. "You are to go before Gabriel to Kadim, making a path through the lower regions. Hold the territory until he returns."

Michael, wrapped in the fiery brilliance of the glory of God, summons his troops with a piercing blast from his blazing trumpet. Their war cry thunders through the heavens, "For the Father, the Son, and the Holy Spirit, that His Bride might come forth."

As each movement of his luminous wings thunders through the heavens, excitement for the impending battle charges the atmosphere and rumbles through the celestial troops. "Yes, that the Bride may come forth!"

Entering the Earth's Disputed Territory

Violent surges of glory radiate from these celestial beings as they charge from the throne room with blazing swords drawn. Soon they are slicing through the thick sulfuric atmosphere as they open a heavenly portal. Penetrating the human realm, the heavenly troop leaves eternity and enters the restraints of time.

Like a fiery ball of light, the soldiers cross from a realm of indescribable beauty and eternal harmony into a world of chaos, war and endless brutal strife. As the light of divine fire pierces the spiritual darkness, the angelic warriors catch the foul demonic swarm by surprise as they battle to enter earth's disputed atmosphere.

Unsheathing their vile swords, demons spew out blasphemous curses that clash wildly against golden torrents of resurrection power. The demonic forces are enraged with the intrusion into the captured territory they consider their own.

Stunned to a momentary halt, the panicked demons are filled with terror. Fiery explosions erupt around them, blasting through their ranks and throwing burning, screeching demon hordes howling back to the abyss. Fiery prayer missiles from earth explode around them and wreak havoc against the satanic host.

Horrific screams frantically signal for more demonic reinforcements. Master Potter's prayers have hit the mark, crippling the enemy and cutting them off. Terror fills the hooded eyes of the gruesome, diabolical spirits as the battle rages.

Suddenly Michael yells to Gabriel, "We've cleared the path, and I'm sending my best warriors ahead to take you in. We'll stay here and hold the ground until you return."

With long, golden hair flying wildly in the spiritual wind, Gabriel sets his chiseled features and noble face firmly in determination to carry out the Father's will. Fiercely majestic, his appearance is disguised in white-hot lightning flashes. He leaves a trail of fiery golden light as his magnificent, shimmering wings carry him on his strategic mission.

MASTER POTTER'S HOUSE

Gabriel flies over the rough, white-capped seas that ceaselessly pummel the shoreline. On the edge of a jagged cliff, surrounded by an ancient cedar forest, sits Master Potter's House. Built into the rock to provide protection from the raging storms, this secluded stronghold overlooks the quaint fishing village of Comfort Cove.

Circling high above, Gabriel sees a pillar of fire descending from the heavens. Like a bright tornado, it swirls around the house—a marvel of wind and glory. This mystery of heavenly flames engulfs but does not destroy the house; it is placed by Father as a hidden entryway into salvation, concealed within the enemy's camp.

GABRIEL'S VISIT

Before the ache of Master Potter's heart can be fully expressed, the movement of wings ushers the splendor of Heaven into the fireside room. Gabriel emerges through the fiery pillar. Overcome with awe and humility, the great angel bows in worship before his Master. The Potter quietly receives his praise and smiles at his unexpected return.

The fellowship of comrades in this most ancient of wars is instantly renewed as Master Potter lovingly touches Gabriel's shoulders, summoning him to stand. Gabriel's smile gives way to joyous laughter as he embraces Master Potter, the beautiful, glorious Son of God.

"The Father heard Your cries and sent me. The enemy, though surprised by our sudden appearance, was firm in its fierce resistance. When we began to feel the weight of the enemy's detainment, Your prayers strengthened us for the final thrust into this cherished realm."

"I knew the battle was raging, so I prayed on your behalf." Gesturing to the shelves, Master Potter says, "The fighting has been violent on the Potter's Field as well, but there are great victories. Many new vessels are lining my shelves. I have planned incredible destinies for each of them."

"They're beautifully designed and each one is so unique. In the heavens we watch with wonder and excitement as You mold the clay into Your own divine image." Gabriel extends the golden scroll. "I must go now; Your Father has additional orders for me."

A knowing nod transpires between them as the mighty angelic being turns and ascends heavenward through the fiery pillar.

Unrolling the parchment scroll, Master Potter eases into His chair and rubs His soft, curly beard as He reads. Sweet memories of intimate fellowship with the Father and Holy Spirit stir deep love and longing within His soul, and He places His hand over His heart and sighs.

His penetrating gaze returns to the hearth, and flames explode in fiery tongues of orange and yellow at the glory emanating from His eyes. The blazing fire and wind envelop and transport Him heavenward toward holy communion.

Fiery passion from the Father's heart sweeps over Him as they run to embrace each other, completing the divine mystery of the Trinity. Softly at first, and then with gentle crescendo, a celestial symphony fills the heavens with rare and unearthly fragrances, touching time and eternity.

Chapter Three

Forsaken

Fleeing down the cobblestone alley behind the old tavern to the outskirts of Comfort Cove, Forsaken stumbles into the dreaded Potter's Field. Moonlight illuminates the broken vessels and garbage heaped on this huge city of worthless refuse. Bloodied and bruised after another vicious beating, she is barely escaping with her life.

Years of trying to fill the empty void inside her soul had led to a downward spiral of alcohol, men, self-loathing and bitterness. Penniless and out of choices, she moved into a shabby room above the fisherman's tavern with a local brawler named Antagonist.

Once the thought of such an individual would have sickened her, but years of compromise made sleeping with even the vilest of men acceptable.

It wasn't long before she became the target of his rage. During one of his many violent attacks he cracked her sides, leaving gaping wounds in her fragile, clay vessel.

I've got to hide. If Antagonist finds me he'll kill me! Gasping for breath and exhausted from running, Forsaken collapses to the ground, convulsing in loud, broken sobs. Wet ocean fog rolls in, slowly turning the Potter's Field into an eerie, otherworldly landscape. The anguished cries of other broken vessels echo sharply across the lonely field.

A terrifying demonic horde creeps out of the dark shadows and through piles of garbage, further wounding the already shattered vessels. Hiding in an open trench, Forsaken grabs her head, trying to escape the recent memory of Antagonist's destructive words and the heavy blows.

Forsaken had regained consciousness and was surprised to find Antagonist passed out on the floor. Reeling from the beating and her own alcoholic stupor, she stumbled down the stairs and out into the night. With no other place to go, her terror drove her down the alley and finally into this field of torment. Abandonment and hopelessness fell over her like a heavy blanket.

The Guardian Angel

Standing close by, a huge figure sadly watches Forsaken; she is crusted in mud, lying among the pottery shards and broken pieces of glass. He longs to help but cannot, at least not yet. The imposing angelic being, Valiant, has looked after her since birth. Somber and still, his features express the years of disappointment and concern over the many tragic choices she has made—choices that have culminated in the scene that now lies at his feet. Once hopeful for her future, he wonders if she will ever turn to Master Potter and be saved.

Meanwhile, Forsaken's heart pounds wildly. *This is worse than I ever imagined! Not only do I have to hide from Antagonist, but what if the legends are true? Since childhood I've heard that Master Potter stalks the Potter's Field at night and lures broken vessels to His home, only to hurl them into the Mountain of Fire. Once you enter this field they say you're never heard from again. What if it's true?*

Drained and exhausted, her body throbbing with pain, she falls into a fitful sleep. Demons dance in and out of her nightmares as she floats off in her alcoholic-induced stupor. Moaning aloud, Forsaken struggles in her sleep as nightmarish visions haunt her with images—her abusive father screaming into her young face, threatening to abandon her in the Potter's Field.

Near dawn, Forsaken stirs awake. Drenched in sweat, her dress clings to her broken and aching body. The rising sun begins to burn off the fog and beats down on the mounds of rotting garbage inhabited by swarming flies. Her mind reels with the reality of actually sitting in this appalling field.

Streams of vapor rise from the refuse, creating a nauseating stench. She sees vultures circling, waiting for the last breath to escape from abandoned and dying vessels just like her. With trembling hands, she pushes herself up, determined to begin searching for a hiding place.

From a standing position, Forsaken is now able to see the vastness of this city of refuse. Jagged mountains of trash, garbage and broken vessels are strewn as far as her eyes can see in every direction. Those vessels that survived the night begin to emerge from their hiding places, driving away the packs of stray dogs and rats who challenge them for scraps of rotted food.

Looking closely at the different vessels she thinks, *I'm just like those other broken pots that have been discarded and thrown away. My whole life is ruined.*

Look at me! I used to be so beautiful and now I've lost everything. This is what my father always said I deserved. I guess he was right! I'm going to die in the Potter's Field.

CLOTHED WITH COMPROMISE

Hours drag on, and Forsaken eventually finds a discarded barrel and climbs in. Peering through the cracks, she sees hundreds of other shattered vessels carelessly discarded across the field. As her mind screams with tormenting thoughts about her many bad decisions, she tries to push back the guilt and shame by blame shifting and rationalizing them away. *I wouldn't be in this mess if it weren't for Antagonist! Why couldn't he treat me right? He's just like all the rest.*

Trembling with fear, Forsaken feels the haze of her alcoholic stupor clearing. She crouches lower in the barrel, covering her ears in a futile attempt to block out the ceaseless, terrifying cries of tormented souls struggling to escape their misery. In the place of broken and forgotten dreams and dashed hopes, dark clouds of depression and the heaviness of despair descend upon everything in sight, covering the Potter's Field in a death-like shroud. Spiritual darkness excites even more demonic activity, and depression consumes the field.

WARRING OVER LOST SOULS

The mighty angelic being adjusts his sword as he scans the dreary scene. His orders are clear: he is not to interfere unless Forsaken's life is threatened. So he stands interceding, waiting to see what the end of the little damaged pitcher will be.

In this chaotic environment, an insidious war over lost souls continually rages. Spirits of rebellion and jealousy breed division in an attempt to annihilate fragile relationships. The purpose: isolate the vessels and make them easy targets. Already strained ties between family and friends are severed and destroyed by the sinister minions, as relationships yield to the destructive grip of demonic bondage.

HOW DID I GET HERE?

As night approaches, Forsaken crawls out of the stifling barrel and bitterly mutters to herself, "It wasn't supposed to happen this way! Just a few years ago I had everything. How did my life go so wrong?"

Her thin, mud-splattered dress no longer conceals her bruises. Blood from the cuts on her forehead and arms has stained her tattered outfit. *I used to be so attractive before I ended up on the docks. I always had a voice like a nightingale, and when I sang for the dinner parties at Madam's inn, just the rustle of my beautiful gown turned every man's head. Look at me now!* Forsaken sobs bitterly as she touches her tender cuts and bruises. *I'm such a mess! No one would ever want me.*

The intense fear of again being found by Antagonist drives her to look for a better place to hide. She slowly picks her way through the field, trying hard not to let panic overwhelm her. Once before she had tried to escape his controlling clutches, and he threatened to hunt her down and kill her if she ever left again.

She sees movement ahead, hope is rekindled and she limps quickly toward another broken vessel. Drawing near, she hoarsely whispers, "Can you help me? I'm lost and thirsty. I just need a safe place to stay for a few days and then I'll be traveling on. You see—I don't really belong here."

DEPRESSION'S DESTINY

The pudgy little mug laughs with contempt, "Oh, you belong here all right. I know all about you. When I worked for the village I occasionally enjoyed dinner with the mayor. That's when I heard you sing at Madam False Destiny's Inn." Sticking a fleshy finger in her face, he continues, "Everyone knew you were a cheap little gold digger—so don't tell me you don't belong here!"

Stung by the harsh words, Forsaken retorts with anger, "Who are you to judge me? I wasn't after Madam's money. Besides, I don't have to answer to you."

"Of course no one blames you, coming from the docks and all. I heard that after you got kicked out of Madam's inn you became a drunk just like your old man."

Her shoulders drop and she hangs her head in shame, causing the gaps in her sides to widen and send jolts of new pain across her fragile vessel. Yes, she had come from the docks, but her natural beauty had opened doors for her. She once believed that she had a chance at being happy and cherished by someone special. Forsaken acknowledges to herself that she had become willing to do anything to escape from her alcoholic father.

Still—it's none of this dirty mug's business. "You keep my dad out of it. I'll never be like him! Besides, did you ever wake up wondering if there would be food on the table? Did you go to school every day with all the other kids laughing at your ragged clothing? You don't know what it's like to be poor! So who are you to judge me?"

"Don't snap at me!" steams the mug. "You think you're the only one who had it rough? Just because I wasn't poor doesn't mean my life was easy. My folks gave me plenty of things, but they never loved me. I was the brunt of everyone's jokes because I'm a squatty little mug. Why do you think they named me Friendless? You're a low grade of clay, but at least you were once pretty and had friends."

Insulted, Forsaken spews out a stream of venom: "So, you think I'm 'low grade,' do you? I see you're in the Potter's Field, too. Why don't you just get out of here? I'm sorry I asked you for anything! Just go away and leave me alone."

Friendless grudgingly kicks another broken vessel before shuffling away. Lifelong companions, demons of self-pity taunt him: "No one cares about an ugly, squatty mug like you, and no one ever will. You might as well be dead. No one would even know you're gone."

Forsaken watches him disappear over a mound of garbage. "Good riddance to bad rubbish!" she angrily yells in his direction. Then she realizes she's alone once more. Immediately, she wishes she had been nicer; after all, he was a man and maybe he could have protected her.

FINDING ONLY FEAR

The rising moon reflects the silhouettes of large, repulsive rats scurrying to gnash at the other devastated lives around her. Delighting in their cruel assignments, vile spirits embed their poisonous talons into the hearts and minds of their helpless victims.

If only I had a drink to calm my nerves and take away the fear. Forsaken digs furiously through the rubbish looking for a discarded bottle with even a few drops of liquor left inside. Frustrated, she throws an empty one over her shoulder and hears a cry, "Hey, lady, watch what you're doing! That hurts!"

Spinning around, Forsaken is startled to see a chipped, stoneware sugar bowl. She recognizes her as the dealer from the private gambling club at Madam's. The dealer had seldom spoken to Forsaken there, except to snap off a mocking, "Yes, Madam," through clenched yellow teeth that invariably held a dangling, somewhat mauled cigarette. Turncoat's movements were always brisk, and her skills with a deck of cards made lots of money for Madam. Her chain-smoking created a brownish-yellow hazy cloud of smoke and putrid odor that clung to each of the high-rolling gamblers.

"Oh, I'm so sorry. I didn't mean to hurt you. I hardly recognize you now. The last time I saw you, you were dealing for Madam."

The dull little sugar bowl stops and studies Forsaken's face. Placing her hands on her wide hips, she rasps, "Well, well. If it isn't Forsaken, the little princess herself! You're not so glamorous anymore, are you?"

"Turncoat, please. I'm new here, and I need help. Someplace to stay for the night at least. You know I don't belong here."

"Listen here, girlie, I might have been a low-ranking employee at Madam's, but we're equal here. You're on your own. I can't help you."

"I can't believe you're doing this. I thought we were friends."

"I was never your friend. You didn't have time for me; you preferred the important people on your haughty climb up the social ladder. But now we see the truth of the matter. No, Forsaken, you're in the right place. You belong in this garbage dump just like the rest of us." Turncoat's lip snarls up just enough to expose her yellow, tobacco-stained teeth.

The demonically fueled words pierce Forsaken's freshly wounded heart, releasing a horde of vile, slimy demons to assault her. Spirits of self-hatred attach themselves to her, driving their sharp talons deep into the tender flesh of her heart and mind. She stumbles further into the Potter's Field. Humiliation and guilt hover over her, battering her with painful memories. Forsaken drops her head into her hands despondently as she succumbs to their vile demonic games. Meanwhile, her addiction is screaming inside of her, driving her in a frantic search for relief.

Chapter Four

The Looking Glass

Frightened at the prospect of spending the night in the open field, Forsaken finds a discarded wagon wheel and slumps down next to it, vowing to stay awake. But in seconds she falls into an agitated sleep.

The great angel, Valiant, her unseen guardian, moves silently through the night, stopping by her side. He tenderly smoothes her wet, matted hair and imparts strength to her fragile frame. Undetected, he recedes back into the shadows, casting a gentle, amber glow into the darkness. He is ever aware of his orders concerning her and prays again to the Father on her behalf.

Moaning in her sleep, Forsaken jerks suddenly and awakens. She pulls herself up with her hands and braces her back uncomfortably against the wheel. Running her swollen tongue over her teeth, she is aware that her bruised, foul-tasting mouth burns with yesterday's bitter whiskey, cigarettes, vomit and dried blood.

Picking up the handle of an old, shattered hand mirror lying beside her, she stares at herself in the remaining fragments. Tears well in the corners of her eyes and stream down her cheeks as she studies her distorted and cracked reflection illuminated in the dim moonlight.

She barely recognizes the woman looking back at her. Brown hair that once looked like soft silk is wildly matted with thick mud and dried blood. Dark, beautiful brown eyes that had once caught the attention of every man in her path now burn with the red soreness of alcoholism, sleeplessness and endless, convulsive crying. Worst of all is the dull deadness that stares back at her from eyes that once sparkled with bright hope. Her empty heart burns with fear, disgust and screaming need. She runs her dirty hand over her once soft and beautiful face, now deeply lined. Each line carries an ugly memory of the hardness of abuse and age. Her youth is squandered—forever lost.

"I vowed as a little girl that I'd never be like Dad. How did I turn out like this? I just wanted to fit in with the crowd at Madam's. I never knew that first little drink would lead me here."

A Look Into the Past

Her eyes are drawn back to the mirror. Dim figures emerge and scenes from her life appear like a haunting stage drama. The luxurious dining room of Madam's inn comes into focus along with the clinking of fine china and crystal goblets. Soft conversation and laughter fill the elegant candlelit room.

Forsaken is wearing a beautiful, rose-colored gown of the finest European silk, trimmed with ivory lace. The plunging neckline and skin-tight fit show off her hourglass figure. Her long skirt sways gracefully with each elegant step as she walks toward a grand piano to make her singing debut. Trembling with nervous energy, she scans the many faces in the dining room until she finds Madam's reassuring nod.

Violins and cellos join with the piano as her lovely alto voice stirs romance in the softly lit room. She is exhilarated by the cheering crowd's standing ovation. Sweet acceptance washes like waves over her lonely soul. As she looks into the exuberant crowd, she vows that she will do whatever it takes to keep this wonderful feeling alive. She curtseys, throws a kiss to the crowd and leaves the stage. *This is what I've been searching for my whole life!*

A wealthy gentleman presents her with a single red rose. Putting his arm possessively around her tiny waist, the handsome escort takes her to his private dining table. Pulling her chair out, he kisses the back of her neck, sending a rush of adrenaline through her quivering heart.

Champagne bubbles into crystal goblets, as the room toasts her successful debut. Still lost in the sweet memory of that night so long ago, Forsaken continues staring into the mirror shards and sees spirits appear around their table—spirits she never knew were there. She watches in spellbound horror as a black spirit of alcohol addiction buries his jagged talons deep into her tender heart.

The scene fades into a smoky haze, and Forsaken snaps back into her wretched reality. She wipes the tears from her red, swollen eyes. *That's where it all started. He was the first of many men who said they loved me, only to throw me away when someone else sparked their interest. All I could do was drink the pain away.*

Years of memories rush into her brain like a flood of pain that Forsaken is no longer able to drown with alcohol. She begins to see the harsh reality. Even those she had previously thought of no consequence have now rejected her. She finds herself swirling though a dark abyss of hopelessness and black despair.

Chapter Five

From Riches to Rags

Shifting her weight to ease the pain in her side, Forsaken feels a hard object under her hand, half buried in the rubbish. Digging it out, she uncovers an old pocket watch with a shattered crystal. The one remaining hand points ominously to midnight. Painful memories of another gold watch flood her mind. It was the night Mayor Lecherous approached her.

Suddenly she's in the upstairs hallway of Madam's, coming out of her bedroom, and finds him outside her door. Using his huge body, he blocks her escape and pushes her back inside.

"Forsaken, I've watched you with all those other men, and I've been patient. Now, it's time for me." His sexual appetites, inflamed by spirits of lust and perversion, are excited beyond his control.

"I can give you more than those other men. I'm very wealthy, Forsaken, and I know how to treat a class act like you. You and I, we like the same things—money and influence, the beautiful things. I can give you all these—if you give me what I want."

It was true, she did love all those things, and for just a moment she entertained the thought of allowing him to provide them. Nevertheless, in the end his repulsiveness was too great.

"Get out of here! I don't care if you are the mayor!"

He shoves her struggling body onto the bed, crushing her beneath his huge hulk. Unsuccessfully, he drops his grotesquely fat, sweating face to hers in an attempt to deliver a slobbery kiss. His breath reeks of old cigars and gin.

Panic overwhelms Forsaken, and she raises her knees and pushes with all her strength. At the same time she bites down on his ear as hard as she can, wrestling free from his unwelcome advances. She rolls out from under him as he howls in pain.

"Get away from me! Not only are you repulsive—you're married!"

Holding his bleeding ear, he shouts, "When did you develop a conscience?"

"You'll never have me. You disgust me! How dare you come into my room like this! I'm telling Madam."

Spying his treasured pocket watch on the bed, she hurls it at him. Barely missing his head, the crystal shatters against her mahogany dresser.

"You're nothing but a whore! I'll destroy you and your reputation. No one treats me like this and gets away with it. Madam won't save your skin this time. Your days are numbered, mark my words!"

Falling Into the Enemy's Hands

Sitting in the foul-smelling garbage and broken pottery shards of the Potter's Field, Forsaken numbly clutches the broken mirror and pocket watch—heart-breaking symbols of her painful past. "I hate him. He destroyed my life!"

Madam's distraught face appears before Forsaken. Her normally beautiful eyes are swollen from tears. "My ruby and diamond brooch is gone! My late husband gave it to me on our wedding day. It was in his family for generations, and it's irreplaceable!"

"Oh, Madam, please don't cry." Forsaken rushes to comfort her. Taking a delicately embroidered handkerchief from her bosom, she dabs Madam's streaking, coal-black mascara that is running down her jowls. "The chief of police has his men combing every inch of the Inn. I'm sure they'll find it. Maybe you just misplaced it!"

Madam's pencil-thin, red mouth forms into a hateful grimace, "No! I wouldn't leave something that valuable lying around. It was stolen! Whoever took it will pay dearly. I'll see to that!" She motions abruptly with her hand, dropping hot ashes from her ever-present mother-of-pearl cigarette holder.

Straightening up to her full height, she throws the black-feathered boa over her shoulder, covering multiple strands of pearls that adorn her thick neck. Her elegant silk dress strains to contain her ample bosom. Dressed like high society but barking orders like a sergeant, she commands the attention of all her employees as they scurry in and out, frantically searching for the lost jewelry.

Tears fall down Forsaken's cheeks. "Oh, Madam, is there anything I can do to help?"

"The dinner guests are arriving. I need your beautiful voice to entertain my customers."

As Forsaken is finishing the evening's final musical number, the chief of police bursts through the French doors leading to the dining room, with a distraught Madam at his side.

"We've found Madam's priceless brooch," he announces. Pointing an accusing finger at Forsaken he yells, "There's the thief! We found the jewels in her bedroom hidden under the mattress. It's the biggest scandal we've had in Comfort Cove since the Feel Good Saloon watered down its whisky."

For a few seconds stunned silence reigns, then gives way to an eruption of frenzied voices. All eyes turn to Forsaken. She scans the room, and familiar faces that just a few minutes ago were smiling adoringly at her are now hostile and suspicious.

The dignified Pastor Compromise, from the Country Club Church, puts down his brandy, stands to his feet, clears his deep voice and incredulously announces, "This is outrageous! After everything Madam's done for you. How could you betray her generosity, Forsaken?"

Blushing deeply, she stammers, "B-b-but, I didn't do it. I'm innocent. I swear!"

He turns back to his dining companions and says, "Not only is she a thief, she's also a liar. I had my doubts about Madam taking her in. I've never seen anything good come from being charitable."

Forsaken elbows her way through the erupting crowd and falls on her knees sobbing. Throwing her arms around Madam's ample hips she sobs, "Don't believe him. I didn't do it! I would never hurt you. You've been like a mother to me."

Mayor Lecherous's yellow teeth appear through his cigar-stained lips as he smiles coldly. He turns back to face the other city officials crowded around his reserved table near the French doors. Shifting his cumbersome frame, he tells them, "I warned Madam about taking in riffraff off the docks. They can't be trusted!"

Madam's heart, pierced with the razor-sharp pain of betrayal, lashes out, "Forsaken, how could you? I rescued you like a sniveling dog off the wharf and turned you into a classy lady who had to fight off suitors. You were like the daughter I never had. This is how you repay me? You've shown your true colors. I thought I'd changed you, but even in the most elegant gown you're still a low-life whore."

The chief of police jerks her roughly to her feet. "Madam, we'll take care of her, and she'll never trouble you or your patrons again! We have the evidence to put her away for a long time."

Sickened by false accusations against her, she pleads, "Madam, don't let them take me. I don't know how it got there! I just know I didn't do it!" Frantically, Forsaken's terrified eyes search the room for help. When she sees the mayor stroking his many-layered chin and mocking her with his gloating expression, she realizes he's made his threats come true.

I'VE BEEN FRAMED!

Forsaken yells back toward Madam as the chief of police drags her away.

"I've been framed. The mayor said he'd ruin my reputation if I didn't let him have his way with me. That's what this is all about! He's behind all this!"

Madam's wounded expression now hardens to stone as she storms toward Forsaken. "First you steal my jewels, and then you accuse an honorable man—my friend for over 30 years. How dare you! Who do you think you are? I want you out of here right now. You're lucky I'm not pressing charges! I never want to see you again!"

Madam returns to the dining room as her friends gather to comfort her. Mayor Lecherous makes his way through the crowd and gently puts his arm around Madam. "You know her background—her dad's an alcoholic—and she's halfway there. What can you expect?"

Just as the village clock strikes midnight, Forsaken is roughly thrown onto the cobblestone pavement outside the inn. She falls hard against the wet street, cutting her face and scraping her hands. People she had thought were her friends are now standing on the porch pointing to her and hurling insults.

Humiliated, Forsaken runs as fast as she can to get out of the condemning eyesight of the crowd and away from the jeering voices. After several blocks, one of her sequined high heels catches in the cobblestone street and sends her sprawling. She pushes herself to a sitting position and looks at her stinging palms. They are scraped and bleeding from the hard landing on the abrasive surface. She looks at her shoes. One heel is broken completely off and the other shoe is marred with a wide streak of black dirt. *Oh, my beautiful shoes.* She takes them off and clutches them to her chest as she limps along.

After a few minutes she arrives at the docks. The sun is setting, and the local tavern is brightly lit and jammed with fishermen looking to unwind after a hard day battling the sea. She walks to the edge of the deserted dock and sits staring at the waves. The day had started so well and was ending so badly. *I can't believe it. My life was finally going somewhere. I was making something of myself. My musical career was great, and Madam was mentoring me in the spiritual readings. I was going to become a rich fortune-teller just like her. I had a natural gift for reading tarot cards...but now look at me.*

Taking a Dark Path

Forsaken remembers the time that Madam led her into the opulent parlor with its overstuffed Victorian furniture and heavy brocade drapes. Forsaken sat down on the plush, burgundy velvet sofa. Madam gave a quick wink and pulled the drapes back to reveal a dark-stained oak door with a golden pentagram painted on the center. She motioned with her arm for Forsaken to enter. Madam pushed open the door. The room was painted black, and with just one dim oil lamp in the dark room it took a moment for Forsaken's eyes to adjust.

She scanned the room; there were no decorations—a stark contrast from the plush parlor. In the middle of the room was a round table with chairs and a crystal ball. Waiting around the table were the town's most influential people—Mayor Lecherous, the Fire Chief, the chief of police and Pastor Compromise from the Country Club Church.

Madam motioned for Forsaken to have a seat at the table. Then Madam seated herself at the head and began the session by picking up a deck of tarot cards.

"Madam," said Mayor Lecherous excitedly as he chomped on his ever-present cigar, "I acted immediately on the last advice you gave me, the business deal with the lumber mill, and the money is still pouring in."

"Madam" began the pastor, "I'd like to contact my dead sister, Rachel. I need to know—

"Madam," interrupted the Fire Chief, "you promised last time that you'd ask the spirits what I should do about my relationship with my wife."

Forsaken was surprised at how they were all in awe of Madam. She watched as they were transformed from the town's most respected leaders into little boys desperate for Madam's attention and advice.

Later that night Madam shared with Forsaken that she was one of the most respected spiritists on the whole seacoast. "Many wealthy people travel great distances and spend huge sums of money for my advice, Forsaken. I can teach you my trade. Someday when I'm gone, you can carry on the family business."

Forsaken nodded her head. She, too, was in awe of Madam's powers. She felt powerfully drawn, seduced into a new world of knowledge and power. "Oh, yes, I'd like that very much," she said, looking at Madam. But Forsaken couldn't see the gnarly, black demon with yellow eyes wrapped around Madam's neck, whispering evil "revelations" in her ear.

Antagonist

Where will I even spend the night? I've lost my room at the inn. I can't sleep here on the docks. Where can I go? Forsaken startles at the sound of breaking glass. She looks up in time to see a huge, burly fisherman crash through the front window of the tavern and land with a thud on the cobblestone street. At first she thinks he's dead, but he eventually staggers to his feet. Forsaken is repulsed by everything about him—his dirty work clothes, the cuts on his face and his drunken mannerisms. He reminds her of her dad, just the type of man she was trying to leave behind. She looks at her scraped hands and laughs cynically, *I guess I don't have to read my palms to know what my future holds*. Standing up from the dock, she smoothes her hair and rubs the tears from her eyes. *It's only temporary*, she lies to herself. Then she kicks her much loved shoes into the water. *I'm no lady tonight.*

Limping off the dock, she hurries to catch him. "Hi. I'm Forsaken." His glazed eyes look her slowly from head to her bare feet and then fix on her cleavage.

"I'm Antagonist," he slurrs, putting his arm around her waist.

Suicide's Assignment

As the vision fades, Forsaken smashes the mirror against the wagon wheel, weeping hysterically. "I hate them all. It's too painful. If I don't get a drink, I'll lose my mind."

Digging frantically through the rubbish, she picks up wet, rotting garbage by the handfuls. Finally, she uncovers an old whiskey bottle. Hands shaking, she presses it to her cracked lips and sighs with relief when a few drops slide down her parched throat.

Shaking the bottle, she tips it up again but fumes are all that's left. Demonic figures move in and out of the murky shadows. Tormenting spirits of self-hatred and insanity continue the taunting flashbacks. The powerful talons of addiction plunge deeper, racking her body with cold sweats and painful spasms. Frustrated, she angrily throws the empty bottle toward a discarded barrel.

The huge gargoyle-like figure of Suicide gurgles with evil delight as he approaches. At the same time, Forsaken's guardian angel draws closer. The sudden approach of this glorious angelic being startles Suicide's demonic ministers who have readied her for the kill. Like neighborhood bullies, they jump up and down enraged, cursing, "You can't have her, she's ours."

The angel, drawing his sword of fire, boldly declares, "You vile deceptive spirits—you do not have permission to take her life."

Suicide spews angrily, "Just watch how we whittle her down. It won't take long now. Madam False Destiny opened a spiritual door in Forsaken's life. We'll kill her before she goes to your Master. It's too late. Madam conjured us up as a curse to destroy her because she knows too much."

"You deceiver. Your power is not as great as you portray. She has free will and a prophetic destiny that will wreak havoc on your kingdom." Taking a shofar from his golden belt, he trumpets a war cry throughout the field. Warring angels position themselves as pillars of light waiting orders from the Father.

Under the prayerful gaze of the angel, the trembling, sniveling demons slither toward Forsaken. "Maybe we don't have the authority to kill her, but watch us convince *her* to take her own life."

The dark spirits whisper in Forsaken's ear, "You're just what your dad always said you'd be, a loser destined for the Potter's Field. You ought to end it all before Master Potter destroys you. Either way you're dead!"

As the foul demon speaks the words into Forsaken's ear, she speaks them aloud simultaneously with evil, choreographed precision.

Hysterically she sobs, "What's the point of living? I've lost everything anyway. I should just die. I don't want to hurt anymore." Nauseating terror turns into dry heaves as hallucinations and tormenting voices plague her mind.

Valiant speaks tenderly to Forsaken, and the atmosphere becomes charged with hope. "There is one who loves you and can save you. Cry out to Master Potter, it's never too late."

His gossamer wings glow with resurrection power as the shining angel opens his mouth, and deep intercessory groans rise into the heavens on Forsaken's behalf.

Realizing heavenly reinforcements are on the way, Suicide quickly slithers around Forsaken, coiling his snake-like body around her wounded spirit like a python, seeking to crush her will to live. Clutched in his serpentine embrace, she yields to his fiendish venom and gives up all desire for life.

The snake rasps, "Master Potter will just destroy you in the Mountain of Fire. Get it over with now; fall on that rusty knife over there. Just one brief moment of pain and then—everlasting peace."

CHAPTER SIX

THE CHALLENGE

In the heavens, the Father, Son and Holy Spirit delight in divine communication of holy passion, sharing thoughts and emotions too deep for spoken words.

In the stillness of that intimate fellowship, the Father answers the deep, yearning desire of His Son, "What I have promised, I will fulfill. Remember when I reached down and scooped up wet clay and fashioned mankind in Our image?"

Holy Spirit blazes with excitement, "You breathed life into the lifeless clay, and instantly flesh began to stir. We continued to watch as the being quivered and pulsated and newly fashioned eyes opened in adoration and astonishment."

Amused and laughing, the Son says, "I remember. The angels were crowded around this created being trying to grasp the mystery hidden in Your Father's heart—that this insignificant piece of clay would one day be My Bride."

The Father responds, "Yes! I gave her the capacity to love You of her own free will. The angels were confused, Satan raged, but We rejoiced."

SATAN ENTERS THE THRONE ROOM

Vile repulsion rips through Heaven as the ghastly yet familiar stench of Satan approaches. Celestial guardians draw their swords, constantly bewildered that this repulsive being is allowed to enter the throne room. No matter how often he comes to accuse the Bride, the angels never get used to his odor and appearance. One who had long ago been beautiful and a much-loved companion is now so dark and hideously monstrous!

Even his voice is ugly and evil in its resonance, as he snarls: "How foolish it was to make man out of clay. Why didn't You form him from bronze, silver or gold, something that would last? Clay is fragile, perishable and weak. It's so easy for me to crush and destroy Your useless clay vessels. Consider Your great casualties in our little war. It takes little more than one deceiving lie to embed my hooks deeply into Your foolish vessels." Satan snarls, spits and laughs shrilly. "And then my weakest demon takes them out!"

Master Potter Responds to the Accuser

"Satan, you can destroy the temporary clay shell, but we both know the fight is greater than that," the Son replies. "What enrages you is that living souls inside the earthenware vessels are made in My image and created to love Me. That's what this war is all about!"

Looking down through the realms of Heaven, Satan points his long, twisted finger of accusation to the Potter's Field on the outskirts of Comfort Cove. "War? You mean this little battle I'm winning! Just look at those shattered, broken vessels! Your image? They resemble me more than You! They're damned already!" His insane laughter echoes through the corridors of time, spewing poison onto the field below.

The Father looks sternly at the diabolical creature. "Satan, you're the father of lies and greatly deceived. Betrayal bought this Potter's Field of broken lives, but My Son's blood will turn this field of despair into a door of salvation."

Spitting foul-smelling liquid from his mouth and convulsing in agony, Satan is reminded of his utter defeat at the Cross. He cowers, lowering his slimy, black form to the ground.

Have You Seen Forsaken?

The Father points to earth, "Have you noticed that little clay vessel named Forsaken?"

Recovering slightly, Satan stands still cowering and looking away. His mocking laughter rings through the throne room. "She is rightly named…Forsaken is what she is and will remain. Your Son's image is so marred in that vessel, Heaven and hell both know You can never salvage that one! I already have a destiny planned for her, and she will be a prophetic voice for my evil kingdom."

The Father is deeply moved with compassion as He watches Forsaken. Her brokenness cannot be denied. Her demonic perversion, sinfulness and utter lack of desire for Himself is obvious, yet He confidently states, "I, too, have a plan, a destiny for this clay vessel you call Forsaken. She will become a beautiful Bride for My Son and will bring many others to the same relationship."

Satan spits yellow foam from his mouth and rages, "This vessel is as much Your enemy as I am! She hates Your religious ways and Your foolish, boring holiness. By the time I'm finished with her, she'll be given over completely to ruthlessness and cruelty!" His red eyes fill with fiery hatred and he screams, "She already belongs to me! She'll never love Your Son. I own her heart, and she will serve me and die in my embrace."

With his heart energized with renewed hatred, Satan is almost frantic to leave the discomfort of the throne room and rush out and fulfill his diabolic plans to destroy the fragile little vessel. But instead of exiting, he looks almost foolish as he stands in humiliation, knowing he can't leave until he bows before the God of glory. Reluctantly he kneels, the Father gives a nod and he is released to his delusions of grandeur.

Hearts aflame with fervent passion for the little clay pot, the Father and Son look deeply into each other's eyes with a knowing smile. Turning to Holy Spirit, they commission Him to descend to the Potter's Field.

The challenge is on!

Chapter Seven

Death Stalks

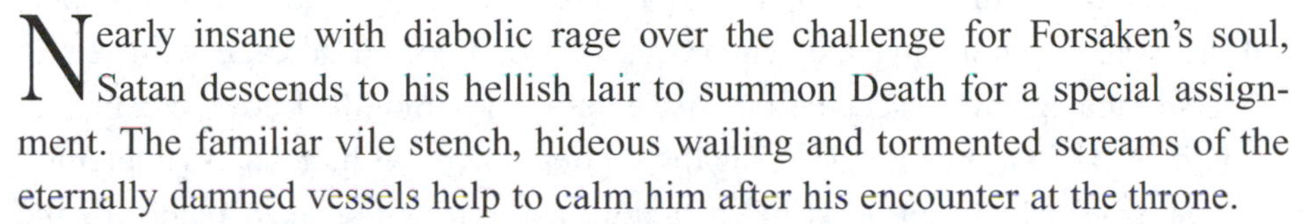

Nearly insane with diabolic rage over the challenge for Forsaken's soul, Satan descends to his hellish lair to summon Death for a special assignment. The familiar vile stench, hideous wailing and tormented screams of the eternally damned vessels help to calm him after his encounter at the throne.

Death instantly appears out of the yellow and green sulfur smoke, bowing slavishly low before Satan, the Prince of Darkness. Although they are friends of no one, mutual hatred and an unquenchable thirst to destroy the work of the Godhead bind the two demonic rulers together in a fiendish camaraderie.

With heaven's fragrance still in his nostrils, Satan seethes with hatred, "I have a project that requires your attention." He spits, "I've just returned from the throne room where I was challenged to a wager that I don't intend to lose."

Pointing to the Potter's Field, the dark figure hisses, "See that sniveling, pathetic little pitcher with the cracked lip? That's the one we're after! I've already done most of your work for you. She's crushed and broken and already ours. Suicide is with her now, and she's very close to giving up—but since the challenge, I'm changing my plan."

Hungry to taste the blood of another victim, Death drools from between his large, yellow fangs. "Wouldn't it be easier to let Suicide finish her off? We know how much you love to see us dragging their pathetic corpses to you."

"Don't be so anxious, I have big plans for this vessel! One of my best spiritualists, Madam False Destiny, began mentoring her. I want her back there for more training. Bringing her to me too soon would be a shallow victory. Killing her now is our last resort."

Totally given over to the loathsome thirst for destruction, the wicked schemers are drunk with hatred and the unquenchable craving for victims' blood. Reveling in their wicked plans they look at the pathetic vessel. "I not only want to win this challenge but I want to twist the knife deep into the Godhead's heart by capturing Forsaken's affections," Satan snarls. "She must be made to love me. We will *finally* triumph over the Son when she becomes my trophy."

He leaps to his webbed, gnarled feet and grabs Death by the throat, slamming him up against the wall. As he dangles, Satan growls inches away from Death's contorted, fearful face, "If you fail me, humiliate me or if I lose this challenge, I'll claw your decaying flesh off your putrid body and leave you to die in The Ancient Caverns."

Death Seeks Forsaken

Shaken, Death ascends to the Potter's Field. His huge web-like wings spew sulfuric vapor, paralyzing the inhabitants of this rejected acreage with terror. Deep guttural growls escape from his gaping, wet mouth. Eerie screams rip through the field as he moves among the shattered lives with merciless contempt.

Suicide's shriveled heart beats rapidly as he sees Forsaken reach for the rusty knife. She tries to summon enough courage to plunge it into her broken heart. Spirits of self-hatred and insanity dance wildly. Completely abandoned to their greedy cravings for pain and destruction, they join Suicide in this diabolical celebration of fiendish joy at another victim's gruesome demise.

Out of view and in deeply recessed shadows, the soft glow of Valiant's presence begins to burn with a golden light. Holy indignation rises in him as he watches the Father's adversaries plot to bring this little pot fully into their evil grasp. He quickly puts up his shield and unsheathes his sword to destroy the vile spirits before they take her life.

Just as he is about to charge into full view of the spirits, Death intercepts Suicide and calls off the attack. "I hate to ruin your little party, but the plans have changed," he hisses condescendingly to the lesser-ranking spirits. "I've been given *this* choice assignment. Satan is battling the Godhead over this despicable, insignificant, sniveling little pot. Why either would want her is beyond me." Pointing to another rejected vessel, he tells Suicide, "There's your next victim. He thinks he's so bad that not even God can save him."

Spitting and murmuring curses at the high-ranking devil, Suicide slowly uncoils his ghastly, snake-like grip from Forsaken. She drops the knife weeping in anguish. "I don't even have the courage to do this right. Can anyone help me?"

False Promises, Lies and Destruction

Death spins around, focusing his slimy attention on Forsaken, and with hypocritical comfort whispers, "Madam saved you once. She could do it again.

Why don't you just go to the inn and beg her to take you back? She loves you like a daughter." Black talons soothe her troubled brow.

Penetrating into the vile darkness of the enemy's camp, Holy Spirit powerfully advances against the dark chaos and confusion that perpetually reign over this field. Contending fiercely for her soul, He releases a vision of Forsaken sitting on her grandma's lap.

In a soft, still voice, He gently whispers, "Forsaken, your Grandma Pearl is the one who really loved you like a daughter. Don't you remember how she told you about Master Potter and that He loves and saves broken vessels?"

Death opens his yellow mouth and pours out verbal poison, "That's a lie! Everyone knows Master Potter throws broken vessels into the Mountain of Fire to destroy them—your own father told you so. The only hope you have is to go back to Madam's."

Covering her ears with her hands, Forsaken closes her eyes tightly, trying in vain to block out the voices and painful memories. "I'm so afraid. I don't know what to do! I can't even think straight!"

MEMORIES OF GRANDMA PEARL

In the midst of the painful darkness and assaulting memory fragments, Forsaken's heart is suddenly warmed by thoughts of Grandma Pearl. *After my baby brother was born Mom didn't have time for me. He was so sick. Thank goodness for Grandma Pearl.*

It was Grandma Pearl who frequently took her for weeks at a time to her small country cottage when Forsaken's father went on his violent, alcoholic binges. She was only seven when Grandma Pearl died unexpectedly. Then she spent large parts of the day roaming the docks to escape her abusive home.

In an open vision, Forsaken sees herself as a fragile child in the little white-steepled chapel on the outskirts of Comfort Cove sitting snugly next to Grandma Pearl. Grandma had on her favorite church hat, a gingham bonnet, always freshly starched and pressed with a blue ribbon tied under her chin, which she wore as faithfully as she prayed or read the Bible.

The sounds of rich organ music fill the vision as she sees sunlight streaming through the colorful stained-glass windows. The aroma of the rustic cedar pews brings Forsaken back to a time long forgotten, a time of sweetness, safety and innocence. The only places she ever felt safe were here and at Grandma Pearl's.

Forsaken's eyes fix on a golden-framed picture of a man on a Cross whose body is bruised, beaten and broken. Forsaken stares, half curious and half repulsed, at the picture. *Maybe He would understand my bruises. Did His father do this to Him too?*

Everyone in church seemed to be singing with gusto on that particular sunny morning, but all Forsaken heard was her own little voice, "On a hill far away stood an old rugged Cross, the emblem of suffering and shame."

Holy Spirit's Counter Invasion

As the vision fades, tears streak down her face. *Oh Grandma, why did you have to leave? I need your help. No one understands me like you do.*

Holy Spirit comforts her. Gently, softly He whispers, "Remember the picture over the altar? Master Potter also suffered evil at the hands of others so that He could save you out of this field of despair. Call out to Him." These revelatory words of truth pierce the darkness with blazing light, challenging the demonic grip on her mind.

Death, sensing that he might lose this battle, screams, "He never saved you as a child, why would He save you now? Where was He when your father abused you? Look at you—you're disgusting, broken and sinful. You're nothing but a used-up, discarded whore. Who would want you? You're too far gone."

"Don't believe it, no one is ever too far gone. Master Potter looks for the weak and broken vessels to heal." Holy Spirit's flaming words of truth illuminate the darkened garbage dump, sending confusion through the lower-ranking demons. They scurry off in fear to avoid the heavenly brightness, finding comforting refuge under piles of decay and rotting flesh. They screech out an SOS, pleading for hellish reinforcements to arrive.

Enraged at Holy Spirit's life-giving words, Death erupts into a fit of blasphemous curses. Yellow-green sulfuric gases explode from his mouth.

A whirring sound like a swarm of locusts is barely audible in the distance but rapidly grows to ear-piercing levels. The skies above Forsaken turn black from a thick backlash of demonic reinforcement. Within moments, the moon appears to dim as it is overshadowed by the churning, pulsing dark cloud.

Demonic Reinforcements

The reinforcements drop from the skies like a downpour. They hit the field and slither toward Forsaken. The archers take careful aim and shoot fiery arrows of accusation. Others hurl spears or throw poisonous daggers.

Angelic warriors, the ground troops, hurry into place, forming a large protective circle with Forsaken in the middle. They face outward. Valiant draws his sword and the tip bursts into flame. In moments his whole being is engulfed by fire, but he is not burned.

"Our God is a consuming fire," he yells.

Extending his sword, he touches the next angel who immediately ignites into a pillar of fire. The holy fire spreads from angel to angel. These living pillars of light form an impenetrable circular barrier against the wiles of the approaching demons.

Death is trapped inside this fiery angelic circle with Holy Spirit and Forsaken. Even though he is cut off from his demonic horde, his focus is undeterred as he tries to capture Forsaken's soul. Seething rage boils within him as he hears the voice of Holy Spirit and sees the fiery angels protecting Forsaken.

Death vehemently spews to Forsaken, "You're mine and always will be. No one has ever loved you."

Holy Spirit continues, "Forsaken, Master Potter loved you and was always there even though you did not know it. He wept over your abuse. No one is too far gone for Him to save."

Death escalates the battle as he brings up painful areas of Forsaken's past.

"Was He there when you lived on the docks? Was He there when Antagonist beat you? Madam treated you better than some invisible God! She's your only family now. You should return to her."

Covering her head with her arms, Forsaken cries out in great agony. "What should I do? Someone help me."

Holy Spirit Speaks

Holy Spirit tenderly begins to show Forsaken visions of the wonderful plans and destiny for her life. "He loves you, Forsaken, and has been waiting for you to come to Him. But you have to say yes. Nothing is too hard for Him. No one is beyond hope."

Suddenly a memory flashes through her mind, a memory long forgotten. She was a small child, playing on the docks with a pack of stray dogs that had become her family. Suddenly a team pulling a milk wagon went out of control. The horses reared up just as an adorable puppy leapt from her arms and dashed into the street. Without thinking, she dashed after him. Looking up at the huge panicking horses, she froze in terror.

Unseen by her, Valiant grabbed the team, held their harnesses in each hand and restrained them long enough for a burly dockworker to scoop her up and carry her safely to the other side of the road. She knew that day she had escaped sure death, but never realized she was protected by Heaven.

Another scene fills her mind. She is lying on the floor, bruised and bloodied under Antagonist's merciless rage. What she never knew was that he had bragged about killing her that night to his friends at the tavern. She sees Antagonist taking bets over her demise while laughing with his drunken, low-life cronies. She had thought it unusual for him to pass out cold from alcohol right in the midst of a beating. Now she sees the same large angel sitting on his chest, pinning him to the floor.

How many times has he saved me? she wonders.

As Holy Spirit continues speaking the truth, Forsaken's demonic-inspired confusion starts to lift; redeeming love begins to stir deep inside her.

Maybe there is hope for me. Maybe Master Potter can heal me.

Death, sensing he may lose this battle and be punished and disgraced before Satan's evil throne, screams in rage at the thought of having to prostrate himself in front of his cruel master, groveling for his life. "*No!* That's a lie. Master Potter destroys broken vessels. He throws them in the Mountain of Fire."

Holy Spirit challenges Forsaken, "That voice is the voice of Death trying to destroy your life and future. Master Potter *doesn't* destroy vessels; He *rescues* them. Just cry out, 'Master Potter save me,' and He will—because He loves you deeply and longs for you to come to Him. Time is running short and you're in grave danger."

From the depth of hell the murderous voice of Satan commands Death, "You fool! She must not come to Him. Kill her quickly or we've lost her soul!"

Frantically, Death snatches her into his gnarled talons, and Forsaken cries out from the excruciating pain. "Master Potter, if You're really who my grandma said You are—please save me!"

Heaven Responds to a Cry for Help

The groans of prisoners appointed to die never fail to inflame the Father's heart of mercy to bring salvation. The name of Master Potter thunders across the field, releasing His violently passionate love, electrifying the spirit realm. Heavenly portals open and an avalanche of praise and worship roars across the Potter's Field, driving the demonic horde into increased frenzied terror.

Valiant swings his fiery sword and shouts to the angelic ground troops on the Potter's Field, "For the Father, the Son and the Holy Spirit that *this* Bride may come forth." They move like pillars of fire throughout the damned field, routing out the hidden swarms of evil strongholds. Demonic reinforcements arrive and the battle is fierce and bloody as the sound of war resounds throughout the land.

In a flash, Valiant takes an ancient silver shofar from his waist and blows a mighty blast, sounding a war cry to open up the heavens. Michael, the archangel, and his magnificent warriors mount their huge white stallions and descend from the ethereal realms to drive back the screaming satanic hordes. Their assignment is straight from the Father—to rescue this lost, broken soul.

Catching the scent of the battle, the horses charge into the fray, obeying the commands of their riders. Muscles rippling with strength, they strike paralyzing terror in the enemy forces as they carry the splendor and majesty of the Lord's own angelic host. The gusty wind of the Spirit blows like a golden whirlwind around them.

Explosions of resurrection power bombard screeching demons as angelic hosts rejoice in the strength of the victory of the Cross. The warriors wield flashing swords and wreak havoc in the Potter's Field. Swirls of fiery glory break the dark fog of oppression holding Forsaken prisoner as the first light of dawn rises in the eastern sky. This power invasion from Heaven annihilates the demonic stronghold in Forsaken's soul.

Death screeches in horrendous defeat and throws Forsaken down. Leaving her barely alive, he flees with his evil regiment of dark angels.

Rejoicing, her lifelong guardian, Valiant, catches her before she can hit the ground and gently lays her down. Angels of glory fill the skies, exulting in praise and worship over Forsaken's rescue. A blanket of holy peace fills the atmosphere as a cloud of glory grows with each exalted verse.

Blazing with fiery determination, Valiant's great expanse of translucent wings cover her. He lovingly stands guard over the broken little heap. Valiant shakes his head in marvelous wonder at the wisdom of Master Potter. He lifts his blazing sword and joins the heavenly choruses of high praise.

The atmosphere changes as golden rays of resurrection light pierce the darkness. Death and his entourage are vanquished. Having tasted of this unstoppable power before, they regroup for another day, another battle.

Chapter Eight

The Crucified Savior

Silhouetted against the rising sun, a man appears in this graveyard of broken lives. The desperate cries of Forsaken's lost soul stir His unending compassionate love. "How My heart rejoices to hear her call My name. I deeply feel the pain of your suffering, My precious one. I'm coming."

Still lying with her face to the ground and weeping, Forsaken hears footsteps. Startled, she looks up to see the bloody feet of a man standing in front of her. Her eyes travel from His nail-pierced feet up His bruised legs. Streams of blood and water flow to the ground from a deep gash in His side. His wounded chest has been ripped open by the lashes of a cruel, relentless scourging, leaving bloodied and torn flesh.

Pain and grief are etched into His features. Black and blue swollen mounds exist where soft brown eyes should have been. Patches of His dark curly beard have been violently ripped from his flesh, leaving exposed muscle. His cheeks are caked with dried blood.

Forsaken is gripped with compassion that wells up within her heart. Hot tears run down her bruised and bloodied face. *His features are so disfigured,* she thinks to herself, *If He were my own brother I would not recognize Him.*

Streams of blood drip from His brow where a cruel crown of thorns punctures His flesh. Overwhelmed, Forsaken cries, "Who are You? I've never seen a man so battered and beaten! Who would have done such a thing?"

This Is Master Potter

Holy Spirit gently says, "You did, Forsaken! This is the Son of God, who took the punishment for your sins. He was whipped, beaten and put to death so that you could be rescued and reconciled to the Father. You've encountered the crucified Savior who died for you. This is Master Potter, who rescues clay vessels from this field of death."

"How can this be Master Potter? My dad said He loved to destroy clay vessels."

Master Potter begins to turn away, and she sees a rugged wooden cross-beam, which is bound to His outstretched arms.

Desperately she cries, "Wait! Come back! Please don't leave me!"

He turns, faces her once again and gazes deeply into her tear-filled eyes. Unconditional love pierces deep into the numbness of her soul with convicting revelation.

Forsaken hears a crack within her soul as the lie is broken and the chains of bondage are loosed. She now *knows* this is Master Potter and realizes that everything her Grandma Pearl had told her was true. He really does love her, and He really did choose to die rather than be without her.

Her heart is illuminated by Holy Spirit's light, and she understands her awful sinfulness and desperate need for this humble man standing before her. Only Master Potter can save her soul and make her clean.

"I'm so sorry. Please forgive me," she sobs. "I've made such a mess out of my life! Master Potter, save me! Help me!" Completely broken, she wraps her arms around His bloody feet.

Safe in the Savior's Arms

Master Potter gently picks up little Forsaken with His nail-pierced hands, and placing her head against His wounded chest He holds her close and weeps over her pain. Cradled in the Savior's protective arms, Forsaken responds to His overwhelming sacrifice and compassion for her with deep tears of repentance that wash her sin-drenched soul.

Embracing Him tightly, she weeps, "Oh, Master Potter, I love You! Please save me! I've wasted so many years and have done so many horrible things. Please forgive me!"

Born Again!

"Forsaken, I do forgive you. I've always loved you and yearned for you to come to Me. I died to save you and bring you out of the Potter's Field. I endured these wounds so that you might be saved and made whole."

Suddenly, her deep repentance causes the fiery seed of eternity to erupt inside her soul! The wonderment! The transforming miracle! Surging resurrection life flows into her being and connects her spirit with His in holy communion for the first time. Forsaken is born again! She's alive—truly alive!

RESURRECTED LORD!

She watches in stunned amazement as His brutally disfigured features change before her eyes, transforming themselves into a radiant face more lovely than any she's ever seen. He is stunning and radiant—altogether lovely. Once He was her crucified Savior, but now He is also her resurrected Lord.

For a brief and shining moment, white light illuminates off His shimmering clothing, and rays of golden glory shine from His face, hands and eyes. He stands before her, transformed into the Lord of glory. All at once, Forsaken's ears are open, and she hears the glorious singing of angelic hosts. Bathed in white light, she looks down at herself and realizes that she, too, is shining with the light of His glory.

THE HUMBLE POTTER

Ministering angels clothe Him in the soft brown robes of a humble potter, and the glow of glory gradually dims into the rugged and handsome face of Master Potter.

Holding her close, He penetrates her knotted muscles with His healing anointing, soothing her painful spasms and calming the horrible effects of alcohol withdrawal. Sweet perfume and fragrance wash over her as she clutches Him tightly to herself.

Such wonder! Such unspeakable grace, that He would choose to save one such as her from the grasp of Death and the destitution of the Potter's Field. Deep waves of glory continue to heal and cleanse her as He joyfully proclaims to the heavens, the earth and the realms below, "No longer are you called Forsaken. I name you Beloved, the delight of My heart!"

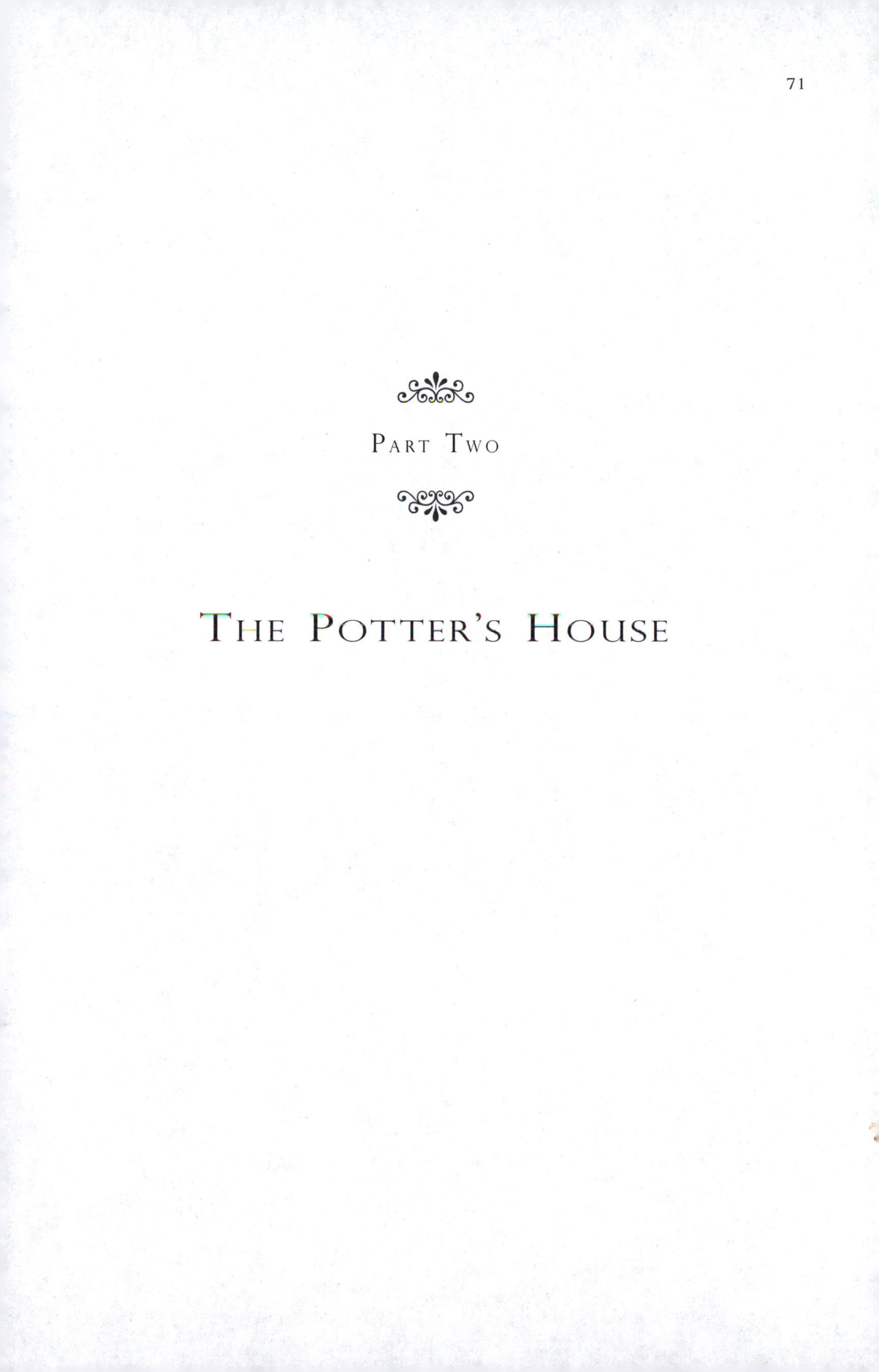

Part Two

The Potter's House

Chapter Nine

First Love

Beloved is leaving behind the name Forsaken and the oppressive atmosphere of the Potter's Field. Master Potter carries her down a rugged dirt road toward His home. His soft musical laughter fills her soul with warmth and peace as her spirit comes alive.

She sighs in relief as Master Potter softly whispers in her ear, "I'm taking you to My home, Beloved. It will be a time of healing and intimacy with Me."

Humming joyfully, they walk beside a meadow of lush green grasses and rolling hills covered with wild sprays of brilliant blue, pink and purple flowers. All of creation seems amazingly alive as the brilliant colors and fragrances from the fields applaud the arrival of Master Potter and Beloved.

Just out of sight, Beloved's guardian angel, Valiant, watches at a close distance. To see him now would amaze and stun her, for his huge, magnificent frame is spinning in circles, hopping up and down, and dancing down the dusty road with heavenly joy.

Other angels are celebrating the miracle of Master Potter's life entering into the little clay vessel. Their laughter and joy ring infectiously throughout the heavens.

Master Potter is eager to show her His Kingdom—her newfound inheritance. So, He gestures toward golden wheat fields glistening in the early morning sun. Brightly attired workers wave to them as they walk by.

"These are My harvesters gathering My wheat." She watches them raise sickles overhead and plunge them deeply into the plentiful stalks. Other workers bundle the sheaves and pile them high onto wooden, horse-drawn wagons.

"Life! That's what My world is all about! Abundant life!"

Lovesick for the Beloved

Lovesick, Beloved can't stop looking into Master Potter's tender brown eyes. Blushing with the glow of first love, her little heart purrs with contentment just to be with Him. When she hears the sound of His voice, her heart races wildly. Oh, the heavenly bliss of being so loved and accepted!

She loves His strong, rugged features and memorizes every part of His wonderful face: His distinctive nose and olive complexion, His brown, curly beard glistening with red and gold, and His sensitive mouth!

The Enemy's Counter-Attack

Still recovering from Satan's unrelenting, violent scourging, Death reappears with his demonic horde, sending them out as spies. They infiltrate the countryside and join the demonic network already in place. It covers Comfort Cove and the surrounding areas, like a black widow spider's web.

These evil alliances create a demonic stronghold over this geographic area. By touching one area of this web, Death sends out demonic communications into this unseen realm to capture Beloved at all costs. Darkness ripples throughout this evil, global network.

A foreboding demonic messenger, Backslidden, bows low before Death. "I am at your command."

"Stand up, you pathetic slave," Death shouts while kicking the demon. "Take a message to Madam False Destiny and Pastor Compromise. The situation is critical. It is urgent that they come immediately." He takes another kick at the messenger and screams, "Go!"

Death paces up and down before the motley, low-ranking demonic crew Satan has given him. *How am I supposed to win a losing battle using this bunch of cast-off, wretched scum?*

He turns to look at their gruesome faces and tries to muster enthusiasm. "Just because Master Potter has her now doesn't mean we can't get her back. We must get her back! The first time He sets her down, as soon as His back is turned, you must snatch her, and we'll send her back to our people."

Looking at them with contempt he snarls, "I'm sending you ahead to hide in the fields and orchards. You must capture her before He takes her to His home."

Armed with poisonous darts of accusation they scurry off to hide and wait for their intended victim.

Death tries in vain to comfort himself. *I know this wretched group will never get her. Master Potter won't set her down until He gets her safely in His house, but she'll leave Him at the first trial. She's never stuck with anything or anyone all her life. When He asks her to lay down her life, I'll be there to snatch her the minute she bolts out His door.*

RESTING IN THE MASTER'S LOVE

Hiding behind some rocks and bushes, the crouching demons finally see Master Potter approaching with Beloved in His arms. Carefully, one pathetic little demon takes aim and blows a poisonous dart towards her.

Beloved's joy is shattered as the dart pierces her heart. "I wonder if Master Potter will reject me someday like all the others?"

Pulling the dart out, Master Potter flings it underhanded back at the demon, hitting it squarely between the eyes. Knocked unconscious, the demon falls off the fence and lands on the ground with a hollow thud, its talons impotently curled in a tight fist.

"Beloved, I will never leave you. You are Mine forever. Always remember, I love you." He embraces her gently, careful to protect her broken handle and many painful wounds as they continue through the fields.

"I love You too. I just can't believe I'm really in Your arms." Grateful tears run down her cheeks.

Brushing her hair back from her bruised face and exposing her cracked lip, He tells her, "Do you know how beautiful you are to Me?"

"But I'm not beautiful. I'm broken and ugly."

"No, Beloved, you're beautiful; just wait and see. Your love and devotion are sweet fragrances that ravish My heart. I love you so very much. You are My little princess."

As they round the corner hundreds of poison darts rain down from a clump of apple trees. As He continues telling Beloved of His undying love He casually brushes them away with His arm. They fall harmlessly to the ground. Still focusing on Beloved, He motions to Valiant, who unsheathes his sword, charges the trees and sends a swarm of demons scurrying off in retreat.

Beloved, oblivious to the spiritual counter-attack, continues to revel in His great love for her.

THE TRAP

Master Potter's eyes sparkle as He looks lovingly at her. His contagious smile so fills her heart with joy. The sheer delight of being with Him is more than enough for the moment. She wants to pinch herself to make sure it's real but is afraid He'll see her and laugh.

Resting in His arms she visually drinks in the colorful orchards filling the horizon with their beauty and fragrances. The warm rays of the noonday sun shimmer through the trees in dappled elegance.

As they round the corner she hears the clomping of horse's hooves. Thinking it's one of Master Potter's wagons she turns and is surprised to see Madam False Destiny and the impeccably dressed Pastor Compromise pull up beside them in an expensive, black lacquered horse-drawn buggy. Beloved can't take her eyes off the beautifully embellished filigreed golden trim.

Madam is smartly dressed, although not as flamboyantly as usual, in a black straight skirt with a ruffled high-necked white blouse. She looks more like a schoolmarm than Madam. Her ever-present mother-of-pearl cigarette holder is also missing. The two make a very handsome, respectable and affluent-looking couple.

Madam sarcastically says, "Well, well! If it isn't Master Potter carrying another broken vessel off the Potter's Field."

Pastor Compromise quickly adds, "You both look so tired. Would you like a ride? We could take you back to the village."

"No, I'm taking her to My house. I have so much to share with her." At the sound of Master Potter's voice the horses let out a high-pitched neigh and violently paw the ground.

Pastor Compromise steps out of the buggy. Gently taking Madam around her ample waist, he hoists her over the side of the wagon, his neck veins bulging as he strains to set her down. Madam lands hard on the ground and casts a quick sneer at Pastor Compromise. She regains her composure, gently smoothes her skirt, and smiles condescendingly at Master Potter, "But Your house is so far away. Why don't You let her stay with me for the night? I've missed you, Forsaken, and—"

"Her name's been changed. She's not Forsaken, she's Beloved." The agitated horses fight their harnesses to get away from Master Potter.

"Oh, of course, of course, she's Beloved now, how nice for her," Madam hisses through clenched teeth. "Well, Beloved, I've been searching day and night since you left. You were right; the whole fiasco with my brooch was all a mistake. You *were* framed, you poor thing. I've missed you so much. We're actually on the way to the church social. We heard that you had been rescued from the Potter's Field so we came by to get you. We'd planned to vindicate you in front of the whole crowd today and let the truth be known. You'd come back into the community in good standing, welcomed with open arms. We're hoping that you will find it in your heart to forgive us and maybe even give us the pleasure of hearing you sing for all of us."

Beloved looks at Master Potter and says, "Oh, I would love to see all my friends. I could go to Your house tomorrow."

Pastor Compromise says, "I totally agree. It would be best, Master Potter, if she returned with us to Comfort Cove for reconciliation. She could even go to Watered Down Village to get some solid biblical training and discipleship. It's just across Stillwater Bridge and we're friends with all the leaders there."

"Now that that little mix-up about my brooch is cleared up, you could stay at the Inn. I've never let anyone take your room. I would love to continue mentoring you, dear. I will always have my home open to you. You can stay with me anytime."

Pastor Compromise clears his throat, "Well it looks like we've all got her best interest at heart and want to see her mature and grow spiritually."

"I've always loved you as a daughter. I missed you so much. I'm the mother you've never had and you're the daughter I never got," Madam gushes as she holds out her arms. "Come here, darling, you've been through so much. My arms are aching to hold you."

Beloved is surprised when Master Potter throws back His head and laughs heartily. "I don't think we *all* have her best interest at heart. I've waited from the beginning of time to hold her in My arms and to enjoy her arms embracing Me." With His eyes full of fire and determination He says, "We have a long day's journey ahead, so we must get going."

Pastor Compromise takes a large side-step in front of Master Potter. "You can't be serious; You're not *walking* all the way to Your house. It's miles from here just to the lower foothills. And once You get partway up the mountain the road ends and You have to go by foot. The rough terrain is nearly impossible. You'll need to conserve Your strength for that climb. Why don't You let us take You to the end of the road? Then You won't be as exhausted as You attempt to make that brutal climb. If You walk, it could be dark by the time You get there and You could get lost going up that treacherous mountain."

"I am the way, the truth and the life. I know the path. No man comes to My house except through Me."

"But the mountainous terrain—"

"I leap on the tops of mountains, and I will carry My Beloved."

Turning abruptly, He heads across the field, jumping effortlessly from one hill to the next, leaving them foiled and cursing.

The need for acceptance and vindication has a stranglehold on Beloved. After the humiliating fiasco at the Inn, Beloved's pride is still badly wounded. "But Master Potter, I was falsely accused, and the record needs to be set straight about what really happened. You could always come with me."

"Beloved, let Me handle this. Things are not always what they seem to be. What you just experienced was a trap to put you back under demonic control. In My time I will vindicate you, but it will not be your righteousness that is exalted."

The Plot Is Foiled

Madam and the pastor climb in the wagon and head back for town. "That didn't go too well," Pastor Compromise says accusingly. "You foiled our chances with your dreadful overacting—"

"I spoiled our chances?" interrupts Madam. "What about you? You have all the compassion of a goat!"

"A goat?"

"Yes, I said a goat."

Death suddenly appears in the middle of the road out of a flash of putrid yellow sulfurish vapor. The two immediately stop bickering and straighten up as if at attention. Death squints at them and hurls blasphemous curses. Waving his hand, he turns the two black horses to gnarly little demons, and the luxurious wagon vanishes in thin air. Pastor Compromise and Madam fall down hard on the dirt road.

The Father's Vineyard

The country road slowly narrows as Master Potter and Beloved enter the ancient vineyards carved into the gentle slopes of the mountain. Gray fieldstone walls separate the terraced plots of gnarled grapevines supporting clusters of dusky purple grapes.

Approaching a beautiful wrought-iron gate of delicate grape and leaf design, they enter the courtyard leading to enormous ivy-covered stone buildings of an ancient winery. Over the entryway is an ornate wooden plaque embossed in gold lettering, "The Father's Vineyard."

In a swarm of activity, workers load heavy wooden casks of wine to be taken to Comfort Cove. Each horse-drawn wagon is quickly loaded and dispatched while another takes its place, waiting to be filled.

"This wine is headed for the docks to be loaded on My ship, which will depart tonight. The captains of My ships depend on the Rock of Salvation Lighthouse to help navigate the treacherous Straits of the Dragon. This ship will bring the wine of healing and refreshing to the Bay of the Martyrs."

New Wine of the Holy Spirit

They stroll under a vine-covered arbor, which opens into a hidden stone courtyard in the back. Beloved gasps as she sees radiant angels. One of the wine casks is open and a multitude of angels led by Valiant are celebrating.

"They're enjoying the new wine of the Holy Spirit, Beloved. He's a good friend of Mine whom you will meet later."

Laughing, Master Potter takes a beautiful goblet from Valiant. "Do you know why they're so joyous?" Beloved, still too stunned to speak, can only nod her head as she stares in amazement.

Valiant offers a toast as the angels raise their glasses. "Master Potter's death on the Cross has redeemed another broken vessel. Today we celebrate Beloved's entrance into new life!" Rousing, joyful shouts of glee exalt Master Potter's great love and sacrifice. Valiant raises his glass again and proclaims, "To the Father, the Son and the Holy Spirit, that Beloved may come forth!"

"Your Grandma Pearl prayed for you every day and wouldn't give My Father any rest until she knew you were safe. She and all of Heaven rejoiced when I rescued you from the Potter's Field, and I wanted to show you just a glimpse of the elation over your entrance into My Kingdom."

Beloved is astounded by what she has just seen. Still dazed, she looks at Master Potter. "Your Kingdom is bigger than what I can see, isn't it?" Master Potter tips His head back and laughs in delight. "You have no idea, Beloved, you have no idea."

Soon they leave the vineyards behind, and the landscape changes from wild flowers into fragrant eucalyptus and oak trees. She snuggles deeper into the folds of His robes, resting and secure in His strong arms.

Chapter Ten

Vessels of Destiny

Hours pass, the noonday sun begins its downward journey and the dense woods give way to a wide clearing. Walking toward a high bluff overlooking Comfort Cove, Master Potter excitedly says in a deep resonating voice, "Beloved, it won't be long before we rest for the night, but first let Me share this with you."

Although Beloved had grown up near the sea, it seems her eyes are opened in a brand new way to the beauty around her. Everything she sees is clearer, brighter and lovelier than she can ever remember. The panoramic view takes her breath away.

The ocean's dancing blue water glitters like diamonds in the brilliant sunlight. The salty sea breeze blows gently through her hair, invigorating her senses as she gazes on the azure blue expanse of the horizon.

Beloved's eyes follow tangles of wild roses trailing down and disappearing over the rocky outcropping. As they move closer to the edge, the busy fishing harbor comes into view.

A demon of fear blows several small, poisonous darts that explode as they pierce Beloved, embedding deeply within her heart.

Suddenly hurtful images from the past flood her mind, terrorizing her. The thought of falling back into her old ways causes her to tremble. "I don't ever want to go back there."

"You will someday, but not before you're ready."

"I don't know if I'll ever be ready."

Master Potter touches her heart with His hand, and soothing heat melts the darts, vanquishing fear. His peace and love once again restore her heart.

"When it is time for you to go, Beloved, I'll go with you. You won't be alone. And you will go back not as a victim, but as My warrior Bride."

The Flagship of the Bridegroom King

Master Potter points at the blue vista of sea and sky to an ancient seafaring vessel destined for Comfort Cove. White billowing sails mounted on tall wooden masts enable the ship to cut through the water in unparalleled magnificence!

Even from this lofty view, the sound of angelic trumpets proclaiming its entrance into the harbor can clearly be heard. Beloved watches fiery messengers on horseback ride throughout the village announcing the flagship's arrival. It is the flagship of the Bridegroom King!

Brilliant flags of scarlet, blue and purple ripple gracefully in the wind displaying the King's royal colors in full governmental splendor. The sleepy village begins buzzing with excitement and activity as people hurry to unload cargo from the majestic vessel.

From this far distance, Beloved can still make out the familiar, weather-beaten faces of the village fishermen hauling in their day's catch. Dock workers who clean and salt the fish shout joyously to each other. Working quickly, they toss the fish in wooden barrels to load onto the great ship.

Others mend torn nets, and Beloved imagines that they are discussing their own exciting plans for the celebration that will take place that night. It's not every day that a ship such as this one comes into Comfort Cove's humble village harbor!

Memories of the Past

Looking down from the bluff, she sees Antagonist coming out of the tavern, heading for the dock. He's wearing his rubber fishing boots with his crumpled and dirty work pants tucked inside. His limp is unmistakable.

Another fiery dart from a nearby demon wounds Beloved.

Her heart is suddenly saddened by the memory of the first time she saw her former boyfriend. He had come crashing through the tavern window on the losing end of a barroom brawl. The relationship had started badly—he could merely provide a place for her to stay, and she could provide what he wanted too—it had ended worse.

She had lost count of the number of times she had vowed to leave him after his beatings. But his sad blue eyes, sincere-sounding apologies, and her fear of living on the docks alone, kept her in the cramped, fish-scented apartment over the barbershop.

He was so strong, but what could have been used to protect her was frequently vented against her. *He's exactly like my father—an angry, abusive drunk.*

She wonders why there were times she felt so strangely drawn to him. She had to admit she was attracted to his lean, muscular frame and tanned face, the result of years of working on the docks. Even the jagged scar across his right cheek, which he got from the broken window, was somehow intriguing.

As she absently stares at Antagonist, Master Potter, aware of her every thought, says, "I'm going to heal your heart of these painful memories. I'm not going to leave you wounded. I'll be your beloved. You will no longer look to men for what they can't provide. I'll give you back the dignity that was taken from you and the dignity you willingly gave away."

She blushes in shame and looks at the ground. Taking her face in His hands, He gently turns it back and replies, "You're on a journey and right now you're broken, but watch what I do. I'll make you a beautiful vessel of honor."

VESSELS OF HONOR

Wooden wagons lumbering down the cobblestone streets create a great racket. The wagons are laden with grains, vegetables, fruits and barrels of wine headed for the flagship.

"Look over there, Beloved! My pottery wagons have just arrived from the Formidable Mountains!" says Master Potter.

Amidst the throng of villagers unloading the pottery, Beloved rubs her eyes, squints and rubs them again to be sure she is seeing correctly. She sees flashes of brilliant light. Watching in fascination, Beloved turns questioningly to Master Potter.

He smiles. "Those flashes are My angels in disguise. They playfully streak through the air of time, flying on the wings of the wind. They're everywhere, all the time, even though you usually don't see them."

Burly workers unpack the wagon, pulling out majestic pots of every conceivable size and shape from the packed straw. Stunning glazes of golden yellows, crimson reds, sapphire blues, emerald greens, burnt oranges, bronze, silver and gold shimmer in the late afternoon sun. Looking down at her own broken, ugly vessel, Beloved's face flushes and she feels she will never be transformed into such beauty that is fit for the Master's use.

REASSURING WORDS

Seeing her face drop, Master Potter instantly understands her fears and reaches out to comfort her. "These beautiful pots were also rescued out of the

Potter's Field. They were as broken as you are, Beloved. This is an exciting day of commissioning for them. They are further along on the journey that you're just beginning. As I did with these, I am taking you to My house to mold and shape your life into a beautiful reflection of My love."

Beloved moans, "But Lord, look at me. How could You ever fix me?"

With deep affection He replies, "I am Master Potter, the creator of all things. I've already seen you as one of those finished vessels that will be sent to the nations. I'm showing you this so you can have faith for your own completion. Remember this day, and know that you have a wonderful destiny that's hidden in Me."

Still held in the Master Potter's strong arms, Beloved has a perfect bird's-eye view from the high bluff overlooking the village. The thought of being a finished lovely vessel makes her laugh with delight. She loves Master Potter even more.

Master Potter turns and carries her into the peaceful and lovely woods, away from the noisy loading docks of Comfort Cove. The excitement of the day slowly fades into the background as they climb higher. The mountainous terrain gradually changes into stately cedar trees pointing upward to the face of God.

Chapter Eleven

The Potter's House

The journey to the Potter's House is nearly complete, but for Beloved it could last forever and she wouldn't mind a bit. Never has she felt so comforted, so loved, so safe and secure. She catches glimpses of gold sparkling through the lush foliage and dense woods reflecting the upland sunlight. She sighs as she nestles deeper into the folds of His robe.

Master Potter approaches a mysterious golden gate with translucent white roses cascading over it. Reaching for the gate, He announces, "Beloved, many have looked for the way but it's hidden. I'm the only one who can take you through this gate."

The gate swings wide open as they enter through wooden gingerbread archways covered with flaxen yellow and pink roses. Lavender and blue lilac bushes emit their intoxicating perfume that hangs like a cloud of incense over the hidden gardens of Master Potter's love.

Sweet peas entangled in iris and hollyhocks climb over a weathered lattice surrounding an old stone bench. The bench seems to welcome them, inviting intimacy and communion as they sit down in the cool evening twilight.

Resting in His Love

"Beloved, I just want to hold you and enjoy your company. Let's watch the sunset together and cherish the fragrance and colors of My gardens."

Iridescent hummingbirds dart from flower to flower, seeking the golden nectar of each lovely bloom. The lively mountain birds gather at pools of living water—springs that bubble up from deep underground wells.

Beloved is overwhelmed with peace and gratitude. "Lord, there is so much life here. For the first time I realize how lost I was."

Master Potter receives her love with great delight. "You've only begun to glimpse what I have planned for you. You've only glimpsed the realms of beauty I long to show you."

As the bright orange sun drops gently below the horizon, Master Potter lifts Beloved up from the stone bench and into His arms and carries her to their final destination. Night is settling in, and the light from the full harvest moon illuminates the path beneath their feet. Master Potter holds Beloved close, and she rests her head upon His chest as they climb the final incline up the mountain.

A Blazing Pillar of Fire

Nearly asleep, Beloved lifts her head to look up in amazement at a blazing pillar of fire swirling over a two-story stone and log house. As they draw near, the atmosphere becomes alive. Suddenly, Beloved is engulfed in a heavy mist of radiant glory, saturated with iridescent particles of golden light. Wispy ethereal hues, colors she's never before experienced, dance around her.

This heavenly portal, which constantly connects Heaven and earth, swirls around the Potter's House. Angelic worship wafts through the air with harmonious cries of "Holy, holy, holy," echoing back and forth between the surrounding mountains. Even the rocks cry out as every object pulsates in a symphony of praise.

"Welcome to My home, Beloved."

This mystical house is made of fragrant cedar logs and living stones. Unseen hands open beautifully carved wooden doors, and Master Potter tenderly carries Beloved over the threshold. Her hand brushes across the beautiful paneled walls releasing the sweet scent of the wood. She looks up to see huge beams of aged cedar and wonders what mysteries they have witnessed in this house.

Will Master Potter permit her to hear the tales of sovereignty and nobility the old ones have seen? What glories have these ancient beams witnessed? What transformations and amazing acts of mercy have been disclosed to these old sages of cedar?

What Is My Destiny?

They enter an inviting room with several large windows. Old wooden shelves line the walls, displaying hundreds of different vessels. The sweet aromas of brewing tea, clay and cedar fill the room. Beloved's eyes are drawn to a large stone-hewed fireplace where a blazing fire crackles and dances. On the great mantel are several large graceful vases, elegant pitchers and sturdy platters.

Looking at all the wonderful and unique clay pots on the Potter's shelves, Beloved remembers the beautiful glazed vessels being loaded onto the ship. Pointing around the room, she says in awe, "Look at those colorful pitchers sitting on those top shelves over there, and those delicate wine goblets. That's a huge serving platter! I love the set of mugs. Will I ever be beautiful like they are?"

A vision appears to Beloved as Master Potter begins speaking to the little pot about her marvelous destiny. She sees herself as a beautiful pearlized white pitcher with royal blue filigree trimmed in gold. She is ministering to broken vessels, saving others from the Potter's Field where she came so near to her own destruction.

In a still, small voice, Master Potter unfolds her destiny. "Beloved, I have called you to be a lovely pitcher, a prophetic voice to pour out My truth and revelation to thousands of others."

Turning slowly around and lighting brass oil lanterns, He settles down into His soft leather chair in front of the fireplace. Master Potter wraps her in the comfort of His arms and begins to softly sing songs of destiny over her.

A deep sigh of weariness escapes Beloved as she slips off to sleep and dreams of the beautiful vessel she will become. Still, she wonders how the ugliness and brokenness of her form can ever be repaired.

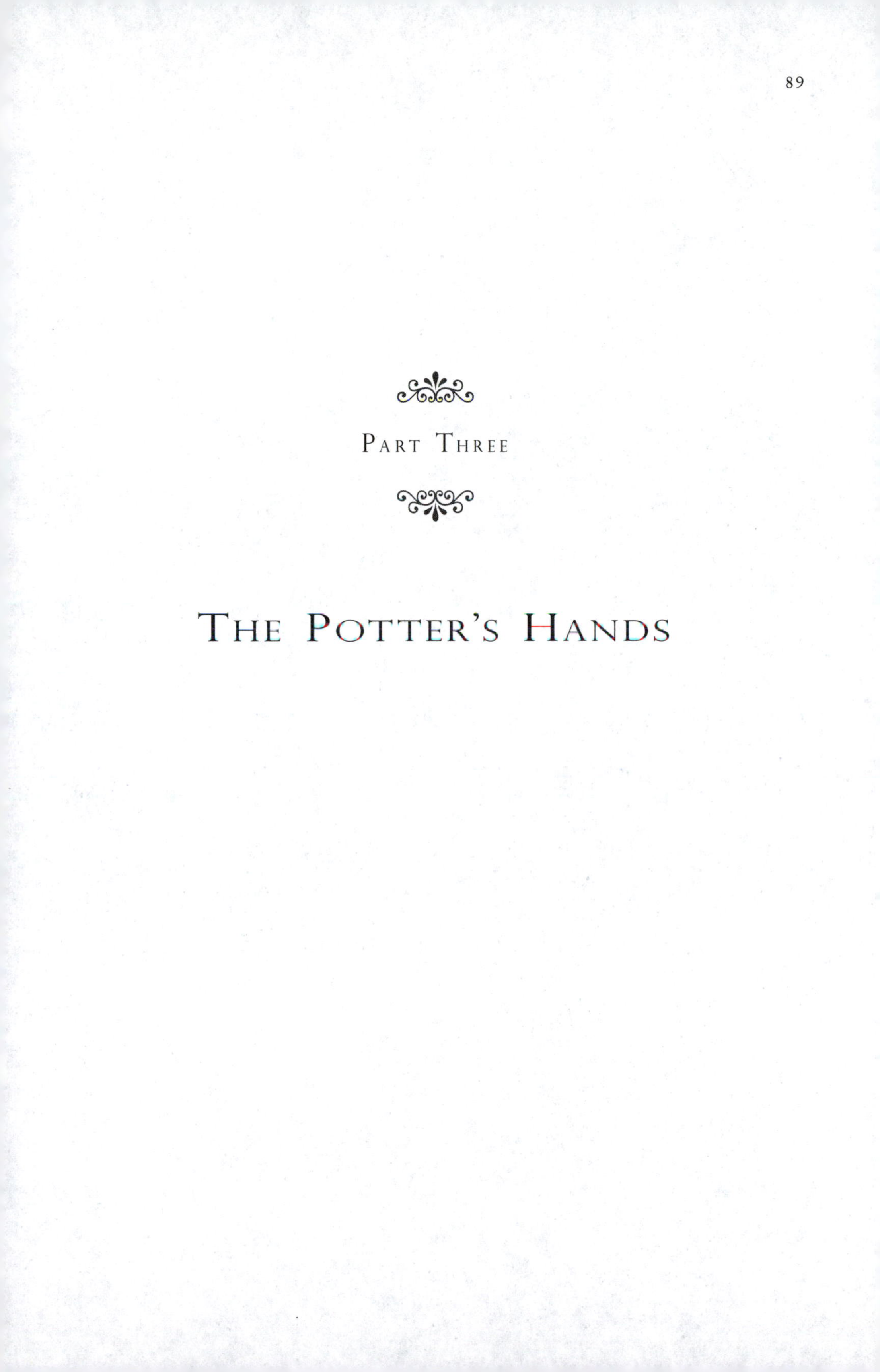

Part Three

The Potter's Hands

CHAPTER TWELVE

UNRELENTING LOVE

Early the next morning after a deep and restful sleep, Beloved awakens to see Master Potter gazing lovingly into her sleepy eyes and wonders if she's still dreaming. Her heart leaps with joy when she sees her own image reflected in His soft brown eyes. His love feels as fresh and new as the brand new morning, and Beloved is astonished all over again by His wonderful love for her.

Master Potter opens the windows to allow the warm easterly winds to bring the sweet fragrances from His garden into the fireside room. The morning sun reflects off tiny dewdrops that glisten on every delicate velvety flower petal outside Beloved's window. Rainbow-colored hummingbirds hover over the blossoms, taking their first drink of golden nectar for the day.

Master Potter lifts Beloved up and carries her to a long hallway lined with closed doors. *I wonder if I'll ever see what's behind them?* she muses to herself.

"Curious, are you?" He asks, as the first one swings open wide revealing the glazing room. A radiant cloud of glory spills out from behind the door. It's so bright that Beloved squints to make out the figures of angels at work painting clay vessels. This glorious vision grips her soul with the beauty and promise of God's handiwork for her own life.

As the door closes gently, Master Potter whispers, "Beloved, someday you'll be beautifully adorned, and then you'll go through the Straits of the Dragon to the Land of Lost Promises."

"What's behind the other doors, Lord? Can I see?" Master Potter chuckles as He hears her thoughts about sneaking a peek into the other doors later that night.

Laughing tenderly He says, "No, Beloved, now is not the time. Each door represents a different season in the process of maturity. Trust Me to lead you in My perfect timing. You must not go in before you're ready. You'll see behind all of those doors soon enough."

Crushed by Holy Love

Carrying her to the back of the Potter's House, He takes Beloved through large wooden doors which open up into a red brick outer court that's attached to the back of the studio. The area is sparse and nearly barren except for a large stone worktable. The barrenness of the courtyard seems to Beloved to be set in sharp contrast to the luxuriant gardens and the warmth of the Potter's House.

Carefully laying her broken clay vessel on the table, Master Potter touches the shattered pieces of her life. With great tenderness, He explains, "Beloved, it breaks My heart how terribly damaged you've become. That was never My intent for you, but sin extracts a high price."

The seriousness of His voice quiets her. Instinctively, Beloved feels the seriousness of the hour and senses that something important is about to happen. Fearing that she may not like it, she says, "Lord, I don't understand. What are You trying to tell me?"

"Beloved, do you remember your vision of the beautiful blue and white pitcher? The one I intend to make of you?"

"Yes Lord, but I'm so damaged with these huge cracks running down my side. I can't even hold water and my handle is nearly broken off. And look at my lip, it's chipped and my words just dribble onto my shoes! How will I ever become what I saw in that vision? You'd have to practically start all over and completely remake me."

Master Potter's eyes look deeply into hers, and large tears well up. Slowly, sadly, He tells her, "You're right, I do have to start over. To fulfill the marvelous destiny I have for your life, I must crush you into fine dust, but I promise I'll not lose even one particle of you. Each particle, like the hairs on your head, is numbered by Me. I will take you to My wheel, and from your dust, make you into that lovely pitcher."

"Please Lord, No! I don't want to be crushed! I don't want to hurt any more."

"This process is a necessary part of making you into that beautiful vessel, Beloved. But you will have to trust Me. The only crushing you've ever known has been abusive and painful; it was intended by the enemy to destroy you. My crushing is deeply rooted in My redemptive love to heal you. It will hurt for a moment, but the freedom and joy it brings will last through eternity."

Lying broken on the Potter's table, she glances around and notices a large object with an inscription on its side. At first she can't quite make it out but as

He moves it closer she sees that it's a stone etched with the words, "Unrelenting Love."

A cold shiver runs up her back. Shuddering, she asks, "Lord, what are You going to do to me? I thought my pain and suffering were over when You took me out of the Potter's Field."

Tenderly He tells her, "I'm going to take Unrelenting Love and crush you into fine dust so I can remove all the brokenness and filth you picked up throughout your life. I know this is frightening to you, but it's necessary to truly set you free. I must break off the sins of the past that hold you in bondage."

"No Lord," she pleads. "Please don't. I don't think I can take one more thing."

"You'll be in My hands the whole time, Beloved. Even in the painful moments I'll be with you. I will never leave you or forsake you. Remember that I won't allow a single moment of suffering or discomfort beyond what is necessary. If you're willing to let Me crush you, I will add My living water and make you soft and pliable for My potter's wheel."

LORD, HELP ME!

Desperately wanting to be free of her past she cries out, "Lord, help me! I want to be willing to surrender to You even though I don't understand. I want to follow You with all my heart. Help me, Lord."

The moment the prayer leaves her lips the penetrating wind and fire of Holy Spirit swirls around her, enveloping her broken vessel. After a few moments, a supernatural empowerment, an enabling grace, rises up in her spirit. It gives her the power to embrace and endure pain at the loving hands of Master Potter.

Beloved closes her eyes, clenches her fists, inhales deeply and blurts out, "Yes Lord, I'm willing."

Carefully raising Unrelenting Love several inches above her, Master Potter strategically brings it down with just enough pressure that the first light tap forms a new crack down her side. She falls into several large pieces.

The breaking exposes the guilt and burning shame of her past as haunting memories sweep over her. Retching rises up in her throat as overwhelming feelings of defilement and sexual abuse bring back the horrible sense of unworthiness. It was a time when her dignity and femininity were stripped away, and the memories torment her.

With heart-wrenching sobs, Beloved cries out, "Lord, I'm so dirty and used up! I hate myself! There's no hope for me! I've ruined my life! No one decent would ever want me now, especially after what Antagonist did to me."

You Must Forgive

"I've always wanted you, Beloved. You must forgive him and all the people who caused you so much pain."

"You've got to be kidding! Forgive him? You know the violent temper he had and how he used to beat me. I barely got away with my life the last time. I hate him! He just used me like all the other men."

"Yes Beloved, that is true. He did use you. But remember you used him too." She sees a picture of herself the night she got thrown out of the Inn. She's getting up from the dock, smoothing her hair and rubbing the tears from her eyes as she walks toward Antagonist. "You approached him because you didn't want to spend the night on the docks. You sold your soul in a failed effort to feel loved and protected. But it wasn't real, and you ended up feeling more hurt and alone."

"Lord, I'm so ashamed. I did awful things, things I don't even want to remember."

"Nothing is hidden from Me, Beloved. I wept when I saw you so abused, but the power to overcome your past is found only in forgiveness. The mystery of forgiveness lies in the Cross. I died to release the power of forgiveness into the earth, which is why you must forgive others as I have forgiven you. I, too, was abused and chose to forgive."

Hot tears stream down her cheeks, "Oh Lord, please forgive me. I feel so dirty and ashamed. I've hurt so many people. I'm sorry I turned to men to fill the emptiness inside of me."

"I do forgive you, Beloved. And now you must forgive Antagonist and the other men who violated you."

Tears well up and sweat beads on her forehead. Beloved trembles and determines to forgive no matter how difficult it feels. "Lord, it's hard, so hard. I have such horrific memories. I even still have bruises and scars, but because You love and forgive me, I choose to forgive him. Even though I don't feel like it, I trust You."

Beloved looks perplexed as she sees tears in Master Potter's eyes. "Beloved, you've captured My heart with your willingness to be obedient. As

I continue to heal your heart, forgiving Antagonist won't just be an act of your will."

REMOVING THE SHACKLES OF SHAME

Firmly, yet tenderly, Master Potter brings Unrelenting Love down on the shards of Beloved's body, crushing her into smaller and smaller bits. "I'm breaking off the shackles of shame and self-hatred. My death on the Cross makes a way for you to come to the Father. My shed blood breaks the sexual and soul connections you have with Antagonist and other men."

Beloved softly sobs, "Thank You for loving me so much! I'm getting clean. I can feel it. I'm getting free, I feel Your love for me."

"Beloved, in your self-protection you become cold and hard, but I'm calling you into a deep, intimate journey of the heart. I'm inviting you to make a holy exchange by giving you brand new innocence in exchange for your worldliness."

MADAM FALSE DESTINY

"Now you need to forgive Madam False Destiny."

"Why should I forgive her? She said that she loved me like a daughter, then she didn't believe me. She threw me out like trash. Anyway, now she knows I didn't take her brooch. It's not like I sinned against her."

"Beloved, we're dealing with your heart, not Madam's. Can you forgive her for her sin against you?"

Deep sobs rise up from the pain of betrayal and rejection. "Oh Lord, I don't know if I can. She ruined my life."

Speaking gently He says, "I know it's hard to forgive, because there was an unhealthy connection in the spirit between you and Madam, and that needs to be broken."

"Lord, I don't understand. What do you mean, 'an unhealthy connection in the spirit'? I just felt there was something special between us."

"There was, but it was fueled by the demonic. I gave you both a prophetic gift. As a young girl, I called Madam to follow Me, but her hunger for power and influence opened the door to the demonic. Instead of becoming a prophetic voice for Me, she took the gift I gave her and became a spiritualist for My enemy."

"Now, she uses her prophetic gifting to manipulate and destroy lives, luring people into false destinies. She recognized your prophetic sensitivity and was assigned to bring you into Satan's service. She mentored you to exploit people for your mutual advantage."

"Oh Lord, You're right. It started out so innocently, but I became intrigued with the power of knowing people's secrets. Madam showed me how to read tarot cards and to predict the future. She taught me to call on demons for the information."

"Beloved, when you experimented in the demonic realm, it opened doors for evil spirits to get their cruel talons into you. I called you to be a prophetic voice to bless people, not to use them."

"Lord, forgive me. Even though I wasn't walking with You, I knew it was wrong to play with people's emotions for my own gain. I'm so sorry. I thought I was the only one wounded, but I've hurt so many people in my life."

"Beloved, you need to renounce your involvement with Madam and the occult. Can you see that was when your life took a downward spiral?"

"How was I so blind back then? You're right; I see it now. The nightmares and the tormenting voices! I couldn't stop them. Help me Lord, I want to be free. Forgive me for allowing Madam to use me. I do renounce all involvement in the occult. I'm so sorry."

Deliverance

Her words of repentance activate the vile demonic spirits of witchcraft and perversion. Fighting to maintain their ground, they screech, "We'll never let her go. She'll always be ours." Writhing in agony she cries out, "Master Potter, help me!"

With holy passion He declares, "Leave her! She belongs to Me! I break your power over her! You spirits of witchcraft and all your evil henchmen leave now!"

Tenderly and compassionately Master Potter takes the stone, Unrelenting Love, and crushes the demonic strongholds.

Infuriated that they must vacate their familiar dwelling, they leave in an explosion of curses as Master Potter's powerful words dislodge their horrendous grasp. Dark sulfuric smoke erupts into the atmosphere as they are driven out to arid lands to begin their search for new victims.

Beloved sobs with relief as heavy layers of demonic oppression are lifted off. "I no longer hear the tormenting voices! Oh, Lord I'm finally free. Thank You, Lord. I love You!"

Suddenly she sees a vision of her past. She's on the Potter's Field, but this time she sees into the spirit realm. She is horrified at the demonic horde tormenting everyone there. Compassion wells up inside her for the other broken and lost vessels. The faces of Friendless, the squatty little broken mug, and Turncoat, the sugar bowl, flash before her.

She realizes for the first time and blurts out, "We are all just broken pots. We were all the same. Without You, we could never get along much less love each other. We only looked out for ourselves, we didn't have the ability to care about anyone else." She turns to Him and their eyes meet. "Thank You so much for rescuing me."

Suddenly the thought of Friendless and Turncoat perishing on the Potter's Field seems like a real possibility and totally unbearable. For the first time Beloved feels true caring toward others. It wells up inside her and she grieves for the lost. She feels Master Potter's pain for them and is gripped in intercession. When she can stand it no more she cries out through her pain, "Won't You go back to the Potter's Field and rescue them too?"

"I have a destiny for all my cherished vessels. You'll find out that the hardest thing, the most heartbreaking thing, is to wait for them to choose life. All they have to do is cry out for Me, Beloved, and I'll move Heaven and earth to be there for them. We have to wait, and we have to pray."

Master Potter tenderly scoops all that remains of the broken vessel, the fine dust of her life, into His protective hands. Not one precious particle is missing.

Chapter Thirteen

Baptism of Love

Dazed from the crushing, Beloved feels somewhat bewildered as Master Potter scoops her off the stone table and carries her from the brick courtyard. "I'm taking you to Abundant Life Falls. That's where the River of Life begins. It flows downstream and turns the wheel at the Settler's Mill where my wheat is turned to flour. Off in the distance she sees a steep, winding trail and a path that leads through the forest to the foothills of a rugged, snow-capped mountain range known by the villagers of Comfort Cove as the Formidables.

She hears the sound of water furiously cascading down a glorious waterfall. The icy water rushes over a sheer cliff, plummeting hundreds of feet onto moss-covered rocks below. Translucent rainbows appear in the hovering mist over crystal clear pools at the bottom of the falls.

Cupping her safely in His hands, Master Potter carries Beloved down the steep path to the bottom of the waterfall to a hidden, gentle pool behind the cascading flow. "These are the Abundant Life Falls and it is here that I will take you through the waters of baptism so that you may rise to new life in Me." Leaning down, He lovingly immerses Beloved.

The living waters soak into her pores. Refreshing! Invigorating! Coming up out of the water she watches a beautiful rainbow of promise emerge in the sparkling atmosphere. He tenderly holds her close once again before setting her down in the pool.

"Rest, Beloved," Master Potter smiles. "I will return for you later." She watches Him walk away until He's lost in the distance.

In the evening shadows, Valiant stands guard with his sword blazing. Smiling down at his little charge, he sighs with contentment as she raises her face in wonderment. The beauty of creation and the majesty of the stars emerge like brilliant diamonds against the deepening cobalt-blue night.

The large full moon illuminates the cascading waterfalls and shimmering pools. Valiant and a glorious angelic choir burst into song as celestial instruments fill the night. Beloved reaches her hands upward to touch the heavens in worship—as her heart touches the face of God.

Chapter Fourteen

Kneaded in His Love

Early one morning, Beloved looks up to see Master Potter returning for her. He gazes at her fondly, kneels down and scoops up her wet clay in His hands. With loving care, Master Potter places her clay back into the singing pools of worship.

Her excitement at finally being ready for the wheel turns to irritation when she realizes she's being put back into the water. She groans, "Lord, when am I going to be made into one of those beautiful vessels I saw being loaded on the flagships?"

Smiling, He reaches down and picks her up again, gently telling her, "It's not time yet. But I'll show you the process all clay must go through to be made ready for the Potter's wheel.

"You are what I call immature or green clay. If I put you on the wheel before you have time to age, you'll be unable to yield to the molding of My hands. Your walls will be thick because your clay will have no elasticity. Therefore, you need more time soaking in My presence to become a beautiful vessel and fulfill your destiny."

Beloved changes her attitude as she realizes there's no way out of the pool and everyone must go through the same process. She adoringly looks up into His face. "I want to be beautiful. If I have to stay here to do it, then that's what I'll do. But how do I become aged clay?"

Seasons of God

"It just takes time, that's all. The process can't be hurried. Clay must sit through hard, cold winters where the water turns to ice. Then it thaws when the spring rains come, bringing new life. Summer heat and warm waters make the clay soft and pliable again."

"Even then the process is not complete. The fall season comes and the dying process begins once more. The freezing and thawing, the breaking down and building up—all of these things transform green clay into flexible aged clay. Beloved, this is the process you must go through. Therefore you must be patient and simply choose to trust Me. One day it will happen. You will reach your destiny, I promise."

"Does it have to take so long? It's boring just sitting in the water all the time! I try to pray and meditate on the Word, but my mind wanders all over the place."

"Beloved, everyone goes through that. Just don't give up. Just keep loving Me.

"Through the many long seasons you'll learn My ways as I strengthen and mature you. All in due season, Beloved. All in due season." Master Potter gently places her back into the little pool of water and returns to the Potter's House.

At times Beloved grows impatient and weary of waiting. "When is it going to be my turn? I'm tired of waiting." Grumbling to herself, she says, "I see Master Potter coming and taking others out of the pools of water. When am I going to the Potter's wheel? I want to fulfill my destiny. I know I must be ready by now. I've been here longer than anyone!" She starts yelling out, "Master Potter, I'm ready. Over here. Did You forget Your little princess?"

More time passes through the seasons, and the years come and go. Beloved works hard at trying to be patient. While she waits, she often ponders in her heart the many promises and dreams that Master Potter showed her. Always before her, deep in her spirit, is the vision of the beautiful vessels being loaded on the flagship long ago. With each passing day it seems longer ago and further away, yet she never lets go—the vision has become the purpose of her life.

Ouch! Lord, What Are You Doing?

Finally, the deep resonating voice of Master Potter beckons, "Beloved, I'm coming for you! You're ready to begin a new season of preparation for My wheel." With a gleam in His eye, He kneels down beside the pool, scoops her into His hands and places her on a large drying board in the warm sun.

"Oh Lord, I'm so excited! I'm ready for anything!"

Suddenly she feels herself being picked up and repeatedly shoved down on the wedging board. As if that isn't enough, He squeezes, kneads, and pounds her into place. He pushes and prods, making her clay soft and pliable in His hands.

"Ouch! Lord, what are You doing?"

"This process is called 'wedging.' It will bring a consistency to your life as I work the air bubbles out of you and knead My love in. Then your clay vessel will not blow up in the firing ahead."

I JUST DON'T MEASURE UP

Master Potter leans back with a satisfied sigh, and with great delight holds the soft yet firm clay ball named Beloved in His hands. He places her on another wooden board alongside other clay balls of various sizes also waiting to be carried to His house.

Eying balls of clay much larger than herself, she asks, "Lord, why am I so small? That one over there is ten pounds and look at that one! It must be 25 pounds! That one has prettier clay than I do. Why didn't You make me rich brown, dark red or yellow clay? Why did You make me this light grayish color? After all I've been through, I'm still so plain and ugly!"

Chuckling, He says, "So you compare yourself to others, do you? Beloved, I know where to find and dig the various kinds of clay. I love their different textures and wonderful colors of red, yellow, black, white, or brown. I also know what temperature of fire is needed for the different types of clay bodies to come forth as beautiful clay vessels. Whether they are earthenware, stoneware, porcelain or china, I have a plan for each one.

"I'm a creative artist and have personally designed each of My vessels. I know their substance and how much clay is needed for every one of them. A pitcher like yourself could take five or six pounds; a platter takes ten to twelve; a cup might take only one; but it is no less valuable because of its small size."

His eyes search the depths of her soul, peering into a future still hidden from her. He declares, "I've measured you, I know your portion, I know exactly what destiny, what mysteries, what assignment of life I have for you. I have a mission and calling for your life. And now, are you ready?"

"For what, Lord?"

"For the Potter's wheel, of course!"

Her heart leaps with excitement, "Finally! At last! I can become the vessel I was meant to be. I can hardly wait! Wheel, here I come."

Fragrances of myrrh and aloe emanate from His robe as He moves toward her. Master Potter picks up the board heavily laden with clay balls and walks toward His house. After so much time being submerged, Beloved is relieved to leave the pools behind. *No more winter seasons for me! It's high time my ministry got started.*

Part Four

The Potter's Wheel

Chapter Fifteen

On the Wheel

Traveling back through the forest, they enter the barren brick courtyard. Looking up, Beloved catches a glimpse of the pillar of fire still brooding over the dwelling. Terrifying in its beauty, the fiery whirlwind fascinates her. Somehow she knows it's Heaven's gateway. They walk into the heavy mist of radiant glory saturated with iridescent golden particles of light constantly surrounding the house.

Master Potter pushes open the back door and the old cedar beams greet them as they step over the threshold, bringing a renewed sense of security to Beloved.

Hope and wonderment explode in Beloved's heart as they enter the studio. *Will this be the day He makes me into that beautiful blue and white pitcher?*

They pass long wooden shelves loaded with glazed, finished vessels and stop before a large urn and exquisite vase.

"Beloved, I'd like to introduce you to several of my friends. This is Courageous," Master Potter says, pointing to a large amber urn. "And this beautiful vase over here is Loving Kindness."

In unison they both call out, "Hello, little one."

Intimidated by their size and beauty, Beloved murmurs to Master Potter, "See, I told you I'm too small! Even they called me 'little one.' "

Loving Kindness warmly greets Beloved, "So, this is your big day. This is a day that you will always remember, a day when you are changed for all eternity."

The deep voice of Courageous booms, "Don't be afraid, little one. I remember the day the Master formed me on the wheel. It stretches you a bit, but His grace enables you to be pliable in His hands."

Loving Kindness glides gracefully over to Beloved and kisses her on the cheek. Beloved tries to hide her embarrassment as she gazes longingly upon her lovely, handpainted roses. "Will I ever be as beautiful as you? I love your soft green finish."

Loving Kindness meets her gaze and smiles sweetly, "Thank you. Of course you'll be beautiful! But remember, I didn't get this way overnight; it takes time to become a finished vessel."

"I know something about time," says Beloved." I've been waiting around here forever!" The two finished pots look at Master Potter with a knowing smile.

On the Potter's Wheel—At Last

Turning back to Beloved He says, "This is an exciting new season we're entering together. Since it's such a beautiful day, I think I'll use one of the Potter's wheels on the deck." Master Potter takes Beloved through the French doors outside to a large wooden deck overlooking the cliff and the pounding surf below. The ocean's breeze on her skin is refreshing. For so long her mind has dreamt of this day, but now that it's finally here her great sense of anticipation is giving way to a growing sense of fear.

Suddenly a trumpet blast announces a flagship's arrival into the harbor below. Leaning over the wooden railing Master Potter points, "Look! One of my ships has returned from the nations to be outfitted for its next journey."

She watches hundreds of earthenware vessels on the docks ready to be placed on board. Turning to Master Potter she says, "As a little girl I always watched as these beautiful ships came in. Did you know I wanted to be a stowaway? I must have planned it a hundred times, how to sneak on board, so I could escape from my dad.

"Many nights I hid behind the barrels on the dock and listened to the worship music coming off the ships. It was so comforting to me because it reminded me of my Grandma Pearl. I can't believe that some day I will actually ride Your ship, with Your permission and blessing."

Tools of the Craftsman

Finally, Master Potter puts on His work apron and sits down on a low stool in front of the wheel overlooking the harbor. He places a bowl of water and some tools on a wooden bench next to Him. "Beloved, let me introduce you to some more new friends."

With great affection He holds up a reddish-brown bowl with the name Servant carved into its side. "This vessel has been glazed and has endured the high fires. Therefore, it's able to hold the living water necessary to form you into a beautiful vessel."

Next He picks up a sponge. "This is Soaking Love, who works with Servant. Most people will forget who they are, but My hands work in partnership with each of them."

Servant smiles adoringly as Master Potter asks, "Are you ready to begin, Beloved?"

"Lord, I've waited so long; it's hard to believe it's really happening."

With a bold kick, the huge stone flywheel at the Master's feet begins to rotate. Picking up Beloved, He looks with soft penetrating eyes deeply into her soul. "I love you, Beloved. Remember, in the midst of being formed into a beautiful vessel, you won't always understand the process. There are hidden mysteries that one day will be revealed to you. Shall we begin?"

"Oh yes, Lord, I've never been more ready."

A Leap of Faith

Unexpectedly, He throws her down on the spinning wheel. Beloved is suddenly falling at breakneck speed. A wave of nauseating fear sweeps over her, causing her heart to beat wildly. She feels as if she's riding a roller coaster that's racing down a steep hill with the wind whipping in her face. "Oh no! I'm afraid. Oh! Oh! Wait. I can't stop!"

With a great thud, Beloved smashes into an immovable object—the potter's wheel.

Without a moment to catch her breath, Beloved is spinning around wildly with increasing velocity as the acceleration speeds up. Faster, faster, faster, faster.

"Lord, help! What's happening to me? I'm out of control!" He squeezes cold water from the sponge, Soaking Love, and it pours over her head, muffling her cries. Gulping and gurgling Beloved yells, "What are You trying to do, drown me?"

Now frantic and terrified, Beloved thrashes about, fighting for her life, and her clay wobbles out of balance on the wheel. In a power struggle over who will be in control, she resists the hands of the One trying to transform her into a beautiful vessel.

"Don't be afraid of the sudden pressures bearing down on you. Some things have to change, Beloved. Faith means giving up control of your life and trusting Me to be more than your Savior but also your Lord."

Her continued resistance throws her off-balance. "Please help me, Master Potter! I'm trying to trust You, but I don't know how!"

"Relax, Beloved; I'm right here and everything's under control. The very universe is held together by the power of My words. All that I ask of you is a heart that is yielded. Are you willing to say yes to Me, Beloved?"

"Lord, letting go is so scary; giving myself totally into Your hands is one of the most difficult things I've ever done! But, I'm trying! See, I'm taking deep breaths and trying to relax."

He enjoys her willingness and her attempts to yield to His hands. He squeezes more water from Soaking Love onto her clay. Firmly, He presses her down even harder, forming her into a shapeless lump, centered on the wheel. Soft clay oozes between His fingers. The pliability was created at the cost of breaking, crushing, soaking and waiting. Pausing for a moment, He cleans His hands in the humble water bowl.

By this time Servant is so smeared with Beloved's excess clay that she can no longer see the letters of his name carved into his side. She's overwhelmed by his great sacrifice for her.

Creating a New Heart

Then the voice of Master Potter draws her attention. "I'm centering your innermost being. I'm taking away the double-mindedness and renewing your soul. My desire is that your heart be an enclosed garden of intimacy for Me."

His skillful hands plunge deeply into the very heart of her clay, making a firm foundation and widening the base. "Beloved, I know your depths. The goal is to form you in My image. Your emptiness will disappear as I fill the tremendous void in your life with My love. As you choose an all-consuming love relationship with Me, I will awaken within you a true sense of belonging."

Her heart melts in surrender and she yields to the pressure of His hands.

"I'm working in the deepest recesses of your being. It's a place no mortal can touch or even comprehend. The beauty of My handiwork is concealed on the inside, but until I bring up your walls, you still appear as a lump of clay."

Jealousy and Competition

Jealousy rises in other unfinished vessels as they see the loving intimacy between Master Potter and Beloved.

A stocky little pot drying on a shelf next to the potter's wheel wisecracks, "I see You're making another doggy dish! Or is this one going to be special and become a spittoon?"

Discouraged, Beloved says, "See? I still look like a formless blob of clay. Why don't You tell them I am going to be somebody? I'm going on one of the flagships as a beautiful blue and white pitcher trimmed with gold. You told me I'm a princess who will touch thousands."

The envious vessels hoot in derision, "It's an ashtray for sure! It's a doggy dish! Ashtray! Doggie dish! I know! She's a flagship thunder mug—a bedpan! Yes, a bedpan," they all agree. "And a dirty one at that."

The harassment continues until Master Potter intervenes. "Well, I see it's time for all of you to be fired! That should work out some of the dross, the impurities of jealousy, bitterness and resentment that are in your clay. Then you won't be making fun of others."

"That's right," Beloved pipes up. "You guys don't know what you're talking about. Someday I'll be a famous prophetic voice known around the world. You watch and see."

Master Potter continues to stretch her walls higher. "Yes, Beloved, in time everyone will see you're a beautiful pitcher, but you too have much to learn."

"See, I told you so. I'm not a bedpan, look how tall He's making me. Obviously, He enjoys working on my clay more than yours. That's why you've been left up there on the shelf to dry out."

"Well, she certainly does have a mouth, doesn't she? I'm sure she'll be a wide-mouth pitcher," they all smirk.

Angry, Beloved yells back. "You're just jealous of the fact that I have all His attention. Obviously, He cares more about me, or you wouldn't be sitting on the shelves all dried up and useless."

Master Potter stops the wheel and says, "Oh Beloved, your heart is getting exposed. It's time to deal with your attitude."

Chapter Sixteen

Piercing Love

Master Potter's sensitive fingers find several air pockets trapped in her clay. He picks up a pencil-thin tool with a sharp needle-like point. Engraved on the tool is the name Piercing Love.

Fear grips her. "What are You going to do with that?"

"Beloved, we need to work on the air pockets of pride and self-promotion."

"Lord, I don't think I'm the problem. Those other vessels are! You heard how they talked to me; and You're right—they need the dross fired out of them. You need to stick *them* with that needle-sharp tool to get the air pockets out of them. After all, my air bubbles are so small compared to theirs. Can't we keep it our little secret? Besides a little self-promotion is necessary in this world in which we live! What do You say?"

Master Potter persists, "Beloved, these air bubbles will cause you to explode in the firing. I'm not making any deals. Are you willing to repent of your attitudes and allow Me to heal your life?"

Squirming, she replies, "Lord, this is going to be embarrassing. Now everyone will see my defects. After all, You said I'm to be a beautiful vessel going to the nations. This could ruin our reputation!"

"Thank you for thinking of My reputation, but I'm more concerned about your manipulation. If you love Me, you need to humble yourself.

"Your upper rim is uneven too. Beloved, you're thinking a little too highly of yourself. I'm going to have to trim it."

"No Lord. I was just getting so tall and I was finally getting some visibility. People were starting to look up to me and realize my gifting. Everyone's watching me grow in stature. It's not fair. Please, no more."

"Beloved," He says gently, "have you ever heard the phrase, 'to cut someone down to size'? The princess needs trimming because her pride is still showing."

"But Lord, I've been through so much. Isn't it fair that I finally get some recognition? After all, I do have a beautiful voice and I'm going to sing in churches now, for Your glory. And You were the one who called me Your princess, not me."

"Beloved, you are and will always be My princess, but true royalty doesn't demand worship from others. True royalty bows low."

Winds of Conviction

Holy Spirit's convicting winds blow over the delusions of her heart, revealing the wrong attitudes that hinder love. With a sigh of resignation she answers, "Oh no, Lord. I blew it again, didn't I? Forgive me for thinking that I was better than everyone else! Make me more like You. I hate this process, but I don't want to lose our intimacy. If this is what You're asking, I know it's best and I'm willing to trust You. Just do it quickly." Tears well up in her eyes.

With great care Master Potter uses Piercing Love to lance her air bubbles. "Ouch, that hurts!" she cries. He spins the wheel and uses Piercing Love to cut off the top rim and discards the excess.

"Beloved, since you submitted, now I can take you higher." He continues the process of pulling her walls up. "I love your yielded clay. This season on the wheel is a time of intimacy—My hands are touching every fiber of your being. But don't confuse intimacy with knowledge. Because you have much zeal without much knowledge, you need to trust Me to lead you. Don't fall back into old patterns that seem comfortable to you."

Beloved does not really understand the full weight of what Master Potter is saying but she's happy to once again feel His presence. As she spins on the wheel, the water dances up and down her growing walls like liquid shimmering light.

Master Potter places His hand into her and begins shaping her vessel. Great warmth and affection awaken her heart. The soft, warm clay glides gently between His fingers. "Beloved, My fingerprints are inscribed on your soul forever."

You Will Be My Mouthpiece

Stopping the wheel He says, "There is one more thing I must do." Taking His fingers He touches the top rim of her vessel and pulls gently, forming a lip. "Beloved, I have such delight in fashioning your vessel into My image. You will be My mouthpiece, My prophetic voice to bring My heart to suffering people."

Looking at Him through tear-filled eyes, she gratefully says, "I love You, Lord—" then is taken aback. "Lord, the words just flow so effortlessly. They don't dribble out on my shoes anymore. You found me so broken and rejected. It's hard to believe You could make me into something beautiful. You really do love me, don't You?"

"I do love you, but you're only just beginning to comprehend the depths of that great love. Beloved, I want to fill your being with My truth so you can easily pour into other vessels and impart My heart. Someday I'll give you a team of mugs and send you off on My flagship, through The Straits of the Dragon and off to the nations."

Chapter Seventeen

Come, Holy Spirit!

The Potter's wheel slows and stops, and Beloved sits there resting for a moment. She hears the breeze rustling through the cedar boughs surrounding Master Potter's House. As she looks out over the rugged cliffs, the wind increases and whitecaps form on what previously had been a placid sea.

An enormous cloud of brilliant light and roaring thunder rumbles across the churning water. Her heart races as the cloud quickly approaches the house. *What could it possibly be?* she wonders.

Suddenly, it engulfs them as she tries to hide in the protection of Master Potter's hands. Swirling gusts of dazzling glory surround them, impregnating the atmosphere with the power of Heaven. Fiery torches appear as flashes of lightning in this supernatural visitation. A divine person cloaked in a mantle of raging fire appears out of the midst of it.

Welcome, Holy Spirit

Master Potter throws His head back in hearty laughter, obviously enjoying the grand entrance of His friend. The Potter's humble appearance is set in sharp contrast with the majestic splendor of Holy Spirit's garments, which flow and transform into fire, wind and oil before Beloved's eyes.

An exuberant dance of glory revolves around the two comrades as They greet each other. Holy Spirit's awesome voice speaks, "It's so good to see the beautiful Bridegroom King."

Holy Spirit's Attributes

Shimmering with light and power, Holy Spirit moves toward Beloved. He is wrapped in celestial garments so that His very being glistens with golden anointing. Admiring the clay vessel forming on the wheel, Holy Spirit joyfully exclaims, "How wonderful that You've made Beloved into a prophetic pitcher. I remember when We first saw her on the Potter's Field, so rejected and broken, but look at her now—a trophy of Your wonderful grace."

She blushes bright red with the compliment and her heart warms toward Holy Spirit as she hears the love and acceptance in His voice. The air around the wheel becomes saturated with heavenly glory. The kabod of God, the weighty presence, surrounds her, causing her heart to tremble.

"Don't be afraid, Beloved. This is Holy Spirit; He's My best friend." Cowering behind Master Potter's hands, Beloved says, "I've never seen anyone like Him. He's so wild and magnificent!"

"Yes, heavenly power flows through Him, but He is not just a phenomenon—fire, wind or oil—but rather a real person. And yes, He will come with those attributes; He has a personality even more glorious than all the supernatural movements that flow from His being. For He is also a Comforter, Teacher, Guide and the one who illuminates the Word of God. I want the two of you to become best friends even as we are best friends, because I can't always be with you. For you will never be alone Beloved, as I have tenderly entrusted you to His care."

Beloved fearfully says, "But what will I do without You?"

"If you have Him living in you, then you will also always have Me."

With great admiration, Master Potter reassures her, "Holy Spirit has a radical passion and devotion to Me. He is on a heavenly assignment from My Father to awaken My Bride—that's you Beloved—to your destiny and birthright. He is on a mission: to prepare His people for our upcoming marriage.

"He brings conviction of sin, deep repentance and salvation to the lost. Do you remember, Beloved, when you didn't know Me in that desolate Potter's Field? There, He came to you and responded to your desperate cry for help. He challenged Death for your soul by showing you the vision of yourself as a little girl in your Grandma Pearl's church.

"He is the third person of the Trinity, equal in every way to the Father and Me. You need to know Him intimately. He is the holy escort into the deepest chambers of My heart. Beloved, someday I'll send you back to Comfort Cove, to tell others about Me—in that day, Holy Spirit will go with you."

Another Best Friend

Shuddering to think that she would ever leave the Potter's House, she says, "I'm afraid to go. I don't even know how to pray."

"He will teach you."

Holy Spirit jumps in, "Beloved! You should have seen the prayer meeting two thousand years ago with a pack of 120 disciples who barely knew the first thing about prayer! I was sent by the Father to come to their rescue. I baptized them with fire so that they had power to preach, witness and move in extraordinary signs and wonders. Three thousand people joined the Church that day! It only takes your willing heart my dear. For when you mix a little bit of persistent prayer with My power, anything can happen!"

Shimmering with light and power, Holy Spirit moves toward her. He is wrapped in celestial garments so that His very being glistens with golden anointing.

Master Potter tells her, "Beloved, this magnificent Holy Spirit is the One who sets you on fire to remove everything that hinders love. After salvation, He brings the refiner's fire to burn away areas of callousness, brokenness, unforgiveness and pain. The ongoing process of sanctification is a radical work of healing, cleansing and deliverance in your life as you transform into My very image."

Baptized in the Holy Spirit

"When you go through the wilderness, with all its obstacles, He is the one who will escort you on a marriage chariot out of that barren wilderness. In order to prepare you for these events, I want to immerse you in His unquenchable fire by baptizing you in Holy Spirit.

"You'll receive an empowerment to commune with Me in spirit and truth. Also, you will receive an exciting new prayer language and speak in other tongues."

She gasps, "Lord, when I was a little girl, the pastor at Comfort Cove said speaking in tongues was demonic. He said it was a device of the enemy to bring confusion into the Church, because not everyone gets it."

"No, Beloved, this prayer language is for all My people. It's a heavenly gift which was part of the tremendous outpouring that birthed the early Church. This is available to all believers today, but it takes a childlike faith to receive it."

"I'm confused. I don't understand. I want everything You have for me, but I don't want to be deceived. I'm not sure what You mean when You tell me that I'll speak in a new language. What's wrong with my old one?"

"There's nothing wrong with your old one, but at times your heart will be burdened, and you won't know what to pray. Then, when you pray in tongues, Holy Spirit can pray through you. It will be in a foreign language either of different nations, or in the language of angels. At first it will offend your mind and sound like babble or baby talk. But soon it will grow to become a beautiful dialect to you, even if you don't understand it. As you pray in this new language your spirit will be edified and strengthened. Your burdens will be released as your spirit and the Lord commune."

Holy Spirit flames with excitement, "Tongues can be prayed silently, said out loud, or even sung. It is used in intercession, spiritual warfare, and many other ways, and it can be done personally or in group settings. The most important thing is, it will deepen your relationship with Master Potter. And I know that is the cry of your heart. So Beloved, do you want this wonderful gift I'm offering you? Do you want to be baptized in Me?"

"Oh yes, I want everything You have for me. I especially want to know Master Potter more."

"Beloved," says Master Potter, "just pray, 'Come, Holy Spirit, baptize me with Your fire!' Then start to praise Me with all of your heart and you'll receive your heavenly prayer language."

Timidly at first but then mounting with excitement, she passionately cries out, "Oh yes! Come, Holy Spirit." Slowly, she feels the fiery mantle of His Spirit resting upon her as sweet abandonment sweeps over her spirit. From deep within she begins to praise Him and slowly new sounds come forth, birthing the beginnings of her prayer language.

Stepping Into the Beauty Realm

The beauty realm suddenly opens to new vistas of celestial colors and rare fragrances intermingled with surges of glorious light as Holy Spirit communes with Master Potter.

Beloved soars on the winds of worship. She sings with all her heart, "I love You, Lord. You're so beautiful. You fill the deepest longings of my heart. I want to be Yours forever." Suddenly her prayer language comes joyously tumbling out.

Master Potter expresses His great pleasure, "Beloved, you're Mine. You've ravished My heart. Will you run with Me to the high places in My love?"

The swirling winds of glory and fire increase as the three engage in glorious harmonies joined by the angelic host. She hears the faint orchestration of flutes and harps in a heavenly chorus and symphony of praise.

The whirlwind diminishes as the visitation ends, bringing a sense of utter stillness. Looking out to the ocean, she notices that even the sea becomes calm once more. The only sounds she can hear are the fluttering of wings and the cooing of a white dove that lights upon the shoulder of Master Potter.

"Beloved, Holy Spirit is not only wild and free but He is also gentle and sensitive—just like a dove."

My Mouthpiece

Tenderly touching her lip, He tells her, "I've called you to be My mouthpiece, a prophetic vessel. But your primary focus should always be spending intimate time with Me. In that secret place I will give you My heart so you can impart it to others."

Beloved gazes into His eyes, and in the moment that their eyes meet, a new revelation of His beauty and goodness sweeps over her. Genuine adoration bursts from her heart, erupting into a chorus of praise as she worships Him in her new language.

Chapter Eighteen

Rite of Passage

After the exhausting events of the day, Beloved feels drowsy. She stretches and yawns, "Wow! You made me into a pitcher, Your mouthpiece. When do I begin my ministry? On second thought, a little nap would be nice, then maybe this evening, I can go off to evangelize all the inhabitants of the Isles of the Dragon's Lair."

With the white dove still perched on His shoulder, Master Potter smiles knowingly, takes a towel, wipes off His hands and stands back to admire His handiwork. "Good idea! That's just what I had in mind for you: rest."

Picking up His cutting wire bearing the inscription Rite of Passage, He applies it to her base, cutting her off the wheel. This happens very quickly! Just a few minutes ago she was spinning with great speed on the wheel. Next she's in His loving hands and placed on a wooden shelf next to the Potter's wheel.

Some dried-out vessels sitting on the shelf smile at each other. "Well if it isn't the princess, she's finally going to join us. We'll see how much attention she gets now."

"Don't worry, I'm taking these naughty vessels into the house," Master Potter says as He places them on a board.

A Rude Awakening

Basking in the warm sun, she notices other pots. "Hello there! I'm new here. I'm just passing through on my way to becoming a vessel of honor, a beautiful blue and white pitcher with golden trim. How long have you been on the shelf?" she asks with great excitement and naiveté. A few bitter and cynical vessels in different stages of the Potter's process mumble among themselves, "Here we go again! Obviously that little piece of clay thinks it's finished. I see a rude awakening ahead!"

Little does Beloved realize that some of these vessels have been on the shelf for many months—even years. She just wants to be included in the conversation and longs to have someone pay attention to her.

"What's wrong with all of you? You certainly aren't very friendly. My name is Beloved. I'm sure you've heard of me!"

A large squatty casserole says, "As a matter of fact, I heard you singing on the potter's wheel. You have a beautiful voice. We wondered if you'd like to sing special music in our church."

"I would love to. Master Potter created me to be a prophetic voice. When I minister the anointing really comes. I probably have some valuable insight into the problems you're experiencing with your congregation. I would love to get together with you. With my help, I'm confident we can solve all your problems."

An older and wiser pitcher interrupts abruptly. "Listen, little one, be careful. Pride goes before a fall!"

Defensively Beloved blurts out, "Pride? I'm not proud, I just know I'm gifted and know what's going on. I'm a prophetic voice. Master Potter told me so! He has already dealt with my pride, and it's far behind me now."

The pitcher continues, "I'm also prophetic. I was famous for hearing from God. They needed me, I thought, but my attitude and pride disqualified me. So, Master Potter put me back on the shelf, unused and unnoticed. Now I can only humbly wait and pray for Him to use me once again."

"You look so dried out; no wonder Master Potter put you on the shelf. My whole life has been humbling! You have no idea where I came from and how broken I was when He came for me. The truth is, nobody in the church has a gift and an anointing quite like mine! I'm His princess. He told me so."

Yawning, Beloved closes her eyes and settles into her afternoon nap.

Chapter Nineteen

Pruning

After a few hours Master Potter returns. "Time to wake up, sleepy head," Master Potter says as He lifts her from the shelf. "Beloved, now that you've dried out we will begin a new process. This will help you prepare for your exciting ministry that lies ahead."

Turning to the vessels beside her, she says, "See, I told you so! He's come for me so I can begin my ministry. You watch and see, I'm going to be famous."

Sitting down on His wooden stool in front of the wheel, Master Potter flips Beloved upside down. "Bottoms up," He says with a mischievous grin as He takes out His metal trimming tool named Pruning.

Embarrassed by the awkwardness of her position, she blushes as the other vessels chuckle with glee, "She doesn't look so proud now, does she? Enjoy the ride, Princess Beloved!"

Pruning

Without hesitation, Master Potter takes Pruning and begins painfully scraping at the bare bottom of her vessel to trim off the excess clay. "Ouch! Ouch! Wait a minute. That's part of me. I thought I was finished. Why are You doing this? Can't You see how everyone's laughing at me? Stop! Please."

"Beloved, this is a time of pruning. You won't be giving words until we deal with some of the pride in your heart."

"Ouch! Do You have to do this in front of everybody? Is it really necessary? Couldn't You at least do this in private?"

"You wanted a platform and to be seen, didn't you? And I've given you a leadership calling. The more public your position, the more you'll be trimmed in public. I'm taking off excess clay to create a foot on the bottom of your vessel to give you stability and a firm foundation."

"It's not fair! Others are being lifted up and promoted and I don't see You trimming their bottoms. Why don't they need to be trimmed too? That one over there has a chip on his shoulder, and just look at that big-mouthed know-it-all. I'm no worse than they are."

Gently but firmly He continues to trim her bottom. "Don't worry about those other vessels; that's My concern. If I don't trim your bottom you will crack as you're drying on the shelf, or blow up in the firing ahead."

Relationships That Trim Us

Master Potter continues, "The trimming tools I use to expose your heart are often the relationships that are closest to you. Family and friends at church or work may misunderstand and judge you. During these times of testing, your challenge is to keep your heart soft no matter what. I'm not concerned about title or position."

"Couldn't you just say, 'Bottoms up,' to them, Lord? I would just love to see one of them get theirs! I could pray for them while it's happening."

"Beloved, you know better."

"Alright! I admit it, but don't You think it's just a little extreme to trim my bottom in public? Okay! Okay! I'm just a tad bit prideful but couldn't it be our secret?"

"Beloved! A tad bit? You need to repent! You've come in here like a prima donna offending and hurting others with your attitudes. You've been flaunting your gifts for position, rather than caring about others."

A sigh of resignation escapes her mouth. "Oh Lord, You're right. I've made such a fool of myself in front of all these people. Can You forgive me?"

"You're forgiven, Beloved. I want you to remember there's no shame when you stumble and fall. It's only a problem when you try to hide your faults and fail to come running to Me for forgiveness and mercy."

With a smile, Master Potter finishes trimming Beloved and turns her upright on the wheel. With an artist's eye, Master Potter takes a small piece of clay in His hands and begins to mold it. He adds water and begins to stretch it into a long graceful handle, which He attaches to Beloved's side. Her shape is beautifully formed. Now she really is a pitcher and she's ready for the next process. "Ah, the finishing touch to make you into a beautifully shaped pitcher," says a joyful Master Potter.

Part Five

The Wilderness

Chapter Twenty

Prophetic Journey

The warm winds turn into cool evening breezes as Master Potter and Beloved watch the fiery sun dip into the darkening waters of the sea. Shielding her from the cold, Master Potter cradles her close whispering, "Come, dear one, it's time to go inside."

The fluttering of dove wings signals the return of Holy Spirit to Master Potter's shoulder as they enter the house. The fire is already blazing in the hearth, and the warm amber glow of the kerosene lamps softly illuminates the room.

Master Potter gently places Beloved on the shelf beside other vessels that are drying out and walks to the wood-burning stove. The iron kettle whistles its joyous praise, which harmonizes with the crackling songs of the dancing fire. Master Potter picks it up and pours boiling water over fragrant leaves in a teapot decorated with henna blossoms.

He brings it over to the low table by His overstuffed leather chair and places it beside a plate of raisin cakes and fresh apples. Beloved hears a deep sigh of satisfaction as Master Potter sits down and puts His feet on the wooden stool.

The warmth of the fire spreads over her vessel, making her feel relaxed and cozy as she continues drying out. Light and shadows flicker across Master Potter's face as He sips His tea. Beloved hears the comforting cooing of the dove perched on the back of the Potter's chair.

Without saying a word Master Potter and the dove communicate deep secrets which are hidden in their hearts. Without warning the dove lifts off and flies around the room in circles. With each circle Beloved senses the increase of the wind and fire. Abruptly, He changes course and flies straight toward her.

"Beloved, will you follow Me?" coos the dove.

He soars by her and vanishes into a scenic picture hanging over the fireplace mantel. Shafts of gossamer light radiate from the canvas, drawing her toward it and warming her heart. She can hardly believe it! She realizes a doorway into another world has opened up to her. The dove becomes smaller and smaller in the painting as if it's traveling into the distance. Scanning the amazing piece of art, Beloved's eyes fall upon an old, worn pathway that winds up a steep hill leading to an old iron gate.

Filled with quiet awe, Beloved once again hears the still small voice of the dove wooing her, "Will you follow Me?"

Her heart desperately wants to go but her mind fights her spirit. "This is impossible. It can't be real!"

A Prophetic Invitation

Master Potter's deep reassuring voice says, "Beloved, this is a prophetic invitation to follow My Spirit."

"Lord, I don't want to leave You or Your house. I thought we would never be apart. I just want to rest here in Your presence forever. It's so cozy and comfortable. If I go, will You come with me?"

"No Beloved. I'm sending Holy Spirit to guide you. But even though we're separated, I'll always have My eye on you. Are you willing to follow Him?"

With great reluctance Beloved says, "Yes, Lord, but I can't get into that picture, it's way too high for me."

Rising from His chair, Master Potter picks up His beloved little vessel, brushes her hair away from her face and kisses her forehead. "I'll help you, Beloved, and I'll be waiting for your return."

Walking to the mantel, Master Potter places her into the living picture. The instant her tiny feet touch down she senses a change in the atmosphere. She takes her first step and is amazed to see she is now on the pathway leading to the old iron gate where Master Potter's purposes and Holy Spirit await her.

Chapter Twenty-one

The Wilderness

Rays from the sun warm Beloved's cheeks, and the pungent odors of autumn excite her senses. Trying to get her bearings, she looks for the dove. The worn path before her is lined with stately oak trees meandering up a lush green mountain clearing. The air is cool and crisp.

The oaks stand at attention like ancient sentinels guarding her way. The brilliant orange, red and yellow leaves spiral downward in a burst of vibrant color, carpeting the earth in multicolored beauty.

At the top of the hill, a shimmering figure stands beside the old iron gate. Her confidence falters as she realizes the dove has vanished and now the figure is beckoning to her.

Pausing, she prays, "Lord what should I do? I wish You were here. I wish You would help me."

The fragrant breeze whispers, "Continue the journey, Beloved."

"Master Potter, I can hear You. I was so afraid I'd lost You. Thank You. Please keep helping me."

"I will, Beloved. I will."

Gathering her courage, she resumes walking, with eyes fixed on the waiting angelic figure dressed in a white tunic, shimmering with light and glory. His glistening silver shield radiates light. His sword is sheathed to his side. Tucked through his golden belt is a shofar. Beloved recognizes his auburn hair with its shimmering golden streaks and his piercing blue eyes. She runs toward him.

Meeting Valiant

"Hello, Beloved. I'm Valiant, your guardian—"

"I've seen you before," she blurts out.

"Yes, I'm your guardian angel. The Father assigned me to protect you on the day you were born!"

"I saw you in a vision. You saved me from the horses when I chased after a stray puppy in the street as a child. And you kept Antagonist from killing me the night I left him. Were there other times you helped me?"

Valiant tosses his head back and laughs. "Just a few. You've actually kept me very busy."

"And I saw you celebrating when Master Potter was taking me to His home."

"Yes. That day lives in my memory as exceptionally sweet. I, and the other angels who had just finished battling on the Potter's Field for your soul, celebrated the Father's triumph over His enemy—your choosing life. Ah, what a sweet victory that was. You could see only our little celebration, but your Grandma Pearl and all of Heaven celebrated too."

"Why am I being allowed to see you now?"

Master Potter is allowing you to see me so I can help prepare you for the challenging journey ahead."

He swings open the gate of faith, motioning for her to enter. She follows him to the top of the hill. At the summit, winds whip wildly at her hair. Her clothes flap freely. Hot desert winds from the vast wilderness below make her dry and fragile as she's exposed to their harsh, unforgiving embrace.

Here she sees a panoramic view of what her future will be: desolate mountain ranges, sun-parched valleys, arid sand dunes and bleak barrenness. The stark contrast of the lush gardens and the warm coziness of Master Potter's House bring a sinking sensation to the pit of her stomach. The desolation takes away her breath.

Quickly turning away from Valiant, she runs back down the path past the oak trees looking for the portal back to Master Potter's House. The portal is closed. Angrily she cries out, "Please don't leave me here! Didn't You promise I would be a beautiful pitcher? I want to go back if this is what it's going to be like! Get me out of here!"

No Escape

Valiant waits patiently until her temper tantrum is spent, and he helps her come to the realization that there is no escape! Knowing her feelings he tells her gently, "Beloved, you need to trust Master Potter's purpose for bringing you into the wilderness. He sent me to strengthen and refresh you for this journey. You're about to enter a season of testing to prepare you for your destiny. You need to trust His goodness even though you can't see Him now. Never forget the times of intimacy you shared with Him. He still loves you like He did when you were there."

Realizing her options are limited, Beloved determines that she will get it over with as quickly as possible. She coyly replies as she walks back up the hill, "Where do we start? I'm sure I can finish this and be back home in no time at all."

Reaching into the leather pouch strapped to his belt, Valiant pulls out a package of small cakes, covered with a substance resembling honey. He hands her an earthenware jug of sweet tea, telling her, "Sit for awhile and be refreshed. The journey is longer than you think."

She bites into the first delicious cake and is soon licking the last crumbs from her fingers. Then she drinks the last drop of tea.

Chapter Twenty-two

Amazing Grace

It isn't more than a few moments before Beloved begins to suspect that the food prepared by Valiant was no ordinary meal. She begins to feel strangely energized, charged from the inside out as supernatural strength fills her from deep inside.

Valiant tells her, "Master Potter has many lessons for you to learn and some of them will take all the strength you possess. So, He's imparting His strength through the food you've eaten. When you think you can go no further, remember this day and call upon His name. He always hears you."

"The journey through the wilderness is to learn the mysteries of the barren places. Master Potter wants you to trust Him and lean upon Him no matter what. This is an opportunity to develop even deeper intimacy with Him. Cry out to Him in prayer. This desert is fraught with dangers and illusions, but He's sending you a guide."

Leaning close to the edge of the rocky precipice, he points down the steep trail, "Here he comes now. As always I'll be with you, but just not visible."

How Sweet the Sound

Beloved looks into the scorching haze rising from the desert floor and sees nothing. Squinting her eyes and gazing longer into the radiating heat, she finally sees him. A hooded figure is fast approaching.

The figure leaps and bounds over the precarious terrain. Finally coming to an abrupt halt at the foot of the mountain path, he stands before her. Valiant smiles to himself and introduces them, "Beloved, I would like you to meet your guide, Amazing Grace."

This mysterious stranger is vaguely familiar and yet Beloved can't be sure if they've ever met. He looks like a desert monk in his brown burlap robe, his face mostly concealed under the folds of the hood. *I wonder who this is?* she silently questions, expecting him to reveal his face at any moment.

Instead he abruptly turns, speaking to her in a voice so low she can barely hear, "Follow me, Beloved."

Turning to Valiant she says, "I don't want to go with him. I want to go with you. Can't you just stay visible for me?" Valiant gestures toward Amazing Grace. "He's Master Potter's choice for your guide. I will be with you all the way; you just won't see me."

The Path of Life

She pauses for a moment, then sees that Amazing Grace is already halfway down the steep descent. *He moves so freely and without any regard for safety*, she tells herself. She turns to complain to Valiant, but he's not there. Not wanting to be left alone she quickly follows Amazing Grace along the narrow mountain trail. She crossly yells, "Slow down; I can't keep up with you. Don't you even care if I get hurt?"

Hours pass and the hot winds whip against her body. She wipes her sweaty face mumbling, "What have I gotten into? I've become so dry and fragile in this scorching heat!" She shouts to Amazing Grace, "Can't we sit down and rest for awhile?"

The hooded figure continues, leaving her with no choice but to follow him as he takes her through unfamiliar and treacherous territory. "Do you hear me? I want to go back to the Potter's House! Why don't you answer me?" she wails, limping along behind.

When she finally catches up, he tells her, "Master Potter has sent you into the wilderness so you can learn to walk by faith. Your only hope is in trusting Him to know what is best for you. You can't rely on your own strength or what you see in the natural. The choice is yours."

Evening brings a chill to the desert, and cold wind sweeps through the barren pass, churning up dirt and sand. Beloved rubs her red, burning eyes. Darkness is falling, and the setting sun and lengthening shadows obscure the trail below. A shiver runs through Beloved as she grabs his hand. Renewed strength immediately flows into her.

A Leap of Faith

But instead of following the path to the desert floor, Amazing Grace leads her to the edge of a deep ravine cut into the mountainside. She catches a glimpse of jagged rocks below in the eerie shadows cast by the dim moonlight.

She cries, "Lord, what kind of guide is this? Just look where we are! Surely you wouldn't take me to the edge of a cliff and tell me to jump off!"

But somewhere deep inside she realizes that's exactly why he's taking her there. Frozen with fear, self-preservation takes over. Her heart pounds loudly as she looks into the treacherous chasm below.

Whispering softly, Amazing Grace tells her, "This is your first big test. Will you trust me when you can't see the way or understand what I'm asking of you? Will you take the leap of faith to the other side of this mountain?"

Crossly she snaps, "Are you crazy? You want me to jump! I can barely walk on my blistered feet. I stumbled all day, or didn't you notice?"

TRAPPED

Beloved plops down on an uncomfortable rock, fighting to keep her lower lip from quivering. Behind her is only darkness. The path is no longer visible! She's trapped! Angry, hurt and feeling deeply betrayed, Beloved makes up her mind she will go no further. From a nearby cliff, the lonely howling of a wolf terrifies her. In order to continue the journey she'll have to jump. She frantically looks for her guide but now he's nowhere to be found.

Should I trust Amazing Grace?

An icy wind blows through the pass and shadowy demonic figures erupt in the darkness, filling the air with their vile accusations. Breathing their foul breath close to Beloved's face, they begin their mockery with taunts and accusations.

"Why didn't you take that ride back to town? You could be warm and well fed at Madam's and surrounded by an adoring public. It's not too late. Madam will still take you back."

"I will never go back to her. Master Potter has me here for a purpose."

"Master Potter has brought you here to die! One false move and it's all over! You don't have to continue this crazy journey. Soon the sun will come up and you can find your way back without your guide."

"No, I can't go back," says Beloved, with her resolve waning.

"But Master Potter left you and that guide deserted you. You will always be Forsaken."

"No, I'm His Beloved."

"He brought you here to die. Your guide abandoned you."

Feeling tightness in her chest, and trying hard not to believe the demonic influence, Beloved takes rapid, shallow breaths as she peers out through the darkness to the other side of the ravine. She can barely make out her guide sitting before the crackling flames.

"I think the guide is by that campfire way over there."

"On the other side of the ravine? He won't even come help you. What kind of guide is that?" screeches the demon.

As she watches, Amazing Grace stands and walks to the edge of the ravine, cups his hands and shouts, "Beloved, you can make it! Just take that first step. Trust me. Don't look with your natural eyes; pray in the Spirit!"

Mustering all of her courage, she prays fervently in the Spirit as the demons taunt, "You're going to die out here."

Beloved cries out, "I will not listen to those voices! I'm going to live." She runs to the edge and leaps into the air. As soon as her feet leave the ground, she knows she'll never make it to the other side. She's certain death awaits her. The few moments stretch out to seem like eternity as she tumbles into dark space. In those frozen moments of terror she cries out the only words she can think of, "Master Potter, save me!"

In a flash, boldness and faith erupt inside her. Peace bubbles up within her from a well deep inside her spirit—a well she didn't know existed.

In moments Valiant's strong arms catch her in midair and she soars like an eagle on the winds of the desert. Finally he sets her down softly on the other side next to the blazing fire.

Amazing Grace wraps a wool blanket around her shoulders as Valiant resumes his unseen post next to her, gazing into the darkness. He turns toward Amazing Grace and they both smile in approval.

Beloved sits, dumbfounded, staring into the fire and wondering if the last few minutes were real, or if she'll wake up from a dream.

Chapter Twenty-three

A Sign in the Heavens

Like brilliant diamonds, stars sparkle and dance across the cobalt blue sky as it quickly deepens into black velvet. Amazing Grace promises he will always be near, but Beloved will have to take many risky steps in the realm of faith as she follows him.

Looking up into the starry night, Amazing Grace singles out one particularly radiant star. "Master Potter has put a sign in the skies for you to follow. It will show you the way back to Him. Remember this—things are not always as they seem, but I will never be far away.

"The wilderness will test you and also teach you of Master Potter's faithfulness. You must follow the star. If you wander from its path, you will be in danger. Always use the guidance Master Potter provides for you."

Wandering in the Wilderness

He quietly departs, blending into the darkness and leaving her gazing at the brilliant star. She watches it move across the deepening night sky, illuminating the path below. Afraid to stay where she is by herself, she quickly follows.

The hot days and chilly nights are uncomfortable and dreary. Tormenting demonic spirits become her unseen companions as she trudges deeper into the wilderness. Lonely and exhausted, she stumbles on into the darkness. Jagged rocks have torn her dress and her legs are cut and bruised from falls she's taken. Every muscle and joint aches with fatigue!

Waves of anger and resentment crash over her tormented mind and hot tears well up in her eyes, "Lord," she shouts, "what are You doing to me? Why have You abandoned me? I don't even know where my guide is. Oh, I'm so lonely. I feel like I'm back in the Potter's Field." She heaves a big sigh and sits down beside the trail to take a break.

From behind the next hill Death spews to his motley army of demons, "We've got her now. This is the opportunity we've been waiting for. I knew she'd give up as soon as she got away from the Potter's House and all His gooey, lovey-dovey compliments. She's tired, hungry and lonely and that makes her very vulnerable."

One of the little demonic imps says, "What she needs is tall, dark and handsome."

"Yes," says Death smiling, "and I've got just the man. Our elaborate network stretches to the community in the valley below. Send out an SOS. They must trap her with the beautiful things this spoiled little *princess* can't live without. Quickly let them know of her presence.

"Once we've got her, Master Potter will never get her back, and I'll be vindicated by my master." He drools at the thought. "Backslidden, Self-Pity, go to her now. Just be careful of her guide and that stupid angel."

The two vile spirits move in slowly, wrapping their long tentacles around her head, whispering poisonous words of despair and doubt into her weary soul. Without understanding what's going on, Beloved succumbs to their evil embrace and wallows deeper into despair.

Days and nights blend together in a blur of confusion as she seeks desperately to follow her star and find her guide. Occasionally, Amazing Grace mysteriously appears leaving water and food. Whenever she spots him she takes off running after him with every ounce of strength she can muster, crying out, "Please stay! I'm so alone and afraid. I could die out here! Don't you care? You're a terrible guide. You're supposed to take care of me!"

As always, Valiant stands close by.

Beloved learns that it's better to travel through the cool nights and sleep during the stifling days. The terrain is difficult and barren. Eventually she can do little more than hobble along on cracked, bleeding and blistered feet. The journey she told herself would be over quickly has now dragged into several months.

She prays to Master Potter and calls out to her guide using every manipulative technique she knows—weeping, crying, beseeching, praying loudly in the Spirit, and even stomping her bruised little feet! Anything to convince Master Potter she's ready to be rescued right now! Immediately! Still, Heaven seems silent to her cries.

Chapter Twenty-four

Enchanter

Late that very night, Beloved sees the dim glow of a lantern swaying back and forth as it winds around the narrow path. As she continues to watch, the amber light draws closer and reveals a dark-haired, handsome man with a curly black beard and mesmerizing green eyes.

Meeting her at a fork in the road he smiles warmly and asks, "Are you the one who is lost? We received word that someone needed help. I volunteered to go out and look while the others stayed to pray. These mountains are dangerous at night, especially for a beautiful woman like you."

Blushing at the obvious flattery, she tells him, "Thank you so much. I've been wandering around for months and seem to have lost my guide."

Taking out a ram's horn, he blows three loud blasts. "This is to let everyone know that I found you and that we will be down shortly."

She tries not to stare, but she can't seem to take her gaze off his tall frame, draped under layers of splendid fabric. His white silk tunic is covered by a loose, purple robe heavily embroidered in golden geometric shapes around the neck, down the front and around the sleeves. His white, flowing head cover is secured in place with a woven black rope wound several times around his head and fastened in front with a large, dramatic silver pin dotted with multicolored stones. Around his neck are several strands of mesh chains with dangling pendants and coins. On his finger is a large gold ring with what she supposes is his family crest.

He gestures toward the wide, expansive desert floor. "Do you see those campfires over there? That's my home. Why don't you come with me?" he says in a seductive, inviting voice.

In the distance she sees large clusters of lights illuminating the darkness. *Master Potter must have sent him as the answer to my prayers. There must be hundreds of tents down there. I need a safe place to spend the night, and I need some food.*

"You can spend the night, and we'll give you fresh provision and send you on your way when you regain your strength. You must be cold and hungry." His warm, inviting voice makes her want to throw herself in his arms so he can take care of her.

Shivering, Beloved looks up to see the brilliant star moving away from the campfires. She looks back to the stranger, "Now I'm confused! Master Potter gave me a guide who told me to follow that star. It seem like it's moving away from here."

"Who ever heard of following a star—really?" said the handsome stranger. "A star will never lead you out of this darkness, for stars *need* darkness to shine! I've lived in this desert for years, and I know the way better than any star. I'll guide you into the light, and to safety and protection."

A gentle, warm breeze rushes past Beloved. Out of the soft wind a still small voice whispers, "Don't trust him, Beloved! Follow the star."

Beloved's immediate needs are all she can think of, and she's feeling quite drawn to the stranger. She brushes the voice aside, reasoning to herself: *It's ridiculous to follow this stupid star. I probably didn't hear my guide right. Anyway he abandoned me, and it's obvious Master Potter sent this man to help.*

Tall, Dark and Handsome

The stranger draws near and Beloved is increasingly impressed by his charm. "Let me introduce myself. I'm Enchanter. My father is Pastor Beguiler, head of the religious community you see below. I know Master Potter, and I'm sure it's His divine providence that we got word you were lost and in need of help."

Amazing Grace's gentle urging intensifies, "It's a trap. My star will lead you back to the Potter's House, Beloved. You must follow me."

Beloved struggles. Should she follow the prompting of Amazing Grace? Or, should she go with this obviously wealthy, olive-skinned handsome stranger to a place of warmth and comfort from the harsh wilderness?

He said he knows Master Potter. This must be a divine appointment! I can't stay out here forever. Looking at the inviting community below and back to the mountainous trail, she thinks, *I'm so dried out. I just need a day or two and then I can get back on the path.*

Finally, she turns to Enchanter, lifts her face up to his and smiling sweetly, looks deep into his green eyes and says, "My name is Beloved."

He slips out of his majestic, purple robe and places it around her shoulders. "Beloved! What a beautiful name. Why, you're shivering! You poor thing! Let me take care of you." Beloved can now see the outline of his lean, muscular frame, cinched in at the waist with a scarlet belt.

Flattered and enjoying the attention, Beloved smiles and warmly tells him, "Oh, thank you. How nice of you to notice—I'm actually freezing out here!"

"Of course you're freezing. That light dress is hardly practical for cold desert nights. You'll be warm in just a minute."

The warmth of the cloak feels so good compared to the harsh desert night. Beloved snuggles into it, wrapping it tightly around herself. At the same time, a cold demonic haze subtly settles over her mind, clouding her spiritual perception. Deep inside her lonely soul she justifies her choices. *I'm entitled to be warm and have new friends. After all, I've been abandoned out here and no one else but Enchanter seems genuinely interested in my welfare.*

Enchanter reaches out to take her hand. Hesitating for just seconds, she finally places her hand in his and they walk down the path toward the camp together by the light of the lantern. He jokes, tells stories, laughs and succeeds in drawing Beloved's attention away from everything else but him.

She finds herself becoming increasingly comfortable with him. Her initial hesitation long gone, Beloved is swept up into his physical attractiveness, charismatic personality, obvious wealth and good breeding.

She begins to secretly wonder, *Is Enchanter destined to be my husband? Master Potter knows my desire for a godly man and He did send him to rescue me.*

An Oasis

By the time they arrive at the oasis, Beloved feels Enchanter is her friend. She hangs intently on his every word. He explains that he is a member of a committed and devout religious commune named Deeper Life. Arriving at the campsite, she's relieved to see friendly people standing around campfires, cooking and warming themselves in the chilly night air.

What a wonderful sight after her lonely pilgrimage in the mountains. Here are people, potential friends, talking and smiling, welcoming her into the group with genuine warmth and excitement. A darling little boy runs up to them and pulls them over to his family's campfire.

They're greeted warmly and invited to the evening meal. It's obvious the family is thrilled to have Enchanter dine with them. They fawn and fall all over him, trying to anticipate his every whim.

He must be really important, she thinks.

Seated cross-legged next to Enchanter around a big bowl of rice and lamb, she can't wait to begin. *It's been so long since I've had a hot meal.* Since she is unfamiliar with these customs, she carefully watches Enchanter's every move. Following his lead she scoops up bites of the food on pieces of flat bread and savors each bite as the spices saturate her mouth.

Feeling happier than she's been in a long time, she rambles on and on to Enchanter and his friends about how he rescued her on the trail.

"Now for dessert," he announces, picking up a plate of dates. "These grew in my family's date grove. We own the only grove here and we have a reputation for growing the finest dates. The merchants that come through with the caravans buy all the excess that the community can't use." He slowly picks up a date and, looking deeply into her eyes, holds it to her mouth. Putting her hand on his, she bites into the date, savoring its sweetness and the sexual tension between them. Deep feelings, which had been long dormant, stir in Beloved.

He puts his arm around her as they watch the young boy dance for them while the father plays a mandolin.

Enchanter makes arrangements for her to spend the night with this family and welcomes her again to Deeper Life Commune before retiring for the evening. "I'll be back for you first thing in the morning."

"Isn't he wonderful?" she asks her new friends.

She snuggles deeply into the cloak he placed over her shoulders and drifts off to sleep in the family's tent.

Off in the distance, overlooking the commune, the shrouded figure of Amazing Grace confers with Valiant as he shakes his head sadly, longing for Beloved's return.

Chapter Twenty-five

Deeper Life

The morning sun is just cresting the mountains. Beloved awakens from what has been her first good night's sleep in months. She feels refreshed, although the rest allowed her to realize how many aches and pains were screaming at her. Grabbing her bruised, swollen feet, she massages them gently.

As she snuggles down again comfortably under Enchanter's robe she listens to the cacophony of noises outside in the distance—people, animals, music. *What's going on out there?* she wonders.

"Beloved, are you awake?" Enchanter's soothing voice coos from outside the tent. "Just a minute," she responds as she does her best to fix her hair and dress.

She gasps as she steps outside into an opulent desert oasis. Lush ferns and colorful desert flowers grow around ornately decorated tents. Golden tassels, silver bells and balls decorate their impressive, huge exteriors. It's immediately apparent that this is no ordinary campsite. Prosperity exudes from the surroundings of this obviously wealthy section of the commune. Huge sand dunes surround them, giving a limited vision of the desert beyond and a false sense of security.

Her attention is drawn to a group of distinguished men entering a large multicolored pavilion. A cluster of majestic palm trees shade the tent from the burning sun. Over the entryway to the tent is a large golden banner with the name, *Deeper Life Community Church*, boldly emblazoned in beautiful script.

Turning her around to face him, Enchanter says, "I would love to show you Deeper Life. But why don't I take you to my mother's first? Freshen up a little bit and then I'll give you the grand tour."

The gentle yet firm pressure of his arms excites her. Gazing into his deep green eyes, she suddenly wonders what she must look like. Beloved quickly drops her head in embarrassment.

Meeting His Mother

Soon they arrive at the most prominent tent, tan in color. The tent's many decorative tassels dangle and sway in the gentle breeze. The entrance, formed by fastening back the two tent flaps, is covered with a billowy sheer silk panel. Ferns and desert plants growing in large, decorative blue and white pots are clustered on both sides of the entrance. Enchanter pushes the sheer panel aside and Beloved follows him into the tent. Two servant girls, dressed in bright colors and with veils across their faces, bow low in greeting.

Beloved looks around at the inside "walls" of rich tapestry brocade in a subtle ivory on white pattern. Light floods inside through the same kind of billowy silk panel that covers the doorway. Looking down, she's surprised to see she's standing on a plush, multihued Persian rug as big as the tent. Its dark, wide border contrasts with the light center of floral design. In the middle of the tent is a low mahogany table, surrounded by overstuffed, multicolored pillows of silk and damask scattered around it. On the table is a huge vase of fresh flowers and greenery and a blue oriental tea set. *I had no idea a tent could be opulent. My room at Madam's wasn't this nice.*

The partition at the end of the tent opens and Enchanter's mother steps out. The two servants by the door bow.

Now I know where Enchanter gets his good looks, thinks Beloved. *Mrs. Beguiler is so attractive she looks more like Enchanter's sister than his mother—the same dark complexion, the same dark hair, even the green eyes.*

"This is the little lost lamb I found in the wilderness. You won't believe what a beautiful name she has to adorn her lovely personality," Enchanter says with his usual flair. "Her name is Beloved. We must be living right to have such a fine vessel come among us. Don't you agree? Mother, we simply must urge her to bless us with her lovely presence for awhile."

Taking Beloved's hand she replies, "You're most welcome here, dear one. You must be tired after your long journey. I'm glad Enchanter was able to find you. I'm not sure how much longer you would have lasted in the desert with those city clothes. You must be from Comfort Cove."

"Well…er…I was. I used to live there," Beloved stammers as she feels her face flush. *What if they know the influential people at Comfort Cove and they find out about my past? Maybe they know Madam or Mayor Lecherous.*

She feels her heart beating and tries to take shallow breaths to calm herself. Enchanter says, "When I was a child our family went to the seashore there, but I haven't been to Comfort Cove for years. Every once in a while travelers come through from there, though."

Beloved is desperate to change the subject. "Well, you're right. This dress didn't keep me warm at all. I see your clothes are perfectly suited to this climate."

"Yes, they are, and I'm sure I can find something suitable for you to wear."

Suddenly Beloved is very self-conscious. She watches the way that Mrs. Beguiler carries herself; she notices the elegant flow of the long dress and jewelry. Every mannerism is refined, graceful and dignified.

Always animated, Enchanter tells them, "I have an important meeting with Father and the elders but I should be back early this afternoon to show you around. I know you'll take good care of our beautiful guest, Mother." Enchanter smiles widely.

"Please sit, Beloved," says Mrs. Beguiler, motioning toward the low table. "The tea is freshly brewed." Beloved crosses her legs and awkwardly shifts her weight to get centered on a royal blue embroidered pillow. With every graceful move of Mrs. Beguiler's hands her exquisite silver bangles jingle like the sound of a bell. As she pours the tea, Beloved gazes at the fine embroidery on the emerald green silk dress. Mrs. Beguiler's dark hair highlights her dangling gold earrings with inset rubies. The matching ruby and gold pendant hangs around her neck.

A BATH—AT LAST!

Clapping her hands, Mrs. Beguiler summons several servant girls. She instructs them quietly. One returns with a plate of dates. The other sits in the corner and plays slow, yearning music on her flute.

As Beloved finishes the last sip of tea, another servant appears. "Please take Beloved to her quarters." Turning to Beloved she smiles and says, "You will find a hot bath and lovely robes awaiting you."

The servant girl leads her behind another section of the tent, concealed by a floor to ceiling damask curtain. The servant silently bows to Beloved and pours perfumed spikenard from a beautiful translucent alabaster jar into the hot bath. From her pocket she sprinkles rose petals. Beloved watches them glide through the air and gently light on the water. She inhales the aromatic spikenard and smiles at the servant, who bows once more and leaves.

Relieved that all of her troubles seem to finally be behind her, Beloved relaxes in the stillness of her perfumed bath. She soaks while listening to the gentle music of a distant mandolin.

Who would have thought I'd end up in such a beautiful place and with such gracious people who love and serve Master Potter? I was so afraid I'd never get out of the wilderness. Oh Lord, I need to trust You more. Just look at where You've brought me!

Chapter Twenty-six

Falling in Love

Later, Enchanter returns to find Beloved elegantly dressed in a long-sleeved red silk dress with golden embroidery and matching gold jewelry. His face clearly shows his pleasure. Standing straight with her chin up, she's aware that he is examining her from head to foot. He brushes her cheek with his fingertips, and a thrill shoots up her spine.

Without taking his eyes from her, he tells his mother, "You've done a wonderful job; isn't she beautiful? I can't wait to show her off. We'll be back for dinner after I give her the grand tour."

Beloved's face turns bright red as much from the touch of his hand as from the welcomed flattery and attention. It has been such a long time since a handsome man found her attractive. She feels the same rush of excitement that she used to derive from the standing ovations at Madam's. Closing her eyes she savors the feeling.

She follows him outside into the bustling commune. He quickly takes her hand into his own as he leads her down the path.

"Beloved, do you know what kind of dress you're wearing?" She shakes her head. "It's called a *Malakat*. It's derived from the word *Malakah*, which means queen. And I must say, you'd make a beautiful queen. The dress is made of the finest silk and even the embroidery is silk thread. See the pattern across the chest piece," he says, gesturing. "Here it's geometric and here it changes to the pattern of a cypress tree," he says, sliding his hand gently across the side of her breast.

Beloved doesn't know whether his touch was an accident or not, but he continues talking as though nothing has happened. "Our family is very proud of this community. My great grandfather established it. I come from a long line of pastors and leaders. I'm the associate pastor and worship leader of the church. One day I'll take the senior leadership as my father did before me. I hope to have a son one day who will follow in my footsteps," he says, squeezing her hand gently and putting it through his arm.

The thought that she might be the woman to bear his children and be the first lady of the commune floods her heart. *Is this my destiny?* She quickly pushes the thoughts away as she remembers where she came from and who she was in Comfort Cove.

They continue walking past beautiful, highly decorative tents. "What's all that noise?" asks Beloved.

"That's the marketplace on the outskirts of town. Do you remember that I told you a caravan arrived late last night? Once a week we have market day. When it coincides with a caravan's arrival, it's quite a sight."

On the Outskirts

As they continue walking, the tents become less and less opulent. They come to a watering hole where camels and other livestock are drinking, and shabbily dressed women and children are carrying water in earthenware jugs on their heads.

Beloved looks at the tents on the outskirts. They are black, and some have patches. They are more like large blankets thrown over a wooden frame, totally lacking the elegance and opulence she'd seen earlier.

"Why are these people so poor?"

"They're not poor, Beloved; they are workers. Every community needs employees. Even in nature, some are the queens, like you, and some are the worker bees. Their husbands work in our date orchards and tend to the animals while the women cook and clean our tents."

"Do they have all the rights that others do?"

"Of course they do. They even have a representative who is a deacon and meets with our board. Look at the children playing so freely. See how happy they are. The kind of care that the children get is a good indicator of the health of the community. They are well taken care of. All communities have different classes of people."

The Marketplace

They turn the corner, and the residential tents give way to a bustling marketplace. Stalls with brightly colored awnings line each side, forming a wide walkway. Everywhere people are milling, children are running and animals stroll as if they have no owners. Beloved can't believe how much chaotic activity she sees. So many people are making their way through; there is barely room to walk.

Sweet and pungent aromas waft from the booths, spices she's never smelled before. Men are playing mandolins, flutes and harps, making music in a style she's never heard before. All around, men and women dress in clothing styles she's never seen. Everywhere she looks it's like a celebration for her senses. *This is a long way from Comfort Cove*, she thinks.

Men gather in front of the vendor who is selling flat bread and fresh lamb roasting over a spit. As they eat they take turns rolling the dice in a friendly game of chance. Between rolls they catch up on the news from afar and the local gossip, sometimes having to raise their voices to be heard over the ruckus.

Heads turn when they see the striking couple walk by. Several wonder aloud who the beautiful woman is on Enchanter's arm. Women look on with jealousy as the curvaceous Beloved walks arm-in-arm with the most eligible bachelor in Deeper Life. A sense of power and satisfaction floods her emotions as she realizes she's commanding the spotlight with her beauty and sensuality.

The first booth she stops at displays fine, handwoven rugs. The carded camel and sheep's wool has been dyed in rustic and vibrant colors. It feels so soft and plush as she rubs her hand against it. The next stall carries hammered metal and brass wear—incense burners, lamps, bells, plates and bowls. The next has all manner of wood products, from tiny carved toy camels to large pieces of elegant furniture.

Every inch of every stall is packed with wares—on, under and behind the counter and hanging from the support poles overhead.

Beloved notices that the merchants engage in aggressive banter and bartering with everyone walking by, in an effort to make a sale—but no one has tried to sell her anything, even when she picked up a piece to examine it. *How strange*, she thinks as she continues walking arm-in-arm with Enchanter.

Braids of garlic cloves hang from a booth where several women are clustered. Large gunny sacks with the top rolled down display yellow, red and rusty orange spices behind the counter. "Here, come here for the freshest saffron. This capsicum is unusually potent. Come, come sniff these cloves," the spice vendor cries out.

Women are buying large sacks of rice and carrying them away balanced on their heads. Some have their faces covered; most are heavily adorned with jewelry. Beloved loves the exotic look of the ankle bracelets that many of them wear.

Enchanter guides Beloved to the left, and they sidestep two black and white kid goats following their mother and the little boy running after them.

She can't believe the exquisite hand-made jewelry with brightly colored semiprecious stones. Displayed against a dark background, they glitter and sparkle as the sunlight bounces off the lovely pieces. *What craftsmanship*, she thinks.

"Over here is one of my favorite booths," says Enchanter. "We trade our dates for these fine fabrics," he says as he motions to the elaborate display of solid and printed bolts of cloth. "You probably noticed how beautiful our clothes and even our tents are. This is where it all comes from." Turning to Beloved he asks, "What's your favorite color?"

"Blue."

He tells the merchant, "Please have every bolt of blue fabric delivered to my tent. I think it needs a woman's touch to update it."

"That was easy," he says as they approach a lavish display of fruits and nuts. "Beloved, would you like to have a date with me?" She pauses, unsure if he means the fruit or companionship. "Well, which would you prefer?" he asks teasingly.

Working up her courage she says, "Both."

"Good," he replies, "both can be arranged."

On the counter are olives, dates, figs, raisins, pomegranates and other strange-looking fruit she can't identify. Enchanter points as the merchant fills a bag full of dried delicacies and gives it to him as a gift.

Just past the fruits is a table displaying perfumes, oils and incense. Several ladies have congregated there admiring the multicolored, hand-blown perfume containers. Other vessels painted with beautiful flowers contain powders and ointments. The vendor calls out, "Frankincense, myrrh, spikenard, rose of Sharon and lily of the valley." Recognizing the ivory-colored alabaster jar from her bath, she picks it up and inhales deeply. Smiling, Enchanter says, "Beloved, you do have good taste. This is my favorite also."

MADAM FALSE DESTINY

Beloved sees several booths of religious artifacts, statues, idols, charms, altars, amulets, books and candles. One booth even has a gypsy fortune-teller.

Beloved sets the alabaster jar down and walks from table to table looking at the merchandise.

"Why do you let people sell these things?" questions Beloved, rather taken aback.

"Well, we are on a major trade route and people come from all over the known world. We have a gentlemen's agreement with them and we can't prohibit them from selling any of their wares."

"But people in your community could get deceived from these things."

"Nonsense, we have very strict religious parameters around our people. The elders are the spiritual gatekeepers. These booths are only here on market days when the caravans come through. We can't stop this because we're in the middle of a trade route and we really can't offend them by restricting what they can sell. Besides, whatever path people find that leads to happiness is fine; we all end up in the same place."

"I'm not sure I understand," questions Beloved.

"Happiness is like a mountain with many paths leading to the treasure at the top. Each person must find his or her own pathway to personal purpose and satisfaction. There are many paths with only one destination for all of mankind, Beloved. We all end up at the top."

"But don't you believe Master Potter is the Son of God?"

"Of course I do. But, we are all sons and daughters of God. Besides, we have very strict rules and we forbid them from proselytizing our youth. As I said before, you can tell a lot about a person or a community by how they care for their children."

As they near the end of the market, Enchanter sees Madam at a booth buying a book on spells, several amulets and a large crystal. A knowing nod passes between them.

"This is the end of the market," he says quickly, while turning her around the other way. "We know we won't be buying from these booths, so let me take you back to the tent to rest and I'll pick you up later for dinner with my family."

Chapter Twenty-seven

Pastor Beguiler

Beloved is sitting on an ornate pillow next to Enchanter around the long mahogany dinner table. Pastor Beguiler clears his throat in preparation to speak. Beloved can hardly take her gaze off him. His tanned olive skin, offset against his silver white hair and dark penetrating eyes, commands respect from all.

Enchanter leans over and whispers into her ear, "Father looks very dignified, but don't worry, he really likes you. Do you know how exquisite you look? The sapphire blue of your gown pales next to your beauty." Beloved giggles softly, reveling in the attention.

"Beloved, my son shared with me how he found you in the mountain pass. I'm glad that he and our oasis helped save your life. As the head of this family and the leader of this community, I want to formally welcome you."

At the clap of Pastor Beguiler's hands a parade of servants comes in the room carrying platters of food. Sitting in front of Beloved is a multicourse feast: roasted goat, lentils, bitter herb salad, hummus, goat cheese, roasted lamb, flat bread and yogurt. Beloved inhales the exotic aromas, many of which are completely new to her.

Laughter and warm conversation fill the night air as she is entertained by Pastor Beguiler's stories of how his grandfather founded this religious community. Fraught with bandits, sand storms and other hurdles, he and his followers carved out an oasis for weary travelers that grew into a major trade route connecting various nations.

"Yes, we have been blessed, and this community will pass to our son and someday to our grandson," says Mrs. Beguiler, smiling.

Concealed from view under the table, Enchanter's hand strokes her thigh, causing Beloved's heart to race.

Enchanter says, "Let's toast the arrival of this lovely lady to our community." Lifting an ornate brass decanter, he pours rose water into several brass goblets embellished with floral decorations. "To this wonderful gift from Master Potter."

Beloved blushes and sips the rose water. A feeling of acceptance floods her senses. *I've never felt this loved before except at Master Potter's House. This must be a confirmation from Him that I have a permanent place here among these people.*

A servant brings the final course, a dessert of Sweet Uppuma, a crumbly fried dessert with cashew nuts, cardamom and sugar served along with hot tea, cream and spices.

Pastor Beguiler claps again, and musicians and dancers entertain them. The new culture, new sights, smells, sounds and tastes fascinate Beloved.

Pastor Beguiler's deep resonating voice rivets her attention. She's held spellbound by his charisma and warm invitation. She sees an older version of Enchanter, and imagines herself and Enchanter 25 years from now, seated at the same table with their own children. As Enchanter takes her hand, their eyes meet and she blushes from the sexual energy that passes between them.

As dinner ends Pastor Beguiler states, "I hope that you will stay awhile and get rested from your trying time in the wilderness. We have a guest room and I insist that you stay here. I'm sure my wife would love the company of another woman." Winking across the table at Enchanter he says, "I know how my son feels, too." She looks up at Enchanter and smiles with contentment.

Glancing toward Beloved, Enchanter says, "Oh yes, I've got lots planned for this lovely lady."

Chapter Twenty-eight

Unholy Fire

As they stroll through the commune after dinner, Enchanter says, "Let's get away from the campfires and all these people. I want some time alone with you. The desert has its own special beauty. I want to show you the dunes by moonlight." Enchanter places his arm around her waist as they walk toward the outskirts of town.

Their feet sink deep into the soft sand as they climb to the top of the dunes. "I have a special spot to show you where I always went as a small boy. Follow me." He takes her hand and they laugh as they run down the backside of the dune. "From this palm grove we can see the majesty of the heavens open above us. If we're lucky we might see a shooting star and we can make a wish."

He takes off his robe and spreads it on the sand, bowing before her. "My lady, please sit."

Sitting down next to her he takes out a silver flask, unscrews the top and says, "I brought some brandy to warm us in the chilly desert night." Beloved hesitates and stammers, "I-I don't think I'll have any. I haven't had anything to drink for a long time."

Standing in the shadows and unseen, Amazing Grace whispers, "That's right, Beloved, you no longer need a drink. It's dangerous to be here with him alone. This is a trap."

"What's one little drink among lovers?" He puts the flask to her lips and tips it up. A demon of addiction slithers around her. "It's my old friend Forsaken. I've been waiting for you." After several sips she takes the flask from Enchanter and they drink until it's empty. A warm familiar feeling comes over her.

The Seduction

Embracing her, he whispers tenderly in her ear, "Beloved, I know Master Potter brought you to me. I want to take care of you and protect you forever."

He passionately presses his lips against hers. She struggles to pull back but is held in his strong arms. Finally she pulls away.

He tells her, "We were meant for each other, but I won't pressure you. I want you to want me. I know all the women in the commune and many have wanted to marry me. But I wouldn't settle for anything but the best. There's something so special about you."

Beloved looks into his dancing eyes and admires his curly black beard and handsome features. She wants to say yes but feels restrained not to appear too eager. "It's all happening so quickly. I just don't know. Can you give me a little time?"

"Of course, Beloved, take all the time you need."

She turns her face to him and asks, "What does your father think about me?"

"Mother told me they are both very impressed with your poise and style. They could tell that you are of good stock and would produce a healthy grandson for them.

"Now, it's getting late and I know I should get you home, but how about one little kiss for this poor beggar boy?" he teases.

Valiant stands atop the sand dune with his flaming sword drawn. He knows Beloved's choices in the next few minutes are critical. He fervently intercedes as he watches the approaching demonic horde.

Enchanter and Beloved embrace passionately and kiss as an unholy fire ignites between them, uncapping deep wells of fiery passion. The pack of demonic figures scuttles across the sand dunes toward them, intent on fulfilling their satanic assignment. The intensity of Beloved's desire scares her and she pulls away.

"You feel it too, don't you?" asks Enchanter, "There's a destiny for us—together."

Enchanter holds her at arms' length and looking deeply into her eyes, says, "I don't want just one night. I want you to be my wife."

Amazing Grace warns, "Don't be deceived by your fleshly desires. This is not what Master Potter has planned for you. Stop this now while you still can."

"This is happening so fast. We're just really getting to know each other."

Enchanter replies, "But I feel like I've known you forever, Beloved. It's like you're a part of me. I didn't know what true love was until you showed up."

Beloved rationalizes, *Enchanter loves me and wants to take care of me. I could some day be his partner as the head of this commune. I want to have his son. This must be Master Potter's plan for me.*

Amazing Grace continues, "Beloved, you are on a journey to learn Master Potter's ways. This looks good on the outside, but it's full of deception and evil intent to destroy your destiny. Don't do this. It will cost you dearly. It could set your divine destiny back years."

Enchanter pulls an alabaster jar of spikenard from his pocket. "I bought this just for you because you are so lovely. I saw the way you looked at it in the market today. Spikenard is rare and very costly; it's the fragrance of the bride. Beloved, anything you want I can give you, anything."

He gently rubs the ointment on her wrists and kisses each of them, slowly, sensually, then rubs spikenard on the sides of her neck, followed by kisses, and finally he pulls his finger across her lips and whispers, "Your lips are so full and inviting."

Demons squeal with delight as they tether Beloved in their destructive cords, igniting burning, sexual desires.

Valiant, filled with righteous anger, sees the huge demonic being peering out through Enchanter's eyes orchestrating Beloved's downfall. He waits anxiously for Beloved to call for help.

The urgent voice of Amazing Grace says, "Beloved, cry out for Master Potter. Pray in the Spirit! Flee this situation! The enemy wants to destroy you!"

I won't let it get out of hand, I promise. Just a little bit more; it feels so good to be desired again.

Beloved's body responds to the waves of passion, and she struggles between her lust and the warnings signs in her spirit. "Beloved, you need to leave now and follow the star again. Don't even go back to Deeper Life. Don't be deceived, all actions have consequences." Her mind recoils at the thought of going back out into the harsh desert.

Enchanter pulls her body close to him as the demons froth at the mouth and prepare to dig their talons deep into her tender heart.

Seductively he whispers, "You're so beautiful. Please say you'll be my wife. I'll cherish you forever. Let's become one tonight and seal our commitment under this beautiful canopy of stars." He kisses her mouth ever so softly as his hands start to caress her sensuous curves. "I love the feel of your soft skin."

"Beloved, listen to me," Amazing Grace warns. "It's crucial you stop now. Enchanter is a liar, sent to deceive you. You're in grave danger! You're being lured into a deadly trap."

No, no. He loves me. I love him. I don't believe he's bad.

"You've come too far to return to your old lifestyle. It's not too late. Don't throw away your future for one night of pleasure."

Enchanter presses, "Will you marry me? Please say yes now. Why should we wait?"

It will be okay since we're going to get married anyway. I can serve Master Potter in this religious community. We can minister together and raise godly children. It will work out. I know it will.

"Yes. Yes, I'll be your wife. I want you, too."

Enchanter gently leans her backward onto the soft sand as the seductive fires of the enemy consume them. Carried away by her passion, Beloved surrenders herself fully to him, losing her innocence once again.

Lost Destiny

Amazing Grace weeps with grief as he watches Beloved abandon her prophetic destiny to fall back into the old patterns of her former life.

In the midst of their sexual encounter her mind disengages from her body. Her passion quickly gives way to those familiar feelings of being used by men. Demons cruelly strike her with their poisonous darts, causing flashbacks of scenes with Antagonist and other men who exploited her for their own gratification only to discard her later.

Lying on her back looking up, she's surprised to see the bright star she followed leaving. A tiny tear flows from the corner of her eye as it disappears out of her sight.

Then she remembers Master Potter using Unrelenting Love to heal her sexual brokenness. *I felt so clean and free.*

Beloved feels dirty again and is disgusted with herself and with Enchanter. What had seemed so exciting, irresistible and enticing just a minute ago is now bitter.

What have I done? What have I done?

Chapter Twenty-nine

Midnight Rendezvous

Ten years have passed. Beloved silently walks through the deserted marketplace into the outskirts of the commune. She is grateful for the moonless night. Sadly, she thinks about the women who look upon her with such envy. She came in as an outsider and married Enchanter, the one they all wanted.

Maybe I should be grateful! I have the name, the money, and the influence, but it's not what I thought it would be. I'm so desperately lonely! Enchanter's never home and when he is, he's always angry and yelling at us. I'm just a prisoner in fancy clothes.

She continues walking toward the dunes. *What am I doing out here? Am I crazy? Why should I believe what those women whisper? They're just jealous. I'm sure that what they're saying is nothing but idle gossip anyway! These past years haven't been easy, but still, he wouldn't do anything that would hurt our children.*

She continues down the path leading to the sand dunes and the grove of trees where she and Enchanter secretly met before she discovered that she was pregnant with Purity.

The still desert air carries a familiar voice, and suddenly a hard knot of fear rises up and lodges tightly at the base of Beloved's throat. The soft sand gives way under her silent steps through the dunes. Struggling hard to hold her emotions in check, she prays she won't find what she fears may be ahead.

Tormenting spirits creep along beside her in the dark shadows; sinisterly they whisper, "He never really loved you! Why should he be faithful to you anyway? If you hadn't gotten pregnant he never would have married you in the first place. Just be grateful he gives you a home and a name for the children."

But it wasn't supposed to turn out this way! I thought he was a godly man. He said we would have a ministry together and build a wonderful life. That never happened. Now, I question if he's really even saved. What I live with at home is so different from what everyone else sees. I'm so sick of the games he and his family play, pretending to be so spiritual, acting like they're worshipers of God. They pray eloquent prayers in public, but they never pray at home.

BETRAYED!

The familiar laughter of sexual intimacy comes from behind the last dune. The emotional impact hits her with such force that she drops to her knees. Frozen for a moment, betrayal—a knife sharper than any other—stabs deeply into her heart. Overwhelmed, she must acknowledge the lie of the past years.

Crawling to the top of the dune, Beloved makes out the dim outline of two figures embracing below. She has come face-to-face with the stark reality of truth, and it tears into her soul like the thrust of a spear. She drops her face in her hands and begins to weep. "Oh no, it's true!"

Enchanter's voice is carried on the wind. "I feel like I've known you forever. It's like you're a part of me. I didn't know what true love was until you showed up." She's assaulted with the same treacherous lies he used to seduce her so many years ago. "Please God, help me! I don't know what to do. If I don't confront them, he'll just deny it all."

Making her way quickly down the dune, she gathers all her courage and wipes the tears from her face. Angrily, she shouts, "Enchanter! What are you doing?"

Enchanter jumps up quickly, grabs his robe and covers the figure beneath him as he yells, "Beloved, get out of here! Who do you think you are, spying on me?"

Walking up to him she yells, "If you were home like you were supposed to be I wouldn't have to spy on you." She shoves him aside to see the shocked face of one of the young teenage singers in the choir. Embarrassed, the girl tries to hide from Beloved's gaze.

"Enchanter! She's just a child! This girl is not much older than Purity."

Livid with rage, Enchanter shoves her back, causing Beloved to stumble and fall to the ground. "Go home! I'll deal with you when I get there."

Picking herself up, she screams, "Deal with me! You have more to deal with than just me! I'm calling a meeting of the elders. Let's hear what they have to say about your midnight rendezvous with a 14-year-old. You're nothing but a child molester!"

Grabbing her arm and pulling her face close to his, he seethes, "If anyone's reputation is ruined it'll be yours. No one threatens me, especially my wife!"

Numb with shock and humiliation she stumbles into the night as the terrible betrayal pierces old wounds, and she sobs, "Lord, everything I've lived for these past ten years has been a lie. How could I have been so deceived? My life is falling apart! Where are You? Please talk to me."

Heaven listens intently but silence is the only thing she hears. The howling desert winds carry away her own groans of misery and loneliness.

Chapter Thirty

Paradise Lost

The atmosphere around Beloved's life is drenched with an eerie sense of foreboding and the days pass without any word from her father-in-law except a refusal to meet with her. She is praying fervently to Master Potter throughout the long days and nights, but she's heard nothing.

Finally she's summoned to Pastor Beguiler's tent for the meeting she's requested. Discouraged by his silence she apprehensively approaches the ornate dwelling.

"Lord, give me favor with the elders. Let them hear the truth. I know Pastor Beguiler will do everything to protect his son and his own reputation. I feel so alone. Lord please, help me."

A Meeting

Unseen by Beloved, Valiant protectively walks beside her as the servant girl shows her into the pastor's office. Smiling warmly and rising to meet her, Pastor Beguiler offers her a chair next to her husband. "Beloved, so good to see you! I've missed you. Enchanter has already filled me in on this little misunderstanding between you. I'm sure we can work it out—just the three of us."

Moving her chair away from Enchanter, she asks, "Where are the elders? I requested a meeting with them so everyone could hear my side."

"Now Beloved, that won't be necessary; this isn't a trial. After all, we're family."

"But this is too serious for just the family. This concerns the whole community. You don't understand, I found him out in the desert molesting a 14-year-old child."

Enchanter calmly defends himself. "Molesting! What a lie! She's the one who seduced me and she's hardly a child! She's old enough to know what she wants and it just happens to be me. It's not like she was a virgin. She came on to me for months until I just couldn't help myself! After all, you've not exactly been warm and inviting lately. Besides, I would never do anything to hurt you and the children."

"I'm not a fool. You've been doing this for years. I've turned a blind eye because I didn't want to believe it. But I've heard the whispers and seen you exchanging looks before."

"You've always been jealous of me, Beloved. What does a look have to do with anything?"

"What about the late night meetings? I pretended not to smell perfume on your clothes or question your whereabouts but I always suspected you were unfaithful."

"You're blowing this whole thing out of proportion. I provide you and the children with a good home. I put food on the table and clothes on your back. I would think you'd be grateful! I'm entitled to a little fun now and then."

"I don't call molesting a child 'a little fun,' even if she was coming on to you. You're a grown man and should have stopped it."

"Listen, Beloved, I got ambushed! This was unexpected and I admit it got a little out of hand, but you need to forgive me and just get over it. You're always so emotional! Let's just move on with our lives."

"I want you to move on, and move out of our home. I don't want to be married to you anymore or have you around our daughter." She turns to Pastor Beguiler. "He needs to be exposed and disciplined in front of the church to protect the young girls of the commune. Maybe then he'll get some help and do something about his problems."

The two men exchange knowing looks. Pastor Beguiler places his hand on Enchanter's shoulder. The smile leaves his face and his eyes flash with a hard glint as he tells her, "We were hoping you would just forget this little matter and come to your senses. If anyone goes before the elders of this church it will be you."

"I'm not forgetting anything. This is not going to be swept under the carpet like you do everything else!"

A Threat to Destroy Her

Walking to his desk, Pastor Beguiler picks up a file with her name written across the cover. The tone of his voice changes from condescending to threatening, "I know your history; Madam False Destiny and I are old friends. She's willing to come and testify about your character if need be. Do you really think the elders or anyone else would believe you after they hear what she has to say?"

The color drains from her face as she realizes she's been trapped once again in a web of lies and half-truths. Rallying all of her courage she defiantly says, "I don't care what you or Madam says, your son is a child molester!"

"Just so we understand each other, you have no case, Beloved. That young girl is no longer part of this community. She was sent away a few days ago. So where's your proof?"

"I don't need proof! You know it's the truth or you wouldn't have sent her away! You're all sick! I want a divorce! I'm taking my children and leaving this place!"

Joining his father, Enchanter tells her, "Divorce? That's not a problem! But if anyone is leaving it's you—without my children. I won't have an unfit mother raising them."

"Unfit! You're the one who molests children and commits adultery. I won't leave without Purity and Crusader!"

Moving towards her Enchanter rages, "No one is taking my son! You no longer have any rights here, as my wife or their mother. Purity is already showing signs of following in your footsteps and needs my fatherly protection."

"Protection! She needs protection from you. I'd never leave them with you."

"It's no longer your choice! You're leaving today without them," says Enchanter, pointing to the file on the table.

Looking at her father-in-law, Beloved pleads, "Please don't let him take my children. They're so little and they need me. I won't tell anyone, I promise! I'll do anything!"

He mockingly smiles at her. "It's too late, Beloved. I can't trust you."

"No, no! I'll be good! I promise. Don't take my children."

Beloved begins to tremble. Looking up to Heaven, she cries out, "Please Lord, don't let them take my children."

Pastor Beguiler picks up a goat's horn and summons the elders telling her, "Master Potter doesn't hear the prayers of thieves and whores!"

Shoving her outside the tent and knocking her to the ground he blows the horn again. "You wanted a meeting with the elders? You've got it! But you're the one on trial."

Chapter Thirty-one

The Outcast

Knowing she has only minutes, Beloved frantically scrambles to her feet trying to make it home. All she can think of is how to get to her children before the elders arrive.

Enchanter yells out, "Bring her back!"

Her heart races wildly as she hears pursuing footsteps. Gasping for breath she arrives home to find two elders standing guard at her doorway. As she tries to push her way through they grab her, and she sobs, "Let me go! Let me go! I want my children."

Hearing their mother cry, little Crusader and Purity rush toward her. Bursting into tears, they cling to her skirt as the elders tear them away and drag Beloved to Beguiler's tent.

Thrown at his feet, she looks hopefully at the people of Deeper Life crowding around her. Astonished to see the beautiful and pampered wife of Enchanter being dragged by two of the elders, the stunned crowd seems sympathetic.

Beloved tries to defend herself and rally their help. "Please listen to me. I didn't do anything wrong!" Pointing to her husband, she shouts, "This man is a child molester! They want to cover it up and get rid of me. Please help!"

Enraged, Enchanter grabs her by her shoulders, shaking her violently. He stuns the crowd as he strikes her across the face. "Shut up! No one is going to ruin our family's reputation, least of all a little whore like you."

Pastor Beguiler gives his son a disapproving look before turning to the people. "Don't be shocked at the display of raw emotion by my son. He's been terribly betrayed and deceived by this woman. I've called you here to discuss this situation because it affects the entire commune."

"As you know, my son found this woman wandering in the wilderness. We took her in and treated her like a member of our family. After just a few weeks, she managed to seduce him as many of you suspected. She claimed my son was the father of her child, Purity."

Beloved can see her daughter being restrained by the elders. She searches Purity's little face for reactions to the awful lies of her grandfather. Heartbroken, Beloved strains to make herself heard.

"He is your father! Don't believe those lies, Purity."

"Unfortunately we know that's not the truth," counters Beguiler. Holding up the file, he tells them, "I have proof right here of her character and what she did before she came to our community.

"She lived over the mountains in the seaside village of Comfort Cove, the daughter of the town drunk. She worked at Madam False Destiny's Inn. Madam is a splendid and upright woman, whom I happen to know personally.

"She loved Beloved like a daughter, and took her in out of the cold, just like we did. Beloved used the cover of her establishment for a prostitution ring in order to seduce the most wealthy and influential men of the community.

"In addition to being a whore, she's also a thief. Madam was shocked to discover her family heirloom jewelry had been stolen by none other than our own little Beloved."

The Crowd Turns Against Her

The crowd of sympathetic faces turn to frozen glares as Pastor Beguiler weaves his evil web of lies. A blanket of demonic energy charges them as they look at Beloved and remember how she came into their community and so quickly married into the Beguiler family. Long-buried jealousy and envy rise to the surface. Beloved had achieved wealth and prominence so effortlessly—the very things they work so hard for, but never achieve. Their frozen glares shift to angry accusation.

Beloved's emotions are ragged. Panic sets in as she realizes she's lost whatever sympathy the crowd had for her. "Don't listen to him. I didn't do it! I didn't do it." She drops to her knees, overwhelmed by her inability to counter Beguiler's lies.

"They found the jewelry hidden in Beloved's bedroom. Out of the goodness of her heart, Madam decided not to press charges, but this sad story doesn't end there."

Pastor Beguiler now points his finger at Beloved. "If that weren't bad enough, Madam told me confidentially how Beloved tried to seduce even the fine mayor of Comfort Cove. She threatened to ruin his reputation if he did not leave his wife."

Anger boils through the crowd as they shout their responses to his words. "I always suspected something was wrong with her."

"She came in here so haughty and seduced Enchanter right under our eyes!"

"She never really fit in; she was always holier than thou."

"Well, I'm not surprised; I always said she was no good."

GUILTY AS CHARGED!

"That's right," Beguiler continues. "My poor, inexperienced son didn't have a chance against such a seductress! He never suspected the truth of her past until I revealed it to him. And, oh, it broke his poor heart in two. By then it was too late, but he decided to make the best of it. God only knows how hard he has struggled to make this marriage work. I don't believe she knows who the father of this child really is."

Beloved rallies her emotional and physical energy for one last defense. "I wasn't pregnant when I came here. Enchanter seduced me just as he did Harmony the other night. Please believe me. Why do you think they sent her away? I made some mistakes, but everybody has and that was before I met Master Potter. I'm not the kind of person they say I am. I've lived here for ten years; you know me."

Sensing some of the people have remained sympathetic toward her, Beguiler continues, "Sent Harmony away? That's ridiculous! Just ask her father, Elder Self-Righteous. She was accepted at the prestigious music academy in Comfort Cove and will just be gone for a year or two."

The senior Beguiler goes in for the kill. "She hasn't changed! She's always had a hidden life. She wasn't satisfied with just Enchanter! When my wife was away Beloved actually tried to seduce me. I threw her out of our home, and now you must throw her out of this good community so that her poison cannot infect anyone else."

Beloved's tears won't stop. She buries her face in her hands, realizing that she cannot unseat the Beguiler's satanic grip on the community.

A gray-haired elder steps up and continues, "She's like a foul disease that will contaminate our young sons. She'll not rest until she's gone after all your husbands. We have righteous laws concerning this kind of behavior. We must not chance the wrath of God on our fine community. We must enforce His holy commandments."

STONE HER!

A gasp ripples through the crowd as dark demonic spirits stir the listeners into a state of rage. Several women close to Beloved yell, "Stone her! She's unclean! No family is safe with the likes of her around!"

"Take her to the Field of Blood and stone her."

Pushing and shoving, the crowd turns into a frenzied mob hungry for blood.

Breaking free, little Purity runs into her mother's arms, sobbing, "Stop it! You're hurting my mommy!" Beloved flings her arms around Purity, who buries her head on her mother's chest.

Beguiler throws more fuel on the fire. "Enchanter was determined to give Purity our name. But, she's not a Beguiler! Our blood does not run through her veins. Throw her out with her mother!"

Dark, vile spirits move among the crowd inciting them into a hostile mob. The crowd rushes in, pushing them to the outskirts of the commune, shouting, "Bad blood is bad blood! She may be only ten years old, but soon she'll be just like her mother."

The crowd throws rocks at the two figures but Valiant deflects most of them. They struggle free from the mob and run. "Mommy, why are they hurting us? I'm afraid."

"It's going to be alright. Master Potter will help us. Just keep running!"

One large stone hurls through the air and strikes Beloved's head. Stumbling, she pulls Purity down with her. Beloved throws herself over her daughter as the angry crowd surrounds them, pummeling Beloved with their stones. Her head is bleeding and she can feel bruises forming on her body and face. Pleading, she yells, "Please, don't hurt my little girl. She has done nothing to you."

The silhouetted figure of Pastor Beguiler stands over them gloating. Beloved tries to get hold of her emotions. "Please, please, please," she begs, "just give me Crusader and we'll go."

Sensing the sympathy of the crowd beginning to shift toward Purity, Beguiler shouts, "I wouldn't think of letting the children die with you in the wilderness. Leaning close to Beloved he whispers, "Purity will make a fine servant in my home. Of course, I'm changing her name to Promiscuous."

Yanking Beloved to her feet, he shoves her into the restraining arms of Elder Self-Righteous as he rips Purity out of her grasp. He orders his elders to take the now hysterical little girl back to his tent.

Fighting to get free, Beloved screams, "Never forget, your name is Purity! It's Purity! I love you."

Enchanter pushes through the crowd with eight-year-old Crusader, forcing him to look at his now dirty, disheveled and bleeding mother. "Son, I don't want you to ever forget what you're seeing today. This is what a whore looks like and this is what the Holy Scriptures tell us we must do to whores. Your mother has brought shame to the family. I know it's painful to lose her and this might seem cruel, but you will understand when you get older."

Looking into the pale, expressionless face of her son, Beloved feels her heart rend in two. "Son, please don't believe them! I'm innocent! I didn't do the terrible things they're accusing me of. Please, Crusader…."

Crusader looks at her blankly for another moment before Enchanter grabs his hand and disappears into the mob.

Chapter Thirty-two

Signed, Sealed and Delivered!

Beloved fights back with all her strength as Beguiler pulls her small bruised frame into his vise-like grip. One of the elders yells, "Silence!" Raising his other hand, he motions to the mob to stand back.

The oppressive atmosphere suddenly fills with a foreboding stench. Beloved battles to get away as the dark, grotesque, disfigured face of Death emerges before her horrified eyes. Pastor Beguiler nods to him. "Here she is, signed, sealed and delivered! I've lived up to our part of the bargain! You can have Purity too, when I'm through with her."

Thrashing violently to free herself from his awful grasp, Beloved finally cries out, "No! No! I'll go with him. Just don't let him have Purity."

"You have nothing to bargain with; you're already his."

Death opens his foul mouth, and long strings of yellow drool drip from between his yellow fangs. His jagged mouth spews his furious hatred. "So we meet again, Forsaken!"

With every beat of her heart, her body throbs in pain. She staggers and regains her balance. With a boldness that surprises her she hears her voice say, "My name is Beloved! Master Potter changed it when He defeated you in the Potter's Field."

"That was then—but He won't help you now. You turned your back on Him a long time ago. You chose to live a lie these past ten years. Why would He want you back?"

Hot tears stream down her face, stinging her cuts and abrasions, as Death's river of ugly taunts washes away her resolve to fight. Drunk with the prospect of finally destroying her, Death hisses, "What about all those promises that you would become a prophetic voice? And all those grandiose visions and dreams you bragged about? What a pathetic joke! You'll never see your children again. I've destroyed everything you've held precious."

Beloved pleads again with Beguiler for her children. "If I can have my children, I'll stay and never tell anyone about this."

"No, Beloved, you're not part of the family any more. I can't trust you. But, you know how merciful I am," Beguiler says with a smirk. "I'd hate to see my grandson's mother die in the wilderness. Madam False Destiny has graciously offered to take you back and work out your rehabilitation. If you cooperate with Madam and make good progress, then maybe I'll let you see Crusader and Promiscuous."

Beloved's heart leaps at the thought of seeing her children again. *Maybe I could go back and just pretend, then I could see Purity and Crusader again. Master Potter would understand that I don't believe in that lifestyle any more.* Her mind whirls in confusion as she tries not to let go of the idea of seeing her precious children again.

Suddenly she flashes back to the first day in the wilderness and what the angel told her, "When you come to the end of yourself, remember what happened this day, and call upon the Lord."

I could never go back to Madam False Destiny—that would mean denying Master Potter. He saved me!

Her last flicker of hope to see her children again dies inside her. Her body begins to tremble and by an act of her will, Beloved declares through her tears, "Master Potter may not want me back, but I will never renounce Him."

Beguiler scoffs, "You would be willing to lose your children for Him? You fool! You'll regret that decision when He won't take you back."

Death snatches Beloved from Pastor Beguiler's grasp. "We had a deal. She's mine! My master is waiting for her." Beloved's strength is spent. Unable to even struggle against Death, she hangs limply in his gnarled grasp and whispers, "Master Potter, please, help me."

Chapter Thirty-three

Winds of God

Beloved's unseen guardian angel, Valiant, rushes into the fray on behalf of his charge. Moving toward Death with the power of resurrection glory, he unsheathes his gleaming sword and cuts Beloved loose.

She jerks suddenly, yanking loose from Death's firm grasp. Shock comes over her face as she realizes that she is free.

The eastern sky quickly changes from pristine blue to a dark brown, as an ominous torrent of sand and wind sweeps across the desert, blowing directly toward the commune. The crowd panics at the blinding force of the approaching sandstorm.

Flashes of fire and lightning illuminate the darkening desert sky. The Father's thunderous voice rolls across the heavens, challenging demonic spirits. The hot sand pelts against Beloved, stinging her broken body and lashing at her open wounds.

Protecting her eyes, she peers through her fingers to locate Purity. She catches a glimpse of her being dragged away, screaming and fighting. Beloved watches in horror until Purity and her captors are engulfed in the sandstorm.

The frightened crowd flees the Field of Blood and runs for shelter as the heavenly whirlwind engulfs them. Now the wind intensifies and the air becomes thick with sand, making it almost impossible to breathe.

Death screams in agonizing pain when Valiant scorches his vile being with the burning glory of his sword. Throwing his grotesque head back, he howls bitterly and blasphemes Master Potter.

Valiant moves quickly to shield Beloved from the scorching sand. Convinced that Master Potter could never love her now, she clutches her torn robe and curls into a ball in the side of the dune, sobbing.

Activating the Unseen Realm

Beloved's nearly forgotten prayer language erupts from deep within her spirit, but her frail voice is lost in the roaring wind and pelting sands. Thinking she might die, she desperately pleads for Master Potter to forgive and rescue her. "Lord, please forgive me! Help me."

Beloved's prayers to Master Potter activate warring angels who charge into battle. Throwing a huge, fiery golden net over Death, the angelic warriors hurl him into the engulfing storm through the power of the Cross's vindication. As Death is thrown down, the angels shout wildly in victory.

Soon, the sound of pulsating demonic wings and clashing swords fades to a distant rumble. But many curious angels crowd together in glorious light and hover over Beloved, waiting to see what will become of her.

The sandstorm whips up into a whirlwind of dazzling glory and fire before calming to a soft, gentle breeze. Opening her eyes, Beloved sees the dear figure of Amazing Grace striding toward her. Then she loses consciousness.

He lifts her into his powerful arms and carries her back into the mountains on the outskirts of Deeper Life.

Amazing Grace

When Beloved wakes up disoriented and in pain, she sees the compassionate face of Amazing Grace looking down at her. "Amazing Grace! I thought I'd never see you again. Was it all a bad dream?"

"I'm here, Beloved," he says, gently wiping blood from her forehead. "And, no, it wasn't a dream."

A look of horror contorts her face. "My children, my children!" She tries to sit up and winces as a sharp pain immobilizes her. Amazing Grace gently lays her back down. She clings to his robe, crying, sobbing so deeply that Amazing Grace can't make out her garbled words. He continues to comfort her, praying for the Father to send her peace.

Finally, Beloved regains enough composure to be understood between her gulping sobs. "Please, please, release the warring angels right now to rescue them. They need me!"

"No, Beloved, they need Master Potter."

Panic-stricken, she shrieks, "They need me more. I'm their mother. I can help them."

"Beloved, there's nothing else you can do for them right now. The only way you can help them is to pray. When you lost your children your responsibility changed. I'm going to teach you to intercede for them, and that will release Master Potter's protection. The question for you now is, will you follow me?"

Beloved is hysterical over Amazing Grace's reply. Her high-pitched voice screams out at him, "But I can't live without them! What will happen to them?" Not waiting for his response, she continues screaming out her frustration at Amazing Grace. Her rage momentarily dulls her pain and she pushes herself to a sitting position.

Kneeling beside her, he continues praying as Beloved's wild, ranting accusations toward him finally decrease enough for him to respond.

"It is not for you to know the outcome now. Purity and Crusader's destinies are hidden in the councils of the Trinity. These are secrets that will unfold in time."

"No, the time is now! I'm so afraid for them. Help them—help them now!" Her voice grows louder as panic sweeps over her again.

"The question is still, will you follow me?"

She grabs his robe and pulls him close. "Without my children? I can't! Let's go get them. You can take angels. Don't you care? How can you let them die at Deeper Life? Do something, now...." She releases his robe as she pushes him backward. He puts his hand down in the sand in time to regain his balance.

He waits patiently as her hysterical raging subsides into deep sobbing. She is furious over her inability to manipulate Amazing Grace into action. He reaches out to touch her and she turns away and lies back down. In a futile attempt to comfort herself, she curls into a fetal position, her back to him.

"Beloved, I can tell you that your children are precious to us. We'll move Heaven and earth to save them."

"I don't believe you. If you loved them, you'd save them now."

There is silence for a long time. Beloved is still facing away from Amazing Grace. He watches as her shoulders begin to heave. Her body trembles and finally she bursts forth in deep, guttural sobs. Uncontrollable weeping wrenches her body and she wails in agony over the loss of her children and her inability to rescue them.

With no other options, she finally allows Amazing Grace to gather her into his comforting arms. He rocks her gently and whispers words of hope as he helps her to pour out her anguished heart until all she feels is the empty void of her children's absence.

Emotionally spent, she falls into a fitful sleep in his arms, giving her aching mind and body some much needed relief. When she awakens a few hours later, Amazing Grace is once again lovingly attending to her.

Beloved blushes and looks away, ashamed of her past choices and her recent tantrum. "I made a mess out of everything, didn't I? I'm so sorry I didn't listen to you. Can you ever forgive me?"

He gently reassures her, "Yes, Beloved. I forgive you. You were never out of my sight. I've longed for you and grieved that you didn't follow me but I never left you."

"Why couldn't I see you?"

"I wear many disguises, and you've seen only a few. I've come to you as a voice in the wind, tongues of fire, a dove and even a cloaked guide."

Revelation dawns on her. "Holy Spirit? Is that You?

"I come in many different forms and manifestations. But it's imperative that you learn to recognize My voice and obey Me."

"But why didn't You show Yourself? If I had known it was You I would have followed!"

"No, Beloved! You wouldn't have followed Me. You chose to take the easy way out of the wilderness. Pain and discomfort seemed an unnecessary hardship to you at that time, but in the end it would have brought you life. The *easier* path you chose was an illusion of lies producing only death and great loss."

"I came into the wilderness all healed up; now I'm divorced and I don't have my children. I'm such a failure. I made a mess of everything, didn't I?"

"Yes, but Master Potter has marvelous ways of restoring the enemy's devastation and our wrong choices."

"But, my whole life is destroyed."

"Master Potter still loves you, and we need to go to Him. So, I'm asking you again, will you follow Me?"

Faces of her children crying reappear before her eyes as she struggles with the thought of leaving them at Deeper Life.

Feeling overwhelmed with grief, she buries her face in the folds of Amazing Grace's brown robe, sobbing uncontrollably, and recommits herself to the journey.

"Yes, I want to go to Master Potter."

"We'll stay here a few days until you are well enough to travel and then we'll continue your journey."

After weeping for a long time, Beloved struggles to regain her composure. "It's…just so…it's just so hard…to leave them."

Putting His comforting arms around her, Amazing Grace rocks her back and forth. "I know, Beloved, I know."

Beloved sleeps fitfully off and on for the next two days as her body tries to regain its strength. Her restless dreams are filled with visions of Purity, Crusader, Death, Valiant, Amazing Grace, the angels and the awful events of her last hour at Deeper Life.

Before the sun comes up the third morning, Amazing Grace awakens Beloved and they slowly disappear into the dawn, leaving her children and Deeper Life Commune behind.

Chapter Thirty-four

Dressed for Battle

Numbness fills Beloved's broken heart as she stumbles and falls in her weakened condition. Supporting her weary and fragile frame, Amazing Grace helps her walk over the sand dunes toward the steep mountain trail ahead.

They create a strange spectacle. Amazing Grace, still wearing His long, brown hooded robe, looks like a cloistered desert monk. And Beloved, tattered and bruised, looks like a little wandering waif He's found.

Once they are a half-day's journey from the commune, the two wilderness wanderers stop to rest. Amazing Grace gives her food to eat and water to drink from His leather pouch. After she's eaten, He tenderly bandages her head and applies ointment to her swollen and blackened eyes. Saddened that she's so wounded from the violent encounter at Deeper Life, He speaks soft and gentle words of encouragement.

"I missed you so much. It's so good that you are back with Us."

The tender ministry of her desert friend imparts renewed strength in her weary body and mind. He lifts her to her feet and holds her close.

Unbeknownst to her, suffering and pain are doing a mysterious work of drawing her into deeper levels of prayer and trust with Amazing Grace. Once their respite is over and night is falling, He quietly resumes His place in front of her on the narrow desert path. Leading her deeper and deeper into the wilderness, He turns and looks into her eyes.

An unspoken understanding passes between them as He points to the brilliant star twinkling overhead. Beloved blushes and they both smile at each other and chuckle. "I understand," she replies. "Don't stop following the star, no matter what."

"Remember, Beloved, I will never leave you, even when you can't see Me. You're never alone; My eye is always upon you. Valiant is with you too."

"What are You doing when I can't see You?"

"Watching and interceding on your behalf."

Beloved smiles and gazes up at the star. When she looks back to the trail she realizes that Amazing Grace has vanished.

"I will follow the star," she states resolutely as she begins down the path.

Alone but Never Alone

Hours pass and her steps become laborious. The cold night air brings its own kind of misery to her stiff, aching muscles—a misery she had forgotten long ago.

Death and his demonic horde hide in the barren rocky pass waiting to cruelly ambush and torment the fragile vessel with their poisonous river of lies.

Death screams at his demonic troop, "After ten years of waiting, I had her in my hands. Now she's back in the enemy's camp!" Sneering viciously at a nearby cohort, Death vents his anger with a swift kick to the demon's stomach. "Master is not going to be pleased. We can't return until we have our trophy, whether dead or alive. Her body is tired again so we must go after her now. Her greatest vulnerability is her children. That is how we shall attack. Each lie must be carefully designed to wear her down a little more."

The demons position themselves along the trail and begin their accusations. "What kind of mother are you, leaving your children behind? They'll hate you forever for abandoning them. Crusader already does! Did you see how he looked at you?"

"Why don't you turn around and beg Enchanter to take you back?"

"Oh Lord!" she cries through muffled sobs, "What have I done? Maybe I should go back!"

The twisted words tear at Beloved's heart and mind. The taunts continue, "You always told yourself you wouldn't do what your mother did, but you turned out just like her! She never protected you, and you aren't protecting Purity and Crusader!"

"You're no better than she was!"

Their lies reverberate against the steep cliffs, creating evil echoes of destructive accusations.

"Your life is over! There's no point in living without your children!"

Beloved covers her ears and lets out a painful groan, "I can't bear it, Lord! I want to die!"

Ambushed by Suicide

Her mind succumbs to the attack of the hypnotic voices until she's drawn off the path to the edge of the steep crevice. Suicide's raspy voice whispers, "All you have to do is take one step off this cliff and you'll have peace. They'll be glad you're dead! Those children have already forgotten about you anyway!"

"Yes, I want peace! I can't live without them. Purity! Crusader! I know this is the best thing for all of us. Lord, please take care of them."

Moving closer to the edge of the cliff, Beloved takes a deep breath. Looking down at the long drop onto rocks and brambles makes her dizzy. She closes her eyes, holds her breath and prepares to step off.

Suddenly Amazing Grace appears and slips His arm around her, pulling her back to safety.

"Beloved, fight for life! I'm here to help you. You don't wrestle against flesh and blood, Beloved, but against demonic principalities and powers."

The words of Amazing Grace impart hope and faith. She cries out, "I don't want to die! I want to live for Master Potter and my children!"

Turning to command the dark forces He declares, "She has resisted you. You must leave now!"

The enemy sullenly retreats for a moment and Amazing Grace walks her back to the path.

"Beloved, you're in heavy spiritual warfare, and the enemy is trying to kill you; but you must always remember that Master Potter loves you, even in your weakness."

"But I keep messing up His plan for my life," says Beloved.

"Master Potter has a destiny for your life and the lives of your children. You are the only one who can thwart Master Potter's plan; the enemy cannot steal it from you unless you give up the fight. You must put on the whole armor of God to resist the fiery darts of the enemy."

As He speaks, ministering angels gather around to dress her for battle. A form-fitting bodice of golden mail is slipped over her torn dress. It has a delicate appearance but takes on an invincible power as the breastplate is strapped on.

Then they place a silver crown of salvation upon her bruised head to protect her mind from the lies of the enemy. A golden belt of truth is girded about her waist and leather sandals are placed on her feet and laced around her calves. They hand her a glorious shield of light with the word "Faith" emblazoned in scarlet.

Now dressed as a warrior bride, Beloved receives from Amazing Grace a sword with "The Word of God" engraved on its golden handle. He tells her, "As you speak the Word this sword will be activated. You are armed and dangerous. You are My Beloved—no longer a victim, but an overcomer." In the spirit realm Valiant nods with approval, like a proud parent, as a holy glow emanates from Beloved's being.

A Second Attack

No sooner has Amazing Grace disappeared than the demonic horde regroups and attacks again. A throaty voice sneers, "Do you really think speaking words into thin air can make a difference?"

Two or three others join in, mocking, "Obviously your prayers haven't done any good in the past; just look where you are now!"

"Divorced! Childless! Homeless!"

"Poor Forsaken. Poor, poor abandoned trash," the scorn increases.

"A complete failure! You couldn't even follow a star!"

Beloved stands against the onslaught at first, but wears down quickly. Soon her heart once again faints. "I've failed everyone, including Master Potter."

Quickly Amazing Grace reappears and says, "Don't agree with the enemy. Put your shield up, get your sword out, and release the Word, Beloved. Remember how much Master Potter loves you and your children. With His weapons, you can win the day."

The mocking, venomous assault continues. "The reality is that Master Potter doesn't care about your children. If He did, He would have rescued them."

"He sent you back to the wilderness to die."

"Die."

"Die, die, die, die," the voices get louder and louder.

The Sword of the Spirit

Fear assaults Beloved's mind and she takes several backward steps. Touching her bruised heart with His fiery hand, Amazing Grace ignites flames of truth concerning the mysterious plan for her and her children. "Remember, Beloved, you're not on your own. We are comrades in battle. All of Heaven is for you."

She feels strangely warmed and shakes her head as if waking up from a dream. She hears the clear voice of Amazing Grace as He proclaims, "Master Potter will rescue your children. The Word says, '*He will contend with those who contend with me, and He will save my children.*' "

Supernatural anger rises up within her and she repeats His words with authority. She boldly declares to the demonic realm, "Master Potter will rescue my children. The Word says, '*He will contend with those who contend with me and He will save my children.*' "

"Good, Beloved, speak the Word again. Let your voice be heard," coaches Amazing Grace.

As she continues to proclaim the word of faith, the sword in her hand becomes activated, giving off a brilliant, pure white light.

Screaming, the demons declare "Divorced! Childless! Homeless! You'll always be a disappointment to Master Potter. You're a failure, Forsaken!"

Amazing Grace proclaims, "You are His Beloved, forever. You can never lose His love. The enemy is a liar."

"I'm not Forsaken, I'm Beloved. You're a liar and the father of all lies. Master Potter has a destiny for me and my children." As the words flow from her mouth, she is amazed at the power and unction behind them. *Where did that come from?* she wonders.

"That's great, Beloved, you're doing well. Remember the authority of God is behind your confession. Your speech is a powerful weapon. It builds your faith and cripples the enemy's power."

She slices through the darkness, causing surges of resurrection power to explode into brilliant flashes of light. Her sword cuts through the atmosphere, leaving vaporous trails of sulfuric smoke as she wreaks havoc in the evil entourage.

Warrior angels energized by Beloved's prayers of faith charge into the battle on her behalf. Boldness arises from deep within her, courage she has never possessed. Constantly encouraged by Amazing Grace, she is fearless in the skirmishes that continue throughout the long cold night. "Look at them run, Beloved; you're doing great. The battle is the Lord's."

The clash of the angelic army and the demonic screeching hordes being driven back cause spiritual sparks to fly into the night. Glistening swords clash and wounded vile spirits explode in red sulfuric vapor. The Father looks down, pleased at the fireworks display on the desert mountains below.

Amazing Grace mentors Beloved in spiritual warfare and the use of creative spiritual strategies. As she comes to trust Him, a deep camaraderie develops between them. They wage war against their common enemies as they continue to follow the star along the mountainous trail.

Chapter Thirty-five

Joyous Celebration

The star fades as the first light of dawn peaks over the desolate mountains. Beloved painfully limps along the rugged trail. Her armor is dented from the many arrows hurled by the enemy but still in place.

Her beautiful robe from her elegant wardrobe at Deeper Life is now beyond repair. It is caked with dried blood and smudged with dirt. The rips and tears expose the scrapes and bruises on her frail body.

Her brown hair is matted with blood from the head wound she received from the angry mob. The piece of cloth Amazing Grace so lovingly applied to bandage her head has slipped off during the night skirmishes, and she rewraps it as well as she can.

As the warmth of the sun's rays rise above the surrounding mountains, she looks for a place to rest before the desert heat becomes unbearable. Beloved hears faint sounds from far off in the distance and her spirits rise slightly. Maybe she can find friendly people and shelter.

As she gets closer she realizes it's a song and thinks that maybe she recognizes it as one that Master Potter sang over her at His house. *Am I hearing things?* Despite her exhaustion, she pushes herself harder, struggling up the mountain path as quickly as she can.

She catches phrases of the song as it is carried softly on the wind. "The Lord your God is with you…I am mighty to save." Her heart leaps for joy. *Could it really be true? Could Master Potter be here?* Forgetting her wounds and how tired she is, she runs with a renewed energy.

As she gets closer to the top of the ridge the song wafts over her. "I take great delight in you. I will quiet you with My love and rejoice over you with singing."

Is the journey through the wilderness over? It's been ten hard years.

Meeting Master Potter

From the top of the ridge she looks down and sees a wide valley hedged in on three sides with reddish rugged cliffs. Beloved is astonished to see a majestic white tent set up in the valley below.

It's engulfed in brilliant glory with the same blazing pillar of fire she saw over Master Potter's House years ago. On each corner and in the center of the beautiful tent are tall golden flagpoles glistening in the high morning sun.

Colorful flags of purple, scarlet and sapphire fly at the top of each tent pole. They remind Beloved of the Master's flagships anchored off Comfort Cove. The center pole flies a flag bearing Master Potter's family crest of the lion and the lamb etched in gold. The lovely design work stands in stark contrast to the desolate sands and rock-strewn mountains surrounding it.

Deep longing erupts in her heart as she sees Master Potter running towards her with His arms open wide, and it takes her breath away.

In a deep tenor voice He sings out, "Come away with Me, My Beloved." Leaping upon the mountains and skipping upon the hills, He is suddenly in front of her. Scooping her up, He affectionately embraces her, and she collapses in His arms. He swings her around in joyous celebration as she becomes covered in His flowing white robes. His fiery eyes of love look deeply into hers.

He whispers lovingly, "Rise up, My love, My fair one, and come away with Me. For the winter is past and the time of singing has begun. I've missed you so." He sings softly, "Beloved, Beloved, you are My Beloved."

Chapter Thirty-six

The Tent of the Lord

With great love and gentle tenderness, Master Potter carries Beloved down the rugged mountain into His tent, singing all the way. He gently lays her on a long, cushioned couch covered with pillows. She opens her eyes and is astonished to see into the realm of eternity. There is no roof on the tent, only an open heaven. A thick, heavy cloud of glory and light saturates the tent and connects to the pillar of fire swirling above.

Celestial music of flutes, harps and stringed instruments waft down from the throne room. Hovering angels join with the heavenly choirs. The unearthly music has a life of its own. It penetrates her body, infusing strength and renewed hope.

Looking behind Master Potter, she sees two ministering angels. The first holds a golden bowl and has a linen towel draped over his arm. The other holds a golden tray with alabaster vials containing exquisite fragrances of flowers, sweet spices and oils. She also recognizes the small honey cakes that Valiant gave her at the start of her wilderness journey.

With great distress she cries out, "I had no idea this was waiting here for me. It's beyond anything I could ever imagine. If only I'd followed the star a little bit longer, I would have saved myself so much pain. I could have been here with You ten years ago. I missed You so much. I'm so glad to be with You again. Oh, Lord, forgive me. Please forgive me."

A sick feeling rises in her as she waits to hear His response. Gently, He strokes her face and speaks the words her painful, tattered soul needs so badly, "I've missed you so much, Beloved. I love you, dear one." He sits her up and puts His strong arms around her. Reveling in His warm embrace, she weeps even harder.

"I've longed to see your beautiful face, Beloved."

Looking down at her bloodstained dress from Deeper Life, she bows her head in shame. Sobbing even harder she cries, "How can You say I'm beautiful? Look at me. Look at what I've become. I left Your house all healed up, and now I'm broken again."

Master Potter's eyes are filled with tears. "Beloved, it wounded My heart when I saw you suffering. How I wanted to spare you! I called to you many times, but you would not come."

Touching His face with her bruised hand, she wipes the tears from His cheeks and cries, "Oh Lord, I'm so sorry. I did hear Your call, but didn't realize how much I hurt You until now. Please forgive me."

"I do forgive you. I know this was a painful journey for you also."

The ministering angels come forward and Master Potter takes off her dented armor piece by piece and hands it to them. He pours precious oils into the golden basin of living water; then taking her old friend Soaking Love, He begins to cleanse her wounds.

Her Healing Begins

Reclining on the couch she begins weeping.

"They lied to my children and took them away. All I wanted from them was to be accepted and loved. They're evil and cruel. I hate them all. They practically killed me out in the desert."

"Beloved, I understand. I, too, was taken outside the city and judged for things I didn't do. I was beaten and cruelly betrayed as you were."

"I hate them—all of them—for what they've done. They've destroyed my life."

"Beloved, your hatred will destroy you. Forgiveness has greater power than vengeance. Pastor Beguiler and Enchanter deceived them too. Let Me show you how I see them."

Prisoners of Religious Compromise

Suddenly the religious commune materializes in front of her eyes. The illusion of abundance and wealth gives way to a barren wasteland of poverty and need. The oasis mirage fades and she sees a slave camp.

"Beloved, do you see the pain and devastation of their lives? They're prisoners and don't even know it. My heart aches for My people to come back to Me. Will you show them mercy and forgive them?"

She watches as beautifully dressed people she has known for the past ten years change into tattered beggars fighting over a cup of water. Shadowy demonic figures move around stirring division and hatred. Her eyes are opened to the reality of their tormented condition, and she is saddened by the misery and hopelessness of their religious compromise.

Tears well in Master Potter's eyes as He tells her, "Beloved, they were also rescued from the Potter's Field and began the journey across the wilderness, but they never came back. By refusing to continue through the wilderness, they exchanged My leadership for an illusion of comfort and ease."

For the first time ever, she begins to see the anguish Master Potter feels for them. She realizes they are His beloved children, too. Touched by His deep sense of grief and loss, she cries out under conviction, "Lord, I forgive them. Will You forgive me for hating them?"

As the vision of the commune continues, she sees shimmering angelic beings moving throughout the people and tents. Master Potter says, "It's the enemy's prison, but My forces have been there all the time, waiting to show the way out to those who are willing. You could have left anytime."

She realizes that she was as deceived as they were. "You're right; I was a prisoner too. What appeared to be glamorous in the beginning turned out to be a prison. I can't believe I was seduced by the wealth and power of the Beguilers. I had warning signals all along, but I didn't want to give up the affection, attention and power. I'm as guilty as they are. Please forgive me for doubting You. I'm so grateful to have gotten out. Now I understand how much I hurt You when I did the same thing."

"I will always forgive you, Beloved. You can never exhaust My abundant unending supply of mercy, and by forgiving them you have chosen the way of My heart. When you extend mercy it releases not only them, but also you, from judgment."

Master Potter takes off the bloody bandage applied to her head by Amazing Grace. "Beloved, your forgiveness has enabled Me to heal these wounds." Taking Soaking Love, He gently washes the cut on her head and applies a healing salve scented with the fragrant lily of the valley and aloes as He sings over her.

WHAT ABOUT MY CHILDREN?

Beloved becomes panic-stricken. "Lord, what about my children? My children live in that slave camp. You have to rescue them. They're being raised by deceived and disillusioned people—many who hate You!

"Enchanter lied about me and made them think I'm no good. He sacrificed his own daughter—he doesn't even admit Purity is his! What is to become of her? They'll never know the truth."

Beloved's mother-heart aches as she sees Purity and Crusader sitting side by side holding each other and weeping. Their sobs cause an unbearable anguish in the depths of her soul. She clutches her chest and cries out, "My babies! My babies! Save my babies. They're so innocent. Why do they have to suffer?"

"In the midst of the storm they will find Me. I will not abandon them. I promise you I will protect them. Your children have a destiny in Me, but you have to trust that I'm going to work this for good."

Through her tears she sees two huge guardian angels appear behind them, with fiery swords drawn ready for battle. As she watches, they unfurl their huge glistening wings and extend them into a canopy of light and protection over the children.

Amazing Grace appears, wrapping his comforting arms around them. He whispers gently in their ears, "Master Potter loves you both so much and so does your mother. Never forget that. Even though you feel alone you're not abandoned."

He brushes the hair back from her daughter's face. "Remember, Master Potter named you Purity, not Promiscuous." Turning to Crusader, he says, "Remember your mother, as she really is someone who loved you and wanted to protect you. Someday you will see her again."

As she watches, the children get down on their knees and pray. "Lord, we want our mommy back. Please keep her safe. Don't let her die in the desert. We love her so much."

Grieving Her Loss

Master Potter holds Beloved in His soft robes while she grieves the loss of her children. "You've taught them well how to love Me and come to Me with all their problems. You must continue to believe that I'll take care of them and that I have a destiny for them. You need to release them into My care, Beloved. Every part of your life needs to be given to Me, especially the great losses and the shattered dreams."

Sobbing, she admits to herself that she has no other options. "Lord, I give them to You. What else can I do? Take care of my little ones. I know the only safe place for them is in Your embrace."

He gently takes off her worn sandals and uses Soaking Love to wash her feet. He massages her sore muscles and applies more healing salve to her cuts and blisters. "Beloved, I feel your pain for your children. I share it with you. I will help you bear this burden."

"Thank You, Lord," she says as He wipes away her tears.

"There is one thing you can do. It's the key to your children's well-being."

"What is it, Lord?" she asks with excitement.

"First, let Me tell you what it's not. It's not worry and complaining," He says with a grin. "It's your prayers on their behalf. I know that on the earth it sometimes feels like your prayers are floating in the atmosphere. You wonder if they're really making a difference. Such questions and doubts come from the enemy. I'm going to give you a wonderful gift. I'm going to pull back the veil and give you a glimpse of what goes on in Heaven when parents pray."

Chapter Thirty-seven

Open Heavens

Beloved looks up, and the atmosphere of the tent begins to change. She's drawn upward into this whirlwind of glory, passes through the pillar of fire and soars to the Gates of Heaven. She feels no fear as she's carried in Master Potter's arms into this realm of unspeakable beauty.

As they pass through the ancient gates, the throne room appears before her. She sees vistas of celestial colors and surges of brilliant light. The uncreated, glorious Father, clothed in radiant garments of light, sits on a fiery, sapphire throne, surrounded by a rainbow. Dazzling white purity of unspeakable holiness emanates from Him, and resurrection glory swirls around His throne.

Beloved counts seven lamps of fire burning and moving around the throne and sees something like a sapphire sea of glass, like crystal.

Without warning, tremendous surges of lightning, sounds and peals of thunder burst forth from the throne. These explosions of indescribable splendor and raw transcendent power reflect His fervent passion. Flowing from His being are music and messages that change time and eternity.

Surrounding the great throne are 24 elders in white robes, wearing crowns. Each elder holds a harp and a golden bowl representing heavenly worship and intercession.

In the center and around the throne are four living creatures full of eyes and blazing with fire. These burning ones glisten with dazzling light as they fly around the face of God. Raging infernos of glorious worship, they're consumed and alive with the fire of His presence. Lightning and fire shoot back and forth among them in magnificent splendor.

Night and day, they never cease their adoration and ministry as they gaze upon and unfold His beauty. Overcome by each revelation they cry, "Holy, holy, holy! Lord God Almighty." They release the new vision of His beauty to the 24 elders, who fall down and cast their crowns at His feet, saying, "Worthy are You, our God, to receive glory and honor and power; for You created all things, and because of Your will they existed, and were created."

They join all of creation in worshiping the One who sits on the throne. Millions of words and harmonies become one magnificent song! A symphony of sounds never heard by human ears echoes throughout the throne room. Beloved sees multitudes from every tribe and nation consumed with glorious worship and alive with the fire of His presence. As far as her eyes can see, glorious angels bow low in worship, crying out, "Holy, holy, holy."

A Golden Censer of Incense

As Beloved watches in stunned amazement, a powerful angel, his entire being shimmering with divine light, stands at the golden altar before the throne. He holds a golden censer.

Master Potter says, "Now listen." Suddenly, the worship fades into the distance, and she hears a crescendo of thousands of voices in all languages passionately pleading for salvation, healing and deliverance for their children.

"Lord, please save my child. She's not following you."

"Oh, Lord, my husband is drinking too much and is abusing the children terribly. Please help us."

"Father, the doctors say he's only got a month to live. Heal him, Lord. We need a miracle."

Tears fill Beloved's eyes as she listens to the desperate pleas for these hurting children.

Beloved is gripped as she watches the Father give the angel a great quantity of incense. The steadfast angel adds it to the prayers of the parents upon the golden altar, which is in front of the glorious throne. The fiery smoke of the incense, with the prayers of the saints, rises up out of the angel's censer. Swirling before God as a sweet-smelling fragrance, it mingles with frankincense and other rare aromas.

Then the mighty angel fills the golden censer with fire from the altar and throws it to the earth, answering the prayers.

With each utterance of prayer, power is released in the heavenlies, bringing answers on earth. Thunder rumbles and lightning flashes as mercy, justice and loving-kindness are poured out from the throne, bringing vengeance on the enemy. The release of salvation, deliverance and miracles forces the demonic to retreat.

"Beloved," says Master Potter, "the purpose of an incense offering was to please God in the hope that He would respond with favor regarding the requests or needs. When the Father adds the incense to the prayers it signals His willingness to answer."

FIERY IMPARTATION

Back on the couch again, Beloved is too stunned to speak. She merely looks toward Heaven and back to Master Potter. He smiles. Touching Beloved's spirit, He gives her an impartation of intercession for her children. Surges of anointing go through His hands into her spirit as deep groans of fervent prayer begin. Sounds of travail, birthing and groans she's never before heard go out into the heavens and war for her children, calling forth their destiny.

As her words burst forth in her prayer language, angels carry these precious petitions up to the golden altar where they are mingled with incense and are received by the Father. Finally, after several hours, Beloved's heavy burden for Purity and Crusader lifts.

"Beloved, the very heart that you have for your children is only a infinitesimal reflection of the vast oceans of love that the Father has for them. Yes, you birthed them, and you'd sacrifice anything in this world for them. But He created them and painted the entire universe just for their pleasure. His love knows no bounds."

Taking her face in His hands He solemnly tells her, "You are not in this battle alone. Do you understand that the Father does not take your prayers lightly?"

Beloved, still overwhelmed, smiles sheepishly. "I do now."

Master Potter takes a golden chain with a small flask of delicate perfume attached and places it over her head. Opening the vial she responds, "Oh, it smells wonderful. This smells like Heaven."

"Beloved, this fragrant oil is frankincense—it represents deep intercession. It is one of the smells of Heaven. This necklace is a symbol for you, a reminder of what you just saw. Never stop praying for your children. The Father always hears your prayers on behalf of His young ones."

Chapter Thirty-eight

Forgiveness

Solemnly, Master Potter tells her, "There is one more very serious matter to be addressed." Beloved looks apprehensive.

"You need to forgive Enchanter."

Shock and indignation tear through her soul as she sits up on the couch. "How can you expect me to forgive him?"

"Beloved, I forgave—"

"That's different; You're Master Potter! You're the Son. He lied to me! From the day I met him he was unfaithful! He was abusive and cruel to the children and to me. He twisted and perverted everything when he called me a whore in front of the whole commune and our children."

"Beloved, I do understand your suffering and betrayal, but no matter how unfair, no matter how painful it was, you still need to forgive."

"And what about that 14-year-old girl I caught him with? He needs to ask for my forgiveness, but I know he never will. So why should I even bother? I hate him! He instigated the mob to run me out of the commune to protect his reputation. I still have the bruises to show for it! I'll probably never recover! My vessel is too broken!"

"Beloved, this is a great test of your heart. It was abusive and he was wrong. But, I begged you not to go there. What happened was part of the consequences of your disobedience. Aren't you glad I forgive you?"

"Yes, but it seems like Enchanter gets off free."

"Hardly, Beloved. Enchanter sold his soul for demonic power like his father and grandfather before him. He's like Madam, part of the same demonic network that carries out Satan's work in this area. I had a calling for his life too, and it grieves Me to see what he has become. Don't be deceived, for judgment always comes when there's no repentance."

"I still hate him."

"Hate and bitterness fuel the demonic. No matter how evil and cruel all of this is, it has to go to the Cross or your wound will continue to fester. It will become an open invitation for demons to attack you. Surrender is your key. If you want to live as I live, Beloved, you must let go. Otherwise, your unforgiveness of Enchanter will destroy you, not him."

"I can't forgive; it's too hard. I'd rather die. I want to see justice done."

"Then you will never fulfill your destiny, Beloved. I'm training you as one who can bring salvation and deliverance to many who are ensnared by this network. Part of your destiny is to become a powerful warrior bride to do battle for souls on My behalf. If you cannot forgive, the enemy has you bound and gagged. I'll still love you, but he will be victorious in your life, and My purpose in creating you is thwarted."

WOUNDED FOR HER TRANSGRESSIONS

The vision of Master Potter on the Potter's Field, bloodied and beaten beyond all recognition, comes back to her. With it He tells her, "Was it justice for Me to be judged unfairly and innocently slaughtered for your sins? There is something greater than even justice—My unconditional love. Love keeps no record of wrongs. I suffered unfaithfulness and death at the hands of those who should have loved Me. It wasn't just, but I chose to love and forgive My enemies. If you want to follow Me, you must do the same. Will you now choose to forgive Enchanter?"

She remembers the day Master Potter rescued her from the Potter's Field, how He lovingly embraced her and took her to His house. She remembers the mercy she received and how undeserving she was. Beloved receives a deeper revelation of His suffering on her behalf. Her heart starts to soften as she identifies with Him in her own betrayal and pain.

She whispers, "Lord, I'm so angry and hurt. I have so many terrible emotions warring inside me. Even though I don't feel it in my heart, I choose to forgive him—but only because You require it. Please help me. I do want to be like You. But I'm just not free of the pain of it all."

Looking down at Beloved with pleasure and immense love, He tells her, "With mercy and forgiveness comes healing, Beloved. Even though you still have anger and hatred in your heart, you made a choice to forgive. That decision released you from the enemy's bondage in your life, and the process of healing and forgiveness can begin."

He begins to take off the torn, bloody outer robes and hands them to the ministering angels attending her. "Forgiveness always releases healing virtue. Now I can heal the festering wounds of betrayal in your spirit from Enchanter. This will close a door of attack from the enemy. There is no wound too deep; there is no betrayal so severe that My cross cannot heal."

He takes the healing oil of myrrh and anoints her. "This myrrh speaks of the sweetness that comes out of suffering and My cross at work in your life. This oil is very costly, and so is the process. It will cost you everything."

Suddenly, penetrating sensations of resurrection power surge through her body, releasing waves of healing energy. A miracle occurs as her bruises diminish and her swelling disappears. Her face returns to normal again. The pain leaves her fragile body, and peace floods her as she's physically healed. The aches and pains she felt just a moment ago vanish. Her terrible fatigue is gone, replaced by a renewed strength.

But Master Potter's face is now distorted with her injuries. Black and blue bruises cover His face, and blood drips down into His now blackened and swollen eyes as He takes on Beloved's wounds.

Beloved is undone as she looks into His battered face and hears those words spoken through swollen and painful lips. "Every stone and every fist that was hurled against you, I took as well."

She throws her arms around Him and sobs, "Oh, Lord, how You love me." Then she feels resurrection power flow from deep within Him as the second miracle takes place. His face becomes radiant and beautiful once again, His swollen eyes heal and the bruises disappear. He whispers to Beloved, "I'm so proud of you. I have a wonderful calling and destiny for you."

"But Lord, how can You ever use me? I've wasted ten years. I'm an outcast. I'm vulnerable and weak. Just look at me. I've lost my children, failed as a mother and I'm divorced. How can I ever be in the ministry now?"

Turning her face gently toward His, He says, "Beloved, I will make a way for you where there is no way. It's not about your strength anyway; it's about My power in you. I designed you as a clay vessel because My power is best displayed in weakness."

"But I wasted ten years. Aren't You mad at me?"

"I knew the choices you would make in the wilderness before you ever left My house. I grieved for the pain you experienced while you were at Deeper Life, but it didn't make Me love you less."

I Betroth Myself to You Forever

"I, the uncreated second person of the Trinity, I who with My Father spoke and made the heavens, I make a covenant to betroth Myself to you—forever. I give Myself entirely to you. I don't just give you My blessings—I give you Myself.

"I know you don't understand the depth and the fullness of My love for you. It's a progressive journey of the heart. But I have paid off all your debts, and all the demands of justice have been met in My death. I have paid your dowry and I am committed to bring you into wholeness. I am preparing you to be My Bride."

He takes out a beautiful white linen robe and puts it on her. "Not only are you utterly forgiven, but I will restore your dignity. I will remove your shame. I make you a chaste virgin. I covenant with you forever to protect you.

"Our relationship is not based on your failure or attainment. Our relationship is based on My mercy and My deep love for you. I will be faithful. I am trustworthy. If you are faithless, I am faithful still.

"This is the bridal oil, spikenard, a rare and costly fragrance. I anoint you with this oil and seal My irrevocable betrothal to you with a kiss."

Lovely perfumed aroma emanates from her earthenware vessel, and now His fragrance is hers.

"Beloved, it is imperative that you understand this: One of the greatest blows to the enemy kingdom is when you become confident in My unfailing, unconditional love for you. Even in your weakness, I desire you. I passionately pursue you.

"Oh, Beloved, you do not realize the destiny you have in Me. Watch how much damage you, My weak clay vessel, My little princess, My warrior Bride can do to the enemy when you finally believe that."

Another angel appears holding new, shiny armor. "You must always wear the full armor of God, to resist the fiery darts of the enemy." Master Potter gently dresses her in the armor and stands her to her feet.

Wiping her tears with the back of His hand, He continues, "I will satisfy you. I know your dreams; I know everything about you. Watch what I can do with your life! Watch the beautiful destiny I have for you come forth!"

She is surprised to see tears in His eyes. He gathers her into His arms and emotionally whispers, "Beloved, look at what you sacrificed for Me. You could have seen your children again if you'd only gone to Madam's. But you chose not to compromise. I love the way you love Me. You may feel like an outcast and failure, but you are worthy to be My beautiful Bride. Just one glance of your eyes ravishes My heart."

Drifting off to sleep that night, she dreams of the joyous day she will be reunited with her children.

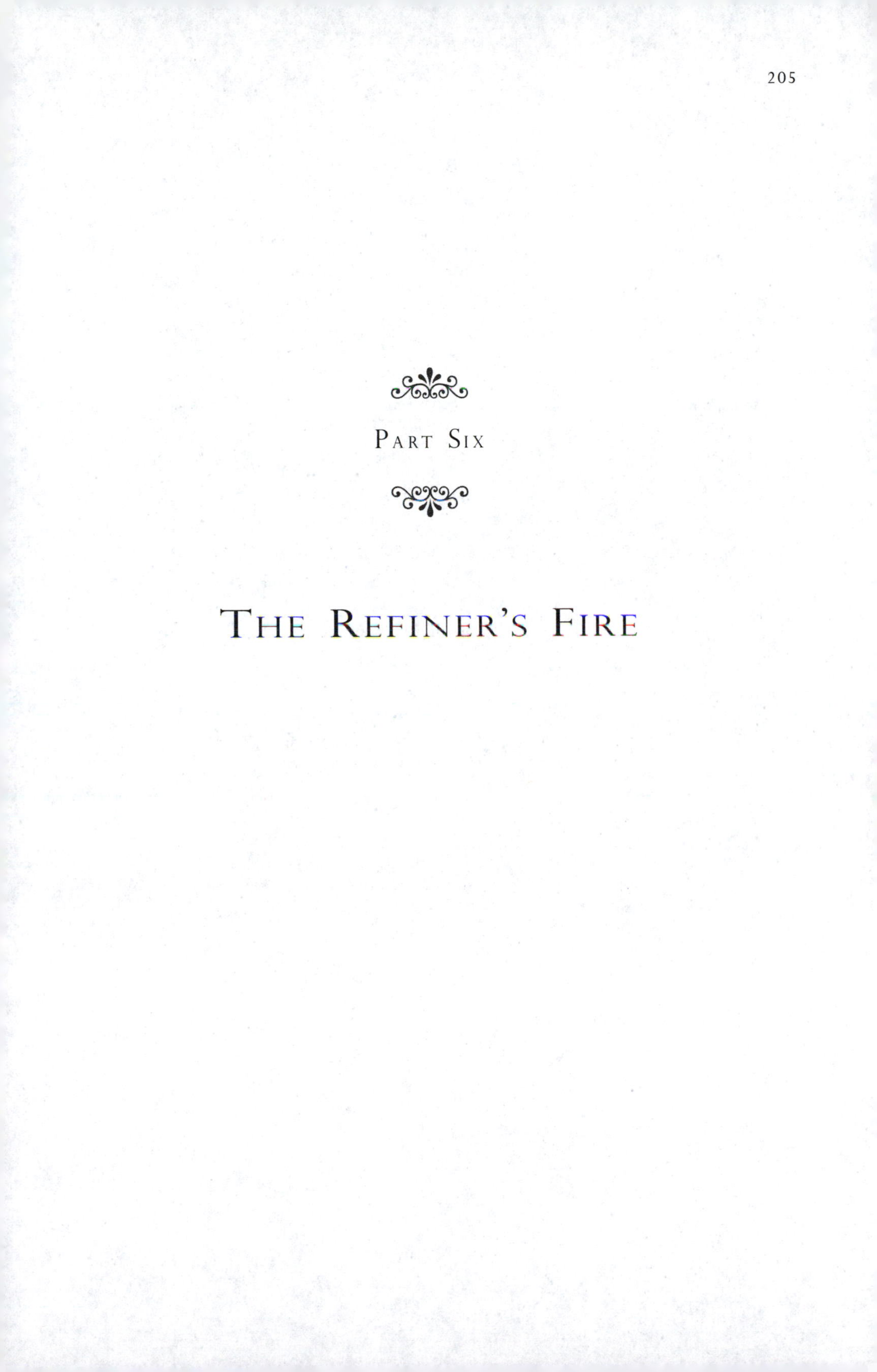

Part Six

The Refiner's Fire

Chapter Thirty-nine

Trophies of Grace

The next morning when she awakens, Beloved is pleasantly surprised to find herself no longer in the tent but in the familiar surroundings of the Potter's House. Rubbing her eyes, she rehearses the events of her journey back to this wonderful, safe haven.

The glowing embers in the fireplace, from last evening's fire, have almost gone out. She looks around to see if anything has changed; and for a brief, confused moment she even wonders if her entire journey through the wilderness was only a dream. But her children are no dream, and they are gone. The familiar, wrenching pain of loss floods over her again. Looking up she sees the ancient beams of cedar and is comforted by their presence.

Time for Promotion

The early morning light shines through the windows as Master Potter picks her up, saying, "Beloved, it's good to have you home again. Now that you've made it through the wilderness, it's time for promotion."

Carrying her over the threshold into a brick room lined with shelves, He carefully places her on a shelf with hundreds of other vessels. Glancing around from her perch on the top shelf, she sees dozens of pitchers like herself, but in various shapes and sizes. On other shelves below there are large urns and planters. On the other side of the room are plates, bowls, cups and saucers. Everyone looks like they just came from the wilderness, brown and dry.

She turns and notices a large dried-out canister next to her. "I'm Beloved. What's your name?"

"I'm Harvester."

"I'm so glad to meet you, Harvester. I'm from Comfort Cove. Where are you from?"

"I grew up on the outskirts of Watered Down Village, next to the Valley of Indecision."

"I've never been there; I've only been as far south as—er—the Potter's Field."

"That's where I ended up too. I was a fisherman on The Bay of the Lost. When my boat got destroyed in a storm I got washed up on the Potter's Field. I'm so glad Master Potter rescued me."

Beloved nodded, fully understanding.

"Do you know what this room is used for? I've heard from other vessels around here that we've all been promoted."

Beloved smiles up at him. "Master Potter just told me the same thing."

A familiar-looking mug on her right pipes in, "We've talked among ourselves and we've decided that we're definitely in His trophy room. Why else would we be displayed so prominently on these shelves?"

Fearless, a sturdy wine carafe, butts in, "I don't want to be a trophy. I want some action. I'm already bored sitting around here collecting dust."

Beloved looks back at the little squatty mug, trying to think where she knows him from, but Harvester interrupts before she can ask. "Comrade, you have so many friends and always hear the latest news. Give us the scoop!"

Beloved continues, "For a moment I thought I knew you, but I've never met anyone named Comrade."

Awkwardly he replies, "Oh, that's alright, I just have that kind of face. Everyone thinks I look like someone they know. We've probably never met, or I'd remember."

Suddenly, Beloved turns to him with a look of surprise as she remembers that same voice yelled at her in the Potter's Field.

"Wait a minute! I do remember you! Your name is Friendless! I know who you are."

Sheepishly, Comrade looks down at his shoes and sighs in resignation before looking into her eyes, "My name used to be Friendless, just as yours was once Forsaken—before Master Potter rescued us. I was afraid to tell you who I was, because I thought you wouldn't want anything to do with me."

"Don't be silly! All you did was yell at me in the Potter's Field, and I forgive you for that."

A Painful Confession

He drops his head, unable to look at her. "Listen, I did something you don't know about, something that was just awful. But you have to understand that Mayor Lecherous was going to tell everyone about my past if I didn't do what he wanted. I knew I'd be finished in Comfort Cove."

"I don't know what you're talking about! What did you do?"

"I was the one who took Madam's jewelry and hid it in your room."

Beloved's smiling face falls into an expression of shock. Disbelief fills her eyes. "You did what? How could you? Didn't you know what would happen to me?"

"I wasn't worried about you, Beloved; I was only concerned for my own skin. I don't know why Mayor Lecherous was after you, but he said he was going to destroy you. If I didn't help him he would ruin me too!"

Beloved asks, "What could he possibly have against you? You seemed to be one of the most upstanding citizens, and you certainly weren't poor."

The mug explained with a quivering voice, "I was addicted to gambling and skimmed money off the village's revenue to pay off my debt at Madam's. When Mayor Lecherous discovered what I'd been up to, I became his pawn. He forced me to set up a second set of books for him so he could steal money from Comfort Cove's treasury. He called it 'our little business arrangement.' "

Comrade's face turns bright red with shame as he looks into Beloved's angry eyes. He gulps, and braces himself for a tirade.

The sharp pain of betrayal stabs right into her core. Beloved is stunned and furious. Hot tears roll down her cheeks, and she can barely breathe, reliving the pain of that night and the betrayal she suffered.

Comrade continues, "You're not the first person he took advantage of. But I went home that night and could not sleep, knowing I had helped to ruin you. Later, I actually confronted the mayor. Me, can you believe it? I threatened to expose him. Well, he just laughed at me in that mocking way of his, and in the end he got me fired in disgrace. He planted the thought in everyone that I couldn't be trusted with their money. He didn't even have to say what I did. All he did was give a certain look, and they all went along with everything he said."

Cleansing Streams of Forgiveness

Listening to Comrade, the old hurts flood her and anger is all she can feel. She blurts out, "It serves you right after what you did to me."

Hot tears begin to roll down Comrade's pudgy cheeks. "I'm really sorry. Can you ever forgive me?"

"I don't think so. You don't deserve it after what you put me through."

A warm wind swirls into the room, and Holy Spirit gently whispers, "Beloved, you've been forgiven much; now, you must love much."

"But Lord, we're not talking about me; we're talking about what he did to me. Why should he get off the hook and be forgiven so easily? I want him to suffer for a while. He deliberately ruined my life!"

"Beloved, long before you ever met Comrade you ruined your own life with the choices you made. The enemy used him, but he also used you to hurt people. Are you willing to forgive him and give grace, like Master Potter did with you? You're both very different people now."

"I just can't, Lord. It hurts so much. In my heart I just hate him," she confesses. "I'm willing but I'm not able. Lord, if You put forgiveness and grace in my heart, I'll do it. I can't forgive in my own strength; it's impossible."

"That's right, Beloved. You can't forgive without My empowerment; therefore, I'll fill your heart with compassion and forgiveness." With those words, Holy Spirit touches Beloved's heart once more, and a warm sensation penetrates her entire being.

Sadly Comrade begins to walk away. Beloved sighs, "Wait a minute, Comrade. Don't leave. I guess if I were in your shoes I probably would've done the same. I remember how I was in those days and the terrible things I did just to be accepted."

"I did that all the time. It was how I lived. I wish we could start over and I wish I'd never hidden the jewelry and caused you all that pain. Can you please forgive me?"

"I do forgive you, Comrade—because Master Potter's forgiven me for the way I treated people back then."

Little Comrade begins to jump up and down as guilt and shame fall off his shoulders. Taking her hand, he breaks out in a grateful smile, "I'd like to be your friend, if you'll let me."

Sovereign Friendship

Holy Spirit turns and whispers in her ear. He tells Beloved that her friendship with Comrade is a sovereignly chosen friendship, and just as Comrade's name means loyal friend, so he will become one to her. Extending her hand to him she tells him, "I like your new name. It's so much better than Friendless!" Beloved gives Comrade a warm loving embrace.

A tear trickles down Comrade's round face.

Smiling warmly, Beloved says, "So much has happened to me since those days at Madam's, but right now I want to hear about you."

Walking and talking together for hours, the two friends share tales of their journeys since they last saw each other on the Potter's Field. Beloved's heart grows increasingly warm in the presence of her new friend. She soon finds that she trusts him enough to share her painful journey about the loss of her children and failed marriage.

A bond of friendship forms between them, and finally they join a group of vessels on a lower shelf who are in an intense debate about where they all are.

TROPHIES OF HIS GRACE

Steadfast, a large oval serving platter who loves to talk, yells across the aisle, "Comrade, I don't think we're in a trophy room! Do you think we're in a trophy room? This looks like a church to me. Haven't you noticed we're all lined up on the shelves? Row upon row, it's just like the pews in a church. Maybe we'll have a guest speaker; I wonder who it will be? Mark my words, it's definitely not a trophy room."

"Well, obviously He's gathered us in one place for some special purpose," the fragile perfume vial Sweet Adoration adds in a voice so soft the other vessels must strain to hear her.

A tall, forlorn-looking vase murmurs, "We barely survived the wilderness and it sure doesn't look like a trophy room to me. I think it's a setup! We're in for more crushing or breaking or another wilderness trek. Or, we're going to be left on the shelf for a long time again. Oh, I hated that part the most." She moans loudly, "Oh no! Here we go again!"

Always cheerful, Comrade rescues the moment. "That's just Long Suffering; don't pay any attention to her. She's always the party pooper."

"Well, I can certainly see why Master Potter would promote us after all we've gone through," Harvester yells out in a booming voice.

The bantering gets louder and louder as all the vessels begin talking at the same time. Each vessel is boisterously voicing his or her opinion about where they are and how they got there.

Thinking about her children and the people she left behind, Beloved says, "Shouldn't we be grateful that we're here? After all, some people didn't make it out of the wilderness."

Joyful, a little wine goblet, chimes in, "Beloved's right. Some of my friends and family are still back there. I wouldn't have made it if it hadn't been for Master Potter."

Soon the group is talking excitedly among themselves and sharing adventures of how they almost didn't survive. They've all forgotten how dried out and tired they were. Isolated and discouraged for so long, they are thrilled that Master Potter gathered them together for some great purpose.

Deep friendships form as the vessels sit on the shelves. They spend the time worshiping, studying the Word together, and building families and homes. Greatly relieved that they're out of the wilderness, they sometimes wonder what the next journey will hold.

Angelic Reunion

In the unseen realm, Valiant and the other guardian angels are having a great time as they move among the shelves. Playfully, they call for more of the glory as they peer into the open heavens above them. Eternity answers back with indescribable beauty, glory and worship. Living light radiates from them and grows as they draw strength from the endless worship around the throne.

They love it when all the angels gather together. Talking and laughing in small groups throughout the room, they share their own war stories and tell how they kept their charges safe in the wilderness.

When the angels hear the Word being quoted or the name Master Potter, they gather around the vessels quickly so they don't miss anything. They love the worship and join in dancing and singing His high praises.

With an open Heaven above the vessels and angels dancing between them, the vessels are oblivious to the supernatural realm as they boast of their spiritual maturity.

CHAPTER FORTY

A CUSTOM-DESIGNED DEATH

The harsh realities of the wilderness fade away as the years pass. They are replaced with restlessness and boredom. Vessels compete for the best places on the shelves, jostling each other for better positions. It seems that certain vessels only want the space that another vessel has. But, when it finally gets the coveted spot, it loses its great longing for it, only to begin pining away for someone else's place.

Eventually a pecking order arises from within the ranks of the group. Cliques form within the different groups as they fight for leadership of the trophy room.

SPIRITUAL PRIDE DEVELOPS

The vessels begin to brag to each other, "We're a cutting-edge church! After all, we survived the wilderness! That's why others come to us."

In the midst of their expanding spiritual pride they don't notice Master Potter and His ministering angels tightly closing all the doors and windows before turning a few strategically placed knobs. Fire emerges from the floor as a barely visible flicker and slowly builds into red-hot flames.

At first no one wants to admit what's happening, so they pretend to be enjoying the rise in temperature. Comrade whispers to Beloved, "It's sure getting hot in here! Are you okay?"

Sweat pours off her as she answers, "Yes, I'm all right but I can't figure out what's happening. Is it warfare or hot flashes? I can't tell!"

Joyful overhears and butts in, "It must be warfare!"

Other vessels loudly complain, "It's getting awfully hot in here. Let's leave. I'm sure there's a better trophy room down the street."

"Hey! Who has the key? The door's locked!" Fearless complains as he tries to make a way of escape for the vessels.

Fire, Fire, Fire!

Harvester howls, "Ouch! Fire is coming through the floorboards and in between all the shelves. Somebody call the fire department."

"Fire, fire, fire!" the yells rise up in unison from around the room.

Sweet Adoration wails, "Look, there's fire climbing the walls! Someone tell Master Potter! He'll help us! He'd never allow this!"

A chaotic chorus of shrieks and howls can be heard. "This is warfare!"

"Let's start a bucket brigade," shouts Comrade. "Everyone line up." The vessels scurry back and forth and finally, under Comrade's leadership, end up single file in a line.

"Now what?" asks Beloved.

"Now we pass the water down the line in the buckets!" shouts Comrade.

"But we have no buckets!" yells Long Suffering. "And we have no water either. We're all going to die. I just know it."

Fearless takes leadership, barking orders over the confusion. "Everyone start praying and binding the enemy! The room is on fire!"

Shouts arise for Master Potter to rescue them from the clutches of the enemy until Long Suffering chastises them. "Are you all a bunch of dimwits? Quit over-spiritualizing. It's not a trophy room—it's a kiln! You obviously didn't notice, but Master Potter is the one who turned the fire on!"

Slowly truth begins to dawn on them and panic sweeps through the vessels as they frantically run around shouting out advice and orders and bumping into each other.

In the midst of the chaos a glorious figure appears in the swirling flames. Recognizing their friend Holy Spirit they cry out, "Help us. Turn off the fire. What are You trying to do, kill us?"

In an awesome voice that penetrates their very beings He declares, "That's exactly what We're trying to do. Master Potter has placed you in this blazing kiln to purify your hearts. Because you're dry, fragile vessels you'll break under pressure unless you're fired. You'll never be able to contain My glory. This painful firing is for the fulfillment of the incredible callings on your lives. You are all truly vessels of honor. Submit to the intense heat and let it promote you to the next level." He throws His mantle of consuming fire over them before He disappears.

In their misery the vessels all blame each other. Gossip, slander, and division come to the surface in this holy fire. Relationships with family and friends are strained and become increasingly painful as the dross in their clay is burned up. Impurities of jealousy and competition arise to the surface.

The flames intensify, and Beloved looks disdainfully at the sweaty people next to her. She begins to complain bitterly about them. Uncomfortable and short-tempered, she suddenly dislikes most of them.

Walls of Division and Separation

Many experience persecution at work and intense difficulties in relationships. The ensuing tensions raise walls of separation and division. Communication is strained in the consuming fire.

Out of the smoky flames ugly demonic voices emerge accusing Master Potter. "So where's your God now, Forsaken? He could speak a word and deliver you out of this inferno, but He was the One who put you in the fire. Why don't you just go back to your children? I'm sure they miss you!"

Holy Spirit whispers, "Remember the lessons of warfare from the desert? Put on your armor and use your authority, Beloved!"

I need my helmet of truth to stand against the enemy's lies, thinks Beloved. She wonders, *Where's my armor? I just had it last month! Oh, here it is on the back shelf.*

"In the future keep it on, Beloved. One of the enemy's strengths is surprise."

The tormenting voices brutally assault her as they hiss through the intensity of her suffering, "Look how He treats you, Forsaken! He really doesn't care what happens to you."

The heat advances, causing perspiration to drip from her weakened body; but she grasps her sword and shield and feels renewed strength surge through her. She stands to her feet and is amazed when the fiery arrows of accusation hit her shield and fall harmlessly to the ground.

Beloved looks at Comrade and says, "Did you see that?" She begins shouting, "Everyone, listen to me. Put on your armor. It's the only way we can defeat the enemy's attack."

"Great balls of fire!" booms Harvester. "How could I have forgotten?"

There is more commotion as the vessels run to find their long forgotten armor while trying to dodge the enemy's fiery darts.

"I'll never find my armor in all this smoke. I'm doomed," wails Long Suffering. "I can't even remember the last time I used it."

"Oh, I feel better already," says Sweet Adoration as she straps on her breastplate.

Harvester bends over to put on his gospel shoes and yells, "Ouch! Comrade, watch where you point your sword."

Holy Spirit continues His encouragement. "Great, Beloved! Now command the demonic spirits to leave."

Taking a deep breath she yells, "We belong to Master Potter and in the authority of His name I order you to leave—now!"

"That's right, Beloved, use Master Potter's authority. They'll screech and complain, but they have to go."

"Yes, you have to go," shout some of the other vessels as they finally get their armor on.

Unseen swords battle on behalf of the vessels as Valiant and the other guardians give a war cry and enter the fight. "Vengeance is the Lord's!"

The Weapon of Worship

Holy Spirit says, "Now Beloved, don't forget one of the most powerful weapons you have—worship."

Beloved's beautiful voice leads the vessels in hymns of battle and triumph as she boldly proclaims the enemy's defeat with music. They sing in the Spirit, and faith is restored. Wisps of sulfuric smoke erupt through the chimney of the blazing kiln as the dark spirits flee.

The pots, dressed in full armor, all look at each other and erupt in whoops of joy and celebration.

"Let's see 'em try that again," yells Fearless as he jabs his sword toward the chimney.

Watching through the spy hole, Master Potter rejoices to sees His children maturing. Tenderly He says, "You're learning My ways. I'm so proud of you. Never go to battle without your armor or you will be at the enemy's mercy, fighting in your own strength. Always stand against the enemy with your full armor and in My name."

Master Potter checks the fire, reads the temperature and then turns the knob to release even more heat.

"When the temperature is exactly right I'll turn off the kiln and bring you out. I not only fire one vessel at a time but I also take families, churches or groups of friends and set them all on fire until the dross is burned out. Through the fire of your circumstances I will custom-design each of your deaths until your character becomes more like Mine. This temporary fiery affliction will pass, and you will carry My eternal weight of glory, My abiding presence, in your vessel."

He smiles to Himself as the fire goes from a low red heat and shoots into blazing orange flames.

CHAPTER FORTY-ONE

REFINER'S FIRE

Holy Spirit joins Master Potter as He stands outside the fiery kiln. "I wonder if they understand how much You love them and that there are only two choices on earth—either the refining fire of God, which brings life, or the destroying fire of Satan, which brings death!"

Master Potter lovingly responds, "I'm so delighted that these vessels are willing to be fired. Otherwise, they'd fall apart at the slightest pressure and wouldn't be able to hold my oil, grains and fragrances. I know Father is proud of them."

A VISION OF CHILDHOOD

Holy Spirit blows His fiery winds through the kiln, raising the temperature even more. "Beloved, I want to bring you into a deeper place of healing."

In the midst of the flames, suddenly the face of her father appears. Startled, she cries out, "Lord, I never wanted to think about him again. I just want to forget how much he hurt me."

Holy Spirit opens the old wounds locked deep inside her soul. Shocked at the bitterness and rage exploding within her, she cries out, "Lord, there's so much pain in me, I'm too afraid to go there. Please help me! Make him go away!"

The fire intensifies and works its way into the walled-off memories as a vision appears of her childhood home. From her hiding place in the bushes she sees her dad stumble into the house. In his hand is the familiar brown paper bag from the tavern.

Beloved's heart races and she's paralyzed by the fear of those old feelings. It's as if the Holy Spirit has opened up a chamber in her heart where the feelings and memories have never changed. Suddenly, she is a small, powerless child again and she is overwhelmed by the same terror she felt growing up.

Holy Spirit reassures her, "Don't be afraid, Beloved. You're safe with Me."

"But, You don't understand! He was so cruel! I hate him! He never wanted me or even loved me." Beloved falls down and sobs uncontrollably, releasing years of pain that were deeply pent up inside her soul.

"Beloved, I was there and heard your cries in the night when you were only four years old. I felt your pain and I know the abuse that took place, but only Master Potter can heal you. Will you let Him?"

It's a struggle for her to answer, for the pain is very deep. Yet, in the end, her need to be healed overrules her fear. "Oh yes, I just want the pain to go away. I just want to stop hurting and being so afraid. Help me, please!" she wails.

Looking into the vision again she sees Master Potter with His arms outstretched and herself as a little girl running toward Him. She burrows her head deep into the folds of His robes and clutches His legs.

Master Potter picks her up and cradles her in His arms, smoothing her hair and wiping away her tears. "He won't be able to hurt you this time, Beloved, but you need to go back into the memory so you can face the truth and receive healing." He holds her close and walks toward the house.

Revisiting the Past

The strong, familiar odors of smoke and alcohol invade her senses, causing old emotions to rise up in a wild torrent of pain as they enter. Standing in the stark living room, Beloved relives the poverty of her childhood and the constant ache of loneliness and shame.

Walking down the dark, narrow hallway she hears the sobs of a little girl behind a closed door. Beloved throws her arms around Master Potter's neck and buries her head in His shoulder, pleading, "Don't make me go in there! I'm too afraid! I don't know if I can bear it! It was my fault, I was a bad little girl!"

"No, Beloved, you were just a child who was terribly abused and it was never your fault. I'm so sorry this happened to you, but I'm here and he can't hurt you anymore. If you'll trust Me, we'll walk through the door together. Healing will come as you allow Me to take you through the pain to forgiveness. But we can't go through that door unless you're willing."

Pausing for a moment, Holy Spirit reminds her of Master Potter's faithfulness, how He saved and delivered her from the Potter's Field and fashioned her into a beautiful pitcher. For her to become the glorious vessel of destiny, she must face the roots of her pain and be deeply healed. Only by seeing her childhood in the light of Master Potter's truth can she truly be set free.

Cradled in His arms, Beloved stands together with Master Potter before the bedroom door. She trembles as the voice of her drunken father rises above the pitiful sobs coming from the little girl named Forsaken.

Tearfully Beloved cries, "I want to go in there but I just don't think I can. I'm too afraid!"

"I'll keep you safe in My loving arms, Beloved," says Master Potter reassuringly.

Nestling close to Him, she takes a deep breath and cries, "Okay, as long as You're with me."

Painting the childhood scene, He reminds her, "It began the night when your mother left to give birth to your baby brother. She left you in your father's care hoping that he would stay sober."

She cries hysterically, "But he didn't! I begged him to leave me alone, but he hurt me anyway! I tried to tell mom when she came home, but she wouldn't listen to me! She just ignored me and told me to go play."

Suddenly the veil of time is removed and she sees her mother as a little girl suffering the same abuses she had to endure. Master Potter tenderly continues, "In her heart she knew, Beloved, but because she was so broken she could not stand up to your dad. You see, her dad was just like your own father. Out of great fear she made wrong choices and remained a victim of the generational sins of her family line. Holy Spirit hovered over her and wooed her many times, but to no avail.

"Sadly, your mother chose to live in a place of denial and unreality instead of allowing Me to usher her into liberty and destiny. In the end she couldn't help herself. But in the deepest core of her being she loved you desperately."

"But she didn't have time for me after my brother was born. He was so sick and demanded all her attention. I was left alone to cope with dad. After my brother died, she was always in bed, too depressed to do anything. I became the mother and wife. That's when the nights became so horrible."

Master Potter and Beloved survey the various scenes from her childhood. In her parent's room she sees her mother in bed with her arms covering her face. Behind her, Beloved sees what she had never seen before: evil, sinister talons piercing deeply into her mother's mind and heart. A spirit of grief and depression had gained complete control. A wild-eyed spirit of insanity circled the room mocking and jeering at her and spouting nonsensical rhymes.

"Beloved, after your brother's death she never left that place of grief. Insanity crept in and then took more territory each time she repelled Holy Spirit. She lived in such fear and agony that all she really wanted was to die. She felt like such a failure as a mother and a wife.

"After you ran away to work at Madam's, your mother finally asked Me to save her and now she is reunited with your little brother. I've passed on to you and your future generations the family blessings I ordained for her. Nothing is lost."

Replacing Anger With Compassion

Deep compassion for her mother bursts forth from Beloved in great gulping sobs. "Oh Lord, I didn't realize she was so afraid. All I knew was that she wasn't there for me. And it really hurt because I thought she was rejecting me. I thought that I wasn't a good enough daughter."

"She never meant to reject you, Beloved. She really loved you. She just wasn't well enough to express it."

"I really did love her; I just tried to protect myself by pretending I didn't. I thought it would hurt less, but that didn't work."

"Will you let Me take the bitterness and all the pain that's behind it?"

"Yes Lord, now that I understand that she only did what she could. It makes it so much easier to forgive her."

"Beloved, I am so proud of you. You have done so well. Every time you deal with one of these heart issues you come closer to your destiny," He says as they exit the bedroom door and walk down the hall. "But part of your heart is still shut down. You need to trust Me and be willing to go through this next door."

Chapter Forty-two

Golden Keys of Forgiveness

The heat in the kiln continues to intensify in the all-consuming refiner's fire.

Recognizing her bedroom door, Beloved panics. "No, no, not there. I don't want to go in there. Please, don't make me," she pleads as she clutches Master Potter and buries her face in His shoulder.

Tenderly holding her He speaks, "Beloved, he can't hurt you anymore. I'm in control this time and I'll protect you. Will you trust Me?"

With her face still buried, she hesitantly nods.

Turning the door handle, He carries Beloved into the darkened room. They enter just as her father is getting up from the bed, leaving little Forsaken weeping under the covers. Time freezes in the fiery vision and Master Potter tells her, "He doesn't have the power to harm you anymore. Now you can tell him what you've always wanted to say."

Still feeling vulnerable, she turns slowly to face her father. She stares at the floor, trembling in fear.

Master Potter says, "Go ahead, you're not Forsaken anymore, you're Beloved. Tell him what Forsaken, as a defenseless, helpless little child never had the power or voice to say."

Beloved hesitates, unable to make eye contact, and in a timid voice asks, "Why did you hurt me and make me think it was all my fault? I was just a little girl!"

Realizing that her father is locked in the past and can't hurt, hear or see her, she begins to feel safe in Master Potter's arms. "Year after year you came into my room and hurt me! You said it was our secret and I couldn't tell anyone."

"That's good, Beloved. You can say anything you want to. What are you feeling right now?"

Uncapped anger surfaces, and she blurts out, "You lied to me when you said mom would leave if she found out. I was so scared she'd go away and I'd be left with you."

Looking at Master Potter, as hot tears pour down her face, she says, "I felt so dirty. I don't think I can ever forgive him. He was so mean to me. I finally had to leave home just to get away from him. That's how I ended up at Madam's. He should be begging me to forgive him, but he's not even sorry! I want him to feel pain like I did! I wish he were dead!" Suddenly the flames flare up as her anger fuels the fire into a raging inferno.

Sitting down in the old rocking chair next to the bed, Master Potter holds her close. She lies like a limp rag doll in His arms and sobs until she can't cry anymore.

"You're safe now. He can't hurt you anymore. It broke My heart to see you suffer," says Master Potter as He continues to rock her.

Looking up with her big brown eyes into His tear-stained face, she cries, "I was so innocent. How could he do that to me?"

"Every person has free will. Each person's choices have the power to destroy or to bless. It wasn't right, and it wasn't My plan for you to suffer such devastation and betrayal, especially from your own parents. But My Cross has the power to bring life out of this terrible anguish. Your part now is to forgive."

"It's too painful. I could forgive the others but I can't forgive this. I can't do it. You're asking too much. Besides, You're all I need. I never want to see him again."

The purifying fires are unrelenting as Master Potter continues, "Beloved, I created you to experience deep intimacy with Me. The enemy has tried to prevent that by using your father's brokenness and perversion to shut down your ability to love and trust. Your fear of intimacy blocks our relationship, because painful memories and unforgiveness have locked the door of your heart."

Evil Consequences

Now weeping softly, she sighs and tells him, "I want You more than anything, but I still want my father to pay for what he did to me. He belongs in jail!"

"He already is, Beloved. Let me show you."

The scene changes and her father no longer appears so big and powerful. She notices how his outdated, tattered clothes hang on his emaciated frame. His eyes are sunken into a thin and bony face covered with a dirty, scraggly beard.

Once tall, strong and handsome, Beloved's father is now bent over with age and the burden of his sinful life. His eyes are dull and dead. She remembers looking in the cracked mirror in the Potter's Field and seeing that same look in her own eyes.

Prison bars crash down around him as she watches. Now, a heavy iron door slams shut with a loud, thundering boom. Her father looks around, eyes filled with terror and dread, as tormenting demons laugh cruelly at his captivity.

Beloved recoils in horror as she watches long, sharp talons sink even deeper into his mind—winding and vining around other talons that have long twisted and controlled it. Terrifyingly little is left of the soul God created; talons of perversion, rage and addiction have grown large and formed a thick, tangled system of demonic control.

Overwhelmed with sadness and grief, Beloved feels compassion well inside her for the first time as she realizes how deeply he is suffering. "That's why he acted like he did. The demons were fueling his addiction just like they did mine. He looks like he's going to die. Lord, can You free him?"

Master Potter gestures toward him. "I want to free both of you, but only your forgiveness and his repentance will open the prison door. Remember, the battleground is in your mind and heart. In this test you will become bitter or sweet. How you respond determines whether you will fulfill your ultimate destiny. You can disqualify yourself from your high calling by harboring judgments and bitterness, which will keep you captive to your past. Will you choose love, Beloved?"

I CHOOSE LOVE

The vision of her father disappears and she looks into the face of Master Potter. Softly weeping in His arms she says, "Yes Lord, I choose love."

Gently He leads her, "Will you forgive your father?"

Haltingly, painfully she weeps openly as she says, "Father…Father…I forgive you for abusing me and not taking care of us." She pauses and takes a deep breath, "I hated your cruelty, but I choose to forgive you." The hardness of her heart breaks open, releasing painful blockages of shame and devastation. She bursts into deep convulsive sobs as the years of bottled-up pain are released.

Mercy and compassion flood her as she cries, "I'm sorry I hated you. I don't want you to hurt anymore."

Master Potter strokes her hair and says, "Beloved, your hatred and judgment toward your father imprisoned you as well as him. You needed to ask his forgiveness for your hatred in order to break the curses of your own words."

Holy Spirit gently places His mantle of fiery conviction over Beloved. "Father, I was also wrong for hating you. I used to hide in my room at night and wish you would die. I want you to know Master Potter the way I know Him! Please forgive me."

The Lamb That Was Slain

As her words go forth in the unseen realm of the Spirit, golden keys of forgiveness unlock ancient doors of bondage.

She watches in horror an open vision of Master Potter as a spotless, innocent lamb being slain in darkness—before the foundation of the world. Unable to stop the slaughter, she watches the light glisten off the plunging knife blade. His life departs and His blood pours out.

Loud cracking noises rumble throughout the earth as generational curses shatter. Beloved feels shaking, like an earthquake under her feet. She grabs Master Potter to steady herself.

Angels apply His blood to the doorposts of past and future generations of her family, bringing deliverance and freedom. In the distance she hears the blast of an ancient shofar. The voice of His blood cries out, "Mercy and forgiveness. Mercy and forgiveness for all who ask."

The voice of the blood reverberates in the heavens, through earth and into the darkest abyss of hell. Satan and his angels scream and writhe as it renders the enemy's kingdom impotent. With no way to overcome its power and no place to hide, they curse and blaspheme as the blood's voice cries out again, pronouncing freedom for Beloved and her father.

Thunder, lightning, and whirlwinds of glory swirl around her. Radiant light illuminates through her clay vessel as the kiln turns into a golden furnace of healing. The dross of unforgiveness, bitterness and anger is demolished by His all-consuming refiner's fire.

Beloved feels the shackles of her judgment fall away. Freedom is released in her spirit and joy floods her being. She feels as light as air. She continues clutching Master Potter for fear she might float away. She revels with Master Potter in the new-found freedom she is experiencing as they laugh and continue to watch the celestial glory and light show.

Intercession

"Where is my father now? Did he get released from his cell?"

"No, Beloved," responds Master Potter. "You forgave him, but he can't be released until he repents." The vision of her father reappears and she watches as he cries out, "I want to die." He rattles the bars again and again, unable to free himself. She recognizes the tormenting voice of Suicide saying, "That can be arranged," as his python-like body slithers toward her father, seeking to crush what little remains of his will to live.

Beloved, who just a few minutes ago was wishing her father dead, screams out to Master Potter, "They're going to kill him. Do something." Master Potter replies, "I won't let them take his life now. I'm giving him another chance." He turns to Suicide, who is just beginning to coil around Beloved's father and with a whisper says, "Be gone."

The vile snake jerks his head toward Master Potter and drops to the floor. It writhes as if mortally wounded, rolling from back to front, hissing and gasping until it shrivels and is finally consumed in the fiery kiln. The vision of her father fades.

Awed at the power of Master Potter's words, she says, "You make it look so easy!"

He looks at her affectionately and chuckles. "Beloved, there's power in My words, power in My blood, power in My name, power in forgiveness—and My power resides in you, but you just don't realize it yet.

"There is real warfare for your father's soul. You need to continue to release My power as you intercede for him so I can deliver him into My Kingdom. No one is too lost to be found by Me."

Deep agonizing groans of intercession rise from her spirit as she cries out, "Save him, Lord!" His power through her prayers begins to break through the heavy oppression of the prison cell.

Chapter Forty-three

Glorious Reconciliation

As her intercession subsides, she is surprised to hear muffled weeping and looks around the room to see where the crying is coming from. Master Potter rises out of the rocking chair and carries Beloved to the bed.

"There's someone you need to meet. This is you when you were four years old. You've blamed and rejected little Forsaken and considered her your bad side in order to deal with the abuse. Your father convinced you that it was your own fault and said that you were a bad little girl."

As she looks down at the quivering heap, the sobs of little Forsaken under the blanket tug at Beloved's heart. "Help me Lord; I don't know what to do."

"You need to reconcile with the little girl inside of you, to forgive her—to forgive yourself."

Sitting down on the bed, He gently pulls back the covers and lifts Forsaken on His other knee. He puts Beloved's hand into hers. Looking at Forsaken, Beloved sees her dirty little smudged face and sad eyes. Compassion wells up in her. She begins to tremble and her breath comes in short uneven gasps. Beloved tries to hold back some deep traumatic emotion but is unable to as hot tears pour down her face.

"Forsaken, is that really you? You're so tiny and vulnerable. I didn't realize how little and helpless you were."

Forsaken shrinks back and tries to hide in Master Potter's robes.

Beloved is overwhelmed with the painful losses the little child has suffered. Beloved realizes how beautiful she really was and longs to know her.

"Lord, I don't understand, why is Forsaken separate from me?"

"Beloved, many times when someone is traumatized they wall themselves off and disassociate while the trauma is going on. You are really only one person, but that was the only way you knew to survive. It was as though you saw the little child in you, Forsaken, as the bad girl so you didn't have to feel defiled."

"But she's so damaged. I don't know if I want to be part of someone who is so damaged."

Master Potter replies, "But she is the part of you that you shut down. Through My blood you can forgive yourself and be healed, reconciled and made whole."

Beloved looks at little Forsaken and says, "Oh Lord, I do want to be reconciled. She's been through so much."

"Beloved, you need to embrace her."

Tenderly Beloved pulls Master Potter's sleeve away from Forsaken's face and says, "I'm not going to hurt you. Will you come out?"

Shyly little Forsaken tells Beloved, "I thought you didn't want me. I was trapped in that dark secret place where demons tormented me. They said you didn't love me or want me to live."

Beloved softly answers, "I'm so sorry. Will you forgive me? I thought you were bad, but I realize you were a victim like I was."

Forsaken hesitantly searches Beloved's eyes and finally nods. Beloved stretches out her arms invitingly and Forsaken buries her head on Beloved's chest and a torrent of pent-up emotion is released as tears wash down Forsaken's cheeks.

Beloved feels overwhelmed with Forsaken's pain and continues, "Please forgive me for rejecting you and for even hating you. I blocked out all those years because the pain and shame were too great for me. It wasn't your fault either." She gently rocks Forsaken as she continues to embrace the little sobbing girl.

As Beloved forgives herself, little Forsaken's voice comes forth. Beloved watches as she transforms from a dirty little waif into a beautiful little girl.

Master Potter looks tenderly at little Forsaken and Beloved and proclaims, "I break the code of secrecy and silence over your lives and I free both of you to have a voice again, to feel again, to live again, to play and laugh again."

Beloved says, "You're so beautiful and you have such life about you. I think I left all my childhood playfulness behind."

Giggling, Forsaken says, "Maybe I can teach you how to play. Bet I can beat you at jacks!"

"You can not!"

"Can so."

Holy Spirit appears as smoky golden flames, bringing the fire of glorious reconciliation to rest upon Beloved and Forsaken.

Forsaken leans over and motions Beloved closer as if to tell her a secret and touches her shoulder and says, "Tag you're it," as she jumps down off Master Potter's lap.

Squealing with delight, Beloved chases Forsaken around the room.

Roaring with laughter, Master Potter watches them embrace each other and merge into one.

CHAPTER FORTY-FOUR

SPIRIT OF ADOPTION

Beloved questions Master Potter, "Why has my life been so hard? It could have been so much easier! Why didn't you give me a normal father and mother? Why has there been so much pain and loss in my life?"

"Beloved, I chose the exact time and the family into which you were born. All fathers and mothers fail miserably, for you were born into an evil, sinful world. Even so, the kindness of God is well able to deliver you from generational curses and lead you into eternal life. If your life had not been so difficult, if all your needs were met by them—you wouldn't need Me.

"Only I can fill that God-given void in your heart. My Father and I purposefully designed all vessels to find complete satisfaction and joy in only one place: the Father heart of God."

LOVED FROM ETERNITY PAST

Beloved sees herself in the spirit as a pulsating golden light, an unborn destiny, being sent forth by the very breath of God into her family line. Even her generation was chosen and ordained by Master Potter before the foundations of the earth.

Suddenly she sees herself hidden deep inside her mother's womb and she feels Master Potter's hands forming and molding her. At the time of her delivery, she hears her parents arguing, and she cringes back in the birth canal, not wanting to be born. But the voice of Master Potter woos her, "Beloved, I want you to experience life. I have loved you from eternity past, and all the days of your life are written and scheduled in My book.

"I want your life to be as beautiful as it was in My mind's eye when I first conceived of you. I have redemptive purposes in the circumstances of your life and the family I place you in, so come forth little one. You are not a mistake—your name, Beloved, is written on the palm of My hand."

Beloved gasps with wonder as she watches the spectacle unfold in the vision before her eyes. In just moments she realizes that the truth presented in the vision is changing her from deep within.

A demonic shroud of generational spirits of rejection and death dissipates as Master Potter's words penetrate her spirit, freeing her to choose life. Weeping turns to laughter and celebration as the heavy oppression lifts.

She shouts, "Lord, You wanted me to live and even to be in this family. You have a plan and prophetic purpose for my life. It doesn't matter if I don't totally comprehend it all. I just know You love me and want me. That's all that matters."

Beloved feels whole for the first time in her life. Her senses seem to come alive. Her vision becomes crystal clear. She's captivated by new smells. She can almost feel the spiritual energy flowing around her. The dark blanket of numbness has lifted and even her thoughts seem clearer. For once in her life, she can truly, honestly feel like herself!

Brooding over her, Holy Spirit releases divine revelation of the spirit of adoption and the Father's love for her. In her spirit she is hit by wave after wave of His liquid love. She hears, "This is My daughter, Beloved, in whom I am well pleased."

Deep within her mended heart, a cry comes forth: "Oh, Abba, my Father. I will love You forever."

Chapter Forty-five

Lord! Turn Off the Heat!

The fiery yellow and white flames shoot through the floor of the brick kiln, licking and climbing the walls and exploding out of the chimney. The rising fire and smoke mingle above the Potter's House.

The vessels inside are white-hot and phosphorescent, and they groan as they endure the refiner's fire. A literal chemical change takes place inside of each vessel. They will never be the same, for they are changed forever as His cross is applied to their lives.

Grumbling and Complaining

"This is just ridiculous!" Steadfast, the chatty serving platter, grumbles from the back of the kiln. "Who came up with this bright idea? If this is what the Potter calls promotion, I want to go back to the wilderness! It was uncomfortably warm, but nothing like this. Let's make our requests known. Come on everyone, join in."

All the other vessels beg Master Potter, "When are You going to turn off the heat? We're all dying in here!"

The rich baritone voice of Harvester bellows above the din, "Lord, have You forgotten us? It's not for myself, You understand, but it's for all these little, fragile vessels. Hey Comrade, are you still alive?"

"Just barely, my friend. I know Master Potter made me a squatty mug but I feel more like one of those hot, fiery stones in the throne room."

Long Suffering moans, "I don't think we'll ever get out of this fire. We're doomed for sure."

Sweet Adoration, the delicate perfume bottle, shyly warns, "Haven't we learned by now that murmuring and complaining only bring more fire? Lord, don't listen to her—really, we're as happy as we can be."

Joyful, the wine goblet, chimes in, "Yeah! Praise the Lord!"

The voice of Fearless rises above the roar of the fire, "Quit whining, and quit pretending that everything's okay. These fires are only a season He has allowed. Remember? It's all a part of our preparations to become beautiful vessels. Don't let your hearts faint! At just the right time He'll turn the fire off and open the door."

"Of course you're right," says Harvester, as sweat pours off his vessel and drips onto Comrade's head. "I keep forgetting that this is all part of the process of becoming vessels of honor."

"I don't know if anything is worth this," says Long Suffering, fanning herself with last week's church bulletin.

A Prophetic Vision

Looking into the relentless fire, Beloved sees a prophetic vision. She watches in amazement as she sees the magnificent flagships being loaded at Comfort Cove. Beautifully glazed vessels of all shapes and sizes sparkle in the sun.

As the men load the vessels, she sees a wine carafe and realizes it's Fearless and a team of goblets being packed into wooden crates headed for the nations. She sees purple grape designs on their sides and the sun glistening off their pearl white glazes.

Beloved yells across the kiln to Fearless, "Master Potter just showed me a vision of you and your team. You were being sent out to the nations with eight wine goblets. They were just like you, beautifully glazed, wearing their armor and ready to go."

Hearing Beloved's vision, the vessels now have renewed hope that they'll be on the flagship.

"All right, Fearless!" says Steadfast, slapping him on the back. "You'll even have a team of goblets!"

The vessels' excitement builds. "Wow, a pearl white glaze. What a change."

"I love grapes," says Joyful, the wine goblet. "Maybe I'll get them too."

"Did you see me? Did you see me, Beloved?" asks little Comrade. "Was I being loaded on the ship too?"

As the fires continue to rage and more time passes the vessels grow increasingly impatient, generating a new level of frustration. They complain loudly, desperate to be heard over the fire's roar.

"I don't see a ship anywhere around," says Fearless, sulking in the corner. "I've been waiting forever and still no ship. Not even a dinghy. I'm not pearl white either; I'm still this dreary grey color. I think you just made that whole story up, Beloved."

"Why would I make that up? I really saw it."

Harvester jumps to Beloved's defense. "You apologize to her. She's my friend and I know she wouldn't do anything like that."

"Why should I apologize?" asks Fearless, approaching Harvester, who towers over him in a confrontational manner.

Harvester picks him up and draws his fist back. Fearless's feet dangle above the floor.

Master Potter peers through the spy hole. "Is everything okay in here?"

Harvester drops Fearless, and they stand side-by-side like best buddies, talking a mile a minute over the top of each other. "Everything's great."

"Really."

"We were just having a little fun."

"Right, fun, fun, fun with my friend," says Harvester as he pokes Fearless on the arm.

Master Potter says, "I was just checking to see if you're done or if you maybe need a little more time."

All the vessels rush toward the spy hole as one unit, jostling each other and yelling about their excellent maturity levels and how well they all get along.

"Yes, we've really learned to love each other," says Joyful as all the pots vigorously nod their heads in unison.

"My dross is gone. It's a miracle!" shouts Comrade.

The vessels all shake their heads and agree that their dross is gone too.

Harvester bellows out, "Please Lord, turn it off! We're finished. I'm sure we're cooked."

"Well done, even," adds Fearless.

"I've heard your cries and I know the pain you're in. Just a little while longer and you'll be released." Turning the knobs slowly He shuts down the kiln.

Even with the fire off, the kiln is still like an inferno with the walls and floor glowing red-hot. They continue to cry out, "Lord, if You love us then turn off the heat! We've been interceding, like You taught us, day and night!"

"Why don't You help us? Why don't You turn off the fire?"

"It's off," Master Potter gently answers.

"I think He's hard of hearing. Yell louder, everyone."

Their voices rise up in unison, "Open the door! We can't take any more!"

"We're dying in here!" yells Comrade.

"It's off," He responds patiently.

"No, Lord, You don't understand! It's still hot. If You loved us You would turn off the fire and get us out of here. Please open the door!"

Waiting on God

"I know it doesn't feel like I've turned it off, but I have. You need time to heal after your heart surgery. If I open the door before the kiln cools and fresh air rushes in while you are still red hot, you will crack or even explode."

Valiant and the other guardian angels are enjoying the vessels' perplexity. They know that only through the vessels' faith and patience will they inherit their promises. Still they are ever on the alert to carefully guard the destinies as joyful servants fulfilling God's purposes in the lives of each individual.

In the slowly receding heat they minister sweet sleep and refreshing to the exhausted vessels. The vessels dream of being beautifully glazed, admired by everyone and moving in powerful signs and wonders.

Chapter Forty-six

Holy Spirit Intervention

Not everyone in the fiery kiln is experiencing pleasant dreams. While the other vessels sleep peacefully, Beloved tosses and turns. A dark stream of frightening images and foul odors assaults her mind. The enemies of her soul that have stopped her throughout her lifetime are quick to question the healing of her abusive past. The nasty horde sends a demonically fueled nightmare to challenge the work of Holy Spirit. The haunting dream is a familiar terror she has relived many times over the years.

It starts off as usual with the musty odor of unwashed sheets and blankets. The air hangs still and heavily oppressive, making it difficult to breathe. She feels a disruption and agitation in her spirit and then the old fear rises slowly from deep within. Suddenly her muscles tense in a primordial readiness to run from her enemies.

The door to her room slowly opens and the nauseating odors of whiskey and cigar smoke assault her senses. Her stomach churns in revulsion. Slow stumbling footsteps approach her bed and the face of her father emerges through the darkness towering over her.

Putting his fingers to his mouth he shushes her and drops down hard on the bed. The old metal springs rattle and the thin mattress slopes to one side under his heavy weight. She can feel his clammy hands touch her bare skin as he pulls up her nightgown.

She tries to scream and run away but as always terror holds her bound in its paralyzing grip. Struggling to wake up, she sees her father's ugly contorted face transform into Pastor Beguiler's paunchy face. The little girl on the bed becomes her daughter.

Spiritual Warfare

"No! Don't touch her! Stop! Stop! Master Potter, help!" In that place of being not quite awake and not quite asleep, she wars in the Spirit, struggling on behalf of her daughter.

Many miles away, Purity puts her nightgown on after another lonely day. Since mother left, life has become a matter of survival. She has grown up quickly under the stern discipline of Grandfather Beguiler.

Whenever she finds a quiet time she dreams about those years before mom had to leave; sometimes it makes her feel better. But tonight she wonders if she'll ever see her again, and the memories only bring her into a deeper depression.

Grandfather Beguiler took her to his house and gave her the name Promiscuous before she even understood what it meant. She remembered what her mother told her and had refused to answer to that name but in the end, and after many beatings, she began responding when called.

Enchanter remarried immediately and started a new family. He never acknowledges Purity as his daughter and only speaks to her to issue an order, as he would any servant. Usually he just ignores her, while her stepsister and stepbrother are lavished with attention. For three years, Purity has had to pretend he isn't her father. Love has been replaced with only loathing for him.

Grandmother is so cowed by Grandfather Beguiler that Purity feels only pity for her. Sometimes Grandmother slips her a secret delicacy from the kitchen and smiles at her or leaves a surprise under her pillow. Purity always knows it must go unacknowledged, but she clings to those little moments of pleasure and fantasizes about what might have been.

Purity has just turned 13 years old, and she is now beginning to fill out her clothes with new curves. Confused about the physical and emotional changes taking place, she longs to talk to someone, and yearns for her mother even more.

Oh Lord, if only she were here! She'd explain what's happening to my body and why Grandpa stands at the entrance to my bedroom at night and stares at me. I'm so afraid! Please bring my mommy back. I'll be good if only you'll do this one thing. Crusader is the only one who really talks to me but he's too little to help.

Familiar Spirits Attack Again

Beloved awakens frantically from her nightmare. Sitting up quickly she feels defiled and unclean. She immediately becomes aware of an evil presence in the room. "Master Potter, save her. Please save her!"

The familiar family spirit screeches, "He isn't going to save her; she's just like you—promiscuous! Like mother, like daughter. Right, Forsaken? I'll always be here to remind you how much you enjoyed those nights with your father!"

Holy Spirit charges into the fray, telling Beloved to put on her armor. "Stand in your healing and hold your ground."

Trembling with familiar fear, she looks to Him for help.

Holy Spirit hands her a new weapon, an ancient shofar. "Release the sound of the Blood, Beloved. Remember your forgiveness broke the generational curses. As long as you allow them, those familiar spirits will return. But you now have the authority by the power of the Blood of the slain Lamb to command them to leave."

Dressed for battle in her armor, she is consumed by righteous anger. She blows several blasts on the shofar and commands the evil spirits, "By the power of the Blood I command you to leave and never come back. I am healed. I am His Beloved. You no longer have any authority over me or my children."

Falling to her knees Beloved intercedes for Purity.

"Please Lord, send warring angels to protect her from the enemy. Don't let Pastor Beguiler harm her. Please protect my little girl. You said You would do battle for my loved ones, so now I'm pleading with You—please, please, do what I cannot."

Chapter Forty-seven

Visitation in the Night

Activated by Beloved's prayers, a cool gentle breeze sweeps down from the mountaintop swirling and drifting into the commune. Leaving dazzling trails of sparkling light against the black sky, it wafts into Purity's small room at the back of the tent. Unobserved by Purity, two huge warrior angels enter the room and stand in front of the mat where she sleeps, their flashing swords drawn and ready for battle. Their glistening wings extend to form a canopy of light and protection over her.

She quietly weeps, "Mom, where are you? They call me bad names and say I do bad things. They tell lies about you and say you died in the desert, but somehow, I know you didn't. You told me to take care of my brother but I can't. I can't even talk to him unless we sneak to the outskirts of the oasis."

"It used to be so wonderful—the way you would hold me, sing to me and tell me stories about Master Potter. I don't understand! I know you love me, but I'm just so lonely. I wish you were here with me. You always told me to be brave, and I'm being as brave as I can. But why can't you be brave and come and get me?"

Her pillow is soon drenched with tears as little Purity sobs out her frustrations and fear. The terror of grandfather's nightly visits has left her cold and trembling under her blanket. Steeling herself against what is sure to come, she continues to sob.

"Grandfather makes me feel so awful when he looks at me. He's accused me of being with one of the boys. He said I did dirty things with him. But I swear I didn't, Mom. I really didn't. You told me Master Potter would take care of me. Where is He now? I need someone to help me."

The Assault

The flap to her room opens. Purity holds her breath and closes her eyes, wanting desperately to escape. She pulls the cover over her head and curls into a fetal position as she prays for a way of escape. Terror rises up in the pit of her stomach and travels to her chest, finally lodging in a silent scream.

The horror of little girls from generations past convulses within her. *Mommy, mommy, help me! You always told me what to do. Please tell me now.*

Purity can hear his heavy breathing as he approaches and stands staring down at the pitiful little mound before him.

Maybe if I don't move and pretend to be asleep, he'll go away, she thinks. But then he gruffly whispers her name. "Promiscuous, wake up." The throaty sound of his voice sends chills down her little frame.

Trembling, she pleads softly, "Please, please don't do this, Grandfather."

She feels the cover being pulled away and as he bends down his hot breath nauseatingly drifts over her. Purity cries out, "Please, Master Potter, make him go away! Mommy said if I cried out to You, You'd help me. Please come!"

Many miles away Beloved enters into a place in the spirit realm where time and distance no longer exist. Gripped with travail, she wrestles against the demonic forces assigned to her children, with moans and groans erupting from deep within her inner being. "Master Potter, please save her."

The resurrection power of Heaven backs Beloved's words. Unseen by Purity, the two angelic warriors suddenly throw her grandfather against the tent wall. Peeking out from under her cover, Purity can only make him out dimly in the dark room and is too stunned to figure out what just happened. She can only stare in wonder as he curses and starts back toward her mat. Once again, unseen hands throw him violently away from her. Picking his frame off the floor, Grandfather Beguiler runs out of the room in terror.

Purity's voice crying out had brought the household out of their beds in time to see him exit her room. In a terrible rage he orders them all to clear out, except for his wife.

False Accusations

Nervously wiping his brow, he orders his wife to sit down. Pausing for a moment to gather his thoughts he paces around the room and then sits in front of her. Looking at the distraught face of this woman he once thought beautiful and now finds repulsive and old, he tells his story.

"I heard a noise and went to investigate. It was coming from Promiscuous's room. I entered and found her with a young man. I ordered the scoundrel to leave, which enraged Promiscuous. She threatened to tell everyone that I had tried to rape her. That's when she cried out. I turned to run and that's when everyone saw me in the hall leaving her room."

Pastor Beguiler's tirades usually leave his wife gazing at the floor and submitting to whatever he wishes. But this time her sad eyes never leave his face. Slowly his voice becomes less angry and more pleading. He realizes she knows the truth.

Without saying one word or asking what his wishes are, she summons her servant and orders her to take Purity to another household immediately.

Back in her room, Purity can't understand what happened but she knows it was Master Potter who came to her rescue. Tears flow again, but this time in gratitude as the servant enters her room and packs her few belongings. She no longer has to worry about visits in the night from Grandfather. Love and gratitude toward Master Potter fill her. The huge angels take their place at her side and follow her into the night.

Beloved prays for hours until Holy Spirit tells her that victory has been gained. Now the excruciating pain of their separation overwhelms Beloved. *Lord, thank You for the assurance that all is well, but please let me go to Deeper Life and get Purity and Crusader.*

The anguish lying just beneath the surface of her consciousness sweeps over her in wave after painful wave. Sobbing until there are no more tears left, she finally falls to sleep, utterly exhausted.

Valiant steps in from the shadows and touches her brow, bringing rest and peace to Master Potter's Beloved.

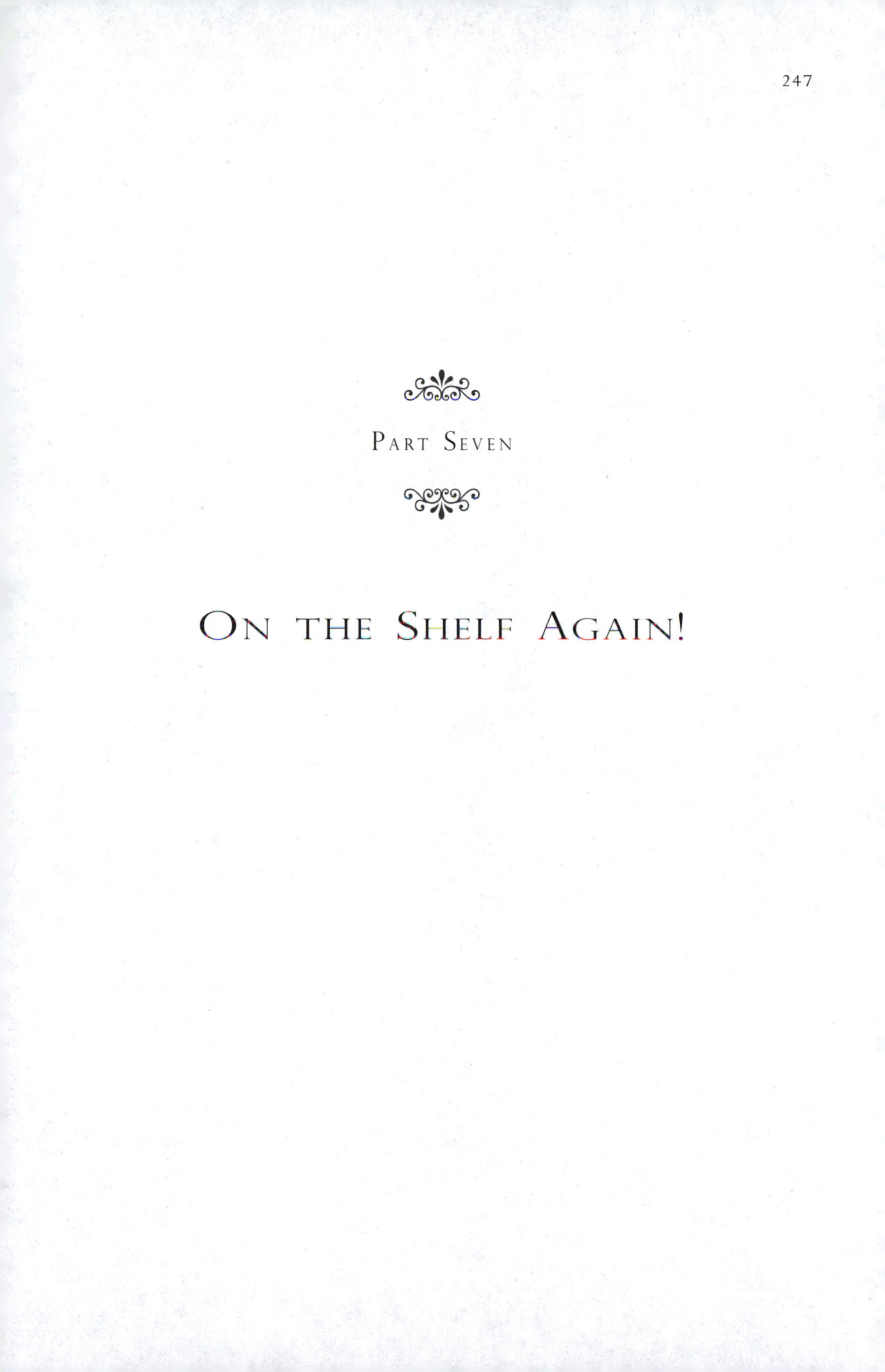

Part Seven

On the Shelf Again!

Chapter Forty-eight

The Good, the Bad and the Really Ugly!

Sitting inside the cold, dark kiln the vessels awaken to the sound of metal rods being loosened on the outside. They hold their breath as the door slowly creaks open. Light comes streaming in, momentarily blinding them. Master Potter smiles as He watches them squinting, trying to see how beautiful they have become.

Master Potter pulls them out into the bright daylight and places them next to each other on a long wooden board.

"You've passed this test! I'm very proud of you all."

A shock runs through the vessels as they realize how bare and naked they look. Beloved tries to conceal her astonishment when she sees Comrade's new appearance and quickly looks at the other vessels around her. Dismayed, she realizes all of them are ugly, and she feels miserable as she wonders what she must look like. *We're just dull; I thought we'd be shiny with beautiful colors reflecting off our glazes. What happened?*

Sweet Adoration, the perfume vial, cries out as she is carried into the sunlight, "Am I beautiful yet? Am I done?"

Long Suffering replies, "Honey, you just look old and dry. You're not even glazed, just like the rest of us. This kiln experience is like a nightmare I can't wake up from."

Disgusted, Harvester bellows, "I can't believe it! After all the fire and pain I've been through, and I'm not even glazed. This is unbelievable!"

Arguments erupt as the vessels try to figure out what went wrong.

Fearless yells, "I thought we were supposed to have some color and be ready to go by now! Hey, Beloved! You just prophesied I would have a purple grape design on a beautiful white glaze and be off to the nations! Talk about missing it! What happened?"

Embarrassed, Beloved drops her head. "Honestly Fearless…really, I saw you and your wine goblets being loaded onto the flagship! I promise."

"Come on you guys, don't be so hard on her, she's just learning. She probably got her prophetic timing mixed up—by ten or twenty years," says Comrade, coming to her defense.

After a while, Master Potter quiets them. "Beloved, the prophetic word you had for Fearless was right."

Turning to Fearless, Master Potter continues. "Beloved never said *when* you'd go on the flagship. Prophetic timing can be a major stumbling block because My ways are hidden! Just because I show someone a vision today doesn't mean it will happen tomorrow. My words are to give hope and encouragement for your destiny. Although accurate, they are still in the future."

Another Firing?

Speaking to the group of disappointed vessels He says: "You're right; you're not glazed yet. This was only the first firing. You are now in the stage I call bisqueware. But you have all been changed and matured by My refiner's fire."

Long Suffering turns to Beloved. "This doesn't sound good. Did He just say there's more than one firing? I don't think I could live through another one!"

Sweet Adoration looks lovingly to Master Potter. "But Lord, we're so ugly! Just look at us! No one will even notice us except to laugh and poke fun."

Master Potter holds her out proudly for the others to see. "You look wonderful to Me, but others will not see your beauty until you're glazed. You must go through a higher firing to melt the silica, which are small particles of glass in your glaze. They melt only at extremely high temperatures. This molten glassy finish will seal the surface of your porous earthenware vessel and enable you to hold My substances."

Placing her back on the board, He tells them, "Tonight, I will pour golden healing oil into Sweet Adoration, but it will evaporate rapidly because she has not been glazed."

Shuddering, Beloved asks, "Do we have to go back into the fire right now?"

"No, not right now. I have other plans for you. You're all coming into a new season of refreshment."

"I'm ready!" shouts Joyful the wine goblet. "Let the celebration begin."

As He finishes speaking, Master Potter opens the large studio windows, allowing the gentle sea breezes to bring sweet fragrances from His gardens into the fireside room. Then Holy Spirit swirls throughout the room in a gust of wind, bringing refreshing and mirth. A mighty anointing of joy bubbles up within the vessels, bringing relief from the hot fires as they celebrate the new season ahead.

The vessels pray for each other, giggling and chatting, and then finally settle down to rest on the shelves.

BACK TO THE POTTER'S FIELD

Master Potter says, "I'm assembling groups to go down to the Potter's Field and rescue other broken vessels. Fearless, would you like to head up a team and take Joyful and some others with you?"

Joyful, the wine goblet, excited and wobbling a bit, says, "Wow! I'd love to go with Fearless! Who else wants to go? What about you guys over there?" Delight bubbles up and spills onto those around her. "I can't wait to introduce my old friends to Master Potter!"

Steadfast and Harvester, always ready for adventure, follow Joyful's lead. Harvester yells, "I've been waiting for this! I've got the tracts."

"Follow me, troops," Fearless shouts while heading out the door.

Sweet Adoration yells as she runs to catch up. "What are the 'Four Spiritual Laws' again? I keep getting points two and three mixed up! Hey, wait for me!"

Master Potter smiles and shakes his head. "Aren't you forgetting something?" Fearless stops abruptly, and the vessels following his lead all plow into him and end up in a pile on the floor. Master Potter gently helps them to their feet.

"What did we forget? We're ready, willing and able," says Harvester.

"I think I know," replies Sweet Adoration. "It's our armor, isn't it?"

"Yes, it's your armor. I don't think you want to fight the enemy on the Potter's Field without it, do you?" asks Master Potter.

"About face, troops," yells Fearless. "Everyone, run—don't walk—to get your armor." After a short delay to find and sort their armor, the vessels help each other dress.

"Wow, this is really tarnished," says Comrade, looking at his breastplate.

At Fearless's command, they all line up to take inventory. "Everyone got their shields to quench the fiery darts of the enemy?" The vessels all wave their shields wildly above their heads. "How about your swords?" After a quick check to make sure everyone is fully clad, they turn and march out the door.

"Now this is what I call an army," bellows Harvester. "Lookin' good, troops!"

"To the Potter's Field," yells Joyful.

"Yes, to the Potter's Field," they all shout in reply.

The group left in the fireside room chatter excitedly as they swap war stories from their fiery kiln experience and wait for the others to return.

Reconciliation

At the end of the day, the weary yet ecstatic troop returns. The room bursts into joyous applause when new vessels snatched from the Potter's Field are placed on the shelves. Master Potter carefully places a broken sugar bowl on the shelf beside Beloved and Comrade. "Look who they brought in! You knew her as Turncoat, but I've always called her Faithful."

Comrade tells her, "We were rescued too, Turncoat. Oops, I mean Faithful! You knew me as Friendless at Madam False Destiny's Inn, but Master Potter changed my name to Comrade. Do you remember Forsaken? She was a singer for Madam. Her name is now Beloved!"

Faithful looks away as her face flushes. She stares at her feet. Beloved remembers the argumentative interchange they had on the Potter's Field and tries to figure out how to put Faithful at ease. "I guess we were both really desperate last time we met."

"Oh yes," responds Faithful. "I had just arrived at the Potter's Field myself, and I was so scared. I-I'm sorry I couldn't help you."

"I was frightened too. In the Potter's Field we were both just trying to survive. Neither of us was thinking about anyone else's well-being."

"But Forsaken, I mean Beloved, I'm sorry I was so mean to you that day. I was always jealous of your position at Madam's. I was just an employee, but you were like her daughter. You sang so beautifully and had the spotlight and Madam's attention. I was glad when I saw that day that you had ended up like I did."

"Oh Faithful, I was so mean to you at Madam's. I felt you were beneath me. I really was a snob. I'm so sorry."

"I'm sorry too," says Faithful. "I should have at least tried to be nice to you, even if I couldn't help."

Beloved hugs the sugar bowl. "I'm so glad you're here! I forgive you. Will you forgive me too?"

"Yes, of course."

Beloved responds, "What's past is past. We both have an exciting journey ahead."

"I'm so happy to be out of the Potter's Field and here with some familiar faces," Faithful tells Comrade and Beloved.

I WANT THE BEST SEAT

Whistling softly, Master Potter returns with other vessels from the kiln, arranging them strategically. He sets a large sturdy casserole dish named Diligence next to Comrade.

Diligence complains to the other pots: "I don't want to be over here! I'm sure Master Potter put me on the wrong shelf. That group over there is more my style, and, besides, they have a much better view of the harbor. They appear to be wealthy, and not everyone is gifted to work with the rich. Don't take this personally, but I feel called to pastor folks like them."

Abundance, the large fruit bowl on the shelf above Beloved, joins in. "Come to think of it, I wonder why He didn't display me on the mantel? As a woman, I certainly deserve as much exposure in the church as the men are getting. Don't you think so, Beloved?"

"Well, I think that Master Potter is the One who—"

"After all, that mantel looks like a platform of prominence and authority! I know I've been in a dry season, but He's called me as an evangelist, and I've already started moving in signs and wonders!"

Comrade turns to Beloved. "Pay no attention to Diligence and Abundance; they just like to complain. Besides, have you noticed that they're really ugly? They're uglier than we are, that's for sure!"

THE DISCIPLINE OF FASTING

"Hey," Harvester's booming voice captures the attention of everyone in the room. "I just read this great book on fasting. It said that we could attain spiritual maturity by going on a fast. Isn't that great?"

The excited vessels all crowd around pledging their participation. "That's a great idea!"

"I want to fast."

"Me too."

"Let's do it!"

Finally, the excitement settles down and Comrade questions sheepishly, "What's a fast?"

The vessels all look perplexed until Harvester explains, "A fast just means going without food for a while."

Smiles fade, and the vessels all look at the floor or the ceiling and finally just shuffle away. "Fine," yells Harvester. "Just fine! I'll do it myself if none of you want to be spiritual! I'll show you! I think I'll do a 40-day water fast. How hard could it be?"

Exciting News

Finally, only Comrade and Faithful, the newly saved sugar bowl, are awake.

"I'm much too excited to sleep! I can't believe Master Potter came for *me*. When I looked into His eyes for the very first time, I knew that He loved me. It's hard to explain—He loved me just for who I am; I didn't have to pretend to be someone else. What a relief! I can't believe I'm here. And I can't believe that people from my past are here, and they've all got a new name, too."

"I can remember when you were back at Madam's shuffling the cards. I lost lots of money to you," Comrade says with a grimace. "I had a gambling problem then, and it got me into a lot of trouble. I don't even like to think about it now. It seems like it was another person then, not even me."

Faithful looks away.

"What's the matter? Did I say something wrong?"

"Oh, Comrade, I didn't always shuffle the deck straight. You were set up so many times. I used to get a percentage of the winnings at the Inn. I really needed the money. Could you ever forgive me?"

Surprised by his own response, Comrade tenderly looks at the broken sugar bowl and says, "I forgive you…you are no longer Turncoat, remember? Now you are Faithful! We both have a lot to put behind us. Who would have thought that we'd both end up here together? Master Potter is so merciful."

"I never knew what happened to Forsaken, I mean Beloved. After we had that big fight, I never saw her again. I was in the Potter's Field off and on for years. One day, someone came looking for Beloved. She was very disappointed when I told her that she had been gone for years. I had no idea—"

"Her? Her who?" Comrade babbled.

"I don't know. A young lady, she was really pretty—"

"We've got to tell Beloved!" Comrade jumps to his feet, loses his balance and tips over backwards. In his frazzled embarrassment, he blurts out, "D-d-don't just stand there—do something!"

Clambering to his feet, he grabs Faithful's hand and drags her over to where Beloved lies sleeping. Faithful says, "What's happening? Why are you so excited?"

Beloved was in the middle of a wonderful dream. She and Master Potter were flying over Comfort Cove. "Look at all the houses below. Each house represents at least one person that I want to bring into Father's Kingdom." As Beloved looked down at Comfort Cove and then to the horizon, she heard Comrade's voice in the distance..."Beloved, Beloved, BELOVED, BEEE-LOV-ED—WAKE UP!"

Trying to conceal her irritation, and trying to cling to her dream, she mumbles, "Not now—sleeping."

"But you have to hear what Faithful has to say."

"Tomorrow."

"No, now. Tell her, Faithful; tell her."

Faithful looks at Beloved and back to Comrade. "I think I'll come back tomorrow." She tries to hide her nervousness by holding her body rigid, but her lid starts to rattle. "Oh dear," she says.

Comrade steps in front of her to block her exit. "Now, Now, NOW! This can't wait!" he says.

"Well," began Faithful, raising her voice slightly to be heard over her rattling top. "Once when I was in the Potter's Field, it was probably about a year ago, maybe a little less. Anyway, I was digging through the trash, and someone wanted to know about you."

Comrade is shifting his weight from one foot to the other. Unable to contain himself any longer, he blurts out, "It was a girl. It was your daughter. It was Purity!"

Chapter Forty-nine

The Settlers

For a while, it was quite an exciting adventure for the teams who went back to Comfort Cove on mission trips. They marveled at how they could actually hear Holy Spirit telling them what to do. They visited the taverns and fishing docks, bringing in more and more vessels.

Beloved and all her friends were constantly looking for Purity when they went to town, but they were unable to find her or anyone who had seen her.

Sitting on the shelf again after one of the trips, Beloved looks toward the familiar stone-hewed fireplace. She remembers her own beginning with Master Potter and the lessons she learned at His hands. *I remember sitting in Master Potter's lap in His big leather chair. He held me close to His heart and sang over me as we watched the fire dance.*

Lost in thought, she reminisces about her wilderness journey and the children she left behind. Tears well up again, and Holy Spirit reminds her it's time to pray.

Suddenly her children's faces appear before her, causing her mother's heart to ache, especially when she sees the deep sadness in their eyes. Silently interceding in the Spirit, she prays for protection and strength in the battle that is being waged against them. She weeps softly until she senses an assurance from Holy Spirit that all is well.

Beloved fights discouragement by remembering what Master Potter had showed her in the tent of the Lord about praying for her children. She never stops interceding for them.

The Grumpy Faster

As each day passes, Harvester not only becomes thinner, but he also becomes grumpier. He spends more and more time to himself and develops a bit of a holier-than-thou attitude. He begins making frequent mission trips into Comfort Cove alone and brags about his newfound spirituality through fasting.

"I thought fasting was supposed to make you godly. It's just making him mean," says Patience.

"I think that each day he fasts he becomes less like Master Potter," says Long Suffering.

The Seasons of Change

Beloved enjoys the frequent trips where she and her friends snatch other broken vessels from the demonic hordes roaming the Potter's Field. Always mindful of how hard the process was for her, she's quick to make friends and encourage them. She enjoys watching Master Potter lovingly take these new pots through the same processes and seasons she has been through.

One day, Master Potter gently picks up her old friend Faithful. "Goodbye, Beloved. I'll see you again," she says as she is carried through the double doors and out into the brick courtyard. Beloved waves and remembers only too well the crushing, but also the freedom, she received from Unrelenting Love.

She longs for the day that she will see Faithful again but knows that she will be soaking under the waterfall for a long time.

She remembers how painful the wilderness was to her and always intercedes fervently for vessels making the perilous journey.

Breaking His Fast

One day Harvester returns from a solo trip to Comfort Cove. Tense and defensive, he storms off by himself to a lower shelf. Concerned for his friend, Comrade cautiously approaches.

"Hi, Harvester! Mind if I sit down?"

Harvester motions with his hand. "What do you want?"

"I just want to make sure you're okay. I mean, you seem moody lately."

"I'm fine."

Comrade leans closer to Harvester. "Say that again."

"I'm fine-fine-FINE!"

Comrade bursts out laughing. "Oh Harvester, I can smell fish 'n chips on your breath. You've been stopping by the tavern for lunch on the way to the Potter's Field, haven't you?"

Finally the story comes out. "I thought I could fast for 40 days, and after I made that boast in front of everyone, I was too proud to admit I couldn't. Since day five, I've been sneaking off and eating one meal a day at the tavern. I'm so ashamed."

"Oh Harvester, let's go tell the others. We've got to get some more food in your stomach and get you back to normal. We miss your enthusiastic personality and encouraging attitude. I promise you, the group will be thrilled that you've given up your 40-day water fast."

BORED, BORED, BORED

Months turn into years, and the vessels grow familiar and bored, moving into predictable systems of order and routine by playing it safe. Preferring the comfort and safety of the shelves, they venture into the Potter's Field less and less frequently, and eventually not at all.

"After all," they complacently boast, "we've made it through the most devastating fire. We've paid our dues and brought many to salvation. It's time for those new pots to go out there! We'll just stay in the Potter's House. Everyone knows we're proven warriors, skilled in surviving spiritual wars."

The unglazed vessels make lots of wrong choices as they unconsciously draw back from risk. Their reputations and comforts begin taking priority, even over rescuing others from the doom of the Potter's Field. Promotion and self-protection become the gods of their lives as they jockey for rank and position. The offense of the Cross is gradually forgotten, replaced by cheap grace that allows them to live unchallenged. Their fiery zeal is replaced by compromise.

Beginning with one small decision and then another, over the days, months and years, the dark cancer of apathy spreads slowly and subtly into the hidden recesses of their thoughts.

THE SUBTLE SNARES OF SATAN

Satan does not forget the challenge and fights with ancient tools to infiltrate and cloud their thinking. They tell themselves self-righteously, "We're radical and live on the cutting edge! Others may be pharisees, becoming controlling or religious, but not us. We survived the fire and know too much to fall into that old trap."

Evil shadows of legalism and complacency form cataracts on the eyes of their hearts, clouding their gift of discernment and subtly veiling the truth of their condition.

Believing the lie, they tell each other, "It's wisdom not to be controversial. After all, we're His gatekeepers, and we don't want to lose our people to error."

Their guardian angels are becoming increasingly bored as they watch this uneventful existence. The vessels no longer position their lives to need clashing swords and heroic deeds for the sake of the Kingdom. The angels are helpless to fend off the attacks of sickness and affliction in the Church. Diligent to watch over the vessels, they wish Master Potter would do something to wake them up.

After the vessels spend years sitting on the back pews and entering into the Church's compromise, all the songs and sermons begin to sound the same. Beloved feels a painful ache in her heart, and she asks, "Lord, what has happened to me? I'm so bored. I used to be able to feel Your love. We've had so many adventures together—vessels were saved, healed and delivered—but we haven't done that for so long. Why have You left?"

A Prophetic Lesson

Excitedly, Valiant stands to attention and awaits orders. "Lord, she is stirring."

Holy Spirit whispers, "Master Potter has never left you. You've made choices to back away from Him. You've become comfortable and very adept at retelling old war stories. Even in the church, you no longer pray for people and you refuse to give prophetic words."

Convicted, Beloved becomes defensive. "I just have to make sure it's really You. I don't want to operate in error and ruin someone's life. I want to be careful and use wisdom."

Holy Spirit counters, "You've mistaken wisdom with compromise, Beloved. You've been deceived by the enemy's schemes and your own desires to be accepted into the religious system of position and titles."

"But that's the only way to get promoted into leadership and become useful."

"Whose leading are you following, Mine or man's?" She pauses, unable to respond as the truth sinks in.

"I'm so sorry! Help me to know the difference, and give me the grace to step out when You prompt me. I'm sorry I care so much what others think."

Answering her request, He re-ignites her prophetic gifting. Beloved receives a vision and a word of encouragement for a lonely teapot sitting on the shelf by the big double doors.

Afraid of being judged by the other vessels, she looks around to see if anyone is watching. "I can't give a word. What if I mess up the timing again?"

"The question is, do you love Me enough to be misunderstood and risk losing your reputation? Don't allow pride or fear of failure to keep you from My school of the Spirit. There's a learning curve, and at times you will make mistakes, but that's part of the training."

Spotlighting the lonely teapot named Golden Incense once again, Holy Spirit says, "Look at her. Can't you see her hopelessness? She so needs to hear Master Potter's heart for her."

STEPPING OUT

Beloved slowly walks to the double doors and introduces herself. Then she tells the teapot, "Master Potter showed me a picture of you as a beautiful intercessor. You had gold trim on your lid and spout. You had lovely lavender roses handpainted on your sides. I saw you traveling with a team of matching teacups and saucers carried on an ornate silver tray."

Beloved continues, "As a little teapot, you feel insignificant, like you can't contribute. But the steam of your prayers can open city gates. Your prayers are so much more powerful than you ever imagined. He showed me that He's going to send you to many nations to bring salvation and deliverance. Steeped in His glorious presence, you will impart strategic information to governmental leaders. This will help to change laws and bring justice and mercy to the poor."

Watching nervously for confirmation, Beloved awaits her response.

Golden Incense's face becomes animated as she attempts to whistle. "This is an answer to years of prayer and fasting. I was beginning to think I was too old. I've been sitting on this shelf for so long my hair has turned gray. I can hardly wait for the glazing to get it colored! Maybe it will be a royal purple or eggshell blue."

She and Beloved hoot with sheer delight as they witness the accuracy of the prophetic word and the faithfulness of Master Potter.

Chapter Fifty

Help Has Arrived

Evening approaches and the warm glow of flickering light from the fireplace casts dancing shadows around the room. From the shelves where they sit, the vessels watch Master Potter take off His work apron. Settling into His brown leather chair with His nightly cup of tea, He puts His feet on the wooden footstool, relaxing at the end of another day. Humming to Himself, He picks up a pad and sketches designs for beautiful new vessels.

Beloved tells Comrade, "This is my favorite part of the day. Don't you love the coziness of the fire and the sound of the wood crackling? The glow of the fire is so warm and toasty."

Steadfast moves closer to the edge to get a better view of the fire. "How very wise of Master Potter to contain it in the fireplace. It makes it safe for all of us to enjoy. Not like that fiery kiln we went through. I hated that kiln, didn't you guys?"

Stretching, Master Potter puts down His tea and throws more wood into the hearth. It crackles and sizzles, causing red-hot embers to explode and sparks to fly, making little Comrade jump back and hide behind Harvester.

"Quick, Beloved! He's big enough to hide both of us!"

Harvester's bellowing laugh fills the room, and others join with him. "Great balls of fire, Comrade! It's just a little spark!"

Comrade blushes with embarrassment as he peeks out from behind the big canister. "Gosh, it really did look like one of the enemy's fiery missiles to me. That reminds me, I wonder where I left my armor?"

Fire, Fire!

Suddenly, the vessels hear yelping dogs and galloping horses off in the distance. Apprehension ripples through the fireside room. The clamor increases with the sound of clanging brass bells and urgent voices yelling, "Make way! Make way! The Potter's House is on fire!"

Quickly looking toward Master Potter for reassurance, they gasp in astonishment as He throws even more wood into the already blazing and spitting fire. The sparks shower into the room as the clay pots cringe as far back as they can on the shelves. Then He uses an iron poker to stoke the fire even hotter!

The thunder of galloping hoofs stops, and the wagon pulls up outside the big double doors. The barking dogs now compete with the loud clanging bell that announces the arrival of the fire wagon. Fists pound heavily on the doors, and gruff voices yell, "Hurry up! Open the doors before the house burns down! Open up or we will have to break it down!"

The vessels are now checking nervously to see if their shelf is on fire. Joyful jumps up and down with excitement crying out, "Help has arrived! Yeah, we're going to be saved! Quick! Open the doors!"

The vessels anxiously watch Master Potter's every move as He walks to the doors. Smiling serenely, He asks calmly, "Shall we see who it is?"

Unexpected Visitors

Burly men dragging fire hoses push their way into the fireside room yelling, "Fire, fire! We're here to rescue you!" Cold water makes contact with the burning logs and red-hot embers, creating heavy, billowing smoke. Sooty steam fills the room and splatters onto the vessels and shelves.

Spirits of fear and intimidation permeate the room as they prowl around the shelves, bringing a dark foreboding presence. The panicked vessels frantically search for Master Potter, but, unable to find Him, they will settle for anyone who will save them.

Appearing like an apparition out of the midst of the choking smoke and rising steam, the tall, commanding figure of the Fire Chief towers above them. Dressed in a yellow slicker and red metal fire hat, he stands with his feet firmly planted and his arms crossed. His penetrating hazel eyes seem to look right through the vessels. His dark olive complexion and handlebar mustache make him appear very distinguished. A frisky dalmatian sits obediently by his side.

At the sound of his voice, men scurry to obey his orders, checking for any hidden outbreaks of fire. The courageous firemen move around, carefully picking up vessels and checking between the shelves for smoldering flames of revival.

Sighs of relief can be heard throughout the room as the vessels realize that order is being restored and someone has arrived to tell them what to do.

The charismatic and handsome Fire Chief removes his red fire hat and runs his fingers through his perfectly styled, coal-black hair. Clearing his throat, he calms the remaining chaos with his authoritative voice. "You can all relax now. The situation is under control. We're here to help you."

Something about the Fire Chief is hauntingly familiar to Beloved. But she's so relieved to be rescued that she dismisses the prompting of Holy Spirit as He faithfully whispers to her heart, "Beloved, you need to discern what's happening. Where is Master Potter?"

Chapter Fifty-one

Fire Insurance

Shaking his head and sighing in frustration, the Fire Chief begins pacing. "We've been here many times before. Master Potter will just never learn. He's always starting dangerous fires that we have to put out." The faithful, well-trained dalmatian stays close, walking submissively by his side.

Fire Chief's voice appears to be filled with deep concern as he continues, "You wouldn't be in this mess if Master Potter had only listened to us. But He insists on setting fires. I highly recommend that you leave this house, but if you insist on staying and playing with fire, you really need to take my advice and get some fire insurance.

"If you feel you must have fire, it should be contained, controlled and used only in a safe environment." The Fire Chief orders his men to sweep the hearth of any remaining embers. Then, lighting his own strange fire, he turns to address the dirty, smudged vessels.

The room darkens as it fills with dense smoke. Long, eerie shadows silently creep through the room as the Potter's House is taken over.

"I've brought along my trustworthy assistant, who has many years of experience in squelching fires. I think you will agree with me that he is an expert on this."

Fear of Man

A heavy, ominous presence invades the room as the Fire Chief yells excitedly, "Please welcome Fear of Man!"

The curious vessels applaud and cheer the entry of this tall, impeccably dressed, well-groomed figure. Exuding authority and commanding respect, he turns toward the shelves. Fire flashes from his piercing blue eyes.

Abundance, a fruit bowl, blushes and practically swoons. Fanning herself, she says, "Oh, is it hot in here, or is it just me?"

The forlorn little vase Long Suffering mutters, "If you have any more hot flashes, you're not going to need another firing!"

Most of the vessels run to the front of the shelves eager to hear his recommendations as he sets his briefcase down and takes out the fire code and safety manual.

"We have this situation under control. Rest assured that you are now safe. The Fire Chief has already updated me, and I'm fully prepared to help you so this type of perilous situation never threatens your safety again."

Looking down in disdain at the vessels, he holds up the manual, shaking it over his head, "Why haven't you followed the safety rules? That's the only sure protection against dangerous fires. Didn't Master Potter have you read it?" Spirits of guilt and manipulation slither onto the shelves, digging their talons into the vessels.

"Fires can happen even in the best situations." He pulls out large stacks of official-looking documents and says, "So I have brought some fire insurance policies to protect you and your loved ones against future disasters."

Religious Ritual and Law 'n Order

"Insurance is expensive! So I offer several policies, each depending upon how much protection you feel you need. My assistants, Religious Ritual and Law 'n Order, are here to pass out the forms. They will even help you fill them out." Smiling, he continues, "We'll assist you in any way that we possibly can."

His two well-dressed assistants walk among the crowd. Many of the vessels are impressed with Law 'n Order. The slightest movement causes the numerous medals displayed on his chest to clang together like chimes. Each medal signifies a victorious battle won by extinguishing fires.

Religious Ritual, in his expensive three-piece suit and salt-and-pepper hair, exudes respectability and intellectual prowess as he passes out forms. "My expertise is to train your leadership to work for our organization. If you follow our guidelines, we can just about promise you financial success and an impeccable reputation in your lovely community."

Policy #1

Fear of Man continues, "I have four policies in mind for this group! The first one is called the Safety First Policy and is priced very reasonably—if you are willing to have no more than three logs in the fireplace and only once a month. We will train some of your own people as deputies to monitor your fires to make sure they don't get out of control.

"Plus we'll send my assistant, Law 'n Order, to instruct you in the proper techniques of using buckets of water and wet blankets to put out flying sparks that may start other fires. As I am sure you have discerned by now, we are experts in fire prevention."

The shelved vessels look at each other and nod.

"They sure seem like experts to me. I'll bet they've had years and years of training," says Steadfast. "Years and years and years of training."

"I wonder if even Master Potter knows this much about fire?" asks Diligence, the sturdy casserole. "First He makes a wrong decision on where He sets me, and now I find out He's failed to tell us about this wonderful insurance."

"Yes, fires are really dangerous; He could have burned the house down and us along with it," says Abundance, the large fruit bowl, as she addresses the other vessels.

Nodding, Fear of Man continues, "We've found that people are relieved not to have to worry about fires that could indeed burn down their houses. Another benefit of this policy is that it makes very efficient use of your valuable time. In fact, advertising a once-a-month special revival fire meeting pulls bigger crowds, brings in more offerings, and allows for less time spent on cleanup."

"No cleanup is good," mutters Long Suffering. "I hate it when I sweep the hearth and ashes fly up my nose."

"Oh, a little hard work never hurt anyone," mutters Fearless under his breath.

"Well then, maybe you can clean the fireplace next time," replies Long Suffering curtly. Bickering erupts between the two pots.

SPIRITUAL WARFARE

Sitting in the dismal room, Beloved musters her courage to ask, "What if we want to have more than one fire a month? It can be dark and cold without a cozy fire!" Other vessels agree with her and raise questions regarding the policy. Her courage is becoming contagious.

The long arm of Law 'n Order wraps around her shoulders, and he whispers in her ear. "You will do just fine without a fire," he says, nodding his head. "We are the experts and know what is best. After all, we're just here to help you! Why don't you just sit down and let us men handle this. Who ever heard of a woman firefighter? You don't want to be a troublemaker!"

The oily voice of the Fire Chief fills the room. "Oh, she's not stirring things up. We do value women's input, even though they're usually overly emotional. I totally understand her concerns. Beloved is your name, isn't it? I've had my eye on you for some time."

Fear of Man reaches out to paralyze Beloved's heart, but she shrinks back from his grasp in alarm and begins to pray silently.

Holy Spirit appears in soft feathery smoke swirling around her. "Don't be afraid Beloved; just keep praying. This is heavy spiritual warfare. I'll give you discernment as you press through."

Beloved turns to Comrade, Harvester and her new friend Golden Incense. "It feels so oppressive in here without Master Potter's fire. I can't even see what's going on through all this thick smoke. Let's pray for Master Potter to come back."

Joining together, they cry out, "Help, Lord! We're confused and not sure what to do! We need You."

Holy Spirit releases wisdom and revelation for strategies to defeat the enemy. "A great deception has been loosed in the fireside room. You must pray for discernment so that the enemy's plan will be uncovered. It's not just these assistants; you're really fighting spiritual wickedness in high places."

They cry out, "Lord, uncover the plans of the enemy. Show us who we're really fighting."

The smoky, evil haze of deception begins to lift as their earnest prayers hit the atmosphere. The powerful intercession scorches the gnarly hides of the slithering, infiltrating demonic horde. Aware that he is losing ground, the Fire Chief snarls for his henchmen to get back to their oppressive tasks.

The spirit of fear infiltrates the intercessors. Afraid of being discovered, they shut down and disconnect from each other. Spirits of depression cover them like a heavy blanket. Battle plans fall to the ground as each one becomes isolated and silent.

Policy #2

As the prayers subside, Fear of Man recovers quickly. "Our second policy, at a small additional cost, is the Family Discount Policy wherein we supply an ornate, glass firescreen. This maintains a controlled temperature. It also gives full protection for you and your children to keep from being burned by the fire. I'm sure you'll agree, the safety of your children is one of your paramount concerns."

Looking at each vessel he continues, "Master Potter is foolish and dangerous the way He builds fires, and you must protect yourself and your families against His recklessness. A responsible parent would do everything to protect his or her child from Master Potter's damaging flames."

Most come into agreement with this wisdom as Law 'n Order craftily directs the demonic hordes around the room. Spirits of accusation and unbelief subtly move among the vessels.

"After all, Master Potter was the one who started the fire in the trophy room. You barely survived it, and then He starts another one! What was He thinking?"

The Fire Chief commands the room's attention once again and says, "Remember, we're the ones who saved you. If Master Potter really cared about your safety, we wouldn't have had to rescue you. Where is He anyway? Why did He put you through so much and then abandon you?"

Beloved feels Holy Spirit's grief at the accusations against Master Potter. She tells the others, "But as clay vessels, if we didn't go through that fire we would be fragile and not able to hold His substances. Master Potter did what was best for us because He loves us. Don't listen to them; there's something wrong here!"

The vessels take sides for and against Master Potter. Comrade shouts, "Beloved, I'm with you! He's always been faithful and even gave us Holy Spirit to guide and help us!"

"I don't know," says Abundance. "He did put us in the kiln, and now He's abandoned us."

"That doesn't sound so loving," Diligence agrees.

Sweet Adoration cries, "Master Potter does love us. After all, He rescued us from the Potter's Field. We all need to pray!"

In their confusion, the pots don't notice that the Fire Chief is barring the exits.

POLICY # 3

Fear of Man shouts, "Quiet! Quiet! I'm totally for Master Potter! Please do not misunderstand me. In fact, our third policy is called, Monuments of Master Potter's Past Glory. We recognize some unenlightened people still like fire, but this is the safest way to enjoy it—or at least the memory of the last great revival fire.

"So my assistant Religious Ritual will supply large, hand-tinted photographs illustrating historic moments when Master Potter brought signs, wonders, and even healing miracles. These moments are forever embedded in our memory, as I'm sure they are in yours, even though the last great revival fires offended many people and brought terrible division to your churches."

Undetected, spirits of deception begin to move among the vessels, wrapping their steely bands around the clay vessels' minds. He continues, "This very popular plan includes sweeping the hearth clean and having no messy, dangerous fires at all! You have no wood to chop, split, or haul, no soot, no smoke, no ashes—no work or mess to clean up! You know how messy division in the church can be. Avoiding it in the first place is certainly wisdom. Don't you agree?"

"Well, that makes sense," says Diligence. "It seems like wisdom to me."

"I agree," says Abundance. "It's always best to avoid conflict."

Religious Ritual continues, "In the spring time, we supply greenery for the fireplace—artificial of course, but it looks so real that no one will know the difference, and it's so fashionable. All the best churches have it. What's important is for you to have no upkeep. Who wants to be seen shoveling out dirty old fireplaces? Aren't you above that, really? Master Potter called you to be leaders."

"I like this plan," says Joyful. "I like remembering how powerfully God has moved."

"That's what this plan is all about—God's past move of the Sprit. We should be proud of and grateful for these memories. What a rich and vibrant history we have. All you have to do is choose this plan, Monuments of Master Potter's Past Glory, and we will go through the archives and get photographs from the last century when many of your ancestors moved in signs and wonders. We will display these along with some of the crutches, braces, and wheelchairs right here in this room. After all, the Word says to not forget His works."

HOLY SPIRIT STRATEGY

The voice of Holy Spirit resonates through the vessels: "The past works of Master Potter are not dead monuments to be remembered. You are not to be an audience, but activists to bring the Kingdom of God to earth *now*. It's not enough to just look at past revivals; you must pray and uncap these ancient wells of anointing for your generation and your children.

"Stand on the past victories and come up higher and go further than they did. Don't be content to sit here and reminisce. Go out and do your own radical exploits as double-portion sons and daughters."

Directing His voice toward the ones snoozing in the back, He releases conviction and says loudly, "Awake, you sleepers. Arise and uncap those ancient wells of anointing for today."

At the sound of Holy Spirit's voice, the heavy oppression starts to lift off Beloved and the intercessors. Other vessels awake as out of a daze.

Comrade looks to Harvester, "Why do I have such a bad feeling about this?"

Harvester replies, "I'm no fan of fire. If I never saw the inside of that kiln again it would be okay with me, but Master Potter's fires in the big stone fireplace are different. They bring refreshing. I don't like all this talk about sweeping the hearth clean."

Policy # 4

"Quickly, let me go over our final and most up-to-date policy. This fourth plan is called Cleanliness Is Next to Godliness. It is our most expensive, but most effective policy, as it does away with the old-fashioned fireplace and totally modernizes your church. This is undoubtedly the finest plan we offer. After all, everyone knows fire is a dangerous and archaic custom anyway!

"In fact, we not only train your people to be fire deputies but also to be bricklayers so they can actually close up your drafty old fireplaces, first in this house and then in your neighborhoods and cities. And, as an added bonus, the most gifted—*and you know who you are*—will be sent out to assist our team in locating fires and putting them out. Fighting fires is an exhilarating career. For some of you men who are tired of sitting on the shelves waiting, I promise you, you can't find much more excitement in life!"

Smiling at the naïve little pots, he tells them, "Plan one, two, three, or four, any combination is fine. It's so easy, just like falling off a log, so to speak. Just talk it over among yourselves, and sign on the dotted line. Remember, my two excellent assistants, Religious Ritual and Law 'n Order, will be moving among you to offer any assistance or advice you may need."

Chapter Fifty-two

The Great Deception

Diligence, the sturdy casserole, yells from across the room: "I want plan number two, the Family Discount Policy. It's the best protection and the safest for the children and the whole family. My church elders would approve of this plan."

Abundance tries to be heard above the din. Waving her handkerchief to get Fear of Man's attention, she shouts out, "Over here! I'll take that plan too, but I want the Safety First Policy tacked onto it. A once-a-month revival meeting is great. I can even invite Auntie Killjoy. She wouldn't be offended or uncomfortable in any way. Three logs are perfect; it gives some heat but won't burn the house down."

Having lost their spiritual discernment, the vessels intensely argue over which policy to sign up for. Each is convinced that the one he or she has chosen is the very best and is unwilling to hear others' opinions. Stubbornly and selfishly they attempt to drown out each other's words. A mean-spirited attitude has entered the group of vessels, although few realize a change is taking place.

Cloak and Dagger

Quarreling and strife consume the vessels as they turn on each other. They begin to play the dangerous game of cloak and dagger. In the shadows of the church they hide under the cover of their title and position. While they smile and act spiritual, they knife their companions in the back, then tell themselves they are doing God a favor.

Terribly deceived, they become self-appointed vigilantes, slandering vessels that move in the freedom of Holy Spirit's fire that they once loved. In so doing, they come into deeper bondage to the spirits of control and legalism orchestrated by Fear of Man. Deceived, many eagerly sign fire insurance policies without reading the documents.

In the suffocating haze, passivity invades the shelves and the vessels become comfortable in the growing darkness. Spirits of lethargy cloak their minds, draining their energy and squeezing the life out of them. Rocking them in their loathsome arms, the demonic choir mesmerizes the little church to sleep singing, "Rock a bye baby, never grow up!"

Bring Back the Fire

Grieved by the dissention, deception and lethargy, Holy Spirit urges the intercessors to reconnect with each other and to agree together in prayer. "Join together with each other. I'm calling you to return to your first love. You need to repent and cry out for Master Potter. Look what's going on around you. Your companions are being deceived by the enemy."

As they gather together again, a tenderizing fire begins to erupt in their hearts. Finally they can contain it no longer and the huddled, scared group begins to cry out.

Beloved wails, "Yes, Lord. We want Your fire and Your presence. Forgive me for my fear and apathy."

Golden Incense, gripped with groans of deep repentance, enters in. "Forgive us. We need You as a continual blazing fire so that we can be carriers of Your glory."

The fervent prayers of the saints rise as golden perfumed incense before the throne. Each petition and cry cracks the oppressive, invading darkness.

Softly, Beloved's beautiful voice leads the praying vessels into worship. Gentle tears flow as they're caught up in praise. Others move into prophetic songs.

Heaven responds by releasing refreshing winds to the intercessors, imparting revelation and a new faith level to fight for revival fire. The windows of Heaven open and gusts of glory sweep through the room.

The holy fragrance of adoration and the heavenly glory violently assault the demonic. While dodging the missiles of glory shot from canons of praise, the Fire Chief growls at Fear of Man to seek out and destroy the source of the hated worship.

Terror flashes through Fear of Man's piercing blue eyes as he panics, afraid he will have his master's rage unleashed on him. Quickly he rounds up his assistants, Law 'n Order and Religious Ritual, and assigns each of them a regiment of demonic spirits to try to regain control of the room.

Unable to locate the intercessors, they grasp the other pots in a vise-like grip. Murmuring and spitting they say, "The dreadful fire is the last thing any of you need! You know from your past experience how painful it was to suffer that fiery ordeal. Do you really want to do that again?"

Some of the vessels agree with the lies of the gathering demonic horde, telling each other, "No! We should never have to go through something like that again! We remember how horrific the fire was. Don't forget that Master Potter orchestrated it Himself. We want to sign up for some fire insurance."

Paralyzed by Fear

Frightened by the counterattack, Beloved and the intercessors start to lose hope. They shut down and stop praying once again.

Having regained control of the room, Law 'n Order notices Beloved and comes over and says, "We have safety procedures here for everybody's well-being. And I know you ladies don't want to be rebellious. You really shouldn't break the rules."

Beloved cries out, "Don't listen. His rules are bondage."

Law 'n Order snarls with sarcastic glee, "There's always a big-mouth woman around who struggles with the issue of submission. Challenging proper authority is not only wrong but sets a dangerous example for others."

Golden Incense says, "Beloved, I think you're right. We don't want to get caught up in rules and regulations and lose our first love."

Joyful says, "I love Master Potter and I want His fiery love. I want Master Potter to come back. Where is He?"

Fear of Man joins the group and puts his arm around Law 'n Order. Shaking his head sadly, he says, "How many times have we seen this? Women who have a Jezebel spirit, who think they're doing the right thing but just stir up contention and bring division to the group."

Law 'n Order responds, "I know, the bad thing about being deceived is that you don't know it."

"Oh my goodness," wails Long Suffering. "I knew I was deceived. I just knew it. Now it's confirmed in the mouth of several witnesses."

Religious Ritual struts over to join his demonic henchmen. "I know in your little hearts you girls want to do what's right. But remember, it does say in the Word that a woman should be silent and not in authority. It's dangerous to have intercessor groups without someone experienced to be accountable to."

Beloved and Golden Incense look at each other with confusion.

Fear of Man says, "We're bringing in wisdom to govern this terrible mess that Master Potter left you in and then you four challenge our leadership. Unless you learn to submit you'll never be able to move into your destiny. Unless you grow up into maturity, by listening to your God-given authority, you will always grieve Master Potter's heart."

Beloved starts weeping and says, "I don't want to be rebellious. I just want Master Potter. I don't know how to do this. Help me. It must be better for me to just shut down and not say anything than to cause others to fall by questioning leadership."

"That's right," says Fear of Man, nodding his head and smiling.

Other dark political and religious spirits swirl around Beloved and her friends, shutting them down with their insidious accusations.

"Now ladies," begins Law 'n Order, "which one of the plans that we're offering today, or which combination of them, would you each like?"

Joyful stares at her shoes and tries to discern what to do. "I don't want to cause problems but I want more than a once-a-month revival meeting."

Fear of Man growls, "Stop being a troublemaker. Didn't you just hear what I said? You have four options and only four options. Master Potter is dangerous; His fires are out of control. They're not an option."

Diligence, relieved that the intercessors seem to be coming into line says, "You don't want to be rebellious; after all, the Fire Chief knows about fire too. He's an expert. We don't want a fire that's out of control. Really, choosing one of these plans is the best for everyone."

False Submission

Wanting to do what's right and moving under false submission, the ladies stop praying and begin questioning their motives. They retreat into self-examination and morbid introspection.

Joyful painfully blurts out, "What if we're praying wrong? I don't want to stir up trouble for the group."

"I never can trust my motives," says Long Suffering. "Whenever I think I'm doing the right thing, it turns out to be wrong. It's so hard to know."

"I guess that's why we have leadership over us," says Joyful. "We're all new to this. If I learned anything from this it's that my discernment isn't as good as I thought."

As tears run down her cheeks Beloved says, "I always make a mess of everything. In the wilderness I fell into the enemy's trap and believed it was

God's will. Now I resist the very people that are here to help us, thinking it was the enemy. I'm a total mess. I'll never grow up into my destiny."

"I assume if Master Potter wanted us to have His fire He could certainly bring it. He didn't need us to pray for it before," adds Golden Incense.

"I guess having positions of leadership is not what God has for us women," says Joyful. "I think I'll just serve in the nursery and let the men put out the fires."

"I can cook the Wednesday mid-week dinner," says Beloved. "Everyone loves my tuna casserole."

"I think I'll volunteer to clean the pastor's study," Long Suffering sadly says. "I guess that's how I can contribute to the Kingdom."

"Well, we can all get together and have a prayer meeting each week. We'll hold up the men in prayer as they are out doing powerful exploits," says Golden Incense.

Holy Spirit shouts, "No, don't shut down and come under false submission and legalism. You want Master Potter's fire. This is a deception. The Word says that My sons and *daughters* will prophesy. You are neither slave nor free, Jew nor Greek, male nor *female*. Each of you was called when you were in your mother's womb with a special destiny. You are not limited because you are a woman. You are only limited by cultural and religious prejudice. Master Potter wants to use you powerfully to preach and teach the Word and move strategically in government, not only in the Church, but in the secular arena as well. You all have a great destiny in God."

PROPHETIC DESTINIES

"Joyful, you were created to be a prophetic singer. You will take the music of Heaven and bring it to earth. I will give you rhythms and notes that will set captives free and bring great healing to families. You will write songs that will impact generations."

"Wow," says Joyful, perking up.

"Long Suffering, you have suffered much in your life and allowed those sufferings to work a depth of maturity and love in your heart. I have given you a love for the Word. I have called you to be a powerful teacher. You are one who digs up the gold buried in My Word and gives it as treasure to both men and women."

"I-I can't believe it," stammers Long Suffering.

"Golden Incense, you are a prophetic intercessor for the nations, a freedom fighter! You will repent for the sins of the fathers, uncapping ancient wells of revival to open geographical areas. I will give you keys to unlock city gates and strategies to break curses from generational bloodlines that affect entire people groups and nations."

Golden Incense's lid rattles in excitement, and she blows off several blasts of steam from her spout. "Did you hear that? I'm going to intercede for the nations, not just the men going out from here!"

Beloved is excited for her friends, but tears well up in her eyes as she remembers her past failures. *I'll probably never reach my destiny since I have a Jezebel spirit.* Bracing herself for bad news, she waits for Holy Spirit to speak.

"Beloved, I am bringing you to a place of great authority, a place of kingly anointing. I'm training you to confront the Jezebel spirit, for I am calling and training you to the office of the prophet.

"I will take you to the realm of the Spirit that goes into the places of principalities, powers and dominions of the air. I will show you strongholds over nations, and the enemy will scatter and tremble like the mountains as you bring down and release My purposes. I will show you My divine chessboard, and you will prophesy, putting the players into place. You will partner with Holy Spirit to move in manifest demonstrations of My power and authority. You will be My voice of fire.

"The warfare that you are all up against right now will train and prepare you for your future. In the midst of the battle, I will teach you to hear My voice and be victorious over the enemy."

Beloved looks up weeping and Holy Spirit says, "There's one more thing, Beloved. Your destiny is far bigger than tuna casserole."

The women hug, laugh and weep together as the spiritual restraint and deception are broken off. "Come on, ladies," says Long Suffering. "There's a war going on, and we're needed in the battle. Let's pray."

Chapter Fifty-three

Prayers of the Saints

The yellowish-green fire in the hearth casts haunting shadows across the once handsome face of the imposing Fire Chief, transforming it into the dark, grotesque face of Death. The dalmatian beside him barks ferociously and turns into the huge gargoyle-like figure of Suicide. Gurgling with evil delight, he taunts the deceived vessels.

Sinister laughter fills the room as Death throws his head back in sadistic glee over his seemingly victorious quest. Picking up vessels who signed his policies, he violently throws them into his strange, morbid fire. Vomiting his damnation and ridicule of the duped vessels he spews, "You didn't want the fire of Master Potter! So, how do you like mine?"

The dark horde rudely shoves the vessels, knocking some off the shelves. They fall and break as casualties of war. The room fills with laughing, mocking devils that join together in an evil taunt. A sickening hysteria takes over the wicked celebration.

Pray Without Ceasing

Confident of his victory, Death orders his evil henchmen to move throughout the room to destroy any remaining intercessors. Huddled together in the back, Beloved and the newly inspired women intercessors rally the troops. "Fearless, Comrade, Harvester, we need your help. Get the others. We're losing our friends."

Agonizing over the fate of the lost vessels, Beloved and her growing group of prayer warriors fervently cry out for Master Potter to come back before more vessels are lost to the evil lies of the enemy.

Heavenly glory invades the room as their unrelenting prayers ascend to the throne. The Father releases His warring angels into the battle below. The angelic army explodes like fiery comets, showering glory and splendor. Charging through the atmosphere on the way to the Potter's House, the mighty angels fight valiantly to overcome all demonic obstacles in their path, leaving a wake of black sulfuric carnage behind.

The intercessors continue to cry out as the battle rages: "Forgive us Lord, for we let the fresh fire of Your love go out. Make our hearts fiery once again. We want shining, burning lives that reflect your glory so others will come to You."

Harvester quickly joins the group, and falling to his knees, pleads, "Master Potter, where are You? We need You!"

"Help us to overcome the deception and unbelief that blinds them before it's too late," says Golden Incense. "So many have already fallen away and become prodigals, and the fires have gone out in their hearts."

Through tears, Comrade sobs, "Don't let our friends be deceived and compromise their destinies."

As Death continues to torment and destroy the backslidden vessels, others join with Beloved and her friends as they battle to drive out their enemies. A powerful intercessory group is birthed, and their faith increases as they become united and focused, bringing frustration and confusion to the dark horde.

Holy Spirit equips the growing number of prayer warriors with powerful strategic plans. "Don't be afraid; I'm with you. Praying the Word and worshiping are your most formidable weapons against these dark powers."

Mobilized into an army of intercessory voices, they wield their swords and declare boldly, "Come, Holy Spirit! We cry out for the resurrection power of the Cross to take back the land and destroy demonic strongholds in our midst."

Invaded by Heavenly Glory

Their prayers activate huge unseen angelic warriors, who enter and position themselves strategically throughout the Potter's House. Fully armed and ready for battle, their fiery eyes search out the demonic horde.

Shouts and prophetic declarations go forth like a mighty trumpet blast, breaking open the heavens as the vessels cry out, "In Master Potter's name we break the power of the demonic hold and call forth the power of the Blood that defeated hell."

Valiant and the other guardian angels in the fireside room start to radiate with heavenly light as they eagerly join in the battle. The sounds of clashing swords and ferocious cries from the angelic warriors can be heard once again in the fireside room as they respond to the Father's orders and battle on behalf of the vessels' prayers.

Suicide, tormented by the constant intercession and worship, relentlessly paces back and forth, cursing the angelic troops from the Father's throne released by the fiery intercession. Before he can respond, a huge warring angel charges him, driving his sword through Suicide's gnarly hide. Instantly, a gush of black sulfuric smoke pours out as the evil demon shrivels and becomes transformed into a small, sniveling dalmatian pup. With tail between its legs, it slinks away from the battle whimpering.

Activated from the throne, the blazing pillar of wind and fire, which constantly connects Heaven and earth above the Potter's House, descends into the fireside room. A formidable weapon, this mysterious heavenly whirlwind, this life-giving fire, engulfs the strange demonic fire and extinguishes it.

Stark, cold terror grips Fear of Man and Law 'n Order as they are bound and swallowed up in the holy fire of vengeance. Terrified of being consumed by this heavenly glory, they shout blasphemous curses. Angelic warriors throw these strong men into outer darkness where they writhe and spew their agonizing groans.

The unquenchable swirls of penetrating fire route the enemy forces with unstoppable glory. A deep, guttural growl escapes from Death's jagged mouth as he sees his troops annihilated. Infuriated, he searches for the culprits, knowing his time is short. Tearing through the shelves in a horrendous rage, he blasphemes Master Potter until he triumphantly finds Beloved and her friends huddled in prayer.

Lunging at her, he viciously snatches her up in his gnarled talons. He spews his foul breath into her face. "I knew it was you, Forsaken. You've been rescued for the last time. I have you now! You won't cause us any more trouble! Your fate is the same as those I just threw into my fire."

As the heavenly glory increases, amazing peace settles over Beloved. She prays in the Spirit and enters into that secret place of refuge. Holy Spirit brings to remembrance the times when Master Potter rescued her from Death's cruel grasp in the Potter's Field and again outside Deeper Life.

FIGHTING BACK

A holy violence emerges from her spirit. Knowing that Death has already been defeated at the Cross, her voice becomes resolute. "My name is Beloved, and I belong to Master Potter." She then proclaims, "You have been defeated by the blood of the Lamb and the word of my testimony. You must leave—now!"

The power of the Blood explodes into the room like a torrent. Death, in his horrendous frenzy to escape, hurls Beloved toward the hearth. She closes her eyes and screams in terror. "Master Potter, save me! I'm going to shatter."

Master Potter suddenly appears in front of the fireplace and catches Beloved in His loving arms.

Frantically leading his screaming, terrorized horde through dark portals of escape, Death turns back to meet her eyes. In one last hellish challenge, he screeches, "I'm not finished with you yet, Forsaken!"

Safe in Master Potter's embrace, she sobs quietly as He tenderly tells her, "Well done, Beloved. I'm not finished with you either."

Chapter Fifty-four

The Warrior Bride

A heavy blanket of radiant glory covers the room as the sweet fragrance of Master Potter saturates the atmosphere. Imparting peace to the frazzled vessels, He brings divine order to the chaotic shambles of the fireside room.

The desperate cries of tormented vessels that were captured in the strange demonic fire draws His attention. "Master Potter, we're sorry. Please rescue us. We want to return to You."

Excitement reverberates throughout the room as He snatches each one out of the fireplace. The vessels shout joyfully as He places their traumatized companions—the plates, cups, bowls and saucers—back on the shelves. Safe again, the happy vessels jump up and down, cheering Master Potter's return.

"Everything will be like it used to be. It'll be like the good old days. Just like the good old days," says Steadfast, smiling.

The Glory Fire

Fresh wood is stacked in the hearth and ignited. Light and warmth fill every crevice and corner of the shelves as the grateful vessels snuggle once again in the comfort of Master Potter's safety and protection.

Chuckling, Master Potter says, "Well, I see you've had quite an adventure here."

Long Suffering smiles. "It was another test, wasn't it? I knew it was a set-up! I tried to tell them, but do you think they would listen to me?"

Joyful dryly asks, "Is it time for refreshing now? I could use another drink!"

Walking toward Beloved and the other intercessors, Master Potter commends them: "Father heard your prayers and released an angelic legion to rescue you from Death's demonic horde. You're learning to follow Holy Spirit's promptings. I'm really proud of you. However, there was one thing: you could have defeated the enemy right away if you had been wearing your armor."

All the vessels groan and look chagrined.

Pressing On to the High Call

"Many vessels decide to camp out in My fireside room and are only fired once. They remain as privates in My army, sitting on the shelves as unsightly dry bisqueware under the shadows of the church system."

Pacing among the shelves, Master Potter sounds a challenge: "Where are My captains and My lieutenants? Where are My colonels and generals? Who will fight in My war against Satan's diabolical troops? I have promotion for many of you, but you must be willing to go into the next firing—My higher glory fires!"

Harvester stands at attention, clicks his heels together and salutes Master Potter. His deep voice bellows, "Right here, Sir. I'm right here! I'll be Your general, Sir! I'm ready to decimate the enemy's kingdom. Pass out the weapons! What's the strategy? Where's the battle plan? Sir, yes Sir!"

Fearless and Comrade nod their heads and also salute. "Where's our armor? We're not going to war again without putting it on and wielding big swords."

Puffing up his chest, Fearless replies, "Follow me, men!"

Comrade yells in his higher-pitched voice, "Let's go take some territory right now!"

Sweet Adoration watches the three vessels march around passing out combat boots and barking out orders. After a moment she yells, "Boys, I'll take a size two please."

Beloved, joined by the delightful teapot, Golden Incense, is helping everyone get into his or her armor.

"Now don't forget your shield, Steadfast. You'll need it to stop the enemy's fiery darts," says Beloved.

"Let me just tighten up your breastplate of righteousness," Golden Incense says to Sweet Adoration.

Creating Air Cover Through Prayer

Master Potter tells them, "Your intercessory prayers provide air cover for My ground troops, enabling them to establish beachheads. At times you'll soar high in the Spirit above the battlefield and do reconnaissance reporting on what the enemy is doing. At other times, you'll be in the trenches holding ground or storming the hill. All of this is to save lost, dying souls and to reclaim cities and nations for Me."

Oh Lord, I want to help take territory. Will I be one of the foot soldiers? Going to battle on a big steed would be a lot easier, Beloved muses.

"I need to practice my marching," Comrade says as he and Joyful strut up and down the aisles. They grab Beloved's arm to pull her along.

Joyful and some of the musically gifted vessels grab drums and bugles as they sing and play, "Onward Christian soldiers, marching as to war...."

"Come on everyone, join in with us," shouts Joyful.

Watching all the hustle and bustle of His privates passing out weapons and making battle plans, Master Potter smiles and tells them, "Yes, strategic warfare is necessary, but you'll never survive without a deep revelation of My love. I'm calling you to be My warrior Bride."

A HEAVENLY BRIDEGROOM KING

The room is suddenly transformed as heavenly portals open ushering in realms of glory. Awed, the vessels slowly put down their drums and bugles when they hear the soft, celestial wedding music of flutes, harps and stringed instruments resounding from the heavens. As the beauty realm of the throne room opens to them, they see glimpses of rare unearthly colors and surges of radiant light, and they smell rare fragrances.

Swirling gusts of dazzling magnificence surround Master Potter as He transforms into a heavenly Bridegroom King before their stunned eyes. His humble, brown potter's clothing transforms into flaming garments of white light down to His feet. Girded about His chest is a golden band. His handsome and rugged face is like the sun shining in its strength. Torrents of brilliant light reflect from His fiery eyes. His head and hair are white like wool.

The purity of the light blinds the vessels; they automatically hide their faces and turn away from His fiery glory. Holy Spirit sweeps around Him in rushing surges of heavenly devotion. As their eyes adjust to the brilliance, they gaze upon His transcendent beauty in awe and wonder. The intensity of His presence grows brighter. Glory beyond earthly imagination fills the room.

They marvel as a blazing golden ladder is lowered through the portal into the fireside room. Celestial wedding music grows louder as the heavenly musicians playing harps, flutes and stringed instruments descend the golden steps.

Next, a mighty angel carrying a dazzling golden crown covered in precious jewels descends and places it upon Master Potter's snow-white hair.

The next angelic processional descends carrying shimmering white wedding gowns draped over their arms, one for each of the vessels.

The lovesick Bridegroom passionately calls out: "I want a deeper intimacy with you. Will you trust Me and come into the higher fires? Will you not only be My army, but will you also be My warrior Bride?"

An aura of purity and holiness causes the vessels to join with the angelic hosts prostrating themselves before Him in adoration. Overcome by the glorious Bridegroom King, they cry, "Holy, holy, holy!"

Chapter Fifty-five

The Bridegroom King

Master Potter motions for the enthralled vessels to stand. He directs their attention to a beautiful, completed royal purple pitcher with gold trim as she enters the fireside room.

"This is one of My vessels of honor. She just returned from The Land of Lost Promises where she ministered in the Village of Despair."

The manifest presence of the Lord rests upon her with unquenchable rays of celestial light. She is wearing a beautiful, iridescent wedding gown adorned with the rare pearls of suffering. Carrying herself with regal beauty and dignity, she exudes authority and government as she shimmers and blazes with His glory.

As the vessels watch her, a holy jealousy arises. A deep yearning that nothing else can fulfill stirs in the vessels' hearts. This supernatural, heavenly desire erupts in their souls as they long for completion.

Amazed, they question each other, "How did she get so beautiful?"

"There's something about her. What is it?" asks Sweet Adoration.

"Look at her brilliant colors!" says Beloved.

"Great balls of fire," blurts out Harvester. "She must be glazed!"

The Bridegroom's Delight

The delight of the Bridegroom is obvious as He warmly embraces her before placing her on the shelf.

Maybe the higher fire is worth it! thinks Beloved.

Approaching Beloved, the newcomer looks intently into her eyes. "My name is His Desire. You're Beloved, aren't you? You have a calling very similar to mine. You also will be a voice for Him—but one firing isn't enough. You must go into the higher, more intense fires in order to come out glazed and finished."

Beloved recognizes a kindred spirit in His Desire. "I don't know if I can bear it! Isn't there another way?"

"I asked the same question myself. But only His purifying fires will enable a clay vessel to carry His holy presence. I hated the fire and wondered if I would even survive, but Beloved, it was worth it! I'm more passionately in love with Him than ever before."

INVITATION TO THE HIGHER FIRE

"He told us the first fire was called the refiner's fire. What will happen in the next one? Maybe if I know ahead of time I can prepare myself!" Beloved asks hopefully.

"There is no way to prepare to die, except to lovingly cling to Him. You must humble yourself and remember it's His great love motivating your death. It's His faithfulness and mercy to touch every area of your life. His consuming fire penetrates and removes everything that hinders love. You can try, but you can never do that yourself."

Overhearing their conversation, some vessels murmur among themselves.

"We know all the best worship songs, go to the most anointed conferences and hear all the famous preachers. We're on the cutting edge," says Diligence.

"That's right! Besides, if we left, who would run the church programs and work in the nursery?" asks Abundance.

"We have no need of the higher fire; we can keep maturing here," says Diligence. "After all, the Potter's fireside room has all the fire we need, and it's so warm and cozy. If we can't mature at the Potter's House, where can we mature?"

Abundance and Diligence yawn and fall asleep on their comfortable pews as spirits of deception confirm the wisdom of their logic.

THE COST

Looking at Abundance and Diligence, Master Potter cries with deep sadness, "There's a price behind the anointing. So many are content to be lukewarm and refuse to go into the higher fires because they're also hotter. I long for every vessel to say yes and fulfill his or her destiny. Sadly, not everyone does. Yet, some do. Just look at His Desire!"

The vessels watch in amazement as she heals the sick and delivers them from the trauma of the warfare they just experienced. The vessels' countenances are changed as she delivers fiery proclamations from the heart of the Father. Her powerful prophetic words set destinies in motion as the Bridegroom looks on with a gleam in His eye.

Pointing to the beautifully glazed vessel, He explains, "She paid an incredible price for the anointing."

Comrade blurts out, "But Lord, I gave You everything in the Potter's Field. I said You could have my bank account, even though I only had a hundred dollars. I offered You everything I had 15 years ago."

Tickled with his outburst, Master Potter says, "Well, it's 15 years later, Comrade! So, now I'd like to make a withdrawal. Giving Me ownership of everything is part of the next fires I'm inviting you into."

Comrade yelps, "Now You're really getting personal, Lord. I labored all these years for those things. That's my life's work."

"Exactly," says Master Potter, turning his penetrating gaze on Comrade.

Fearless whispers to Harvester, "I think we're in trouble. I can smell a barbeque coming, and I think we're invited!"

Harvester jokes, "He loves the smell of the burnt offering—there's nothing like the sweet aroma of our burning flesh."

"That's not very funny, Harvester. You have a lousy sense of humor," Long Suffering moans.

Master Potter continues, "The higher fires usually take place after you've known Me for many years. Now you're financially successful and have a measure of anointing and a sphere of influence. This is the time to test your heart to see if you really love Me more than you love your lives."

A groan runs through the room as the vessels realize they must make sacrificial choices to fulfill their destinies.

"Remember, it's a custom-designed death to work My character in you. For some, it's tearing down financial strongholds. For others, relationships may be involved. I need to deal with the idols of your heart. Everything must bow to Me. Are you willing to pay the price?"

WILL YOU BE MY WARRIOR BRIDE?

Stopping in front of Beloved, He holds up a beautiful gossamer wedding gown for her to see and gazes deeply into her eyes. "Are you willing to love Me with an insatiable love, no matter what the cost, even when you don't understand My purposes and the mysteries of My scorching fires?"

The uncompromising love of the Bridegroom King beckons to the deepest longings of her heart, uncovering the raw naked ache of neediness and loneliness hidden deep within.

Beloved's eyes are riveted by the glowing purity and translucent beauty of the wedding gown. Lustrous pearls and opulent embroidery symbolize the future sufferings of the high glory fires.

"So Beloved, are you willing to follow Me?"

"I want to, but I'm scared. I don't even know what will happen if I say yes."

"If you say yes, Beloved, it will cost you everything. First you will be glazed, totally bathed and covered in My love to prepare you for what lies ahead.

"Then you will ride with other willing vessels on My pottery wagons through Precarious Pass into the dangerous Formidable Mountains. Hidden there is My Mountain of Fire, which is hollowed out into a huge kiln.

"It will be hotter and more intense than the last fire, hotter than you can even imagine. But when the fires are done and I open the door, you will come out glazed and completed—a beautiful, shimmering vessel of honor. Then you will be in a position to fulfill your destiny."

He looks lovingly at her and asks, "Will you be My warrior Bride?"

She looks away from His eyes in shame as she remembers the pain of the last fire. *How could anything be worse than that? I don't know if I can bear it.* Glancing around the shelves, she sees other vessels that are responding. They are being picked up by rejoicing angels and carried over the threshold into the bustling, busy glazing room.

"I'm ready to go," booms Harvester's loud voice. "Count me in. This is what I was created for. I can feel it in my bones."

"Me too," says a more hesitant Comrade with his voice wavering and ending in a little squeak. An angel picks him up, and he cries out, "Wait, wait."

Fearing he changed his mind, the angel looks forlorn and sets him down. "I've just got to get my armor. I can't be without it."

Beloved watches her two friends as they choose their future and destiny and are carried into the glazing room. She hears Harvester's voice as the door closes behind him.

"Great balls of fire, this is amazing. What color am I going to be? You'll need a lot of glaze. I'm a big guy. Let's get on with it. I have a score to settle with some demons."

She glances at the very back shelves and sees Diligence and Abundance sleeping. They are surrounded by old, dried-out vessels. Inside her spirit, she suddenly knows these friends will grow old and die on these shelves, never being glazed and never fulfilling their destinies.

She turns again and looks longingly at His Desire, the regal purple pitcher with gold trim. "I remember being exactly where you are, Beloved. I was so scared and wondered if it could possibly be worth it. But I can tell you, it was."

"I want to but I-I'm scared," says Beloved, wringing her hands. "I'm so scared of the next fire."

"Your flesh is always afraid of pain and death; that will never change. If you wait until you're not afraid you'll never do it. You have to make the decision in faith from within your spirit."

"I-I…" Beloved stammers.

"Remember what I said before—there is no way to prepare to die except to cling to Him. It's because of His great love and mercy that He sends His consuming fire to burn out everything that hinders love. Only through death can there be resurrection."

She looks back into the Bridegroom's eyes; they are burning with love for her. "That's right, Beloved; only through death can you experience true resurrection life. Will you drink the cup of suffering, as I drank it long ago?"

Beloved is torn between His great love for her and her fleshly struggle to maintain control and avoid the dreaded Mountain of Fire.

Weeping softly, she pours out her heart. "I don't want to sit on the back pew and die. I want everything You have for me. What was I thinking? Besides, I'm ruined! I've already gone too far. I desperately need You. I've lost my children, my home, my dreams of being happily married—everything! But, as bad as that was, it was nothing compared to the joy of being loved by You."

LOVESICK FOR THE BRIDEGROOM

Envisioning herself clothed in the wedding gown He is holding, she makes the final decision to pursue the completion of bridal love. As her body trembles with fear, she hears her voice echo throughout the fireside room, "Yes, Lord. Yes, I want to be Your fiery Bride forever." Hot tears flow down her cheeks.

Valiant stands with the other guardian angels watching her like a proud father. He weeps unashamedly as she agrees to give her all to Master Potter. At her declaration, Valiant says good-bye to his cohorts, who are left fervently praying for their pots, and he lifts Beloved up off the shelf to take her to the glazing room.

"Excuse me, Valiant," says Master Potter, with a smile on His face. "May I cut in?"

The glorious Bridegroom gently takes her from Valiant's loving grasp and sweeps her into a dance. "I knew you would say yes, Beloved. I knew you would."

She is unaware of anything or anyone else. She is lovesick. Time has ceased for her as she revels in the Bridegroom's deep love for her. All has fallen away as He holds her in His strong arms. Suddenly, she is aware that she is dancing in His arms on the sea of glass before the throne. She is dressed in her beautiful wedding gown. Her hair is swept up on her head and held in place by a diamond tiara.

From the corner of her eyes she catches glimpses of angel's wings, glorious lights and blazing lampstands, but she cannot take her eyes off her magnificent Bridegroom to look at them.

Dazzling white purity of radiating holiness emanates from the Father on His throne. He is filled with unspeakable joy at the fulfillment of His Son's desire for a Bride.

Lost in their own world, they dance to the celestial music. The majestic Bridegroom stares deeply into her eyes. "I have loved you with an everlasting love, Beloved. I've been waiting, anticipating this sweet moment since eternity past—before the foundation of the world. Your 'yes' means more to Me than you can understand. I gave My life to purchase it. I betroth Myself to you forever, Beloved."

When the music fades, her surroundings come back into focus. She is wearing her regular clothes, and they are standing together at the door to the glazing room.

As she looks into her Bridegroom's loving arms, He transforms back into Master Potter. Tenderly, He takes her face in His hands and whispers, "I believe it's customary for the groom to carry the Bride over the threshold, Beloved." He gathers her into His strong arms and carries her into the bustling glazing room.

Biography

Jill Austin, founder of Master Potter Ministries over 25 years ago, has traveled nationally and internationally as a conference speaker and prophetic voice in the Body of Christ. She has appeared on The 700 Club, PTL, TBN and numerous radio shows and has published articles in *Last Day's Magazine*, *SpiritLed Woman* and *Women of Destiny Bible.* Jill is also on the teaching staff of the Forerunner School of Prayer in Kansas City, Missouri, under Mike Bickle's leadership.

As an award-winning potter, she combined music, drama and art to depict Jesus as the Master Potter in dramatic presentations throughout the world. Over the last 15 years she has moved from the potter's wheel to the pulpit bringing salvation, healing and deliverance accompanied by signs and wonders.

Jill Austin of Master Potter Ministries has traveled extensively for over 25 years as a conference speaker and teacher. If you would like to have her speak at your conference or church, please contact us at **info@masterpotter.com**. Jill's powerful teaching tapes can be ordered online at **www.masterpotter.com** or by using the form provided in this book.

The Price Behind the Anointing (two-tape album)

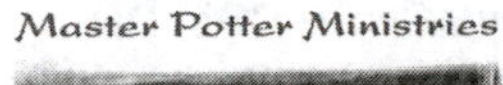

Do you know what kind of vessel you were made to be? Are you a pitcher created to pour forth his prophetic words? Maybe you are a delicate perfume vial that is filled with the fragrance of adoration and worship. Perhaps you are a large platter made to hold the heavy meats of the Word of God?

If you have accepted the call to be a carrier of His glory, you must be primed and shaped into the vessel that He has envisioned for you to become. He has a method of preparation for His vessels, and there is a price that you must pay as He imparts to you the glory of His anointing.

As you may know, Jill Austin was once a professional potter by trade. In this teaching, hear the revelation that the Lord has given her about Himself as the Master Potter. Discover the prophetic symbolism of each Christian as a piece of clay, and the Lord as the potter who is shaping His creation.

Jill shares the steps that go into the process of creating a clay vessel, relating it to her own testimony of being molded to His will. This dramatic account of how the Lord takes us as broken vessels from the potter's field and forms us each into unique creations for His glory, will give you a new perspective on your walk with God.

This is a profound, allegorical revelation of how the Master Potter molds each one of us as a clay vessel and then refines us through His fiery kilns. Recommended for prodigals and those who have been wounded in "the killing fields" of the Church. These tapes will encourage you to pursue God's highest purposes for your life.

Abba Father: The Heart of Forgiveness (four-tape album)

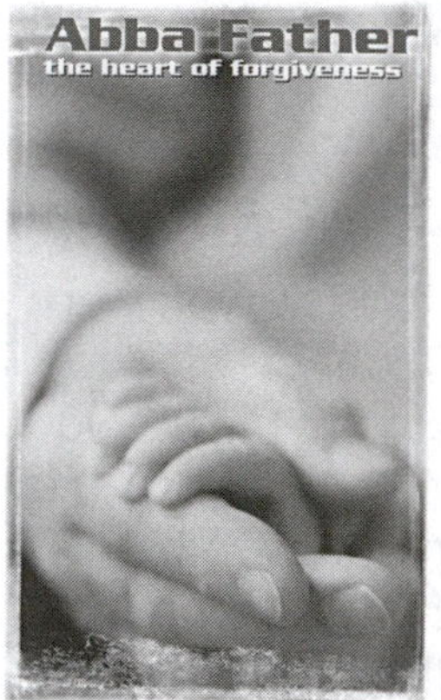

This teaching on forgiveness and reconciliation takes believers beyond "band-aid Christianity" and down to root issues. As most of us know, unforgiveness can be a major roadblock to spiritual growth, leading to frustration and despair.

In this teaching, Jill explores a new approach to healing the heart's wounds, supported by the Word of God. She explains how partnering with the Holy Spirit can bring breakthroughs with personal issues. You will also learn to use prophetic counseling to free others from the unforgiveness that holds people in bondage.

She shares powerful stories of forgiveness, including one about her dying father, whom she had not seen for 20 years. Also included in this teaching are compelling stories about people working through real-life issues to reveal how the Holy Spirit unlocks hearts, allowing the desolate to heal and enter into deeper places of intimacy with Jesus.

A great companion to this tape set is the study guide of the same title available at www.masterpotter.com. The study guide goes into very detailed material on the how's and why's of forgiveness issues. Both the tape set and study guide are highly recommended for pastors, counselors, and the brokenhearted.

Holy Spirit: Preparing the Bride (two-tape album)

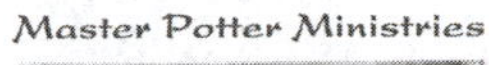

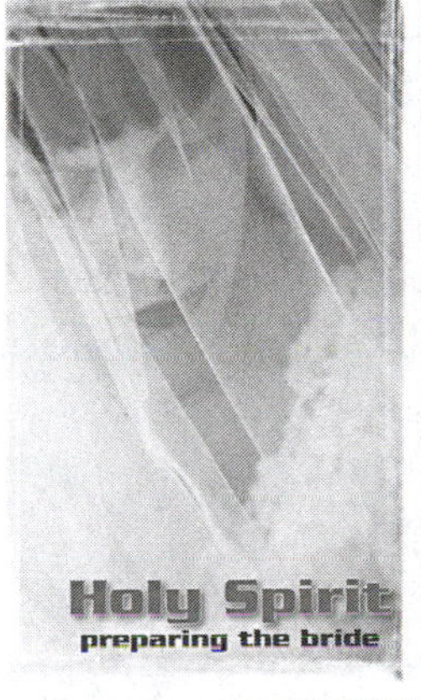

The Best Friend of the Bridegroom

In this tape series, Jill Austin teaches from Genesis 24 and Song of Solomon. Using the story of the servant's search for a bride for Isaac—one who will go willingly to her bridegroom—she paints an incredible picture of the bride that is being prepared for Christ. The story of Rebekah's awakening desire for her bridegroom, woven with burning passion and love from the Song of Solomon, creates a stunning illustration of the way we were created to long for Jesus.

The Holy Spirit is on a heavenly assignment from the Father to go through the wilderness of the earth and prepare a bride for His glorious Son. The Holy Spirit is a dynamic personality who takes us through the wilderness experiences, causing us to lean on the everlasting arms of our Beloved.

From Brokenness to Bridal Love

The Kingdom of God is taken with violence by passionate men and women, forerunners who move in radical exploits. The Lord is calling forth a warring militant bride, a Joshua generation that is willing to venture outside the walls of the Church, seeking to find the Rahabs of the world. Are you willing to reach out to those men and women, disqualified in the eyes of man, who possess a stunning destiny as the Bride of Christ? This is a prophetic challenge for the end-time harvest...will you go?

Taking the Prophetic to the Streets (two-tape album)

Most of us are bold enough to stand in a group of church friends and say, "God is good," but are you bold enough to say it to people outside of church? Assuming you answered, "yes" to that question, let us take it a step further. Are you bold enough to say it to strangers?

The Lord is calling forth an army of prophetic evangelists to reach a lost and hurting world. He is asking if you are willing to take off your blinders to see broken people around you. He is seeking the bold ones who will run to take them His message of love and mercy. Isaiah 61 says that we are to "preach good news, bind up the brokenhearted, and proclaim freedom for the captives."

In this tape set, Jill Austin brings a new kind of perspective to prophetic evangelism. She shares real-life experiences of times when the Lord has given her prophetic words for people in some unlikely places. Through this teaching, you will learn how speaking prophetic words in the workplace and in our everyday lives can bring conviction, salvation, and encouragement to people. You will be stirred to pray dangerous prayers for the release of divine encounters that will radically grip the lost for the gospel's sake.

Additional copies of this book and other book titles from DESTINY IMAGE are available at your local bookstore.

For a complete list of our titles, visit us at www.destinyimage.com
Send a request for a catalog to:

Destiny Image® Publishers, Inc.
P.O. Box 310
Shippensburg, PA 17257-0310

"Speaking to the Purposes of God for This Generation and for the Generations to Come"